THE GREAT DIVIDE

Also by T. Davis Bunn
in Large Print:

The Amber Room
Berlin Encounter
Florian's Gate
Gibraltar Passage
Istanbul Express
The Messenger
The Music Box
Rhineland Inheritance
Riders of the Pale Horse
Sahara Crosswind
Winter Palace
Drummer in the Dark
The Quilt

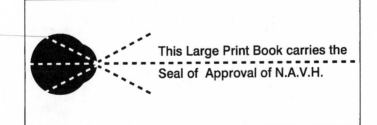

This Large Print Book carries the
Seal of Approval of N.A.V.H.

The Great Divide

T. Davis Bunn

Thorndike Press • Waterville, Maine

Published in 2002 by arrangement with Doubleday, a division of the Doubleday Broadway Publishing Group, a division of Random House, Inc.

Thorndike Press Large Print Christian Mystery Series.

The tree indicium is a trademark of Thorndike Press.

The text of this Large Print edition is unabridged. Other aspects of the book may vary from the original edition.

Set in 16 pt. Plantin.

Printed in the United States on permanent paper.

Library of Congress Cataloging-in-Publication Data

Bunn, T. Davis, 1952–
    The great divide / T. Davis Bunn.
        p. cm.
      ISBN 0-7862-4554-9 (lg. print : hc : alk. paper)
      1. Corporations, American — China — Fiction.
2. Americans — China — Fiction.   3. Rocky Mount
(N.C.) — Fiction.   4. Missing persons — Fiction.
5. China — Fiction.   6. Large type books.   I. Title.
PS3552.U4718 G74 2002
813'.54—dc21   2002028546

FOR ISABELLA
Who gives meaning and joy *both*
to the gift

PROLOGUE

The day and the world were as gray as the sky. Grim and hot and terrifying. There was no escaping how scared she was. Fear gripped her with the strength of an eternal desert. The fact that she was here, that she might actually succeed at what she had planned and schemed over for so long, meant nothing. Not now.

Gloria turned to the next person scuttling toward the gates, and spoke in a voice that she did not recognize as her own. "There, ask this one. Wait, please don't run away!" Gloria wheeled on the cowering interpreter. "Why aren't you asking him?"

The interpreter was a wizened man she had hired in Hong Kong. She had gone through an agency and paid twice what the same services would have cost on the street. But she had wanted a paper trail. If she was being watched, as she hoped, Gloria wanted to make sure they knew she was coming.

The interpreter stared at her with angry defiance. "They not talk with you."

"You need to be quicker, catch them before they enter the compound." She gripped the padded shoulder of his cheap jacket and spun him around. "There, hurry, here comes another busload!"

"Don't touch suit!"

She released her hold. "All we need is one person who works in Factory 101! Just one!"

He muttered an angry expletive, jerked his lapels straight, and stalked toward the disembarking throng.

Gloria risked a single glance at the gates. Guards clustered by the gatehouse and eyed her sullenly, talking among themselves. But none made any move toward her. She turned back, anxious that her plans might fail. Terrified that they might succeed.

She watched the interpreter work the crowd. She knew what he was saying because he had told her. Factory 101, anyone work at Factory 101, we seek someone who has been there or seen inside. Anyone who has spoken to the workers inside Factory 101. Anyone.

In the parking lot's dusty sunlight, the disembarking laborers seemed burdened by the shift they had not yet begun. Some had journeyed from the far reaches of Guangdong Province, traveling as many as ten hours on these rusting, overcrowded buses. They came for a week of dormitory life and ten-hour workdays. Then back for one day in squalid farming villages and families who were desperate for any wages at all, before returning for another round.

Even so, most still chattered noisily as they started toward the Guangzhou Industrial Compound's main gates. Yet as soon as they heard what her interpreter was asking, all animation vanished. Time and time again Gloria watched it happen. Upon hearing the interpreter, the workers showed a single flash of terror, then nothing. The curtain descended. They hurried by, never glancing her way. It was all the confirmation she required.

The interpreter returned to Gloria's side. "They no speak to you."

"Just one. All I need is —"

"Why you no hear?" His English continued to disintegrate the longer they remained. "All have much fear. I too. Come. We go."

"We'll try one more busload."

He motioned angrily at the compound gates. The gesture revealed gray patches of sweat beneath his arms. "The guards ask questions too!"

Gloria glanced around. It was true. The guards snagged passing workers and pointed back to where she stood with the

9

interpreter. The workers refused to look Gloria's way even then. But the guards were bolder. One soldier stomped into the gatehouse, picked up a phone, and watched her through the open window.

"We go. Now."

Gloria blinked through the sweat streaming into her eyes. Why did it not rain? The day draped about her like a dirty, steaming rag. Beyond the tall brick wall, dozens and dozens of smokestacks spewed multicolored clouds, the one directly behind the main gates belching brilliant yellow. The air burned her throat as she said, "We'll try one more time."

Fear turned to rage. "You crazy! These soldiers, they hurt you!"

She swiped at her face. "One more busload. Then we leave."

The interpreter kicked at a stone and stomped away, muttering angrily in Cantonese. Gloria remained standing in the middle of a parking lot several hundred yards wide. The unpaved lot was dotted with signs in Chinese, all for buses to various outlying villages — there were hundreds of rusting signs. Red dust floated over the uneven, potholed surface. Her clothes were stained, her face and hands sweat-sticky and layered with grit. Gloria could feel the soldiers' hostile gaze. She had never felt so exposed. All her careful plans, all her months of scheming, all her urgency and zeal — she could not recall a single thing beyond the rising cloud of dismay.

They had arrived too late. Gloria had planned to set off from Hong Kong before dawn. She had contracted for a car and driver through the hotel, and an interpreter through the agency. She had told the driver, but not the interpreter, where they were going. The interpreter had arrived two hours late, sullen and sleepy in his sharkskin suit, his dull fatigue turning fast to irritation and then to angry fear when he finally learned where they were headed. But he did not refuse, not after she had offered to triple his day rate if he came.

The compound lay twenty-two kilometers east of the Guangzhou city limits, fourteen kilometers north of the river, eight kilometers down a road that went nowhere else. A constant stream of trucks pulled up to a second set of gates farther down the wall, adding their noise and fumes to the already overburdened air. She glanced back at the guards and the factories behind the wall. The compound was as large as a small city. Construction cranes sprouted like diseased trees within a nightmarish garden. She had researched the compound for almost eight months and still did not know how many people worked inside. Some reports said ninety thousand, others closer to a hundred and twenty. She did not even know which was the factory she sought. All she knew for certain was that it was there. A name that conjured shadows and whispery fear even among expatriate Chinese nine thousand miles away, back in Washington, D.C. Back where she desperately wished she was now.

Even so, when the next pair of rolling buses belched black smoke and entered the lot, she almost screamed to the interpreter, "Here they come!"

The man waved one hand and shouted back, only one word of which was in English. "Crazy!"

"Ask them!" She had no choice but to plead. "Just this group, then we go!"

That turned the man around. "Go Hong Kong now?"

"Just this one group more!"

The buses were ancient and scarred and dusted a uniform brownish gray. They rolled and dipped toward the gates and halted almost directly in front of Gloria. She shouted to the interpreter, "Please!"

The man walked over and stood before the bus doors, his shoulders slumped in resignation. Only this time the disembarking passengers neither chattered nor looked his way as he started his speech. Instead, their eyes were locked upon the gates. Their expressions were so taut and so fearful that Gloria had no choice but to turn around.

The first two soldiers gripped her arms and pulled her away from the buses. Two more posted themselves between her and the vehicles. The interpreter had instantly vanished. The arriving workers dispersed almost as swiftly.

Gloria shouted, "I'm an American citizen!"

Another man stepped in close, as diminutive as the others but younger and dressed in civilian clothes. "So, American citizen, who sent you. United Nations? Red Cross?"

"Nobody." Behind the man stood another civilian, bigger and older. The second man had the shape of a bull on two legs — huge arms, no neck, flattened face, eyes as hard as the young man's voice.

"What, you just some little tourist, you come to ask questions about Factory 101?"

"I'm a student at Georgetown University." Wishing she could control her voice, remove the wavering tone. "I'm researching labor practices in China."

"Student? You student?" He said something to the soldiers. The two who weren't holding her arms walked over. One ripped the purse from her shoulder, the other frisked her with rudely probing hands.

"I'm an American citizen! You can't —"

"You be quiet." The young man dug into her purse, tossed her tape recorder and camera to the second man, pulled out her passport, opened it, inspected the picture, came up with her student ID, compared the two to her. "Gloria Hall."

"That's right. I demand —"

A single word from the young man and the bullish man moved so fast she saw nothing, not even a blur. One moment he was behind the young man, the next and her entire face screamed agony. Her vision grayed, almost went black. It felt like she had been hit with a wooden mallet.

"That's good. You quiet now, Miss Student Gloria Hall." He flicked the plastic ID with his finger. She heard it through the ringing in her ears. "Georgetown is place?"

"A university." The blow had dropped her voice an octave. "In Washington, D.C."

The young man spoke once more. The soldiers began dragging her toward the main gates. She shrieked, "Where are you taking me?"

"You come all this way. You want to know about Factory 101." The young man offered a thin-lipped smile. "No problem. We show."

By the fourth week, the work was routine enough for her exhausted mind to wander.

Gloria stood in a line of seventy identical steam presses that ran the width of the building's fifth floor. The walkways ran diagonally. She faced the back of a woman operating a miniature weaving machine, making shoelaces. In front of her was a young man sewing labels inside finished garments. Then came a woman laminating soles on basketball shoes. Each process multiplied by seventy. Three machines in front of the laminator was a set of metal stairs, leading to two glass-walled chambers. The room to the left was the central office, from which they were always watched. Always. The room to the right was empty now. Even so, Gloria could not look in that direction. None of them could. Except for those times when the big man came down the aisles and screamed for them to do so. Then they had no choice.

To every side, lines of dark heads disappeared into the hot and misty distance. The noise was deafening. Many of the

15

machines were brand-new. Others, like the press she operated, were extremely old. Her press hissed and complained every time it was rammed shut. Some of the presses were harder to operate than others. Some of the lighter women needed to grab with both hands and haul the top down by raising their feet off the floor. This was very tricky, as they had to release the handle and hit the floor and jump back before the steam hissed through the padding. After a ten-hour shift with three fifteen-minute breaks, it was hard to find the energy to keep jumping away. Exhaustion reached a point where the pain could not be felt. Gloria had seen in the showers that several of the women had welts around their middle from countless steam scaldings.

Gloria had her own scars, but the worst of them were healing. She bore welts on her right cheek, her neck, her forehead, both upper arms, her left elbow and wrist, and the palms of both hands. Many were from learning how to handle the steam press, but not all. Her right ear still throbbed from a beating two days earlier, and the warmth on her neck suggested it was bleeding again. She did not check. It would do no good. And if she got blood on another shirt, they would beat her again.

The throbbing and the hunger and the exhaustion worked at her mind. Which was not bad. The labor moved more swiftly and smoothly if she did not think too much. Just pull another freshly dyed and washed shirt from the hamper and slip it over the bottom padding. Smooth out the worst creases. Reach and haul down the top, ram the handle shut, squint, and lean away from the steam. Open the press, arrange the sleeves, haul and close and squint. Open the press, fold, close and lean and squint. Open and set the finished shirt in the stack to her left. Pluck out another shirt from the hamper. Repeat.

All this week she had been doing pajama tops for the New Horizons children's line. Which was what had started her thoughts wandering down that particular road. She peered through the steam at one unironed sleeve. Dozens of dancing teddy bears smiled up at her, each framed by the company's famous shooting-star logo with its trailing edge of sparkling rainbows. She opened the press, folded the sleeve in, and rammed the press closed. But hiding the tiny sleeve did no good. For when she squinted through the steam, she saw not the factory but another smiling face, this one belonging to her fiancé.

She shook her head and opened the press and folded the tiny shirt. Now it seemed as though Gary were behind her, moving in close, kissing the place at the base of her neck that always made her shiver. This time, however, the shiver released a flaming tide of regret. For the years and the life stolen from them, for the children they would never call their own. Gloria reached down and caressed the hot shirt, aching from the piracy of losses. So much had been taken from them.

She was ripped from her lamentation by the feel of her ankle being unchained from the machine. She gasped in terror, then released the breath in a cry of panic when she saw the bullish shoulders and the bald head rising into view. She screamed the first words of Cantonese she had learned after her arrival: "I meet my quota!"

The man was called Chou, and it was he who had hit her there in the dusty parking lot the day of her arrival. He had hit her enough since then, and she had seen enough of the others being struck, to know terror just by his approach. To have him come so close and see her not working was impossible. Still, it had happened. Again she screamed what everyone screamed when Chou came for them: "I meet my quota!"

Those were the words they were forced to shout at the end of each shift. Afterward the chains attaching them to their stations were released, and they were led downstairs to the dormitories with the lines of bunks and the bare tables and the stench-ridden toilets. But now the words had no effect. Chou gripped her upper arm with an iron hand and dragged her from the bench. She screamed again and clutched the steam-drenched press. She did not even feel her palms blistering. He wrenched her free and started down the aisle.

No one looked up from their work as she was dragged to the front. No one ever did. Not even the one friend she had made, the woman operating the laminating machine, a former university student with a few words of English. Hao Lin kept her face down and her hands busy. There was nothing anyone could do. To look up would only be a sharing of the terror, and they all carried too much of their own already. They would be forced to look soon enough.

She gripped the railing, the stairs, the doorjamb. Just as they all did. Shrieking and wailing and still dragged into the punishment chamber with its glass wall overlooking the entire factory floor. The steam rose from the presses and the machines clattered with angry laughter at her helplessness. Gloria heard nothing save the rising tide of her own terror.

She babbled pleas in English as she was lashed to the punishment chair. Chou straightened and left the room. He always did. Drawing out the wait was all part of the terror. She continued to moan and struggle and tremble so hard the chair rattled against the concrete floor. Chou returned, this time burdened with an armful of great metal rods. Her moans turned to sobs. She had no idea what it was he carried, only that it would hurt her very much.

He moved behind her and began clattering and banging. The owner's son walked into the room, the slender young man who had spoken to her that day in the dusty square. He carried something too, something that looked vaguely familiar, only her panic was so great she could not draw it into focus. He remained at the other end of the table, setting up what appeared to be a tripod. When neither of the men touched her or even approached, Gloria managed to see through her fear. It was indeed a tripod, and on it he was setting a video camera.

From behind her Chou hit a switch, and suddenly the room was bathed in a harsh light. Gloria flinched as the young man walked toward her. But he merely slapped a sheet of paper down on the table in front of her and commanded, "You read this."

"What is it?" But she was already squinting over the scrabbled writing. And when the words swam into focus, she could not help sobbing.

"No, no cry! You read words!"

But she could not stop. Just four weeks she had been here. Yet it had been long enough for the reason she had come and the nine months of planning and the two years of researching and the loss of her beloved Gary to melt into a puddle of random thoughts and aching remorse. Now, here upon the table before her, the plans became real again. The plans and the hope and the purpose. She sobbed so hard she could scarcely draw breath. She had won.

"You stop tears or we make real pain!" The young man slammed an open palm upon the table. "You stop now!"

"Y-yes. All right . . ." Gloria drew a hard breath. Another. She had to do this. She gave her head a violent shake to clear away the tears. Blinked away those yet unshed. Squinted. Focused. Took a deep breath. And read the words aloud.

As soon as she was done, the young

21

man drew the tape from the video and left. Chou cut off the harsh lights and followed. Soon enough they returned. Chou walked over and released her. An iron hand gripped her arm and lifted her erect. She was walked from the chamber and down the stairs. But not back down the aisle. Instead, Chou pulled her around to a second set of stairs leading to the doors no prisoner ever passed through more than once. She knew this because Hao Lin had told her. Gloria's sobs became louder still as Chou half carried her down and away. She had indeed won.

ONE

"I call Marcus Glenwood to the stand."

Judge Gladys Nicols turned to where Marcus sat, isolated and unprotected. "One last time, Marcus. Go find yourself legal representation."

He scarcely heard her. The meager portion of his mind that functioned normally watched as someone else rose to his feet and approached the witness stand. This other person took the oath and settled into the seat. And waited.

Suzie Rikkers was a tiny waif of an attorney, made smaller by her habit of wearing oversize clothes. Today it was a dark skirt with a matching double-breasted jacket whose shoulder pads were so thick they raised the lapels up in line with her ears. She had been looking forward to this moment for a very long time. "You are Marcus Glenwood?"

"Yes." He had known the agony of two sleepless weeks over what was about to come. Marcus had visualized the scene in such vivid detail that now, filtered as it was through a fog of fatigue, his imaginings seemed far more real.

Suzie Rikkers was an associate in his former firm. He had been instrumental in blocking her promotion to partner. As she walked toward the witness box, she granted him a smile of pure revenge. "You reside in the Raleigh area known as Oberlin?"

"Not anymore."

"Of course." She spoke with the voice of a broken pipe organ, all shrieks and fierce winds. "You sold that house, did you not?"

"Yes."

"And how much did you have in cash after paying off the mortgage?"

"You have the figures."

She spun about. "Your Honor, please instruct the witness to answer the question."

Judge Gladys Nicols had been Marcus' friend for several years, ever since he had joined her in pressing the state bar to pass a measure requiring pro bono work from all big firms. Pro bono meant "for the public good," and signified work done for clients who could not pay. Back when most North Carolina legal work was performed by a tight-knit clan of locals, anyone who refused pro bono assignments was shunned. But nowadays, attorneys who regularly accepted nonpaying clients were classed as fools.

Judge Nicols' expression clearly showed how much she disliked leaning over to tell him, "You know the drill, Marcus."

"About a hundred thousand dollars," Marcus replied.

"Plus another eighteen thousand dollars from the auction of your wife's collection of antiques. Which, I might add, had been valued at around nine times that amount."

"She didn't want them. I wrote —"

"She didn't *want?*" Suzie Rikkers' pacing had such a catlike quality that Marcus could almost see her tail twitching. "You contacted Carol Rice while she was still recuperating in the hospital, and when she did not respond immediately, you sold everything she had brought to the marriage! Is that not true?"

"I gave her a chance to take them. I had no place to store —"

Suzie Rikkers chopped him off. "You were a full partner in the local firm of Knowles, Barbour and Bradshaw. That is, until they fired you. Is that not correct?"

"I resigned. They did not fire me."

"Of course not." Suzie Rikkers continued to stalk about his field of vision. "Would you not say that your rapid rise within the firm was due in large part to your wife's connections?"

"She helped a little." And complained bitterly whenever asked.

"I would suggest that it was more than a little. I would suggest that it was the primary reason behind your being made partner. You were elevated within the firm so that the Rice Corporation and the Rice family name and the Rice family connections would bring in more business."

"That's not true."

She leaned into the sneer, adding all the force of her over-small frame. "So you became the youngest partner in the firm's hundred-year history strictly because of your skills as an attorney?"

He knew why Suzie Rikkers despised him, why she had begged for the chance to represent his estranged wife. Marcus had not been the only partner who disliked Suzie. But he was the one formally to suggest she be fired. And the only one to have declared that the woman was emotionally unstable. Borderline insane was how he had put it at the partners' meeting. Minutes of these meetings were supposed to be strictly confidential. But Suzie Rikkers knew. Oh yes. She knew all right. "That is correct."

She turned so that her laugh could be shared with the man seated directly behind her table. Logan Kendall had no business being in court today, except to watch Marcus bleed. Logan was the newest partner in Marcus' former firm. He had been promoted to take the place that Marcus had vacated. It was only the second time Logan had won a battle against Marcus. He was obviously there to even the score.

Suzie Rikkers went on. "Your claim is hardly substantiated by what has happened since your wife left. You have gone from a partnership in the state's capital to practicing law in the basement of a ramshackle home in a small eastern North Carolina town." She shared her delight over that with Logan, finishing with genuine pleasure, "You have lost virtually every single one of your clients."

"I did not ask them to join me."

"Oh, please." She spun back around. "Spare us the bald-faced fabrications, all right? Your life is a total shambles. You've lost everything. Why? Because your wife isn't there any longer to prop you up."

"That's not true."

Slowly, Suzie Rikkers approached the stand. The next question was put almost delicately. "Of course, there was nothing left of your Lexus to auction, was there?"

"No." To his dismay, the blinding tendrils of fatigue began to whither, leaving him acutely aware of the witness box. Trapped in a wood-lined cage, stalked by Suzie Rikkers. "There was not."

She closed in, and smiled. "Let's speak about the events that led to your wife's hospitalization."

He heard Judge Nicols' chair creak as she angrily shifted her considerable bulk. But she could not save him. No one could. Marcus had no choice but to sit and endure and hope it would not take too long.

At the plaintiff's table directly in front of him, one woman remained seated beside the chair vacated by Suzie Rikkers. His former mother-in-law observed him with cold loathing. Behind her, Logan Kendall watched Marcus' torment with bitter pleasure.

Suzie Rikkers kept to one side, so as not to block his vision of the pair. "You were down at Figure Eight Island for the weekend. You were there with several new clients. Your wife and children were with you. Is that correct?"

His children. The words left him unable to draw breath.

"Mr. Glenwood, are you with us?"

"Yes."

"What happened on the way home from that weekend?"

No answer.

"You were involved in an accident, were you not?"

He nodded.

"Answer the question, Mr. Glenwood. Were you involved in an accident?"

"Yes."

"A terrible accident." Her smile drifted in and out of focus. "Was it your fault?"

"The police said no."

"I didn't ask what the police said. I asked you. Was the accident your fault?"

"No." It was only this hope that made the day possible.

"But you had been drinking, had you not?"

"Not that day."

"The night before. And all the previous day. You had drunk almost continually that weekend. In fact, drinking was pretty much a constant in your life." When he did not respond, she asked, "Do you have a problem with alcohol, Mr. Glenwood?"

"No." Not anymore.

"I suggest that you do." She moved closer so that Marcus could not help focusing upon her. "I suggest that your chronic problem with alcohol fogged your thinking and resulted in a tragedy that wrecked your wife's life and destroyed her hopes for the future. The accident was therefore entirely your fault, Mr. Glenwood. You are the guilty party here. Is that not correct?"

The questions were drawn from the horrors of his dark hours. Marcus struggled but could not find the breath to respond. Which was just as well, since he had no idea what to say.

Suzie Rikkers leaned closer still. "Didn't you feel horrible when it happened? Couldn't you have driven better? Couldn't you have saved their lives?"

The gavel banged with such force that both of them jumped. "All right, that is enough!"

Suzie gathered herself. "Your Honor, I am trying to establish —"

"I know precisely what you are trying to do, Ms. Rikkers. And I will not allow this travesty to continue!" She rose and drew the court with her. "I will see you and Mr. Glenwood in my chambers."

"But Your Honor —"

"Now, Ms. Rikkers. Right this very instant."

Outside the judge's chambers, Marcus kept his distance from Suzie Rikkers by standing inside the cramped cloakroom. On one wall a cracked mirror rose to mock him. The stranger glaring back had the chiseled face of a Marlboro Man's younger brother and the body of a college athlete. Hidden away was a soothing voice, a good mind, a better smile. For years he had treated them all with casual pride. Now they fit like clothes borrowed from an intruder.

The door to the judge's office opened, and the strong voice said, "All right. Both of you get in here."

The office was a narrow jumble of boxes and books and piles of papers. Before Marcus was seated in a chair across from the judge's desk, Gladys Nicols honed in on him. "You shouldn't need me to tell you that proceeding without an attorney is like playing football without a helmet." When Marcus did not respond, she snapped, "Are you paying attention to me, Mr. Glenwood?"

"Yes, Your Honor."

"That's good, because I detest wasting my breath. And I particularly resent such a disruption to my last day in this courtroom." Judge Gladys Nicols had recently been elevated to the federal district bench, the first black female in the state's history to ever achieve this status. Even those who loathed her sharp tongue and even sharper mind had to agree that Judge Nicols was one of the most competent jurists in the state. And one of the toughest. "You've been around these courts long enough to know what happens to *pro se* litigants. Now am I right there?"

31

A *pro se* litigant was someone who insisted on representing himself at trial. Charlie Hayes, Marcus' earliest mentor and former best friend, had once described a *pro se* litigant in divorce proceedings as a person who wanted to light a cigarette while sitting in a bathtub of kerosene. "Yes, Your Honor."

Judge Nicols turned her dark gun-barrel gaze onto Suzie Rikkers. "You have focused your questioning upon some highly emotional issues that are absolutely irrelevant to this divorce hearing."

Suzie Rikkers did not back down. "Your Honor, if you will allow me to proceed to my intended conclusion, the facts will speak for themselves. Marcus Glenwood is a murderer. He deserves to roast in hell. Since we can't arrange that, we will settle for everything he has."

"I'll tell you what the facts are," Nicols lashed back. "Your client out there is rich as Croesus. She's not after money. She's after revenge. She wants to break this man out of spite."

"That is her privilege, Your Honor. And he deserves it."

"Not in my courtroom." She pointed one bony finger at the door. "You get out there and tell your client she has two choices. The first is, I will put this case on indefinite hold until the wife herself appears before me."

Suzie Rikkers showed unexpected dismay. "Your Honor, the former Mrs. Glenwood has granted her mother full power of attorney. She herself has been seriously injured through the actions of Mr. Glenwood. She is in no state —"

"Save it. I don't care if this case freezes up until everybody involved is dead and gone, do you hear what I'm saying? Her alternative is to accept a proper settlement. Say, half of what Mr. Glenwood presently holds in liquid assets." She glared across the paper-strewn desk. "Go out there and tell it to her like it is, Ms. Rikkers. You've got ten minutes."

When Suzie Rikkers had stormed out and isolated them behind a slammed door, Gladys leaned back in her chair and sighed. "Marcus, Marcus, what on earth am I supposed to do with you?"

Because she was a friend, and because she had gone out on a limb to help, he was compelled to respond. "I had no choice. Appointing counsel would only drag this out longer. My only hope was to let her do her worst and get it over with as swiftly as possible."

Gladys Nicols reached for her phone. Up close it was possible to see the fine wrinkles marring her stern features and the feather strokes of silver in her tight

33

black curls. She punched a number and said, "Bring me those New Zion papers, please." She hung up, inspected him anew, and declared, "You were expecting me to stop her, weren't you?"

"I'm not certain I understand."

"Don't you try your foolishness with me. This was all calculated and planned. You knew if Suzie Rikkers started in, with you sitting there all broken and defenseless, I'd have no choice but to pull her up short."

He nodded. "I hoped you would."

"And my last day on the local bench. You ought to be ashamed of yourself."

"They wanted me to have counsel. They wanted me to fight. They wanted to drag this out for weeks." He took a hard breath and finished, "I couldn't take her standing there asking me all the questions I've been asking myself every night for the past eighteen months."

"That accident wasn't your fault, Marcus. I've seen the police report. That truck came out of nowhere."

"I couldn't take days of cross," he repeated, his voice hoarse from the strain of confessing. "My only hope was to agree to whatever she said and get it over with."

"And risk losing everything in the process."

Marcus responded to that by lifting his gaze and revealing to her the hollow core that had once contained his life.

One glance was enough to cause her to flinch and turn away. At the knock on her door, Judge Nicols responded with an almost grateful, "Come in."

From behind Marcus, a younger woman's voice announced, "The writ is complete, Judge."

"Let me have it." She slipped on her half-moon reading glasses. "Marcus, you know my chief clerk, Jenny Hail."

Marcus raised his chin but not his gaze. He licked his lips, but no words came. His throat remained locked around the unspoken — that he had already lost all he had of any worth.

"All right, this looks in order." Nicols reached for her pen and scratched busily. "Based on your argument and the formal appeal, I am hereby issuing a writ of mandamus against New Horizons."

Marcus could only manage a weak, "Thank you."

One of his new clients was a black church in Rocky Mount, his current home. The Church of New Zion had been founded with the first earnings of freed slaves. Their cemetery contained the memories of six generations, the same cemetery that now bordered property owned by New Horizons Incorporated, the world's largest producer of sports shoes, sports fashion, and what their constant advertising called Teen Gear. New Horizons was also the largest employer in a six-county area. Currently they were building a new corporate headquarters on a hill overlooking the church. Well used to throwing its weight around, New Horizons found it objectionable that its boardroom would look down on acres of rainwashed graves. They had asked the local council to condemn the site and remove the tombs.

"As you requested, I am hereby instructing the county commission to respect the cemetery's grandfather clause and allow the current use of the land to continue." She settled the papers back into the folder and handed it over. "Go home, Marcus."

"But we still haven't heard if Rikkers and Carol's mother will accept your terms."

"I'll handle those two. Go home." She offered him a glance of shared sorrow. "Get some rest. Heal. Put this day behind you."

TWO

The afternoon heat lacked August's former fierceness as Marcus joined the frantic coastward rush, everyone desperate to eke out one final September beach weekend. The surrounding cars and SUVs were crammed with kids and luggage, toting surfboards and boats. Ahead of him, two young faces appeared in a minivan's rear window. A boy and a girl waved at him. When Marcus did not respond, they crossed their eyes and mashed noses and tongues against the glass. Marcus watched them, unable to turn from the way fate and the two children mocked his hollow state.

He followed the minivan and the two clowning children to Rocky Mount, and they waved furiously when he took the exit. He drove into his sheltered corner of the world thinking of laughter and simple pleasures, and how easy it all had once seemed.

A pickup stuffed with ladders and tarpaulins and paint cans blocked his drive, so Marcus parked in the street. As he passed the grand magnolia anchoring the center of his lawn, a cardinal flitted by. Five tulip poplars did sentry duty down his property line, while an ancient dogwood and a towering sycamore sheltered the bay window of what would become his office. As Marcus climbed the front steps, he noted with vacant satisfaction that the honeysuckle was finally training itself up the garage trellis. A mockingbird sang to him across his wrap-around veranda, and the day enveloped him with the scent of magnolia blossoms and honeysuckle. On a better man, one who carried less guilt, the magic might even have worked.

He entered the Victorian manor built by his grandfather to a greeting of soft voices, sawdust, and fresh paint. Marcus crossed the domed foyer to the pair of rooms that ran the right-hand length of his house. As soon as they were completed, the front room was to become a library–conference room, the other his office. Now they were draped in canvas and shone with wet paint.

A tall black man with a face furrowed as winter fields halted his painting and looked down from his ladder perch. "How are you doing?"

Marcus surveyed the progress. "Looks like you're almost done in here."

The old man harrumphed and returned

to daubing the ancient crown molding. From the room across the hall a woman's voice said, "I'll be sure to pass on the message soon as Marcus gets in, sir. Thank you for calling." Chair rollers squeaked as Marcus' secretary pushed away from her desk. She walked in to stand beside him and demand, "Well?"

"He ain't saying nothing," the black man offered from his perch.

"That's because you didn't ask him right." A finger jabbed his ribs. "Marcus Glenwood, I'm not gonna put up with any of your nastiness, you hear me?"

The old man halted his painting once more. Marcus looked down at the floor and replied, "It was pretty much as I expected. They staked me out on the courtroom floor and skinned me alive."

The painter's name was Deacon Wilbur, and he was the retired pastor of the New Zion Church. Deacon was his name and not his title, assigned by a sharecropping daddy who could hope no higher for his firstborn, and who had died a happy man after watching his son stride to the pulpit. Like the old-timey pastors of many black churches, Deacon Wilbur supported himself and his family through a second profession. Deacon asked the secretary, "Who is *they?*"

"Miss Rice's momma and that vulture

she hired." Netty Turner had appeared on his doorstep the day after Marcus had moved in, asking for any work he could give. Marcus' secretary attended Deacon's church when she could. "Miss Rice's momma has more money than Wall Street. She never did forgive poor Marcus for stealing Miss Rice away. She hired herself a lawyer nasty as she is. A vulture in high heels. Wears this nail polish the color of dried blood."

"You've never even met Suzie Rikkers," Marcus protested.

"I spoke on the phone with her enough. And her own secretary doesn't like her any more than I do."

"Suzie Rikkers called here?" This was news. "When?"

"Never you mind. I dealt with the vulture. That's all you need to know."

"Netty, if an attorney calls me, you need to pass on the message."

She planted fists on bony hips. "Just listen to you mouthing off at me."

"I'm not —"

"Every time you met with that vulture you'd come back in here scalded. Look at you now, you're close on parboiled." Netty Turner had been a secretary in a previous life, before her only child was born severely handicapped and her husband vanished. Now she needed to remain close enough to respond to emergencies. There were a lot of emergencies with her son. Netty Turner considered Marcus' arrival and his easygoing attitude toward her hours an absolute godsend. "The vulture wanted papers. I sent her papers."

Deacon Wilbur wiped hands, broad and flat as mortarboards, on a paint-spattered cloth. "Still say it was a mistake, you going in there alone."

Marcus tried to shrug off the day's impossible weight. "I can't see how having anybody else witness the ordeal would have made it easier to bear."

"Ain't talking about witnessing." Deacon stuffed the cloth into the back pocket of his coveralls. "I'm talking about being there for a friend in need."

Deacon's kindness threatened to unravel the cords holding his mangled heart in place. Marcus set his briefcase onto a sawhorse and flipped back the latches. He extracted a manila folder and held it up. "The court has ruled on your church's request."

The elderly painter's eyes widened. "It's all done?"

"Signed, sealed, and delivered. Go on, take it. This is your copy."

"No sir. Not before I wash the paint off my hands." He climbed down from the ladder, his eyes never leaving the folder. "Got the hopes of a thousand living souls in that file. Six generations and a whole world of memories, yes, I need clean hands to take hold of that."

Marcus opened the file and turned so Deacon Wilbur could read over his shoulder. "I asked the court to make what is called a declarative judgment. It basically tells both New Horizons and the county commission to leave your property alone."

"Not mine, no. I'm just a trustee for a lot of people, both here and in the here-after." The old man's voice had taken on a preacher's gentle cadence. "You've made a lot of folks indebted to you."

"Just doing my job."

"Yes sir, a lot of folks." Going on as though Marcus had not spoken. "Lot of families gonna sleep better, knowing their loved ones will rest peaceful till the Lord comes with trumpets and chariots of fire. Yes, lots of families." He lifted his gaze to Marcus. "It'd mean more than I can say for these folks to have a chance to thank you personally."

"There's no need."

"Yes there is, now. Strong needs. Strong. Families from all over the county'll want to shake your hand." The dark and brilliant gaze held Marcus from beneath a protruding brow. "Gonna ask a favor of you, sir. Want you to come to our Sunday service."

"Excuse me?"

"You don't have to stay if you don't want. Just come long enough for people to meet the man who's worked to keep their families all resting peaceful. Yes." He took Marcus' silence as acceptance. "Sunday at nine. Much obliged, sir. Much obliged."

As Marcus emerged blinking and stunned from the Sunday service, Deacon Wilbur extended one long arm to draw him near. "Mr. Marcus, come on over here, sir. Like you to meet two dear friends of mine. This is Alma and Austin Hall."

"Nice to meet you." Marcus heard the words as from a great distance. The entire world seemed filtered through the clamor that was no more.

The woman said, "Deacon tells us you took on New Horizons and won."

"That's right." The old pastor did not actually smile, but he unbent enough to nod approval. "Mr. Marcus went in there and saved our families' resting place."

Faces turned in unison toward the cemetery. Today was the first time Marcus had actually laid eyes on the place, and part of him understood perfectly why New Horizons had found it so offensive. The cemetery was not only large, it had a ramshackle air that defied orderly profit-driven thought. Families walked the broad, graveled aisles, pointing out names, watching the children race ahead with bouquets and garlands streaming. Around the outer boundaries, a tumble-down fence fought against the onslaught of weeds. The oldest graves were marked with weathered crosses and bordered by pebbles and seashells and shards of col-ored glass. Sunlight and children's laughter and echoes of the closing hymn danced in the air above the graves like the faint beat of unseen wings.

Alma Hall brought him back around with, "We need ourselves a lawyer willing to do battle with the behemoth atop that hill."

The words hung there between them. Perhaps it was the way Alma Hall ad-dressed him, as though she had been practicing the part for weeks. Or perhaps after that service whatever the woman said, however crude or poetic, would have chimed like crystal bells in the clear September air.

Marcus asked, "You're also involved in a land dispute with New Horizons?"

Deacon Wilbur hummed a single note,

as apparently Marcus' query was the response he had been hoping for. But Austin Hall sighed so long and hard it seemed his wife's words had punctured his heart and drained all breath from his body. Austin Hall said wearily, "Alma, come on now. Don't let's get started on that."

Alma Hall chose to ignore her husband entirely. "Yes, we have a dispute with New Horizons, and no, it is not over land."

Marcus pulled his eyes from Austin Hall, standing there stooped and vacant-eyed. He looked out over the cemetery to what once had been a wooded rise. Along the lower slope pines still fought for space with oaks and sycamores. But the crown had been razed flat, like a giant's hand had swiped away all greenery before pounding the earth so hard it bled clay red. An older metal and glass building squatted to his right. Directly ahead, steel spindles were being planted in the raw clay, lifeless parodies of the growth that was no more.

"This is a matter of great urgency," Alma Hall continued. "Would you please stop by our house this afternoon?"

Marcus turned back around. Alma Hall held to an attractiveness that was as much a matter of bearing as form. She was big boned and spoke with a carefully deliberate air. The sun shone with such strength it made her honeyed skin translucent, as though Marcus could delve through the multitude of layers and see the desperation that fueled her formal tone. "I'll see you about three."

After a solitary lunch Marcus moved about the house, supposedly puttering but in truth accomplishing little. He swept sawdust from the corners of his soon-to-be office and carried Deacon's empty paint buckets to the dumpster out back. Sometimes such idle moments were enough to draw out memories of fonder times. Today, however, the ghosts of bygone eras did not rise to comfort him, and he was glad when it came time to depart.

The Halls lived in Rocky Mount, one of the many new subdivisions cropping up between Zebulon and Raleigh. The recently completed Beltline offered eight-lane access from the poorer east to the richer south and west. Computer technicians and lab assistants and secretaries and low-level executives could buy homes on large lots for money that would have scarcely paid for a doghouse adjacent to the Research Triangle Park.

The Hall residence was airy and light-filled and pleasant, in direct contrast to the welcome Austin Hall showed him.

The man cast a resentful shadow as he silently directed Marcus into the spacious living room, then retreated, leaving Marcus alone.

Marcus stood by the large back window and pretended to take an interest in how the tall sentinel pines filtered the afternoon light. A quarrel between husband and wife carried clearly from somewhere upstairs.

"All I do is ask you to answer the door, and you've got to turn it into the drama of a lifetime."

"I did what you said, Alma. I did it even though I don't want that man in my house, not now, not ever. We don't need him here."

"You heard Deacon. That *man* has taken on New Horizons and won."

"It doesn't change a thing and you know it."

"So what do you want to do, now? Just sit on our hands and let our baby suffer?"

"You don't have any call talking to me that way. None at all. You know that as well as I do."

"What I know is you are the most stubborn man it's ever been my misfortune to meet up with." Heavy footsteps thudded down the hallway overhead. "Now you come on."

"Alma, I'm not —"

"Don't you start. Don't you even try." The carpeted stairs thunked like a muffled bass drum under her angry tread. "Get yourself down here *now*."

Marcus waited to turn around until he heard her say, "Thank you for coming, Mr. Glenwood."

"It's my pleasure." He showed no sign he had heard anything untoward. He had bitter experience of marital arguments carried into the public eye.

"Won't you sit down?"

"Thank you." The furniture, carpeting, and wallpaper were various shades of off-white, deepening to latte-colored wall shelves and a painted brick fireplace. The effect was muted, soothing. Marcus did a quick search for family photos, anything that suggested the presence of children, found none.

"Can I get you something? I've got some fresh iced tea, or I could put on a pot of coffee."

"I'm fine, thanks."

"All right." She watched her husband do a sulky walk into the living room, her face blank as uncarved stone. Only when Austin had seated himself in the chair closest to the hallway did Alma turn back to Marcus and say, "Our daughter has been kidnapped."

The round-backed chair creaked as

Austin Hall shifted his weight. But he said nothing.

Alma Hall gave her husband a swift warning glance, then repeated for emphasis, "Kidnapped."

"When?"

"I can't say for certain. But I would guess it was about six weeks ago."

"Six weeks," Marcus repeated. "And you are only now contacting the authorities?"

"My wife has run herself ragged," Austin Hall muttered. "Talking to every au-thor-i-ty there is."

Alma blasted an angry breath. Marcus took it as permission to inspect Austin Hall. The man was darker than his wife and an inch or two shorter in height. He held to the same dignified authority, only on him it seemed tighter, like he had worked himself into a suit two sizes too small. "What do you do for a living?"

"Me?" The man stiffened slightly, disliking this momentary spotlight. "I teach statistics at State."

"At the Raleigh campus?"

"Yes."

"You're in the mathematics department?"

"Yes. But they share me with economics. I teach two classes in econometrics. I also teach introductory calculus."

Marcus nodded as though the news had great import. "You say your wife has been in contact with the authorities?"

A hand reached for the knot of the tie Austin Hall no longer wore. He still had on a pair of dark suit-slacks and a carefully ironed shirt. His hair was close-cropped, his cuff links gold. Marcus had the impression that taking off his tie was about as informal as this man would ever get. "She started the day we received Gloria's letter, and she hasn't let up. Not for an instant."

"I see." Marcus did not turn back to the wife. Not yet. It would be too easy to dismiss Austin Hall's attitude as that of a severely impatient man. One tired of going through the motions, angry at the disturbances to his tightly controlled world. "Have you contacted an attorney prior to this?"

"Two of them." Austin Hall glanced at his wife, but not for confirmation. Rather to tell Marcus, look over there, that's who you ought to be asking these questions. "One local fellow, he said it wasn't his field of expertise."

But Marcus remained focused upon Austin Hall. "And the other?"

"The man looked into it." He tried for defiant, and failed. "He said our claim was so flimsy we'd risk being countersued by the company for filing a frivolous case. Told us he'd be censured by the court. Wouldn't touch it with a barge pole." When his wife shifted impatiently, he added, "Those were his exact words, Alma. You heard them the same as me."

Marcus remained held not by the man's words, but rather by his eyes. There was a hollow point at the center of his dark gaze, a shadow so deep it bore a hole straight through the man's center. "Do you recall the attorney's name?"

"Larry Grimes with Morgan and Jones."

"They're a good firm. One of the largest in the state." Marcus finally turned from the man and his tightly vacant gaze. He said to Alma Hall, "You believe New Horizons is connected to this matter?"

"I'm not believing anything. They are."

"I see."

Alma Hall had a smattering of freckles across her high and slanted cheekbones. It was the only trace of softness to her face and tone and gaze.

"You're suggesting that one of the largest companies in eastern North Carolina has kidnapped your daughter?"

"That is exactly right."

"Did this take place here in Rocky Mount?"

"No. In China."

When Marcus leaned back, the sofa accepted him like he would never be allowed to get up and leave this behind. "China."

"That's right. Between Hong Kong and a city called Guangzhou." Alma Hall had clearly gained a lot of practice saying that name. "About thirty-five miles over what used to be the Chinese border."

"Mrs. Hall —"

"Gloria has been investigating New Horizons' labor violations for almost two years." Alma Hall had no intention of letting go. "They've been involved in dirty practices since the beginning. Gloria collected all kinds of evidence. She's shown me a whole box of press clippings from just one factory up in Richmond."

Marcus suppressed his list of objections. Sometimes a necessary part of lawyering was waiting and listening until a client ran out of steam.

"New Horizons shows this fancy face to the outside world. Signing on the top stars in every sport you can imagine — tennis, basketball, golf, football, skiing, everything. They spend a ton of money on their advertisements. Slick music, wild lights, everything you can imagine."

"I've seen the ads."

"Of course you have. So has the rest of the world. They pay the stars millions, but they treat their employees like dirt." She was steamrolling now. "Gloria was working to show how they locate their factories in the poorest areas, here and abroad. Places like Rocky Mount, where the authorities will be on their side no matter what mess they get into. And there are a lot of messes."

Marcus asked quietly, "What do you do, Mrs. Hall?"

"I'm dean of admissions over at Shaw University." Shaw was one of the largest black colleges in the state. Alma Hall dug into her jacket pocket, then spent a moment carefully unfolding a sheet of paper and rubbing out the creases. "Gloria is our only child. She left here with a full scholarship to Georgetown University. She took two undergraduate degrees, in sociology and economics. She's doing her master's now in labor relations. The topic of her thesis is New Horizons."

Alma Hall handed over the page. "Six weeks ago, we received this letter."

Marcus accepted the typewritten page, and read it carefully. Then he read it again. And a third time.

He then turned and looked out the plate-glass window. Sunlight streamed through the pines to splash the glass with brilliant light. A gentle wind waved the trees' shadows, weaving black script upon the gold. Gloria's letter was as lucid and determined as her mother. Gloria wrote that she had asked someone named Kirsten to mail this a week after her departure. It was the best way, Gloria wrote, to ensure that her parents did not try to stop her. She was going over to chase down rumors about the New Horizons facility in China. Factory 101, it was called, and what she had gathered so far made the place sound like a glimpse into hell itself. She hurt for those people, Gloria said. She wanted to interview workers from the compound in which Factory 101 was situated. There was a special reason for the timing of this journey. Something that made her mission particularly vital. If they received this letter but had not heard from her personally, they were to contact the United States embassy in Beijing, the consulate in Hong Kong, and the FBI. They should get hold of the best lawyer they could find, and push. Push hard. Her life might depend on this.

Marcus continued to stare out the back window as the pines etched more shadow-script within the sunlight. Marcus spent a long moment searching for a message before deciding the afternoon wrote its mysteries in an unreadable tongue. The air was so still he heard a clock in another room softly chime the half hour. Gloria's repeated use of one word rang with the clock in the sun-splashed air. *Mission.*

Marcus turned back because he had to. Alma Hall read the furtive search for a way out in his features. She cut him off before he could speak by leaning forward and letting desperation clench her throat and rake every word raw. "Mr. Glenwood, my baby is *hurting.* She needs help. I can't explain to you how I know this, but every breath I take, I hear that child crying out from the wilderness." On any other face the gaze would have appeared drawn from the borderlands of madness. "Maybe you were brought to us for a purpose, did you ever think that? You were drawn here because you're the man to bring my Gloria home."

THREE

Monday morning Marcus traveled to and around Raleigh in less than fifty minutes. Where the Rocky Mount highway merged with the Raleigh Beltline, the traffic congealed, but only momentarily. Nine o'clock was a fairly safe time to be headed toward the Research Triangle Park. Techie rush hour began at six and ended at seven-thirty, both morning and evening. This portion of the Tar Heel State prided itself on running to a Silicon Valley time clock.

The Morgan and Jones law firm occupied one of the ultramodern buildings ringing the Park. The exterior was brick, slate, and mirrored glass; the interior was plush and impersonal. After an appropriate wait for someone without a fixed appointment, Marcus was led into one of the windowless interior offices assigned to associates. "Mr. Glenwood?"

"That's right."

"Larry Grimes. Come on in. Sorry about the mess." A black man in suspenders and a hundred-dollar power tie hefted a pile of folders from one chair.

"You take coffee?"

"No thanks."

"Right. Hope you don't mind if I keep packing while we talk. They only gave me until the day after tomorrow to be up and running in Charlotte." Grimes deposited the files into a box, pulled a pen from his pocket, and scribbled on the top. "Your fax said you wanted to discuss one of my clients who's approached you seeking representation?"

"That's right." The office was littered with half-filled boxes and piles of unsorted papers. Nails protruded from an empty power wall, below which rested a box crammed with plaques and photos and diplomas. "Alma and Austin Hall."

An instant's hesitation, then Grimes barked a single laugh. "You've got to be kidding."

"You remember the case, then."

"Sure I remember them. But there's no case. The matter is a total waste of time."

"Alma Hall doesn't think so."

"Alma Hall is an emotionally distraught mother who would do anything to get her daughter back. You met the father?"

"Yes." Marcus watched the younger attorney smooth his tie. Again. Stroking the silk with absent nervous gestures. "I couldn't figure out his reaction."

"What's to figure. The man knows how

to think logically."

"I'm not sure that's the whole picture." Paying almost no mind to his own words. Concentrating on the attorney and his pinstriped shirt with the white collar, his alligator belt, the eyes that danced about the room. "Mr. Hall said you had refused to take their case."

"Like I said, what case? The Hall girl was of legal age, she was known as a troublemaker, she went to China, she decided to stay for a while."

"Troublemaker in what way?"

The attorney's voice tightened. "Look, the claim is groundless. That's all you need to know. The only tie-in between the girl and New Horizons is some hyped-up letter."

Marcus nodded slowly. The man was young, polished, smooth, and under pressure. What Marcus could not figure out was where the pressure came from. "Do you handle many federal cases?"

"Some. Look, I'd love to chat, but right now I'm up to my eyeballs."

"Could I have a copy of any relevant information you turned up?"

When the man looked ready to refuse him, Marcus rose to his feet and added, "I'm sure the Halls would deliver a formal request if I asked."

The man's sudden stillness brought to

mind a nervous quarry. "You can't seriously be thinking of taking this case."

"A girl is missing and nobody seems very eager to have her found. That makes me wonder."

"You're wasting your time." The shrug held the stiffness of a puppet. "But, hey, if you're that hungry, be my guest."

"Thank you." Marcus handed over his card, started for the door, then was struck by a sudden thought. He turned back and hazarded a guess. "By the way, congratulations."

Grimes froze once more. "How did you hear?"

"Oh, you know how these things get around."

Grimes bent back over the box. "Crazy. Kedrick and Walker said I had to keep my partnership secret until their next general meeting."

Marcus tapped on the door frame, his thoughts racing. "I'll expect that file by the end of the week."

Rocky Mount had a divided past and a contemporary chasm. The Tar River flowed dark and sullen through its middle, forming a divide that not even the legal joining of Nash and Edgecombe Counties could bridge. To the west lay Raleigh and wealth. All the town's stores and most of the new investment — private and public both — also lay west of the Tar. To the east, in the area where Marcus' grandparents had built their home some forty years earlier, sprawled a haphazard collection of enclaves. Most of them were black, poor, and bitter.

The eastern side of the Tar River was a time warp to a poorer, harsher era. While western Rocky Mount sported three new shopping centers, nine banks, and a score of new factories, the Edgecombe side remained a one-company town. New Horizons employed almost everyone who held a steady job, over four thousand people and still expanding. Soon after his arrival, Marcus had been told by a black neighbor that New Horizons and the white-run city council liked things just the way they were.

In eastern Rocky Mount, the store windows were boarded up, the roads potholed, the few shops almost empty. People shuffled down cracked sidewalks with tired resignation. This part of town bordered an Indian settlement, three communities established by former slaves, and North Carolina's largest remaining poverty pocket. Marcus had known little of this when he returned after the accident, and he was still learning. At first the black teens who clustered on porches up and down his block had frightened him. Now they were just a part of the scene. The white citizens who continued to migrate farther and farther west referred to this end of town as Dredgecombe.

When his grandfather had built his wife's dream house, the Edgecombe County side of Rocky Mount had been home to the sort of people never fully accepted by their more proper neighbors to the west — sawmill owners and warehouse operators and tanners and hog butchers and landowners whose wealth was built on sharecroppers' sweat. Marcus' grandfather had been a tobacco auctioneer until a stroke cut off his voice and mobility. Marcus had kept the place after they died, mostly because it was his last tenuous bond to a past that held little heritage and even less in the way of family ties.

He turned into his street, which softly hummed sad tales of former grandeur. Decrepit Victorian houses shyly watched his passage, sheltered behind tall oaks. He sometimes had difficulty seeing his place in its newly refurbished state. In a way, he missed how for most of the past eighteen months, returning home had meant confronting a lawn blanketed by sawdust and piles of lumber and sheets of roofing tile and construction tools. Now the roof no longer sagged, the windows did not gape, the huge sycamore no longer probed one dark limb through the third-story cupola, the stairs did not look drunk, and the veranda railing no longer missed the majority of its teeth. Marcus stopped in his drive and regretted the absence of the mind-cleansing labor that had kept him from needing to think of any future at all.

He was halfway up the front stairs when his secretary called through her open window, "You in for a call from Washington?"

"Yes."

"Some lady, I didn't catch her name."

Marcus sidled around where Deacon Wilbur's ladder was set in the middle of the front hall. He asked Netty, "Are the extra computer and fax lines hooked up yet?"

"Been done since last week. Which I told you. Twice."

"All right. I want you to get on the Internet and contact one of the corporate search listings. Doesn't matter which one. Ask for a complete record of everywhere New Horizons operates a facility." He crossed to his makeshift desk in the back corner of Netty's office. He picked up his phone, glanced back, and found Deacon Wilbur had climbed halfway down the

62

ladder to look through the open door. "What is it?"

Deacon asked, "This mean you're gonna help Austin and Alma bring their child home?"

"I don't know anything yet." To Netty, "Once you get that listing, I want you to run it by a legal search engine."

His secretary and the paint-spattered black man shared a glance. Netty said, "Come again?"

"LEXIS is good. Use them." Marcus cradled the phone as he spelled the name. "Have them pull past court records. We're looking for any cases pending or settled against the various New Horizons facilities. Tell them we're looking for a basic track record, just want to query past practices." He waited while Netty and Deacon exchanged another glance. "Well?"

Netty said to the old man, "Sounds to me like real live law is being practiced around here."

He raised the phone. "Marcus Glenwood."

A very nervous voice said, "My name is Kirsten Stanstead."

"The girl mentioned in Gloria's letter?"

"Yes. We're housemates. I'm also Gloria's best friend."

Strung out was the term that came to mind. As though the voice were a viola string, and the tuning knob had been twisted until the wire hummed of its own accord. "Have you heard from her?"

"Of course not." The response was not snappish, though Kirsten held to the haughty citified air of one born to money. She sounded like a woman ready to detonate. "Why would we be going to all this trouble if Gloria had contacted us?"

"Right." Marcus pulled over his swivel chair. "I see."

"I understand you're taking the case."

"I am considering it."

"Considering." The voice twisted one notch tighter. "How fortunate for Gloria that her parents found someone so committed."

Marcus detected a faintly nasal twang beneath the strain. Probably Boston. He wondered what her parents thought of their blue-blooded daughter living with a black woman from Rocky Mount. "First I need to see if there is any case at all, Miss . . ."

"Stanstead. I personally feel that the barest of investigations would show that there is an excellent case here."

"I see."

"Actually, I was calling to offer my assistance. Gloria left some documents you could use as evidence. That was her intention all along."

Marcus bent closer to his desk. "Gloria Hall was preparing a case against New Horizons?"

"Isn't that what I just said?" Kirsten pushed out an exasperated breath. "It was the topic of her master's thesis. Alma told me she had already spoken to you about this."

"I know about the thesis, yes. But not about a case. Or compiled evidence."

"I was assisting her. I have completed a year of law school."

"You're studying at Georgetown also?"

"No." A moment's hesitation. "For the past several years I've been involved full-time in charity work."

"Right." He nodded to the wall. A perfect Brahmin response. When life offered more of a challenge than they liked, the rich hid in charities. She probably organized celebrity jewelry auctions or bridge afternoons. His ex-wife had made a profession of charity wine tastings. "Miss Stanstead, could you tell me what kind of trouble Gloria had been in?"

The tone flashed from tense to furious. "What *is* it with you guys?"

"I'm sorry, I —"

"You've been talking to that other lawyer!"

"It's common practice for incoming counsel —"

"Oh give me a break! I should have known! You're all the same, just money-grubbing parasites!"

Marcus held the phone away from his ear, retreating tortoise-like as he had done so often from his wife. "Not at —"

"You listen to me. The only trouble Gloria has been in came from looking after the rights of people who couldn't look after themselves! Which is more than anyone could ever say about you and your kind!"

The phone slammed down. Marcus sat staring at the receiver. Perhaps this was something mothers taught their daughters in the rarefied atmosphere of the long-term rich. Or maybe it was a genetic thing, this ability to fly into unbridled rage at the drop of a single improper syllable.

He turned around to find Netty and Deacon standing in the doorway. Netty was at the foot of the ladder, Deacon leaning over from halfway up. Both still watching him. "What is it?"

"Seems like an awful lot of trouble," Netty replied, "for a case you're not sure you're taking."

The preacher did not say anything Marcus could hear. Deacon hummed a single note as he climbed back up and returned to his painting. Dipping his brush, the ladder creaking as he shifted to reach a corner, still holding to that one hummed note.

Logan Kendall's secretary said through his open door, "Randall Walker just arrived."

"You set up the coffee, I'll go bring him back. Have Suzie Rikkers join us." Logan hustled down the partners' hallway, then halted by the entrance to the reception foyer to check his reflection. He had once heard his secretary describe him as a middleweight bruiser with a taste for Armani. In truth, the only thing Logan Kendall loved more than fighting was winning. Which was why he was merely a good attorney, but a great trial lawyer. Logan had boxed for six years, choosing his undergraduate school on its strength in the ring. He smoothed his mustache, adjusted his tie and his smile, and entered the lobby with hand outstretched. "Mr. Walker, I can't tell you what an honor this is."

"Randall to you, my boy." The founder of the legal powerhouse of Kedrick and Walker pumped Logan's hand. In the clannish atmosphere of Carolina law, Randall Walker was something of a legend. Two of Logan's senior partners were there to watch his stock soar. "And the honor is all mine."

"I've set up our meeting in the partners' conference room."

"Fine, fine. Haven't been here since you fellows moved. How long has it been?"

"Not quite two years." In fact, they had been the first tenants to sign a long-term lease in the newly completed First Federal Tower, the tallest building in Raleigh. They had rented the top three floors and agreed without a quibble to the exorbitant rent, demanding only two conditions: The firm of Knowles, Barbour and Bradshaw was to be the only law firm granted space in the building, and First Federal was to appoint them outside counsel.

Randall swung easily into step alongside Logan. "This arrangement was Marcus Glenwood's work, wasn't it?"

Logan faltered momentarily. Marcus Glenwood remained a name he despised. The only person who loathed Glenwood more was Suzie Rikkers. And for good reason. "A number of us had a hand in putting the deal together."

"Of course you did. Even so, I'd have to say it was a smart move on Glenwood's part. Very smart. The First Federal contract he brought in more than pays the rent."

Logan bit off the snarl before it could fully form. When Randall Walker's secretary had called to set up this meeting, she had said Randall expected to pay the full hourly rate. For both Suzie and himself. That earned Randall Walker the title of client. And a client was permitted one snide remark. One.

Logan led him into the largest salon in the partnership and said, "I don't believe you've met my associate, Suzie Rikkers."

Suzie Rikkers was an oddity, an outstanding legal analyst and a fair trial lawyer who was constantly on the verge of being fired. What put most people off Suzie Rikkers was her attitude. She alternated between treating life as a battlefield and complaining that people never gave her a chance. Every problem was a personal attack. When she was not angry, her voice clung to an off-pitch mewl. Most of the partners avoided working with her, and the associates and paralegals loathed her. Two things kept Suzie Rikkers on staff — a solid client base, and Logan Kendall. Logan endured her attitude and loved her loyalty. She might be a witch with a buzz-saw voice, but she was his witch.

Suzie Rikkers offered their guest a rail-thin hand. "Mr. Walker."

"A pleasure I've long awaited, Ms.

Rikkers." Randall Walker bowed slightly as he shook hands, then turned to admire the room. "This place is even more beautiful than I'd been led to believe."

The firm's inner sanctum reeked of legal heritage and beeswax polish. When the old courthouse was torn down, the firm had acquired the chief superior court justice's private chambers. Paneling of South American mahogany graced three walls. The fourth wall was an enormous expanse of glass.

Logan turned to the side table where a coffee service of bone china had been set up. "How do you take your coffee, Randall?"

"Black, two sugars." He continued his circuit of the interior walls. A pair of Chagall lithographs and a silk Kashmiri tapestry splashed the room with color. "I believe Mr. Glenwood was responsible for your acquiring the fittings of this room as well. Charlie Hayes, the old chief justice, was a personal friend, was he not?"

Logan's hand jerked hard enough to spill coffee onto the saucer. He set down the pot and used a napkin to dry the stain. His back to the room, he replied, "Like I said, we all played a role in the move."

"Yes, yes, of course you did. And my, what a lovely setting. Mr. Glenwood certainly made a splendid choice. The view from here is magnificent, wouldn't you say, Ms. Rikkers?"

Logan turned in time to watch Suzie grind out the single word, "Great." Marcus Glenwood had twice put his name to her being passed over for partner. And after she had hounded his favorite paralegal until the woman left for another firm, Marcus had spent months trying to gather enough support to have Suzie fired. Defeating that motion was the one battle Logan had managed to win outright against Marcus Glenwood.

"Thank you, Logan." Randall accepted his cup and pointed toward the sunlit day. "Is that White Memorial's steeple I see out there?"

"I have no idea." Logan poured himself a cup and sat down. He did not need to admire the view. The first weekend after being made partner, Logan had spent an entire Saturday afternoon sitting in one of these padded suede chairs. Raleigh was full of parks and trees old enough to blanket all but the tallest buildings. Away from downtown, steeples rose like pointed reminders that this was indeed a city and not merely well-tended woodlands.

Instead of taking the expected seat at the head of the table next to Logan, Randall walked around the conference table and stood up close to the window. After a loud sip from his cup he declared, "Do you know, I can stand right here and point to five of our clients' headquarters. No, make that six. I'm almost positive that's the roofline of the Burroughs headquarters I see out there in the distance." He turned back and beamed at the room. "Must make you feel like the lords of all you survey, sitting up here in this fine chamber. Speaking of which, Logan, I believe congratulations are in order. You've recently been made partner, is that not correct?"

"Yes." Four months tomorrow, to be exact. Some days he could scarcely believe he had made the grade. Most days, however, he felt like he had been at it for a lifetime.

The grand smile turned to where Suzie sat sipping her coffee. "And I have no doubt your own star will soon be rising, Ms. Rikkers." He paused for another slurp, then added, "Especially now that your nemesis has been removed." Randall Walker turned back to the vista. He shook his head in admiration. "My, my."

Logan demanded, "Could you tell us why you called this meeting?"

"Why, I thought that would be clear by now. I wish to discuss Marcus Glenwood." Before they could recover, he continued. "Logan, you have been with this firm for eight years, if my information is correct. And Ms. Rikkers, you've been here a bit longer now, isn't that right?"

Suzie gave Logan a startled glance, searching for her cue. "Almost nine."

"Actually, it's ten next month, isn't that correct?" He continued to address his questions to the window. "Logan, you are from Baltimore, do I have that right?"

"I fail to see —"

"University of Maryland undergrad and UVA law. Married a woman from Raleigh who was studying art history at that fine Jeffersonian establishment. Three lovely children, two boys and one girl who is approaching her second birthday as we speak." Another noisy sip. "And you, Ms. Rikkers, hail from Chicago, our nation's fine and windy city. Undergrad and law school at Northwestern. And still unmarried, a fact I find most astonishing. It must be from preference, certainly not from lack of opportunity." His speech held a courtly air, as though bestowing a royal welcome. "Marcus was born in the Philadelphia area. Although his roots are mostly from these parts."

Suzie Rikkers' voice had the metallic quality of having been pounded flat on an anvil. "Why have you been checking up on me?"

"That's simple enough, Ms. Rikkers. I like to know the people I'm addressing." Randall finally turned from the window and slid into the seat directly across the table from them. "Now perhaps you would be so kind as to give me your impressions of your recently departed colleague."

Logan studied the man across from them. In the space of a few minutes Randall Walker had entered their domain and wrested control, and done so with the kindliest of manners. The man certainly lived up to his reputation. Randall Walker had been the youngest person ever to serve upon the federal appellate bench. After holding that position for eight years, he had formed a partnership that now included two former senators and a retired governor among its ranks. Randall served on the board of over a dozen Fortune 500 companies, and acted as outside counsel to another five or six. He charged 450 dollars an hour, the highest rate of any lawyer in the state.

"Marcus Glenwood is history," Suzie Rikkers snapped. "That's all you need to know."

Randall nodded benignly. "He must have been quite a good trial attorney, to have risen to partnership in less than six years."

"So-so. He had great connections." Suzie's nails did a nervous dance upon the table. "Most of them through his wife. Her family was serious old money."

"His wife, yes. You represented her in their divorce, what was her name?"

"Carol Clay Rice."

"That's right. As in Rice Communications and the Rice Foundation."

Logan disliked being blindsided, and he distrusted the man's courtly manner. He remained silent and let Suzie respond. "Marcus was dirt-poor. I learned that from his former mother-in-law. His parents split up and disappeared when he was about ten. He was raised by his grandparents."

Randall smiled delightedly, as though Suzie was bestowing the wisdom of the ages. "Did you ever work with him on a trial?"

"Once. He went down in flames."

Logan listened to Suzie twist the truth as if she were arguing a desperate case, and wondered how much Randall already knew. For example, did he know that Suzie's account was a pack of self-serving lies, that Marcus had taken over the case from a partner dying of cancer? Logan had been present when Marcus, during his first meeting with the client, had declared that taking the case to trial would do little more than prepare an extremely expensive funeral. The client had subsequently thrown a ton of money at the firm and begged them to save his worthless hide. Marcus had, in fact, drawn from the jury an astonishingly lenient sentence. Logan watched Randall Walker sitting and feasting upon Suzie Rikkers' monologue and decided the aging attorney knew a lot more than he was letting on.

Randall Walker was not an attractive man by any stretch of the imagination. Age had pulled the folds of his face down like melted tallow, until his chin appeared to be held in place by his starched collar and his tiepin. Even his freckles had stretched into age blotches. But his blue eyes twinkled and his smile charmed juries and ladies alike. Randall Walker's reputation did not end in the courtroom.

He even seemed to be working his magic on Suzie. "I can't tell you, Ms. Rikkers, what a fine assessment like yours means to an outsider like myself."

Logan decided it was time to get some answers of his own. "Why are you interested in Marcus?"

"His name has come up in several recent discussions."

He felt a bitter surge. It would be just like his old nemesis to land on his feet and be offered a job with Kedrick and Walker. "Within your firm?"

"No, with a client."

"Marcus is trying to steal one of your firm's clients?"

"Actually, sir, Marcus might be calling a client of mine as a defendant."

Suzie burst in. "Then your client doesn't have a thing to worry about."

The benign smile resurfaced. "And why is that, Ms. Rikkers?"

"Marcus had a total breakdown eighteen months ago." She did not even try to mask her pleasure. "After the accident."

"The accident, yes, how tragic. To have lost both his children like that. It must have been a terrible blow."

"Marcus went to pieces. I watched it happen." She actually smiled. "The firm was going to let him go."

Logan started to correct her, decided there was no point.

Randall said, "He resigned of his own volition, I believe."

"Only after the firm carried him for almost a year. Marcus was dead weight."

"And you say he still has not recovered?"

"You didn't see him at the divorce hearings. He was pathetic." Suzie was cheered by the recollection. "If Judge Nicols hadn't stepped in I would have eviscerated the man."

"Most interesting." Randall Walker rose from his seat, walked around the table, and took Suzie's hand in both of his. "Ms. Rikkers, I must thank you for a most enlightening little chat."

"My pleasure."

"Logan, perhaps you'd do me the kindness of walking me out."

Randall left the room, still very much in charge. Once the two men were alone, he went on, "I can well imagine you must share a taste of your colleague's venom for Mr. Glenwood."

"Marcus and I weren't friends."

"Indeed not. I understand he was your principal adversary almost every step up the firm's ladder." A piercing blue glance shot his way. "And won more times than he lost, did he not?"

Logan halted midway down the empty corridor. "Who's your client in this case Glenwood is taking up?"

"There is no case at this time, but I take your point. Some matters are not to be bandied about lightly."

Logan remained silent, immobile.

"No, indeed not." If anything, Randall appeared pleased by Logan's reticence. "Perhaps you would be so kind as to answer one question: How would you like to act on my client's behalf if this unfortunate matter does proceed?"

Logan could not help showing his surprise. "You want me to represent your client at trial?"

"If need be, sir. Only if need be."

"State or federal court?"

"That has yet to be determined. But my guess would be federal."

"And the plaintiff's attorney is Marcus Glenwood?"

"So it would appear."

"Does he have a case?"

"Weak at best."

"To have the chance to shame Marcus Glenwood in federal court," Logan did not need to think that one out. "I'd waive my fee."

This time the smile was grand enough to show pearly capped teeth. "While the sentiment is most appreciated, the act will not be necessary. Of that I can assure you."

FOUR

On Thursday Marcus waited until Netty had left for lunch, then placed the call to Washington. When the tensely cultured voice came on the line, he said, "Ms. Stanstead, this is Marcus Glenwood. We spoke on Monday, I'm an attorney in —"

"How did you get this number?"

"Alma Hall gave it to me."

"You spoke with Alma?" The tension amped higher. "Are you taking the case?"

"That's why I'm calling, Ms. Stanstead. I'm trying to determine whether there is actually a case here at all." He waited, and when another explosion did not erupt, Marcus continued. "You said you'd be willing to help me work through this."

"Yes. All right." A breath pushed so hard Marcus could feel the unease in his own chest. "Tell me what you want."

"I have undertaken a preliminary search for court records nationwide." Marcus drew the two sheaves of paper to his desk's center. "New Horizons has facilities in sixteen states. If my information is correct, there are cases either pending or on appeal that name New Horizons as defendant at fourteen of these sites."

"I know that."

"You . . ." Marcus stared at the wall. Netty had asked Deacon Wilbur to paint her entire office a buttery cream. The color seemed to swim. "May I ask how?"

"I told you." Snappish. Wary. Coldly hostile. "New Horizons was the subject of Gloria's thesis. I was helping her."

Marcus flicked the summary sheets to the page marked with a paper clip. "Apparently the closest case to us here was at their former facility —"

"In Richmond. I know."

Marcus let the pages fall. "You know."

"They were sued five years ago for polluting the James River. The plaintiffs were a couple of local eco groups and the state water board. When New Horizons lost the case they launched an appeal and simultaneously shut the facility." The words came faster now. Impatient. "It's a standard New Horizons revenge tactic, whenever the local government comes out against them, no matter what the reason. You must know that."

"No." He turned to where the wall was dappled with afternoon light. "No, I was not aware of anything of the sort."

"Their headquarters were moved to

81

North Carolina after a similar incident up in Delaware. The suit was brought by the state's employment board and a couple of unions. They were hit with about a dozen labor violations." When the news was met by silence, she pushed on. "Gloria lived for her work, Mr. Glenwood. We were friends. I helped her where I could."

"How long did you live with Gloria?"

"Almost four years."

"My information is derived from an Internet search engine and is sketchy at best." Nervously Marcus ruffled through the printouts. "The appeals against the Richmond ruling were apparently lodged with the appellate court there in Washington. I was wondering if you would search out the relevant documents."

Kirsten Stanstead's voice turned wary. "Are you accepting this case?"

A long breath, then, "If there is a case at all, yes. But I need a lot more information than I have right now to make that decision."

"Then the answer is, I don't need to do any searching. Gloria kept her case documentation very up-to-date." The lofty impatience broke through once more. "I've been through all this with Mr. Grimes. Didn't you discuss this with him?"

Marcus grabbed the folder that had arrived with the morning's mail. "You spoke with Larry Grimes?"

"I told you I had the last time we talked, Mr. Glenwood. I do not like to repeat myself."

"No. Of course not." The folder from Grimes contained nothing but the initial agreement with Gloria's parents, a page of patchy notes, and the letter informing the Halls that there was no case to be brought. "How much in the way of data did Gloria compile against New Horizons?"

"I don't know." Her wary hostility etched the air. "The attic is full of boxes. Gloria was a lot of things, but neat was not one of them."

Marcus sifted through the three spare pages another time, shook the folder, discovered nothing more. "In the letter Gloria wrote her family, she mentioned something about how the timing of her trip to China had become critical. Did she say anything about this to you?"

"No. And I have to go, Mr. Glenwood. I'm already late for a meeting."

Marcus shut the folder, spread his hand out flat over the slick surface. "Would you mind if I came to Washington and had a look at Gloria's work?"

"I suppose not. When would you come?"

"Tomorrow midafternoon, say around

83

four." Closing his hand into a fist. "I'll leave here at dawn."

After lunch Marcus took a drive. His only vehicle these days was a six-year-old matte gray Blazer with a hundred thousand very hard miles — a far cry from his former Lexus. Marcus slowed as he passed the New Zion Church. The whitewashed building was rimmed on three sides by dogwoods and tulip poplars taller than the steeple. The air above the ancient structure still shimmered from remnants of the Sunday service. As he drove past the cemetery and entered the rise of woodlands, it seemed as though Marcus could still hear the call of voices and the constant clapping.

Early September had remained dry, hot, and cloudless. Sunlight bladed through the trees, then flattened across his windshield as he crested the hill. Marcus slowed and turned into the New Horizons drive, unable to read the brick entrance sign for the harsh afternoon light. He pulled to one side of the road and climbed from the car.

Against the backdrop of thundering machinery, Marcus inspected the New Horizons facility. Despite the raw scarring of recent construction, the site had the air of a high-tech campus. To the east stood the oldest buildings, now dwarfed by a behemoth clad in brick and smoked glass. A sign planted in the landscaped foreground declared it to be the new central distribution facility. The two walls he could see were embossed with New Horizons emblems, bright gold stars streaming silver-clad rainbows. Beneath the logos, letters three stories high shouted the latest New Horizons slogan, GET IN GEAR.

Closest to the state road, an old wooden farmhouse and barn had been converted to corporate guest houses. The farm buildings were now connected by a pillared walkway and decorated with fruit trees and blooming trellises.

A half dozen brick factories and warehouses covered the area to his left, all surrounded by pristine gardens and adolescent trees. To his right rose the skeletal outlines of three mammoth buildings. Each was fronted by a sign sporting the world-famous logo, followed by completion dates. The dust and the noise were as constant as the light.

Marcus climbed back into his car and drove up the hill to the office complex. The older building was steel and marble and mirrored glass. The new structure rising to its right was twice its size. As he pulled the Blazer into a visitor's space, he could see down through the tops of trees to where the clapboard church and ancient cemetery shone in the hot afternoon sun.

The first thing Marcus noted when he entered the marble-clad foyer was the battery of cameras. Four of them. Two mounted in the corners behind the receptionist's desk, one over the electric doors leading back into the building, another rotating in the center of the high ceiling. The receptionist's desk also merited a second look — chest high and tiled like the floor. The two men behind the marble counter wore dark blue jackets and cordless telephone headsets. One was white and bulky, the other black and even bigger. Behind them, a waterfall splashed down an aluminum slide. Both men watched Marcus' approach with blank expressions.

The black man asked, "Can I help you?"

"I'd like to see someone from your legal department."

"Do you have an appointment?"

"No."

"Then we can't help you."

Marcus chose his words carefully. "I'm here regarding a union matter."

Their focus upon him tightened. "Which union are you with?"

"None. I'm an attorney."

"Your name?"

"Marcus Glenwood."

"Who are you representing?"

Clearly this was not the first time they had fielded such a request. Marcus side-stepped the question. "I'd rather discuss that with someone from your legal staff."

The two men both possessed the thick-corded necks and sloped shoulders of serious bodybuilders. The black man pointed behind Marcus with his chin. "Wait over there."

Marcus retreated obediently to a series of marble benches adorned with suede pads. The corporate logo was everywhere — the pads, the walls, carved into the aluminum waterfall, tiled in mosaic into the floor. The wall opposite the entrance sported a huge television screen that played a constant stream of corporate ads, all displaying the nation's top athletes making their hottest moves. Between each ad, the shooting-star logo showered sparks that formed the words GET IN GEAR. Flanking the television were back-lit posters covering almost every conceivable sport. The top PGA golfer squinted down the fairway to where a Chicago Bulls former guard slam-dunked a basket. Beside him twirled the women's Olympic gold-medal figure skater. Marcus walked from picture to picture, pretending to ignore the pair of receptionists. Their eyes never turned his way, but he sensed they were constantly watching him.

The back doors sighed open, and a bright young woman walked straight to where he stood. "Mr. Glenwood, did I get that right?"

"Yes."

"Great." She offered him a cheery smile and her hand. "I'm Tracy. Welcome to New Horizons."

"You're not an attorney."

"No way. I'm a summer intern in the PR department. This is my last week. School starts next Monday." She gave a buoyant grimace. "Back to the old grind."

"I asked to speak with someone from legal affairs."

"Hey, I know, I'm so sorry. Everybody is really tied up right now. You wouldn't believe how busy we are."

"Of course."

"But they asked me to give you a company brochure and thank you for stopping by." She handed over the glossy magazine. "Say, do you have a card?"

Marcus hesitated. "I'm in the process of moving."

"Sure. I can understand that. I am too." Another grimace. "That's the breaks, right?"

Marcus allowed her to usher him toward the outer doors. "Have you had a good time here?"

"Oh, hey, the greatest." The blue corporate jacket did not entirely hide her bouncing curves. "You wouldn't believe some of the people I've met. Just last week I helped host Todd Rankin." When Marcus was not suitably impressed, she added, "Quarterback of the Dallas Cowboys."

"I know who he is."

"Sure you do. Me, I'm just your basic sports nut. Guess that's why they said I could come back next year." She halted as the doors slid back. They were instantly surrounded by the grind of construction machinery. She offered another cheery smile and raised her voice to say, "Thanks so much for stopping by."

He walked back to the Blazer, climbed in, started the motor, and sat there a long moment staring down the steep drop to the little clapboard church. He wondered why they had bothered to send the cheerleader down at all. Marcus put the vehicle into gear and pulled from the space.

He stopped at the intersection, then drove past the construction site. The road became clogged with muddy tracks and the rumble of diesel thunder.

That was when they struck.

Marcus caught a glimpse of light

against metal and turned in time to see a pickup hurtle down the graveled rise. He watched in disbelief as the mud-splattered truck hit an unseen slope and bounced all four wheels off the dirt.

Marcus almost left it too late. Then the roar of the pickup's engine spurred him to stomp on the accelerator. Which meant the pickup slammed into his rear fender, and not his door.

The impact flung him across the seat, the wheel slewing under his grip. Before he could recover, he was hammered back the other way. The second truck's aim was higher, mashing in his passenger door and showering him with broken glass.

The driver of the second truck opened his door and leaned on the running board. He wore a sweat-stained cap and a two-day growth. He shouted above the roar, "Your kind ain't welcome here!"

Marcus glanced behind and to his left. The other driver was opening his door and reaching behind him for something hanging in his rifle rack — maybe a bat, maybe a gun.

The man yelled through his side window, "We got ways to take out the likes of you!"

Marcus jammed himself upright and stomped on the accelerator. The Blazer jumped the curb and sent mud and loose gravel spewing out behind. The attacker got off one good whack, splintering Marcus' rear window. Marcus fought for control as the rise steepened, then slid back over the curb and roared away. He took the final corner overtight and struck the brick entrance logo a glancing blow.

Marcus hurtled onto the state road and raced through the wooded section, finally bursting into the green fields bordering the old church. He was shaking so hard he had difficulty lifting his foot from the accelerator and unclenching his grip on the wheel. He searched the road behind him, saw nothing. He turned back in time to read the sign welcoming him to Rocky Mount, home of the new South.

FIVE

As usual, the nightmare came calling in the raven-black hour before dawn. As ever, Marcus rose in weary defeat and started his day several hours before his body was ready.

The year before the accident, one of the firm's senior partners had been diagnosed with terminal cancer. Marcus had taken over the partner's most critical case, one he was destined to lose. Marcus had spent a lot of time with the senior partner — at first because Marcus needed guidance, later because the man needed some tenuous connection with the life he was leaving behind. Over and over Marcus heard the partner refer to his illness as simply, the cancer. Marcus had not taken much note of it then, assuming that the guy was saying it so briefly and succinctly because of Marcus' own sensibilities. Now he knew better. It was all Marcus could do to refer to his own compilation of tragedies as, the accident. To give it any more space, either in thoughts or in words, would have broken him entirely. The same was true of his new nemesis, the nightmare. There was no way to use more words and still contain all the horror and all the pain. The nightmare came every night. It had been thus since the accident. It awoke him just before dawn. It robbed him of his most precious hour of sleep. It drove a spike through the heart of every new day.

Marcus packed his bag, then ate his breakfast standing at the kitchen counter. He took the Beltline around Raleigh to the airport, the night-dark road tense and packed with early techie commuters.

The earliest Raleigh flight bound for National was a prop job operated by United Express. Marcus joined the other boarders, observed their grim faces and stone-hard eyes, and wondered what other demons journeyed with them that day.

Marcus emerged from National Airport in time to watch dawn streak the Washington sky with a hundred different shades, all of them palest blue. He took a taxi into the city, accompanied by fragments of unwelcome memories. He had not been to Washington in eighteen months. He had not left North Carolina in all that time. Before, Marcus had traveled almost constantly. He had come to Washington at least twice a month — sometimes on business, other times to visit Carol's parents.

Like Marcus, his former wife was an only child. He had once joked that this was the single part of their background they held in common. Carol's family was old Delaware money. Very old. One of her direct ancestors had received a land grant from King George III. The deed, with its watered ribbons and royal seals, still hung upon the living-room wall of their Wilmington estate. They also had a summer home outside Annapolis, which had been in the family since Carol's great-grandfather served two terms as a United States senator. The kids had loved this sprawling clapboard manor, the only reason Marcus had ever endured weekends with Carol's parents. They also owned a penthouse on Central Park West and an apartment in a Louis XIV manor on the rue Faubourg St-Honoré — neither of which he had ever been invited to visit. He had never been to Europe at all. It was one of those things he had always promised Carol and never managed to deliver. One of many.

Marcus sat in the window of a Starbucks in Foggy Bottom, pretending to read the *Washington Post*. Behind him, the six employees called a constant cadence and beat rapid tattoos on the coffee machine. Beyond his window streamed a hectic Friday crowd, most of them young and intelligent-looking and focused on the day ahead. Marcus sipped his coffee and found hints of his own past reflected in those intent young faces.

In the early days of their marriage, he had refused the offer of a job from Carol's father for a thousand reasons. The biggest had been that he was too hungry. He had wanted a place where he could scramble and push and fight and make it on his own terms. He had considered the firm of Knowles, Barbour and Bradshaw to be a perfect fit, and for several years it truly was. The firm had been cobbled together from numerous local groups, all merged under the umbrella of what had once been a San Francisco-based firm. Now it was everywhere — offices in thirty-two states and eleven foreign countries. Marcus had thrived on the sixteen-hour days, the ninety-hour weeks, the competition, the breakneck pace, the constant demand to bill more hours. Carol came from a long line of workaholics, and had learned early on not to complain.

He wasn't exactly sure when the marriage had started to unravel. It would be too easy to say, his final year of law school, on the day they had met. But there was some truth in that statement.

Enough to propel him from his seat and out the door and down Constitution Avenue.

At precisely nine o'clock he signed in at the State Department's main entrance on C Street. Five minutes later he was approached by a balding man in his late forties with a bureaucrat's poker face. "Mr. Glenwood?"

"Yes."

"James Caldwell. As you were told yesterday on the phone, there's nothing anyone can do for you here."

Marcus accepted that the man was not even going to invite him to sit down. "It seems to me that an American citizen gone missing —"

"We don't have the resources." The man wore an ill-fitting checked suit of bluish gray and a goatee with more hair than was on the top of his head. "We deal strictly with policy matters."

"— who's gone missing in China would be a vital enough issue to concern our government."

"Right. Mr. Glenwood, in eleven weeks the Vice President and the secretary of commerce are leading a trade mission to China. We've got seventeen places to fill and more than four hundred heads of industry who want to come along. Not to mention half of Congress. We also have to prepare position papers on two dozen different topics."

And this, Marcus realized, was a carefully rehearsed little speech. "Preparatory meetings for this mission would be the ideal chance to bring up the issue of a missing American citizen."

"Not a chance." The words echoed loudly through the voluminous lobby. "Look, maybe you could ask your local congressman or senator to raise the matter."

"The parents have already tried that route."

"Then there's nothing I can do for you."

"I can't believe the State Department would take such a cavalier attitude to a kidnapped American citizen."

The man actually smirked. "You don't know that."

Marcus studied the man more intently. "You know Gloria Hall?"

"Absolutely not. We make it a policy to have nothing whatsoever to do with the lunatic fringe."

Marcus leaned closer. "The what?"

"Gloria Hall was ready to enlist on any side making trouble for the Chinese. As you well know." The man shook his head, a quick motion like a dog shedding water. "Look, Mr. Glenwood, you're wasting your time. Gloria Hall went looking for trouble and she found it. We can't help you."

The young lady at the International Chamber of Commerce was equally direct but far more polite. Her name was Patricia Calloway and she led Marcus through a warren of tiny cubicles to an office with a window. Her card said she was assistant director for Far Eastern policy and the plaques on her wall said she had graduated with honors from Wellesley and Georgetown's School of Foreign Service. When Marcus had completed his lead-in, she demanded, "You've spoken with someone at the State Department?"

"I tried. They didn't offer a thing."

"I'm not surprised. With a major trade junket on the horizon, they're all heads down in the bunkers."

"Even so, it seems amazing how little interest they showed over a missing American."

"Because it's a Pandora's box they don't dare open." She watched him with intelligent green eyes, clearly assessing whether he was worth her time, and whether he would actually listen to what he did not want to hear. "A number of Chinese dissidents hold dual citizenship with the United States. They go back planning to be arrested, hoping their mission will pressure Washington to act on human rights abuses."

Marcus felt a niggling sensation at the back of his mind. *Mission*. It took a moment to recall where he had come across that word before. "A confrontation over human rights abuses just prior to a trade expedition would be —"

"An absolute debacle," she agreed cheerfully. "The State Department's worst-case scenario."

"I seem to recall that this administration included human rights in its election manifesto."

"Maybe so. But now it's trade first, human rights last. And China just happens to be the world's largest untapped market."

Marcus confessed, "I'm surprised at your candor."

"Oh, we're definitely pro-trade around here." She flashed a quick smile. "But that doesn't make us blind to reality."

"Which is?"

"That China has been backsliding on human rights ever since Tiananmen Square. They make no bones about it. The recent arrests of those pro-democracy advocates were highly publicized, both inside and outside China. This was a calculated act. They're telling the rest of the world this is an internal matter, and we're too big and too powerful for you to risk offending us. So don't make an issue of it, or we'll take our business elsewhere."

She offered another quick smile. "That's my ten-cent tour. We dish it up to everybody wanting to tap the Chinese market. Your average American businessman will waltz in here and give us something like, there's a billion people over there and not a single company making widgets. So we go, fine, but are you willing to get your hands dirty? Because nobody who does business in China stays totally clean."

He was listening to what was going on beneath the surface now, and thought he heard a confusing note of concern. "Did you know Gloria Hall?"

"Just by name. We never met. She was making a reputation for herself as more than just another noisy activist."

He leaned forward. "How?"

"These are all just rumors. But you hear things in this business. She was mentioned in a couple of legal suits against Chinese companies, claiming this and that. Usually something labor related. Then there was some Hong Kong issue, a man who'd been injured in a raid, I think it was. And she petitioned my boss on several U.S. companies operating in Tibet."

Marcus mulled it over. "A trouble-maker."

"You didn't hear that from me. But that was the word in the corridors." Another smile, this one tinged with regret. "One of the bad guys."

Marcus began thinking out loud. "So if Gloria Hall did indeed go to China, and if she was investigating a factory for labor violations and disappeared . . ."

The smile vanished. "I'd say she was in serious trouble. And you don't know how serious trouble can be until you hit it in a place like China."

Though situated less than two miles from the White House, the offices for Asia Rights Watch were on the wrong end of Pennsylvania Avenue. In all his seven years of high-powered travel, Marcus had never had a reason to visit this area. His taxi passed the Vietnam Veterans Memorial, skirted the Tidal Basin, and entered the area known simply as Southwest.

The taxi let him off in front of a new four-story structure of colonial brick. There was no sign outside the building, no indication within of who occupied the top three floors. The lobby was carpeted and sterile and quiet as a tomb. Both the entrance and the elevators were flanked by security cameras.

Marcus exited the elevator on the fourth floor and found himself standing before double doors of reinforced steel. The hallway was compressed by a fire-proofed ceiling and thick concrete walls, and was so quiet the air-conditioning shouted a constant hoarse sigh.

He pressed a button alongside the doors. A solemn voice said, "State your business."

"Marcus Glenwood. I have an appointment."

"Look straight at the camera. No, the other one, to your right. Thank you."

The door clicked open. He entered a windowless reception area. Still he saw no sign announcing where he was. The desk and chairs were of light Scandinavian design, the floors and walls a uniform white. The standard drop ceiling had been removed, revealing heating ducts and lighting systems and concrete, all painted a light blue.

"Mr. Glenwood?"

"Yes." He turned and adjusted his gaze downward. "Mr. Gautam, did I say that correctly?"

"Indeed, yes." The man did not offer his hand. Instead, he beamed broadly enough to reveal more teeth than Marcus would have thought could fit in such an undersized head. He waved down the side corridor. "Let us go and speak in my office."

In the privacy of the narrow hallway, Marcus asked, "Why did you take out the ceiling panels?"

"Merely a precaution, Mr. Glenwood. Probably of no benefit." Dee Gautam had a strong accent with American overtones. The diminutive figure led him into a windowless office as austere as the reception area. "Please to have a seat there."

"Thanks. Precaution against what?"

"Attacks from above. Some of my colleagues possess a well-developed sense of paranoia." He gave a merry laugh as he seated himself behind the desk. "Now then. What can I do for you?"

"I mentioned on the telephone that I may be bringing legal action on behalf of a young lady who is missing in China."

"Indeed yes." The man was all stick limbs and thinning black hair and skin the color of milky tea. He wore a neatly pressed short-sleeved shirt over dark trousers. "A Miss Gloria Hall."

"You know her?"

"I can't recall." He lifted his hands from his lap and gave a broad shrug. "I meet so many people."

Marcus' gaze remained fixed upon

where the hands had reached, though they had now retreated back beneath the desk. He was not sure exactly what he had seen, yet it was enough to leave his stomach feeling like jellied ice. "But you might know her."

"I seem to recall a nice young woman who had an interest in China. I have an interest. We met. We talked. Perhaps. Or it might have been someone else."

"Can you recall what you might have talked about?"

The man laughed once more, a jarring sound in this sterile womb. "If we did meet, we probably spoke of *lao gai*. Yes, most definitely it would be of *lao gai*. You know of these, sir?"

"No."

"*Lao gai* are the invisible prisons. The ones you never hear of. Even among ourselves we never say the name very loud. Oh no. Just whisper." He leaned across his desk and breathed, *"Lao gai."* Then laughed once more.

Marcus affected a smile. But his gaze froze on where Dee Gautam's hands rested upon the desk. Both his thumbs seemed to have extra joints, ones that pointed the digits in the opposite from normal directions. Then they were folded back again and extended normally. But what left Marcus feeling queasy were the deep holes midway between the man's wrists and elbows. The scars were well-healed, but still a half inch deep, as though someone had driven spikes through the bones.

"*Lao gai* are everywhere, sir. Oh yes. All the provinces of China, they need places to store those who become nuisances. You wish to pester the provincial government with requests for political rights or rule of law? Fine. No problem. We invite you to be a guest of the state."

The arms lifted and opened wide, the broad smile returned. "Welcome to the grand hotel *lao gai,* you pesky fellow. Perhaps here you can learn proper respect, yes?"

"Yes." Marcus swallowed on a dry mouth, tried not to track the movement of those two arms. "But I thought Gloria Hall was checking out a factory."

The arms disappeared into his lap. "She has told you this?"

"Not me. She left a letter with her parents."

"Which factory, please?"

"I don't know much about it. Just a number. Factory 101. Somewhere outside Hong Kong."

"In Guangdong Province. Yes." The smile was gone, the dark eyes steady, measuring. "What is your interest in this, please?"

"Gloria Hall's parents have asked me to file suit against the factory's alleged American partner." Here in this place, faced with the reality of those vanished hands and all the stains hidden by these whitewashed walls, the statement sounded lame. "To be honest, there's not much of a case. But if a partnership exists, the Americans might help locate her to avoid adverse publicity."

"Indeed. And the American company?"

"New Horizons." He steered the conversation back to his earlier question. "What would a Chinese factory have to do with one of these prisons?"

"The *lao gai* network holds over two million prisoners, Mr. Glenwood. We *think* two million. Maybe three, maybe five. Nobody knows. Not even Beijing. You see, sir, many *lao gai* prisoners are not tried in a court of law. Oh no. No trial, no public record. They come before a party tribunal, or they have a military hearing. They are sentenced, whoosh, the hearing lasts two, maybe three minutes. Then they are gone for such a long time. Years. Maybe forever."

Marcus pressed, "And the factories?"

"So many prisoners, all must be taught to become good Chinese citizens, yes?"

He gave another of his open-armed shrugs. "What better way than with re-education through labor?"

"You're saying an American company is making sports gear with political prisoners?"

"Oh sir, there is so much to learn here. Indeed yes. You ask questions just like Gloria."

"So you do remember speaking with her."

"Yes, perhaps. These questions, and the name. Factory 101. Perhaps." Absently he crossed his hands on the desk and stared into the distance. "This I must check into."

"I still don't understand —"

"These are not simple matters, Mr. Glenwood. Not aboveboard and straight-ahead like American business. The good Western businessman, he meets the Chinese authority. Perhaps the Chinese person is Communist Party, perhaps military, perhaps son or daughter of top official, but always they are factory owner. Always they wear two hats, but show the Western visitor only one." The accent was stronger now, the words spoken to the blank side wall. "The Chinese official says, yes, I can make this for one-tenth the cost of your factory back home. The American, he smells big money. Does he ask, what are conditions in your factory, how do you hire your workers?"

"Not a chance," Marcus replied. "He takes the money and runs."

Dee Gautam gave his grand smile. "Now you understand Chinese business. Very good."

"But why would they kidnap an American student? That doesn't make sense."

"No. Indeed not." Absently the little man began scratching the wound on one arm. Probing gently into the hole, caressing the scar. "Unless Miss Gloria Hall discovered something they must keep secret, yes? Something we cannot be allowed to know."

"Like what?"

"Ah. That we must see if we can discover." He rose from his chair, drawing Marcus with him. "And now you must excuse me. I have an appointment on Capitol Hill. I have been given three minutes to convince one of your congressmen that more visas should be granted to victims of political terror."

Marcus somehow felt small walking alongside this fragile figure. "Where are you from, India?"

"No. Close. Sri Lanka." Dee Gautam halted by the steel doors and offered one misshapen hand. "You will take this case?"

"Perhaps." The deformed thumbs felt like bony knobs as Marcus gripped the hand. "If there is a case at all."

"Then perhaps we shall see each other again, yes? A pleasure, sir. A pleasure."

Marcus asked his taxi to stop across the street from the Chinese embassy. He got out, told the driver to wait, and crossed at the light. The embassy was sixties' red-brick, broad and squat, set back from Connecticut Avenue by a triangular plaza sprouting a few meager shrubs. A security guard stood bored sentry duty by the glass entrance doors. A few people came and went, most wearing dark suits and professional airs. Down the street rose the Washington Hilton, and a few blocks farther was Dupont Circle. Traffic was light, the street sunny and quiet, the sky blue. No protestors, no sinister air, nothing whatsoever to connect this building to all he had just heard. Marcus climbed back in his taxi and gave a Georgetown address.

P Street was narrow and leafy and lined with Federal row houses. Some sparkled from recent renovations, others held the weary look of long years and hard use. The taxi stopped before a house of brick and painted clapboard, well-tended but lacking the freshness of a total overhaul.

The door and ground-floor shutters were painted forest green.

Marcus climbed the brick stairs, regretting the need to meet this woman at all. He knew the type with bitter clarity — too rich, too thin, chin held high on a too-long neck. Clothes purchased from some Fifth Avenue shop known for muted plaids and clunky shoes. Vowels carefully enunciated, consonants spoken with a pretentious nasal twang. Eyes clear and gaze lofty, as if it required great effort to look down to his squalid level. Everything about her would be angled, pointed, and bony. Especially her opinions. Marcus pressed the doorbell, shields up, ready to encounter his former wife's long-lost cousin. Or even worse, a younger version of his ex-mother-in-law. As far as he was concerned, at that moment the worst thing going for Gloria Hall was her roommate's telephone attitude.

The door opened. A familiar voice said, "Yes?"

But the face did not fit the voice. "Ms. Stanstead?"

"That's right." A light flickered. "You're Marcus Glenwood."

"Yes."

The door remained barely cracked open. "You're late."

It was not true, but he found no need

110

to counter the attack. Or any desire. "Sorry."

"I took part of the afternoon off, and was supposed to be back at work an hour ago." Reluctantly she released the door and let it swing wide. Marcus stepped into a narrow foyer with mint green walls and pegged floors of broad planks, probably oak. The living room to his right sported what appeared to be an original fireplace of glazed brick. "Where have you been?"

"State Department, International Chamber of Commerce, Asia Rights Watch, Chinese embassy." His gaze returned to the woman herself. She stood in bizarre contrast both to the house and his expectations. She wore combat boots, overblown khaki trousers, chain belt, a man's T-shirt, and short blond hair gelled into a myriad of spikes. He realized he was staring and glanced down at his watch. "I thought we said four o'clock."

"Then you thought wrong. I have a meeting downtown with our Brussels group in fifteen minutes."

"You said you worked for a charity organization, is that right?"

Tension vibrated the air between them. "This meeting isn't about me, Mr. Glenwood."

He watched a hand reach for her head,

touch the spikes, then drop to her side. He had the distinct impression she was not comfortable with herself. And everything she wore was brand-new. "Call me Marcus."

"Are you going after New Horizons or not?"

"There's not much of a case. All we could really do is blow smoke in their faces."

"Maybe not." She lifted a manila folder from a side table and handed it to him. "This is the information you wanted about the Richmond trial."

"Great." But his attention remained fastened upon the utterly unadorned face. Which was odd. Marcus had not paid attention to a woman in a very long time. Kirsten Stanstead had lips so pale they appeared delicate even when compressed into a hypertense line. Her nose was snubbed slightly upward, her eyebrows as pale as her hair. Her eyes were arresting. Turquoise and big, as though she had been shocked so hard the gaze had become frozen wide. Shocked and saddened both, for hers was a tragic gaze. Marcus had the fleeting impression of sapphires crushed in a blender. He searched for something more to say. "Did you happen to find an address for the plaintiff's attorney?"

"First page."

"I thought I might rent a car and drive down to Richmond and meet him." Marcus flipped open the folder to have something to look at other than her. "Also I need the name of a good China attorney. Somebody who knows the ins and outs of their law."

"I'll see what I can do. But right now I really have to be going." Words and attitude as pointy as her hair.

Marcus allowed himself to be led toward the front door. "You said something about more data?"

"It's all in a jumble. I'm sorting it as fast as I can. I'll send it to you when it's ready." She actually prodded him through the portal. "Now good-bye. And don't call me again unless you take the case." The door slammed in punctuation to the final word.

Marcus stood upon the top step. Silently he asked the sunlit afternoon why Kirsten Stanstead would go to so much trouble to make him detest her.

"Glenwood's done just about what you'd expect."

Randall Walker scowled at the view outside his car window. He hated the need for subterfuge and the special mobile phone used only for these calls. But loved it just the same. It was a paradox he did not need to question. He had long since grown used to the fact that many of the things in life that he adored the most were also things he was vaguely ashamed of. "And precisely what is that supposed to mean?"

"Exactly what I said. He's made the rounds. Met all the right people. Asked all the wrong questions."

"Now you look here." Randall masked his nerves with an unaccustomed bark. He had heard too many tales about Hamper Caisse to feel comfortable dealing with the man, no matter what the cause. "I don't pay you these ridiculous sums for you to feed me opinions. I want facts. Details. Times, dates, evidence you've actually done your job."

"The entire exercise has been a no-brainer." The voice on the other end sounded caught midway between a whisper and a moan. Which suited the man perfectly. Randall stared at the sunlit day and saw the man himself. Small and without a single sharp angle. Wispy mustache and round-rimmed glasses. Suit as gray as his hair and eyes. Utterly without defining characteristics. Anyone glancing his way would not bother with a second look, there was so little to notice. Which meant he was superb at his job.

"Glenwood visited the State Department, the International Chamber of Commerce, and the Asia Rights Watch. He stopped by the Chinese embassy, but didn't have the nerve to step inside. Then he visited Hall's roommate, that Stanstead woman. It looked like she handed him some file."

"That's bad. And the meeting at Asia Rights is even worse." But Randall wasn't sure this was the case. Part of him wanted to agree with Hamper Caisse and his nonchalant assessment. The man had an almost perfect record, both in gathering data and in situation analysis. Which was not what made Randall Walker nervous.

He had heard the tales. Stories were bandied about boardrooms of companies that used Hamper Caisse's services. How he had gained his reputation in the CIA, how he was willing to do anything for a client. Anything at all.

Even from a distance of several hundred miles, Randall felt unnerved by the man's grotesque mixture of docile ruthlessness. "This could mean serious trouble."

"I think you're wrong. Glenwood is strictly a two-bit operator, and he's out of his league." If he took any pleasure in correcting Randall, it did not show. "You come across a lot of these in Washington.

They show up at the occasional low-level function, scrounge for whatever crumbs they can find. One hard knock and they fold up their tents and scurry back to whatever hole they crawled out of."

"All right. Any idea what's next?"

"He was booked on the six-fifteen United flight back to Raleigh. But when he left Stanstead's place he rented a car. Right now I'm following him through rush-hour traffic on I-95. My guess is he's headed down to see that Richmond lawyer who kicked up such a fuss in the pollution suit. What a pair they'll make."

"Stay on him," Randall said. Then, almost to himself, "I wish I knew what was in that file."

"What can the Hall girl have found out? You had me check her, what, three times? She's just another scrounger. Pity Glenwood couldn't meet her. They'd probably have fallen for each other, right off a cliff. Saved us all a lot of trouble."

Randall wanted to believe him. Wanted to accept that his worry was for nothing, that the fire had been put out safely and everything was under control. But something left him uneasy. Something that could not be entirely ignored. "I want you to search the Stanstead place. Find out if there's anything else lying around."

"You're kidding."

"We can't take any risks here."

A pause, then, "It's your money."

"That's right, it is." Randall cut the connection, sat staring out the window of his Mercedes, wishing he knew what it was that had him so concerned.

When rush-hour traffic trapped him on I-95, Marcus used his cellular phone to call ahead. The lawyer in Richmond sounded hostile and half-drunk. Marcus bullied the man into granting him five minutes and his home address.

The hundred-mile drive took three traffic-clogged hours. Following the lawyer's slurred directions, Marcus took a central Richmond exit and entered a wounded city. Darkness hid the worst of the scars, but what the streetlights and shadows revealed was not pleasant. Buildings had the abandoned look of old tombstones. The sidewalks were empty save for those who loitered and clustered and called to passing cars as if they were hailing death.

He turned off the main thoroughfare and entered a gloom so thick he could not see the street sign, much less house numbers. Finally he spotted a front porch with a light, and in the process of reading the number he also observed the bars where the screen door should have been. Marcus drove down another block to the correct address and parked.

Marcus climbed the steps of the attorney's house and heard the tinny voices of a television game show. The noise marked the dark and his own creeping fear. Marcus fumbled for a bell, found none, so he banged on the door. He heard footsteps scraping the sidewalk behind him. He banged harder still.

"Yeah?"

"Mr. Taub, it's Marcus Glenwood. We spoke on the phone." He did not wait for a reply, but banged again. "Open up."

"Hang on." The latch rattled, the door cracked open a notch. "I told you, you're wasting your —"

Marcus pushed inside, almost knocking the man to the floor. "Sorry. There was somebody out there."

Marshall Taub did not appear the least surprised. "Yeah, this is a creepy place. I never go out at night." He waved his hand, sloshing his drink on the already-stained carpet. "You might as well sit down."

The room's lighting was yellow and feeble, the house dank with old smells. Dishes were piled on a cheap corner shelf. The coffee table between the battered sofa and the television bore two empty bottles and a half dozen glasses. Marcus deliberately walked over and cut off the television. "As I said on the phone, I am representing a client who wants to enter suit against New Horizons."

Marshall Taub relocked and latched the door. "Don't do it."

"I have a file on your case." Marcus had managed to scan the top pages while trapped on the interstate. "I'd just like to ask —"

"I'm telling you, don't go after them." Taub motioned a second time with his glass. "Wanna drink?"

"No thanks." The Richmond attorney had the doughy appearance of someone carrying the worst kind of extra poundage. "You won your suit against New Horizons, didn't you?"

"Didn't win a thing. Lost it. Lost it all."

"But the records show —"

"Siddown, why don't you." He took a hard slug from the glass. "Don't believe what you read. Never believe what you read."

Marshall Taub could have been forty, he could have been sixty-five. His graying beard only partly masked the pastiness of his features. He had the shaky hands and blank gaze of a man determined to kill himself slowly. Marcus asked, "What's wrong with the court records, Mr. Taub?"

"Nothing. Not a thing. Except they're a lie." He drained his glass, reached for the bottle on the coffee table, slopped bourbon into his glass and over his hand. "Sure you don't want a drink?"

"Mr. Taub, who is handling further action against the appeal?"

"Nobody. Not a soul." Another hard slug from the glass. "Know how many motions they attached? Forty-seven."

"They're trying to bury the appeal," Marcus interpreted.

"Burying the case, burying the lawyer." He thought that was funny enough for a repeat. "Won the case, lost it all."

Marshall Taub took a long sip, almost toppled over backward, caught himself, and flopped down into a chair whose exposed springs were partially covered by a ratty throw rug. "Don't do it."

Marcus saw the dark stains covering the sofa cushions, decided to remain on his feet. "Tell me what happened."

"Started with threats. Pretrial motions, pretrial threats." The whiskers parted in a bleary grin. "That didn't work, so they went for the jugular. My other clients started heading south. My partners got worried. I got mad, wouldn't let go, so they dumped me. I had New Horizons cold. A great case."

"You left your firm?"

"Yep. That's when it got bad. Real bad." He drained his glass, let it slide to the floor. "They got pictures of me with a lady I knew. Mailed 'em to my wife."

"They framed you?"

"Manner of speaking." He fumbled, managed to grab the bottle, took a long hit. "My wife left me. Took the kids. Walked out the day I won the case." Another bleary grin. "Great victory, huh."

SIX

Marcus arrived at the Hayes mansion in the soft light of early Saturday morning. Before he cut the motor, his battered Blazer was surrounded by three barrel-chested Labs. The dogs clustered and poked him with cold noses as he climbed down. The extremely well-trained bird dogs neither barked at his familiar smell nor pressed their case. Instead they both followed and led at an amiable distance as he made for the open garage door.

Mansion was the only way to describe the eleven-thousand-square-foot yellow-brick dwelling — despite its doors and shutters and pillars and porticoes and garage all being painted a startling sky blue. The four-car garage had one oversize door that belonged on an airplane hangar, upon which was painted the emblem of the University of North Carolina Tar Heels. Behind it hulked an RV larger than a Greyhound bus and painted the same blue as the house trim. As Marcus walked up the drive, the house's owner was loading sky blue dog boxes into the back of a blue Cherokee sporting a license plate that read GO-HEELS. Marcus knew for a fact that the license plate had cost Boomer Hayes a quarter-million-dollar contribution to the UNC football fund, as the tag had formerly been the personal property of the team coach.

"Marcus!" Boomer Hayes had a voice to match his body, big and raucous and pushy. "Did I invite you?"

"No."

"Don't matter. You got a gun?"

"No."

"That's okay too. Go on downstairs and pick yourself out a couple." Boomer swatted at the dogs, who circled excitedly. "Y'all just hold on to your tails. I'll get to you in a minute." To Marcus, "You remember where I keep the gun?"

"Yes." Boomer's gun room was a basement running the entire length of the house. At one end was an arsenal capable of equipping a fair-size insurrection. At the other loomed an entertainment center with fourteen speakers and a 118-inch Swiss-made television. The carpets, drapes, gun cabinets, leather sofas, and walls were all Carolina blue. Boomer Hayes was serious about only three things — Carolina football, his toys, and his family. The order depended upon how well the Tar Heels were doing that year.

Marcus said, "I'm not going hunting."

"Sure you are. It don't mean a thing, me forgetting to invite you." He opened the first cage door and the dogs started whining. They knew where they were headed. "The 'Heels don't kick off till seven Sunday. We got plenty of time to go pack us some birds."

A querulous voice wafted from the house's side door, the one that led up to the separate apartment wing. "He ain't interested in your football silliness and he ain't going hunting!"

Boomer reached for the nearest dog and hefted him into the cage. "Shame how the old man's gone all doddery. Guess before long we'll have to start chaining him to the bedpost."

A man with the fragility of the very old came tottering into view. He carried a cane, but did not use it, as though the stick were there for assurance alone. "Can somebody please tell me where my only son got this fanaticism over something as absurd as Tar Heel football?" Charlie Hayes limped over to where Marcus stood, huffed a single breath, then continued. "I went to Carolina. Twice. Undergrad before the war and law school after. I never felt like the world would end if Carolina lost a game."

Boomer gave the old man a stricken

124

look. "Don't talk nasty like that, Daddy."

"Humph." Charlie peered at Marcus through bifocals so thick his eyes changed shape and shade with each shift of his chin. "First time Marcus comes by in over a year, you don't even offer your old friend so much as a how-do."

"Now that's not true." Boomer closed the gate on the third dog pen, and began stacking leather-cased rifles like cord-wood. From behind their wire-meshed doors the dogs watched with lolling tongues. "I asked him to come hunting. Didn't I ask you, Marcus?"

"You did indeed."

"See there? You can't get any nicer than that, now, can you."

Marcus said to the old man, "You're looking good, Charlie."

"I'm not either. I look like I sleep with death as a bedfellow. You're just trying to suck up to me on account of not stopping by for so long." Charlie Hayes brandished his cane in Marcus' face. "Well, it won't do you a bit of good. I've written you off and that's final."

Boomer slammed the tailgate shut. "That's my pop. All sweetness and light."

"Now that's a shame," Marcus said. "I came back from a trip last night to find I'd been invited to go fishing this morning. I just stopped by to see if you wanted to come along."

"Then I might have to recollect on what I said," Charlie replied instantly. "I'd pay cold hard cash to get off on some body of water and hold a pole in my hands again."

Boomer murmured something that sounded vaguely like old folks' home.

"I heard that. You ship me off to some perfumed death house and I'll come back to haunt you."

"He would, you know." Boomer's eye was caught by the Blazer's mangled side panel. He marched down the drive, then shouted back up, "Dang, Marcus! Who did the number on your wheels?"

"Two redneck goons over at New Horizons."

Boomer continued to circle the Blazer. "Looks like they put you through the grinder."

Charlie moved down beside his son. "They come at you from both sides?"

"Yes." He walked back to join them. The right and rear windows were quilts of plastic and duct tape. Marcus had used the tire iron to peel off what remained of the left rear fender. "Both sides."

Charlie Hayes poked his cane at where the rear bumper was tied in place with a coat hanger. "What'd you do to rile them?"

"I said I was a lawyer representing union organizers."

Boomer laughed, and in doing so he lived up to his name. "Shoot, you might as well have doused yourself with gasoline and asked them for a light!"

Marcus asked, "What do you know about them?"

"I know they're a Carolina textile company. None of their lot takes kindly to unions. Even a transplanted Yankee like you ought to know that."

Charlie corrected, "Marcus' momma's family is just as Carolina as they come."

"Half-Yankee, then. To say lawyer and union in the same breath is like waving red shorts in front of an angry bull." Boomer surveyed the damage. "You're lucky they didn't come after you with pick handles."

"They did." Then to Charlie, "You'll have to slide over from my side, the passenger door won't open."

"Then you're lucky to be alive." Boomer pounded back up the drive in his size-thirteen boots, patting Marcus on the shoulder as he passed. "Good seeing you again, old son. Things have been awful dull around here."

Charlie waited until they were halfway to Rocky Mount before saying, "You

127

want to tell me why you went and did such a fool thing?"

"I was approached by a couple who are accusing New Horizons of kidnapping their daughter. I wanted to see if they were capable of rough tactics."

Charlie fiddled with the cane, a gift from his son. The ivory top was carved in the shape of a ram's head and dyed blue. "Why don't they take something like that to the FBI?"

"They did, but the FBI can't help much. The kidnapping allegedly took place in China."

The fiddling halted. "As in the country way yonder over there, China?"

"The very same."

The old man used both hands and the dash to swivel himself about. "All right. I'm listening."

Telling what little he knew took them into Rocky Mount. Marcus threaded his way through empty Saturday streets, following Deacon's carefully printed instructions to the fields and woodlands on the town's south side. He concluded, "I read through the files last night. Whatever else she might be, Gloria Hall is a fine researcher. She followed the Richmond case from the outset. Had all the relevant data, including a confidential report from the state EPA advisory panel, something the defense managed to keep out of court. New Horizons was dumping a ton of poisons into that river."

The old man's response exhibited all the mental acuity that had made Judge Charlie Hayes a force in the legal establishment for more than forty years. "Long way to travel, from polluting the James River to kidnapping a student in China."

"I realize that."

"Do you have any concrete tie-ins?"

"Not yet."

"Are you accepting the case?"

Marcus spotted Deacon Wilbur's paint-spattered pickup and pulled to the side of the road. "I haven't decided."

Charlie squinted through the sun-dappled windshield, and said idly, "Sometimes you don't have to win a case to succeed."

Marcus turned to his oldest friend in the legal profession. Charlie Hayes looked every one of his seventy-eight years. "What's that supposed to mean?"

"You just think on it a spell." Charlie leaned over and called through Marcus' window, "Deacon Wilbur. If I'd known you were going to be our guide today, I'd have been out here at midnight."

The pastor smiled for the first time Marcus had ever seen outside of church.

"Why, glory in the morning. If it ain't Judge Hayes."

"Get out of my way, son. I want to stand up and shake Deacon's hand." Impatiently Charlie allowed Marcus and the pastor to ease him from the truck. "How are you, sir?"

"Can't complain, Judge. Can't complain." Deacon Wilbur clasped Charlie's hand with both his own. "Marcus told me he was bringing somebody, but I didn't have no idea it was you. My, but it's good to see you again."

"I hooked up with Marcus when he was still a shavetail recruit. Boy came down from some highfalutin college up north. Didn't help him none. He looked ready to drown his first time in a Carolina courtroom." To Marcus, "Deacon and I go way back."

"That's right, we surely do. My daddy fished with your daddy for more years than I know how to count."

"Deacon's daddy was the finest bass guide I ever hope to meet. How long has he been gone now?"

"Oh, he's been laid to rest a whole passel of years. Resting easy, now that Marcus here saw to our cemetery." Deacon then spotted the taped window on the Blazer's other side. "What on earth's happened here?"

Marcus replied, "A long story."

Charlie demanded, "What's this about a cemetery?"

"Another long story."

"Come on, let's get out on the river." Deacon reached for a pole and a tackle box. "Ain't no law says we can't fish and talk. You all right with a little trail walking, Judge?"

"Fine. Grab my cane there, Marcus."

"Ain't far. Just round that bend up ahead."

Within a hundred paces the swamp cypress and medieval oaks had closed in. The air became dank and rich with forest odors, and the morning light no longer accompanied them. The only signs remaining of the previous year's floods were scattered debris and watermarks high up tree trunks. Ahead, the river moved dark and steady and timeless. Marcus helped Charlie down a slippery embankment, taking them farther into the timeless gloom, down to where a young black man held two aluminum skiffs.

"This here's my youngest brother's boy, Oathell. Mister Charlie, why don't you join me right over here. Easy now, hold her steady, son." The pastor slipped into the flat-bottomed boat and reached back, saying, "Hand me the judge's pole, Marcus. Now Judge, you know I ain't gonna let you work, so you can set that paddle right back down. You two climb in that other skiff and follow us on up the river."

The skiffs were both powered by electric trolling motors, silent save for a high-pitched whine. They pushed easily upstream, traveling beneath a canopy of branches and sun-struck leaves. The river ran dark and slow as molasses, shining a ruddy gold whenever sunlight managed to glance through. From the bow of the second boat Marcus could hear the pair up ahead talking softly. Marcus remained content to float in soft silence within this green cathedral. The young man remained silent save for once, when the older pair up ahead almost shouted their laughter. Oathell humphed his disdain and muttered, "Yes sir, Mister Charlie, yes *sir.*" Speaking low yet loud, meaning for Marcus to hear and be forewarned.

They followed Deacon into a narrow inlet that Marcus would have taken for merely another crack between oily black roots. Only this one meandered through water-clad groves and veils of Spanish moss before opening into a hidden cove a hundred feet wide and ringed by gray pillars of long-dead trees. Far overhead nesting hawks cried their displeasure at the boats' arrival. Otherwise the cove was close, fetid, still, and very beautiful.

"They might as well put up a sign," Charlie said quietly over the water to Marcus. "Bass welcome here."

"Wasn't sure what we'd find after the floods. But it seems like all it did was perk the bass up a little." Deacon ran out his pole. "Ain't more than five, six people know about this place. So few it ain't even got a name."

"Them who know don't talk about it," Charlie agreed, grinning and pointing across the water. "Lookit your nephew there. Like he's done died and gone to bass heaven."

The pastor glanced over but did not smile. "Mind you don't tell nobody 'bout this."

"No sir, Deacon." Subdued now. Respectful.

The pastor asked Marcus, "You aim on fly-fishing?"

"It's been a while. But I'd like to try."

"Run on over to that big cypress there to the other side. There's fish been playing between them roots I can't get to with my cane pole."

Their boat flitted through the circle of sun and heat, then returned to the cool shade on the pool's far side. Occasionally whoops erupted from the other boat. Marcus remained content with his own boat's silence. He had more than enough to concentrate on just then, relearning the art of casting.

After he hooked and landed his second fish and Oathell his fourth, the young man said, "Uncle says you want to ask about Gloria."

"You knew her?"

"Guess I did. We had us a thing going till she left for D.C."

"What was she like?"

Oathell was using a spinning rod and a top-water plug. He flicked it expertly between cypress roots. Instantly the water erupted furiously. He pulled, hooked, reeled. Marcus plied the net, then raised the dripping prize over his head for the other boat to offer soft accolades. The bass hung over both sides of the net. "Must weigh over six pounds."

"This is my reward," Oathell said, accepting the net and fish, drawling the last word so it came out, *ree*-ward. "Been after Deacon to show me his secret place ever since I could walk." A dark gaze flitted his way. "Uncle says, I talk to you, he'd bring me along. Wouldn't tell me why he was letting you in on this."

Marcus said mildly, "I expect it's a bribe. He thinks I should accept the Halls' case."

The young man stared openly now,

then turned back to the lake and the fish with a quiet "Huh." A few more casts, then, "Gloria had a wild streak in her. She'd hide it good, then something'd set her off. Man, it was like night and day. You ever met her daddy?"

"Last Sunday."

"What'd you think of him?"

Marcus was abruptly caught by something his grandmother used to say. "He struck me as a man uncomfortable with his own hide."

Oathell laughed once, a quick bark, but it rang through the quiet air long after the sound was gone. To Marcus it felt like an unexpected compliment. "That's Austin Hall, all right. But he loved that girl of his. Loved her like a straightjacket, it seemed to me. Sometimes the fit got too tight, and Gloria'd just go crazy."

"Is that why she went to Georgetown?"

"Partly. Girl was smart, could've gone anywhere." An angry flick of the rod. "I didn't want her to go. We were young, sure, but I was ready to settle down. We tried to make it, me here at Nash Community College and her up there in the big city. Like to have drove me crazy, trying to keep tabs on the woman. Didn't like to think about her going wild up there, with me . . ." Another angry flick of the pole. "That spring I asked Gloria to marry me. She said no way was she ready. We fought. She broke it off." Another cast. "Maybe she'd already met Gary, but I don't think so. She says that didn't happen for another year after we broke up."

Marcus stopped pretending to pay attention to the water. "Gary?"

"Gary Loh. Oriental guy, Chinese parents, born in this country. Med student up at Georgetown. Man had it all. Looks, brains, money. Ran some kinda campus outreach for a local church." A glance at Marcus, flicking like the lure. "You a religious man?"

"No."

"Hear you went to Deacon's church last Sunday. How'd you find it?"

"My ears are still ringing."

Another barked laugh, quiet this time. "I hear you. Gloria didn't have time for no church until this Gary started sniffing around. Then every time she came home it was God this and God that, like to drive you crazy. Then something happened, I'm not sure exactly when it was, maybe a year back. They broke up is what I heard. I tried to get back with her. She wasn't having none of it."

Marcus set down his pole and turned to face the stern. His movements were slow, deliberate. He inspected Oathell, who continued casting and reeling, the motions as constant as breath. "How long ago did you two break up?"

Oathell flung the lure far out over the water. "Six years."

The young man was handsome, even with his features pinched by pain kept fresh with unvanquished love. Oathell was about his own height, a couple of inches over six feet, with broad shoulders and narrow waist. Marcus asked, "What do you do?"

"I'm a technician with IBM out in the Research Triangle. Work on grinding the silicon plates for chips. Been there ever since I graduated from Nash."

Marcus noticed the slight hunch to the shoulders, realized the young man was dreading a further torrent of personal questions. But Marcus had no desire to cause anyone unnecessary discomfort. So he said, "Why would Gloria take on New Horizons?"

The muscles unbunched, the man took an easier breath. "You know the saying, the thing folks love to hate? That's New Horizons."

"So the stories about the way they treat workers are true?"

"Don't know what you've heard, but I imagine they are. Every family in that church has somebody who's worked over there. And anybody who works for New Horizons is sooner or later gonna come into a story all their own." He lifted the lure from the water, sat watching the dripping hooks. "My daddy worked there for nineteen years. Hated every minute of it."

Marcus spoke his thoughts. "So Gloria might have been able to access a lot of in-house data through her contacts inside the church."

"I reckon that girl could've gotten her hands on just about anything she wanted." The pinched expression returned. "Hard to find anybody at that church who doesn't love Gloria."

Marcus thought of his own contact with the company on the hill. "Even so, a lot of people rely on New Horizons for their paychecks."

Oathell shot him another glance, this one as dark as the waters beneath their boat. "We've got a lot of practice eating the bread of folks we despise."

SEVEN

When Marcus arrived at church that second Sunday, it was to the sound of thunder.

Four young women stood on the stage behind the podium, rapping out a message about going astray. The amplified music was so loud he could not hear most of the words. Marcus tried to slip into the back row, but smiles and little hand motions invited him forward. There was none of the sullenness he found on every street corner in Edgecombe County, none of the silent watchfulness. Gentle hands patted his back as he moved toward a seat in the middle of the congregation.

The discomfort he had known the previous Sunday did not return. Not even when the young pastor came to the lectern, raised his hands in benediction, then invited the congregation to welcome the newcomers. Not even when a woman three times his weight turned and engulfed him in lilacs and talcum powder. Not even when her place was taken by a dozen others, all of whom knew his name and welcomed him with an offer of Sabbath peace. Not even when the crowd launched into the next song, and Marcus slid quietly back into his seat.

People nodded his way, smiled whenever their eyes met. He was neither the tallest man nor the only white face. And he was far from being the best dressed. By the time the singing stopped and the prayers began, Marcus had come to recognize that the only discord was that which he had brought in with him.

After the service he noticed Alma and Austin Hall in the parking lot and walked toward them. As soon as Austin spotted him, he turned and walked away. Marcus halted in front of the big-boned woman and said, "I'm sorry I trouble your husband."

"It's not you, Mr. Glenwood."

"Call me Marcus, please."

"It's not you," she repeated, her voice as sorrowful as the gaze that followed her husband's retreat.

"I was wondering if I could come by and speak with you today."

"I have a board of trustees meeting that runs all this week. I'll be tied up in strategy sessions the rest of today and most of tomorrow. Could we just take a turn here?"

He followed her through the parking lot, observing how people noted their closeness and turned away politely. He moved through a tumultuous crowd, yet was shielded even from the children. Parents steered the littlest ones aside; the older children took swift note of their elders' reactions and pretended the pair was not even there. "The people here think a lot of you."

"Gloria was one of their own," Alma said matter-of-factly. She waited until they had reached the path that bounded the cemetery to ask, "What was it you wanted to see me about?"

"You do not have a case against New Horizons." It was not how he had intended to express himself. But the day continued to reverberate with an authority that permitted no glossing over his message. "I've spent a lot of hours going through the evidence. And I am telling you here and now, there is no motion I could prepare that would result in a positive verdict."

Alma Hall continued along the gravel path. The cemetery's waist-high fence was a derelict affair, with many of the iron rods eaten through and weeping rust. The path itself was weed-strewn and unkempt. Thistles and honeysuckle scrambled over the fence and climbed the oldest headstones. The air was scented with wildflowers and blackberries. Families walked the interior ways, pausing now and then

141

to look down at graves and talk quietly among themselves while the children sang and danced about. The atmosphere was subdued yet happy, a pleasant realm of memories and peace.

Alma Hall demanded in her quiet precise way, "Why do I have the impression there is more you want to tell me?"

Marcus took a breath and held it. Kept it locked up tight for what felt like ages, long enough for them to make the turning at the back corner. Which was where Alma halted and turned to him. "Well?"

He squinted out to where girders for the New Horizons headquarters building thrust like giant pikes into the scarred hillside. And released the breath. And committed. "I need to know whether your goal is actually to win a case against New Horizons."

"I want my baby home." A response as firm and solid as the woman herself.

"We might be able to accomplish that just by bringing suit. An accusation of this magnitude would attract a lot of negative attention."

"Do it."

"I'm not promising a thing, Mrs. Hall."

"It's time you started calling me Alma."

"This could backfire in the worst possible way." Almost wishing she would relent and release him. "If New Horizons had a hand in your daughter's kidnapping, this could drive them farther underground."

She stabbed the Sunday afternoon with a finger as straight and true as the distant girders. "Those people over there are snakes. They are evil. It doesn't take a genius to know they're involved. They've lived their entire lives crawling around underground."

Marcus studied the woman. "That's a mighty strong statement."

"You ask anybody who's had dealings with that group. They dress it up with a fancy logo and nice colors, but they're snakes out to make a killing off the young. Creating a world of make-believe, telling kids they'll grow up to be stars if only they buy these fancy clothes and special shoes." The arm dropped to her side. "What about the warning the other lawyer gave my husband, something about the court arresting us?"

"Actually, they would come after me, not you. It's called filing a frivolous claim. And yes, it could just happen."

"But you're willing to go after them anyway? Even after that other lawyer turned us down?"

The sun rested like a gentle hand upon his head and shoulders. "Let's just say I've got a lot less to lose."

EIGHT

The ritual of fearful tremors chased Marcus from his bed long before the light was strong enough to be called morning. After breakfast he took a final cup of coffee out to the veranda. The wrap-around porch was one of the house's many follies, with great open rafters of wild cherry exposing a cedar-shingled roof with tiny fake cupolas at each corner. The pillars were maple, including the new ones Marcus had turned and carved himself, and the floor's planking was ten-inch heart-of-pine. Three of the dozen-odd rockers he remembered from his childhood had been salvaged from termites and wood rot. Marcus was trying to decide which one to sit in when the process server came and went like a ghost from the dreams he had hoped would remain inside. He settled himself just the same, leaving the bulky envelope unopened and unread in the seat beside him.

A morning mist whispered silent fables of autumnal chill. The trees stood as apparitions in the gray half-light. Even the house's own connection to earth seemed gossamer and fragile. Somewhere out beyond the borders of his vision a motor purred. It appeared to approach from all directions at once, the fog was that thick. A bulky shadow pulled into Marcus' drive. A door slammed. A wraith scrunched up the graveled walk and became the old pastor in paint-spattered coveralls.

"Got folks telling me of signs all over the county," Deacon Wilbur said in greeting. "Portents of a hard winter to come."

"Soon as this mist burns off, we'll be back in summer heat," Marcus replied.

"For now." The old man turned and stared over the porch railing, squinting his whole face as though peering ahead through the mists of time. "But the dogwoods are already casting off leaves, like we'd lived through hard frosts for weeks on end. And there's tales of gray squirrels warring over nuts while the acorns lie ten inches deep under the oaks. Nanny goats with winter beards already a foot long. Hoot owls crying the whole night, restless like they was hunting against winter hunger. You ever heard the like?"

"Not in all my born days," Marcus said, liking the old man immensely.

"Don't you scoff, now. Don't you scoff. Such signs and portents are the writing of nature's hand for them who know the tongue."

It was the closest Deacon had ever come to what Marcus might consider the normal conversation of friends. "I could brew up a fresh pot of coffee if you'd like a cup."

"Thank you, no. My back teeth are already like to floating."

"Would you have a seat here?"

"Don't mind if I do." Deacon Wilbur settled himself into the rocker next to Marcus. The chair creaked a gentle welcome, and the floor drummed comfortably as the man set a slow cadence to the morning. "Nice to see you in church yesterday, sitting there among the faithful."

The burnished mist shimmered slightly. "I enjoyed it." Marcus fretted that the words were so insufficient as to be insulting, but the old pastor simply rocked and hummed a quiet listening note. "And the music was incredible."

"I always wanted to sing in the worst way. Only thing I ever got was the worst way."

"Have you ever been to a white church?" Marcus asked.

"A few times. They were just fine, I suppose." Deacon Wilbur chose his words carefully. "Problem wasn't with those churches. It was me. I heard the spirit in there, yes. I wanted to stand up and thank God for the gift. Dance, shout, clap my hands."

"And they didn't."

"Not that I saw. Felt like I was sitting there with the chosen frozen."

"While I was in your church, I felt good. Comfortable." Marcus was stymied by his inability to confess just how rare those moments had become.

"I tell you what's the honest truth." Deacon's words flowed in time to the rocker's creak. "You're welcome. The place is yours. I don't know how to say it plainer than that."

Marcus felt the pastor's gift deserved an honest response, and motioned to the packet in the seat on his other side. "A process server showed up an hour ago with the final divorce decree."

"Right sorry to hear that." The words were spoken to the fog. "Yes, I truly am."

The sympathy in Deacon's voice left Marcus too open not to say what burned his gut like a branding iron. "I'm seriously thinking about getting drunk."

There was none of the condemnation he expected and half-hoped he would receive. "Didn't know you were a drinking man."

"Used to be. Always thought it came with the good life. And it fitted the job.

People unload their problems on a lawyer like they do a doctor. I found bourbon helped ease the blows." He waited for a response, and when none came, the bubbling pressure gave him no choice but to proceed. "I'd been drinking that weekend of the accident. A lot."

Deacon contemplated the fog a long moment before asking in that deep, honeyed voice, "You taken a drink since then?"

Marcus finished off his mug, wishing it held more than cold coffee. "Not after that first week."

The reverend spoke as though reading lines written in the mist. "Afraid if you started you might never stop."

"That's about right."

"Afraid when you hit the bottom of the bottle you'd be staring into the darkness of eternal night. Looking straight into your own personal hell."

Marcus said to the bottom of his cup, "Sounds like you've been there yourself."

"Something I've found on life's hard road. When I'm staring at the great temptations, I'm being turned from an even greater opportunity." He faced Marcus for the first time since seating himself. "You got something that needs doing? Something strong enough to call to your heart just like this hunger is firing your belly?"

To his surprise, the blinding mist suddenly revealed what he had been half-seeing all morning. "Yes."

"Then I expect your comfort is gonna come from going and doing." Deacon rose, and in the process settled a solid hand upon Marcus' shoulder. He turned from the fog, the portents read and dismissed. "My bones tend to settle of a morning. Best to get them up and moving about."

North Carolina State University had once been content to anchor the empty stretches east of Hillsboro Street. Now Hillsboro was a six-lane thoroughfare aimed straight at the capitol, and State's campus sprawled in every conceivable direction. In the fifties it had been nicknamed Cow College, since over half its student body had been Piedmont farm children down to learn the new science of agriculture. Now its atomic-engineering department held seven NASA contracts, the agricultural-genetics division designed pest-resistant seed strains on behalf of the United Nations and eleven African nations, two professors had won Nobel Prizes in biochemistry, and the veterinary-medicine department held over a thousand groundbreaking patents.

Marcus parked by the original stone bell tower and asked directions to the math department. He found Dr. Austin Hall's name on the address board and climbed to the third floor. A secretary took note of his age and his suit, checked the roster, and reported that Dr. Hall had a class but should be stopping by his office in about twenty minutes. Marcus used the time to reread the folder from Kirsten Stanstead.

"Mr. Glenwood?" Despite his stiff demeanor, Austin Hall looked seriously jolted by finding Marcus camped outside his office. "What are you doing here?"

Marcus closed the file and rose from the bench. "We need to talk."

"I'm extremely busy." Keys jangled nervously in the professor's grasp. "I have a faculty meeting in ten minutes —"

"You might just make it," Marcus replied, holding his ground. "If we don't waste any more time out here."

Austin Hall's entire face folded with resignation. "Come on, then."

The professor wore a three-piece suit of charcoal gray and shoes that squeaked as he walked to his door. "I wish you'd just speak to my wife."

"This doesn't have anything to do with Mrs. Hall." He watched the man have difficulty fitting the key in the door, and knew he was right to come. "This is between you and me."

Austin Hall entered an office as clean and tightly structured as his clothing. He dropped his briefcase on the desk and retreated behind the polished wood surface. "All right. What is it?"

Marcus shut the door. "Please sit down, Dr. Hall."

"I told you, I'm in a hurry to —"

"Sit down."

The man's jawline knotted, but he did as he was told. Marcus pulled a chair front and center before the desk, seated himself on the edge, took a breath. Another. Forced himself to expel the air and the words, though he had to clench his hands and his gut to get them out. "Eighteen months ago I was driving back from Wrightsville Beach. My two children were in the backseat. My wife was beside me. We stopped at a diner for lunch. We got back in the car and started off, arguing like we had been ever since we left the beach."

"Really, Mr. Glenwood, I don't see any reason why you should barge in here and unload these highly personal details."

Marcus raised his face a notch. Nothing more. Just let the other man see his eyes. It was enough to shut off the protest.

Austin Hall dropped his gaze, fiddled open his jacket, and began toying with the gold watch chain that arched across his middle. Anything but look back into Marcus' eyes.

Marcus held to the quiet tone, one that sounded almost gentle to his own ears. Like the voice of the doctor who had come to him that day in the hospital. A voice too full of emotion to hold much force. "We entered an intersection, I could have sworn we had the green light but I don't know, the other driver said it was red and my wife and I were still arguing . . ." He searched for air that did not fill his lungs and never would again. "All I saw was a flash of light off to my right, didn't hear the horn or the brakes, though the police report says there was a skid mark seventeen feet long. Just that flash of light off the truck's grill, then he hit us. Just behind my wife's door. Drove in the back right door and . . ."

He couldn't remember why he had started on this story. Only that he had to finish. "I don't recall much about what happened next. In my memory it was as though one instant there came this flash of light, the next and I was on a bench in the hospital, a nurse was bandaging my forehead, and a doctor was leaning over to say something."

He remembered then why he had come. Why this was so important. His head popped above the surface of his ocean of pain, and he focused on the man opposite him. "I didn't want that doctor to speak. If I had owned a gun, I would have killed him stone dead not to hear what I saw there in his eyes."

Marcus stopped then, and waited until the silence lifted the other man's head. Austin Hall threw him one quick glance. A world of terror in one swift look. Marcus continued, "So I'm here to tell you that all you have to do is say the word and I'll walk away. No, even more than that: Unless you *ask* me to continue, I'm going to drop this case. And I seriously doubt that anyone else will ever touch it."

The dark fingers twirled the chain, a glittering spiral across his middle. "It won't do any good. Alma —"

"I won't say a word to your wife about our conversation. This is between you and me." Another breath, the hardest of all. "Father to father."

The gaze that met his own was hollowed by nights of whispering shadows. "I couldn't bear it if my Gloria . . ."

"I know," Marcus murmured, "all too well."

Laughter and loud student voices

echoed from somewhere down the hall, drawing them back from the brink. Austin Hall asked, "Do you really think making a case of this might do any good?"

"It might. I hate to say more than that. But it might. New Horizons lives in the spotlight. If we could even threaten them with publicly staining their reputation, maybe they'd respond." Marcus unclenched his hands and offered them, empty. "But it's a long shot at best."

When Austin Hall's only response was to turn and stare out the window behind his desk, Marcus rose and left the room.

NINE

Logan Kendall's secretary knocked on his open door. "Mr. Walker is here to see you, sir."

"Show him in." Logan waited to rise until the older man was through the door. "Randall, good to see you. You take coffee?"

"Black, two sugars."

"Have a seat here, why don't you." Logan noted the man's flash of irritation at being directed to the chair in front of the desk, and not the sofa in the corner. Good. Cracking that polished veneer was an excellent first step. Logan walked back around his desk and dropped into his chair. "What can I do for you?"

Randall Walker had the easy smile of old Southern money, and eyes of congealed mud. "What say we wait for the young lady to bring my coffee?"

"If you want." Logan made a scene of checking his watch, his desk clock, his diary. "I need to be leaving fairly soon, though. Got a big case coming up."

Randall held to his smile, though his gaze hardened. "Only if you're lucky."

"Excuse me?"

"I'm here to offer you . . ." He stopped as the secretary returned, with a mug this time, as per Logan's earlier instructions. No china service, no boardroom conference, no stage for Randall to control. This was Logan's office and strictly his show.

Randall inspected the mug, then lifted it in a wry accolade. "You learn fast."

"You started to say something?"

"Indeed I did." A sip, a nod of approval. "I stopped in today to offer you a dream come true."

Logan chose to misinterpret the remark. "Sorry. I'm not in the market for a move. I'm very happy where I am."

"That's good. Real good. Because I didn't make this journey to offer you a position. No. I want to offer you a case."

Logan used the padded armrests to push himself erect. "You're going after Marcus."

"On the contrary. Marcus Glenwood has elected to go after us. Or, rather, after a dear and valued client, for whom I happen to serve as outside counsel."

"Which one?"

Randall used his mug as a stage prop, holding the moment with a veteran's poise. He sipped, sighed, sipped again, and finally said, "New Horizons."

Despite himself, Logan was rocked. "Marcus is suing New Horizons Incorporated?"

"He has not yet filed, but it is looking increasingly likely that he will indeed be bringing suit in federal court."

"Who is he tying in with?"

"Apparently the gentleman has decided to go it alone."

Logan had to laugh. "You can't be serious. Nobody in their right mind would try to handle a federal case by themselves. Much less take on a billion-dollar corporation. Who does he think he is, the Lone Ranger?"

"A question I would very much like to ask him myself."

"Marcus is going to get himself squashed like a bug." The prospect brought a great deal of satisfaction.

Randall nodded once. "I sincerely hope so."

Logan hesitated. To gain New Horizons as a client would be a major coup. His status would skyrocket. But still the question had to be asked. "Why me?"

"I beg your pardon?"

"Kedrick and Walker has a hundred lawyers who'd kill for the chance to represent New Horizons in court. Why come to me?"

Randall fiddled with the knot of his tie.

The triangular design was woven with what appeared to be genuine silver threads, for they reflected the light like dozens of tiny mirrors. "I have done some checking up on you. The word in our tight-knit little community tends to confirm what your colleague Ms. Rikkers implied. You were a better trial attorney, Marcus the better rainmaker."

"So?"

"Yet it was Marcus who received the partnership, not you. That hardly seems fair, now, does it?" Randall leaned forward. "I do not seek just any attorney for this case. I want a lawyer with a grudge."

Logan waited, scarcely breathing.

"I want someone who despises Marcus Glenwood. Someone willing to tear him limb from limb."

The tightness in his throat barely left room for a single word. "Delighted."

"I do not mean for you just to win this case," Randall said. "I want Marcus Glenwood to be so humiliated that his name is forever erased from legal memory."

A light flashed, and with it came a slight easing of the constriction. Logan hungered after this chance, but he also wanted to enter with eyes wide open. "It's not Marcus at all. You want to make sure nobody else takes this case up again later."

The words pushed Randall back in his seat. "Marcus Glenwood has no case. It is a nuisance claim. We want it stifled."

"But I'm right, aren't I?"

Randall's gaze had the texture of dirt from a very old grave. "Whatever my reasons, if you take this case it is with the express purpose of leaving a heap of ashes for the wind to blow away."

Logan permitted his grin to show through. "Then I am definitely your man."

TEN

Marcus pulled into the Hayes drive and halted behind a new Jeep Cherokee of midnight blue. His suspicions mounted when he spotted the keys dangling from the rear door. Which was why he forgot and shut his door too hard, causing one end of the rear bumper to break free of its coat hanger and clank to the ground.

"Marcus Glenwood!" A woman's voice shrilled. "You get that cockroach of an automobile outta my front yard!"

"Hello, Libby."

The house door slammed like a rifle shot. "I declare to goodness, if my gardener dared show up in a heap like that I'd fire him on the spot!"

"Nice to see you again, Libby."

Boomer's wife was tanned and fit and strong-willed enough to keep Boomer and three college-aged kids in line. She wore the obligatory Carolina-casual uniform of a pastel Izod shirt, pleated cuffed shorts, an alligator belt with a gold buckle engraved with her initials, and Bass loafers with no socks. She marched down, circled his car, declared, "It's worse than Boomer said."

"Whose Jeep is this, Libby?"

"Yours, soon as you sign the papers." She tsk-tsked her way back to where he stood. "Amazing those hoodlums let you walk away."

"I can't afford a new car, Libby."

A familiar voice snapped, "Save your breath, Marcus." Charlie Hayes limped his way down the drive. The old man lived in a second-floor apartment separated from the rest of the house by a poured-concrete wall. The wall was one of two conditions laid down by Charlie Hayes before he had agreed to move in with his son. The other was that Boomer stop threatening to cut off his oldest boy for electing to study at Wake Forest. "The title's already in your name."

Before Marcus could object further, Libby said, "Boomer wants to do this, Marcus. You haven't ever won an argument with Boomer and you're not going to start now."

Charlie Hayes huffed to a halt and said to the Jeep, "Dang thing would have to be blue, wouldn't it."

"I'm paying for this," Marcus declared.

"Of course you are." Libby smiled up at Marcus. "Charlie told us about the

Hall case. Boomer started feeling bad for everybody."

"I haven't taken the case yet." It was a feeble protest, but all he could muster just then.

"You will." This from the judge. "Get on over here and drive me to lunch. I'm hungry for some collards and fatback. Only thing I get fed around here is chicken with lemon and yogurt glop. Woman takes pleasure from squeezing out the last drop of fat."

"Fat is bad for you," Libby said, still smiling up at Marcus, a secret look in her clear gray eyes.

"Fat is where they hide the taste," Charlie said, climbing into the Jeep and slamming the door.

Libby reached over and patted his arm. "Go fight the good fight, Marcus Glenwood. Do it for all us normal folk. Keep us safe in our cozy little world."

Though he had been coming for years, the Farmers' Market remained new and strange to Marcus. He still recalled the days of traveling here with his grand-mother, carrying bushels of backyard pro-duce in the trunk of their old Chevy. By the ripe old age of eleven he was hauling the tattered baskets of shelled peas and okra and corn and beets, setting them up

162

according to his grandmother's artistic eye. He earned seventy-five cents for nine sweaty hours' work, and counted himself lucky — but not for the money. If he could have, Marcus would have paid his grandmother for the chance to be there at all.

Back then, the old Farmers' Market had been little more than a dusty red-clay field, packed hard by decades of pickups and horse-drawn wagons before them. Because of her age, his grandmother had held a coveted spot under the open-sided shed, shielded from the sun by a roof more rust than metal. There had been a spigot off to one side where the young ones gathered, filling buckets both for drinking and for wetting down the produce. In Marcus' memory, the children around the spigots were always laughing, his grandmother always had a kind word for her boy, and the summer sky was always so clear it appeared black off away from the sun. There had been a red-headed little darling in a flour-sack dress whose family sharecropped down Wilson way, and in his memories she was always there waiting for Marcus to arrive, always hoping for a smile and a word from the tall boy with the strange accent. Marcus remembered that now, as he drove in and parked by the new restaurant, how the redheaded girl could not get over the way Marcus spoke, his Philadelphia accent turning the words into something so foreign just his listing the produce made her laugh. Marcus followed Charlie Hayes across the parking lot and recalled that little girl and the way she would come running up to greet their dusty car with the words, "Tell me something funny, Marcus." If only he could remember her name.

The new Farmers' Market was positively palatial by comparison. The multitude of sheds were broad and painted bright colors, the floor paved with white concrete so it could be easily washed down. Only the farmers seemed unchanged, slow-talking and tight-faced, their skin leathery and their eyes troubled by being forced to focus on prices and change and the strange talk of city-bred folk. Marcus loved to breathe the perfume of fresh goods with the earth still clinging to their roots.

The market now held two restaurants, and they were almost always full. One had trestle tables and a fast-food counter and sold only fish. The fish came only one way — fried. Whatever they had that day — bass, shad, bream, popcorn shrimp, trout — was served with hush puppies and homemade fries and cole slaw. Beans were extra. Nobody who entered the Farmers' Market fish restaurant a second time said anything about calories or fat content or cholesterol. There were three portion sizes to choose from, and the large portion would feed a starving nation for a month.

The other restaurant was his favorite place in the entire world. The first time he came, three days after his return from law school, it had been as the guest of federal justice Charlie Hayes. The gentleman had observed carefully as Marcus took in the concrete floor and the simple tables and the clamor and the aroma. Marcus had finally turned to the judge and said, "If I ever make it to heaven, I expect to find someplace pretty much like what they got here." Charlie Hayes had nodded once and replied, "I believe there's hope for you yet." They had been friends ever since.

Marcus spent the better part of his chicken-and-dumpling lunch describing his journey to Washington and Richmond. These midday discussions had started the year of Charlie's retirement, and were a habit so ingrained that both men took it as natural. For a querulous opinionated man who was impatient with just about everything in life, Charlie Hayes was an excellent listener, as were most good judges. He let Marcus ramble his way through, sorting things out and making verbal notes in the process.

Only over dessert and Marcus' description of his morning encounter with Austin Hall did Charlie interrupt. "I'm not sure you did right there."

"I had no choice."

"Well, now. Maybe you did, maybe you didn't. Some folks delight in leaving the hardest decisions to others. All you've seen is a spat between husband and wife. You don't know if this was just a lifetime's tango they were dancing there."

"And I'm telling you I had no choice." Marcus was certain of that. "Maybe you've got to go through it to understand."

"Don't even think such a thing." Charlie pushed his half-finished dessert aside. "Look at what you've gone and done. Ruined a perfectly good portion of banana-cream pie with your nasty talk."

"You can't finish it because you ate about a pound of calf's liver and twice that of turnips. Even Boomer would be hard-pressed to outeat you today."

Charlie took a long pull on his lemonade, served in a Ball jar. "Boomer may not be much, but he's all I've got. At least the boy showed the good sense to marry well."

"Libby is great," Marcus agreed.

"She is that. Good mother to the children and her husband both. Boomer's a kid and always will be. Thank you, dear." Charlie held his lemonade glass up to the waitress's pitcher. "And the woman is smart as a whip. Back soon after they were married, I got all riled 'cause she convinced Boomer to stop his law studies and come run her daddy's Chrysler dealership. I went over there ready to tear a piece out of her hide for ruining my boy's life. Know what she told me?"

"I can't imagine," Marcus replied, "what Libby Hayes had to say."

"The lady met me square on, said she was saving us both a whole world of misery. She said my problem was I'd never gotten to know the real Boomer Hayes, on account of my always pushing him to be me. But he wasn't then and never would be. Libby told me Boomer was the son her own daddy never had, a man who lived for hunting and fishing and football and family."

Marcus spent a hollow moment pondering such love and wisdom, knowing it would never be his. "That sounds like Libby."

"Then she told me to go out and find me somebody else to push and prod and raise to the skies." Charlie fiddled with his lemonade and changed the subject. "Randall Walker called me this morning."

"You don't say."

"Wanted to know if we were still in touch, you and I."

Marcus pushed his empty plate out of the way and leaned across the table. "What did you tell him?"

"Now and then, I said. He asked what kind of lawyer did I make you out to be. I pretended like I didn't understand the question. He said, 'Well, is Marcus just a paper pusher, or can he carry the ball in court?' " Charlie drained his lemonade, wiped his face with an age-spotted hand. "I told him you were weak as yesterday's dishwater."

"Good."

"Randall didn't think so. Randall said it was a crying shame. They had an opening for an experienced lawyer and he'd been thinking you'd fit the bill." Charlie lifted his chin until he had Marcus pinned in the proper angle of his bifocals. "I told him not to go wasting his time."

"He didn't call about a job," Marcus said.

"What do I look like to you, a fool on a high horse? I knew that."

"Randall Walker is outside counsel for New Horizons."

"I figured it was something like that.

168

Randall Walker is a goat with a good tailor. Always has been." He spooned up the last of his banana-cream pie. "You sure about his being outside counsel?"

"The file Gloria's roommate gave me, it had a copy of the letter confirming his appointment."

Charlie fiddled with his napkin. "Wonder how she got hold of that."

"I'd like to ask her that very same thing."

"Anything else in that file?"

"Yes." Marcus told him what he had found.

Charlie gave his mouth a second swipe, slower this time. "Sounds like you may be better armed than you thought."

"Looks that way."

"You remember what I told you before we went fishing?"

Marcus nodded. "We don't have to win the case to succeed."

"Good. You were listening. I like that." Charlie's fingers scrabbled across the table top for the check. "Sure hope your Professor Hall decides to run with this thing."

Marcus snagged the check from him. "I'm beginning to feel the exact same way."

The sense of anticipation and progress

stayed with him until Marcus pulled up in front of his house, and saw his drive blocked by a scarred and dirty pickup. One that sent his heart thumping into overdrive when he recognized the clay-encrusted sides.

The driver did not look his way. He did not need to. The profile was enough to drown Marcus in fear and rage.

Before he cut his motor, a second man was at his door. He wore a dark suit and a true Southern smile — all teeth and no eyes. "Well, hey there, Mr. Glenwood. Glad you made it home okay."

Marcus snarled through his open window, "I'm calling the police and having that man arrested for assault."

"Naw you ain't." He turned and called toward the pickup, "That's okay, Lonnie. I'll be seeing you around."

Marcus pushed open the door to his Jeep and rose onto the running board, trying to read the dirty license plate. He could only make out two numbers. The driver waved a languid hand and drove away. "What is Lonnie's last name?"

"You know, I don't rightly recall. Ain't memory a funny thing?"

"What's your name?" His breath came in tight bursts clumped together. "You remember that much?"

"Sure do, Mr. Glenwood. Hank

170

Atterly." He started a slow circle around Marcus' new Jeep. "Work with the city council. Got myself a little business in town. Family's been here longer than America's been a nation."

"This is the way you do things around here, using thugs in pickups to make your point?"

"Now that depends. Lonnie's a right nice fellow, long as nobody gets him riled." The man traced a finger down the side of Marcus' new car. "But you get yourself a fancy-pants lawyer come waltzing in here, saying how he's gonna start some union trouble, why, Lonnie's liable to take offense."

"What do you want?"

"Same as Lonnie, Mr. Glenwood." The smile slipped away. "To have folks like you leave us alone. Me, my kin, and the people who put food on my table."

"You're a supplier for New Horizons."

"They told me you were a sharp one. Now you listen up, Mr. Glenwood, 'cause I'm only gonna say this once." He took a step closer, and his voice became a tight growl. "You stay away from New Horizons. Either that or you crawl back in that fancy new car of yours and drive clear outta town."

"I'm calling the police."

"Call whoever you want. Won't do you

171

a bit of good." The smile twisted hard as the voice. "We know all about how you done lost your kids and the missus. Shame how dangerous the roads are around here."

Marcus felt the air punched from his lungs. The man took great pleasure in his reaction, turning slowly, watching until Marcus managed his first breath. "You just think on that a while, now. The next time they send somebody down here, why, you won't even notice till it's over."

Marcus walked slowly across his lawn. Clouds were forming overhead, the air sultry with soon-to-come rain. He could smell the fresh paint from Deacon's latest work as he walked, could see how the shutters and window frames sparkled from the morning's second coat. The off-white trim made the old fired brick seem polished. Deacon sat on the windowsill of the upstairs corner cupola, paintbrush in one hand, eyes solemn and watchful. Marcus didn't say anything because he didn't need to. He walked up the front steps to the veranda. His home. All he had left.

Netty watched him from behind the safety of the screen door. "You all right?"

He opened the door, then turned to look back over the lawn. The dimming

172

light made the grass shine emerald green. "You know who that was?"

"Hank Atterly. I called the police. Not that it'd do a smidgen of good." Her voice held to tired old bitterness. "Hank and his kind are why this side of town stays locked in a past that nobody but them at the top want to keep."

"What about the guy in the pickup?"

"Never seen him before. But if he's hanging around with Hank, you can bank on him being vermin too."

"Atterly claims he's on the city council."

"Is, was, always has been. Him or one of his kind. He rousted you, didn't he?"

"He told me to stay away from New Horizons."

"That's just what I said. You got yourself rousted." She stared out to where the air over the road remained tainted. "Evil breed. Far as the Hank Atterlys of this world are concerned, folks with a darker hide should never rise above grade school and minimum wage."

"I've heard it said that eastern Rocky Mount is poor because the people with money choose to live elsewhere."

"Don't you go believing that lie, not for a minute. Ain't no reason why the same city council can't put in the same roads on this side they got over west of the Tar

River. Ain't no reason why they can't offer free land over here to a shopping center, or build us a couple of them shiny new county buildings, or maybe even a decent school." She gave her head a decisive shake. "You live here long enough, you'll learn."

The phone rang. She turned toward the office and said over her shoulder, "Whole world has changed since your granddaddy built this house. Only thing that hasn't changed is we still got us a city council and a company with muscle that're working hard as they know how to hold us back."

Marcus listened to her answer with his name, heard the rumble of distant thunder as she came back with, "It's Alma Hall."

Marcus walked to his corner desk and picked up the receiver. Heard a voice that was familiar and yet utterly new. "You get yourself over here."

"Alma?"

"Right now, you hear what I'm saying?"

"What's the matter?"

"Don't you be wasting precious time with questions. *Move.*"

ELEVEN

Marcus saw no rain as he drove, yet every surface wept recent tears. The roads were clogged with traffic and rivulets from a storm that had missed him entirely.

He arrived to find a state of affairs that resembled the weather. Alma Hall opened the door, tall and upright and still dressed for work in a dark suit and low pumps. But her face was creased with pain and stained by tears she had not bothered to clean away. Her voice sounded tragic, broken. "Thank you for coming, Marcus."

"You have news." It could be nothing else.

"This way." She led him into the living room, where today the plate-glass window showed a world gone monochrome gray. Marcus had time for a single glance before he spotted a third person in the room, one who stopped him in his tracks.

"I believe you know Kirsten."

He demanded, "What are you doing here?"

"Sit down, Marcus." This from Austin

Hall. The first time he had ever called Marcus by his name. His voice sounded as broken as his wife's. "Over here, where you can see the television."

Marcus did as he was told, his gaze drawn back to the silent Kirsten. Today she wore jeans and a cable-knit sweater whose collar was softly rolled, as if she sought comfort from the folds. Her platinum hair lay short and close to her head. The controlling anger was gone, the spiky hair, the barriers. Only the eyes were the same, violet and dry only because she had no more tears to shed.

Marcus asked her, "Gloria contacted you?"

Alma sat on the sofa next to Kirsten and took her hand. "Can you watch it through one more time?"

"It doesn't matter. I might as well stay." The words emerged hollowed of all tone, all life. "I'll be seeing this for as long as I live."

"All right." Alma took a shaky breath, nodded to her husband. "Go ahead, Austin."

He used the remote to turn on the television and the VCR. Before the tape had started rolling, both women were sighing quiet sobs. Austin's shoulders trembled in tight spasms.

A series of naked bulbs had been strung

behind the person who appeared on the screen, so all Marcus saw was a blurry silhouette. It hurt his eyes to watch, for the camera had captured the glare far better than it had the person. He leaned forward, struggling to see beyond the shadows.

The camera overfocused, drew back, sharpened slightly. It seemed to Marcus that the silhouette was mashed somewhat, especially on the left side. Then he realized he was staring at a person with badly matted hair. Probably a woman.

The voice spoke. "Hello, Mother. Hello, Dad. I am fine. Everything is fine here. I am staying here awhile. I am working. I study hard. I am fine."

The lifeless voice could have been computer-generated. Marcus realized she must have been reading something handed to her. Words written by someone who spoke such poor English he had no idea how wrong it sounded. Or simply did not care.

"I need money for my work. Send money now. Send money and I will be . . . fine. I am happy. Send money. I want to be left alone. But send money. A hundred thousand dollars. Send it to the Hong Kong branch of the Guangzhou Bank, account four-five-five-seven-two-two." As she repeated the sum and the account number, a faint keening erupted in the living room, a sound as natural to the scene as Marcus' own breath. Gloria finished, "I am happy. Send the money. Do it now."

Marcus sat staring at the empty screen until the other three people managed to regain control. Gloria's mother finally said, "That's not my baby."

Marcus did not understand. "The woman on that tape is not your daughter?"

"No, no." She stabbed at the television. "That's what they've *made* her. But it is not my child. They've hurt my baby. Hurt her bad."

Kirsten stared at Marcus with red-rimmed eyes. "You think you've finally got enough for a case?"

"This is not admissible evidence," Marcus said, his voice sounding hollow to his own ears.

"What a perfectly legal thing to say." Kirsten was too spent to give the words more than a trace of bitterness. "Looks like you're safe, then."

"There is no definitive trail of custody, no way to authenticate the tape. We must demonstrate both before —"

"Oh, spare me. What you're really saying is you still don't need to commit. Am I right?" She stood and walked from the room. From the stairs she said, "Let me know when this garbage is gone."

"Don't mind her," Alma said quietly. "Those two girls were close as twins."

Austin Hall sighed his way to his feet, taking it in careful stages. He stepped over to the bookshelves by the television. "Where did you put the photographs?"

Alma replied softly, "Bottom-right shelf, there in the corner."

Austin opened the little doors, picked out one framed print, straightened, then stood there a long moment. His stillness caused Alma to start sniffling again.

Slowly he turned back to the room. Only then did Marcus notice how unraveled the man had become. From the back he was still the tightly wound professor in his vest and starched shirt and suit pants. But the vest dangled open and the tie was gone and the shirt was unbuttoned to reveal a T-shirt and a trace of graying chest hair. He carried the burden back and stood over Marcus, swaying slightly. "Alma put these things away when she saw how it hurt me to look at them."

Marcus nodded. He understood that perfectly.

Austin turned the picture so that it faced Marcus. "This is my Gloria. Not what you saw there on that screen. This is my baby girl. Right here. You see what they did to her?"

"Yes." The woman in the photograph was electric. She laughed so loudly he could hear her voice. More than that. He heard his own children, his son singing in the backyard and laughing like the chimes of heaven.

Gloria Hall wore a cocktail dress of emerald green, probably silk. She was graced by a corsage and the grandest smile he had ever seen. She was a tall enchantress, not beautiful by any means, there was too much of her mother's strong frame and her father's sternly powerful features for that. Her shoulders and arms mocked the fragility of the dress. She was aware of this, and she did not care. Marcus stared at the picture and knew he had never met a person happier with her own skin.

"Whatever it takes," Austin said, his voice burning the words to charred cinders. "You understand me? Whatever you have to do."

Marcus waited through the police inquiry. He handled the Halls' refusal to give up the original video, which meant traveling with them to have it duplicated. This was followed by telephone discussions with various State Department people and a visit from a local FBI agent, all of which were utterly futile. By the time the last police officer left the Hall home, Marcus was more than spent. He was afraid.

He took the first exit into eastern Rocky Mount and drove until he found the first bar. It was perfect for his needs. The place was full of shadows and serious drinkers, men who weightlifted with fork-lifts instead of barbells, women who put up with a tirade-ridden world for six bucks an hour plus overtime. The bartender managed to take his order without meeting his eye. They didn't care that Marcus wore the only tie in the place. He was just another drifter looking for a drink and a jukebox that would cry for him.

By the third drink the shadows were whispering hated memories and the air had turned hard and mean. Marcus bought a bottle of vodka and carried it out with him. Back home, the drinks went down smoother but the air stayed heavy. Marcus drank until the whispers stopped, or at least until he stopped hearing. He stumbled upstairs, the railing somewhere far out of reach.

He awoke in the hard blackness of another predawn. His breathing sighed like a woman weeping, and he remembered then why he had stopped drinking. It wasn't anything so noble as a vow, or a hope of righting the past or trying for something better. None of that. The drink chained him down where he could not escape the nightmares. They were free then to eat at him for hours, long enough to stain the bed with his sweat. Marcus left his bedclothes in a soggy mass on the bathroom floor and went looking for his running gear.

Exercise had once come natural and easy. Except for work around the house, however, Marcus had done almost nothing since the accident. It took him a half hour to find his running shoes. By then his headache had diminished from lightning flashes to rolling thunder.

The first half mile was pure agony. He breathed fire and tasted bile. The second half mile he sweated the remnants of booze and bad dreams. Even so, the mental metronome kept steady count, and when he reached a mile he knew he had to either stop or die.

When Marcus finally caught his breath, he looked around and realized he had no idea where he was.

He took almost an hour to wind his way home. Long enough to grow mildly hungry and to map out the day's work. By the time he had showered and brewed coffee, the rain had returned. He ate his breakfast standing at the counter, watching crystal curtains close down his world.

The phone rang as he was sorting through papers and mail. Netty said, "Jay is having one of his bad spells."

"Then don't come to the office."

"I could make it after lunch, I guess. Right now it's pretty bad."

"Don't worry about it." He could hear a high-pitched howling in the background, a single note that went on and on, as though being born mentally deficient had granted Jay the ability to scream without drawing breath. "Are you all right?"

"I should be asking you that. Was the video as bad as they're saying?"

He tried to tune out the shrieking. "How did you hear about the Halls' video?"

"This is a small town inside a small town. Somebody heard about it at church and called around. Word gets out about everything. Including where you stopped off last night."

"You've got to be kidding."

"Listen up, Marcus. You want to do some more drinking, you do it around friends. There could have been a night rider with a New Horizons paycheck in his pocket last night. Somebody who'd love to brag he was the one who turned you into mush."

"Sounds like a time warp."

"No it doesn't. It sounds like good old common sense. Now, was the video bad?"

Marcus replied softly, "It was awful."

"Those poor people. We gonna help them out?"

He found himself liking the way she said that. We. "I think we're going to try."

"That's real good. You call me if you need me."

"I'll be fine." And for a time after he hung up the phone, he really believed it was so.

Marcus labored all day in his water-enclosed world. His corner of Netty's office became ringed by law books opened and stacked one upon the other. Marcus had purchased them years earlier for his home office, when an attorney died and his widow auctioned his effects. At the time Marcus had felt sorry for the man. The books were dusty and smelled of disuse. After a while the odor faded into the background with the rain. Noon came and went, and hunger became just one more faint rumble upon the horizon, noted but not acknowledged.

By three-thirty he was done. Marcus showered, then ate eggs and toast standing by the kitchen's tall sash windows. Sometime in the previous hour the rain had let up. Now the mist did not fall so much as float in the still air. Beyond his back window, sentinel pines stood patient in the gray afternoon, their branches turned to heavy green crystal. He stood and listened to the patter of drops falling off the roof, the sound keeping time to his quietly thumping head. Marcus set down his plate, reached for his keys and jacket and folders, and departed for the Hall residence.

Alma answered the door and led him into the living room. The tableau had changed little from the previous afternoon, except that Kirsten had reemerged and a few other people had gathered. Deacon Wilbur and his sharp-edged wife both nodded somber greetings. Alma started to introduce him to two other women, one white and the other Hispanic, but decided it was not worth the bother. Another couple he vaguely remembered from church stood close at hand and yet in the background. Deacon took note of Marcus' expression and quietly suggested they give the family a little quiet. For reasons Marcus did not understand, when Kirsten rose, Alma motioned her to stay.

Marcus declined Alma's offer of coffee, waited for her to seat herself next to

Austin, then dove straight in. "There are a number of grave risks involved in proceeding."

"You're going to take on the case?" Alma's voice remained as hollow as the day before. "You're going to help find my baby?"

Marcus waited until she was silent once more, then continued. "As far as the case itself is concerned, our greatest problem is that we have no direct causal link between New Horizons and Gloria's disappearance. Unless I can come up with something concrete, and fast, there is every likelihood the case will be thrown out and I will be sanctioned for filing a frivolous claim."

"The police have come and gone again, this time with a detective and somebody from the FBI office in Raleigh." Alma turned the words into a tragic litany. "And we've gotten three more calls from the State Department. Nobody is telling us a thing we don't already know. Nobody is offering us any real help at all. They just say —"

"Hush up, Alma, honey." There was no sting to Austin's voice. Nor did his eyes leave Marcus' face. "Let the man have his say."

"As I explained on Sunday," Marcus went on, "basically we have no case. But what is our objective here? Are we after some huge financial settlement? If so, we have lost before we've started."

Marcus tapped the manila folder with one finger. "But if what we're really after is to get your daughter back, there is a chance that just by filing these charges, we'll spur them to action. New Horizons might fear the adverse publicity enough to press the Chinese to do what we can't."

Marcus paused, then continued more slowly, "There is another risk. Filing the charges might have the opposite effect. New Horizons might decide it is in their best interests to get rid of any evidence."

He did not say more. Just stared across the glass-topped table. And waited.

It was Alma who erupted. Alma Hall, one of the most composed and distinguished ladies Marcus had ever met, now utterly unraveled. "What else are they doing to my Gloria *now?* You know what that FBI man told me? He was contacting our embassy! You know where the embassy is? Beijing! You know how far that is from my Gloria? Two thousand miles!"

Marcus glanced at her husband, who said simply, "You already know how I'm thinking."

Austin's quiet tone steadied his wife. She looked at him. "You agree with me?"

"There's too much danger in waiting."

This Austin said to them both. "We need to strike the best we can."

Alma gathered up her husband's hand in both of hers, shifting it over so she could clench it in her lap. Hold it tight. She said to Marcus, "What will you do?"

"With your permission, I will leave here and drive straight to the federal courthouse in Raleigh. On your behalf I am filing a civil action against New Horizons and unnamed Chinese partners." His voice sounded strong in his own ears. Professional. Lacking any hint of the apprehension he felt inside. "The charges are false imprisonment, labor and human-rights abuses, and intentional infliction of emotional and physical distress."

Marcus slid the folders across to them. "One of these is for me, another for the court, the last contains your copy. The first page is a letter of agreement assigning me the role of counsel. Because there is an issue called diversity of citizenship, where our legal action holds national and international dimensions, this is a federal case. I am asking for both compensatory and punitive damages. You need to read all this carefully."

"No I don't." Austin Hall extricated his hand and flipped open the folder. "Let me borrow your pen."

"Mr. Hall —"

"Call me Austin and give me your pen. Time enough for reading later."

Marcus relented. "You need to sign all the copies. You too, Alma."

Austin scribbled and shoved the folders aside with angry jerks. Alma watched him, one hand on his arm, and said quietly, "I lay in bed all last night listening to my Gloria cry for help. You go do this, Marcus. Do it now."

TWELVE

The only reason Marcus heard Kirsten's arrival at all was because he was listening to the night chorus outside his open window. The first sound was a faint hint upon the boundary of hearing, a swish across the lawn, a scrape upon his stairs. For some reason, it only occurred to him much later that the noise might have warned of coming danger. As though on some level far beyond the realm of sight and sound, he knew the noise heralded something good.

He arrived on his front veranda in time to see nothing but a blond head bobbing into the night. Then he spotted the box resting by the door, and understood. Marcus bounded down the stairs and out across the lawn, calling softly, "Kirsten!"

She spun around. For one brief instant, the streetlight illuminated a different Kirsten, one of soft angles and tremulous needs. Then the hand gripping her throat lowered, and the harsh angry tone returned to her voice and her features. "Don't sneak up like that!"

He found no need to point out that she

had done the sneaking. "Sorry."

"I just wanted to drop off some more data on New Horizons."

She said nothing more as he fell in beside her, perhaps because the night was so still and so dark, perhaps because she was ashamed that she had parked two houses down instead of pulling into his drive. "Did you file the case?"

"I just got back a couple of hours ago."

"Everything go all right?"

"It's a pretty surefire procedure. I dropped the papers through the courthouse mail slot."

Kirsten halted by a nondescript Nissan. She fitted in the key and pulled up the trunk, revealing two more boxes. "I don't know why I brought this stuff down from Washington. All along I figured you were going to drop everything. Just like that other lawyer."

Marcus realized it was the only apology she was ever going to offer. He hefted one of the crates, surprisingly light for its size. "A friend of mine pointed out that some cases are won even when they're lost."

For some reason the words caused her gaze to become even more revealing. But she said nothing, merely lifted the final box and waited for Marcus to reach out and shut the trunk. Together they crossed the lawn, the house yellow-red and welcoming ahead of them. Kirsten said, "Alma told me this was your grandparents' house."

"And mine. It's the only home I ever knew." Strange how the night and this closed woman could open him. "My parents weren't much into parenting. They drank. My dad left when I was nine, just didn't come home one day. My mom lasted about a year longer, then one night I woke up and heard her screaming on the phone at her mom, my grandmother. Telling her how she couldn't take it, couldn't raise me, either my grandma came for me or she was leaving me in an orphanage."

The response was so quiet he almost missed it. "That's terrible."

"It was the best thing that ever happened to me." The words were stripped of all pain by the night, and emerged so matter-of-fact that Marcus did not even question why he was speaking at all. "My grandpa had suffered a stroke a year or so earlier. He couldn't get around anymore, so I started helping out the day I arrived. He'd built this house for my grandmother back when times were good. She loved this place. Wouldn't ever think of selling it, not even when we were down to living off my grandpa's Social Security check and what we could raise in our backyard garden. But my grandmother was one of those women who just made everything all right. I don't know how else to describe her."

He climbed the front stairs, lost in the memory of how good it had been to come home and find on the other side of that screen door an old woman who always cared. Quiet and loving and strong and always there for him.

Only when he dropped his case on top of the first box did he realize Kirsten had not climbed the steps. Marcus turned back, and quietly asked, "What happened to your family, Kirsten?"

"My parents were killed in an automobile accident." She managed the first step, did not give any notice to his coming down and taking the box from her arms. Just stood there holding the night. "I'd met Gloria about four months earlier. She helped me. So much."

He dropped the box by the others and returned to her. "And now you're trying to help her."

Kirsten reacted as though slapped, wheeling about, eyes focused now and flashing. She opened her mouth, shut it hard, said simply, "I have to go."

Marcus watched her turn and vanish into the night, wondering about the

193

sounds filling the air. His heart seemed to hum a silver chord he had not heard in so long he could not even think of what it meant.

But the night was not done with him yet.

Marcus wrestled over the information Kirsten had deposited until almost dawn. With every passing hour his mood shifted, from astonishment to outrage to morbid curiosity. At half past four he had done all he could, save for one final call. He looked through his personal directory, came up with the name of a process server he had used in the past, a former federal agent based in Washington, D.C. He did not bother about the time. Process servers were known to live without the regular habits that governed the rest of mankind.

The man answered as always. "What now."

"This is Marcus Glenwood."

"So?"

"I want to serve interrogatories on officers at New Horizons."

"There's been work on them before."

"By you?"

"No. But somebody who attracts that many flies, word gets around."

Marcus glanced at the evidence now

strewn about his office. It carried on into the next room, draping the floor with silky outfits the color of overripe rainbows. "Does the word say anything about how hard it was to track these people down?"

"Close on impossible. They've got a lot of practice at running. You looking at something big?"

"Very."

"Then my advice to you is go for everybody right down to the night janitor. Because that's about the only one you'll get into court."

THIRTEEN

The next morning Randall Walker listened on his mobile phone as Hamper Caisse reported in. "I did what you requested and entered the Stanstead woman's house on P Street." The voice was as laconic as ever, as gray as the man. "There are no further files."

"You're sure?"

"I searched the house for over three hours. I copied everything she had on the computer — hard drive and floppies. Spent another seven hours going through those. You'll see it on my bill."

Randall had his office swept weekly for bugs, but still never spoke to this man except on the mobile phone listed in a paralegal's name. The paralegal had no idea she was the owner of a digital satellite line. Even so, talking to this man left Randall apprehensive. "You found the Hall girl's thesis?"

"Exactly the same as before. Drafts of three chapters. Utterly innocuous material. She knows nothing of any interest to us."

"I want a hard copy."

"You're wasting your time. And mine."

Randall hesitated, then admitted, "You're probably right." Hamper Caisse usually was.

"It's what you pay me for. To be right about these things."

But the worries would not be denied. "Then why does my gut tell me otherwise?"

There was a brief pause. "You're still worried?"

Randall found mild pleasure in having the gray man show any reaction whatsoever, even if it was only mild surprise. "I am."

"I suppose I could go back and bug her apartment. But you'd just be wasting more money."

"Do it anyway. And her car."

He hung up the phone, stared through the floor-to-ceiling windows at the forested view beyond the parking lot, and wondered why he continued to be so afraid.

FOURTEEN

Suzie Rikkers had not slept well in three days, not since she learned from Logan that they were going to fry Marcus Glenwood in front of the federal magistrate judge. Every time she shut her eyes and drifted off, the thought of what was coming down struck her like an electric current. Wham. She'd jerk awake and lie there staring at the ceiling. Staring up into the dark and smiling.

Suzie Rikkers paced the sidewalk in front of the federal courthouse and smoked and chafed at the wait. She was very big on payback. As a little kid she'd watched her dad knock her mom and her older brother and sister around. A lot. She'd learned to hide whenever the rough voice and the boozy odor announced that her daddy was home. He hadn't hit her much, mostly because by the time she grew too big to hide under the bathroom sink her sister had taken an apartment of her own. Left home and taken her brother and sister with her. Tried to take their mom too, but the woman wouldn't

198

come. Suzie had been very glad about that. As far as her eight-year-old mind was concerned, her mom was as much to blame as her dad, since she'd never managed to stop the bad times herself.

Suzie carried that load of early hate with her always. She had earned it. It was hers to wield. Anybody who stood in her way got chopped off at the knees. Especially men. Suzie Rikkers loved nothing better than taking down some smug self-righteous pea-brain who assumed because she was small and fine-boned she was an easy target. Apply the scalpel judiciously, that was her motto. Teach them to sing in a higher key.

The unquenchable lust for vengeance served her well in court. Suzie Rikkers entered the courtroom as she would a battlefield. There was nothing she liked more than legal assault. But her attitude created difficulties elsewhere. Especially inside the firm. The secretaries and paralegals were terrified of her. No problem there. They couldn't do a thing except refuse to work with her. The problem area was the partners. They expected a little bowing and scraping. Even the two women partners. But the only partner who had ever dared attack her directly was Marcus Glenwood. The name alone was enough to frame her vision with fire. Marcus Glenwood had twice used the semiannual partners' meeting to lodge official requests to have her fired. Marcus Glenwood had called her an affront to the legal establishment, a walking time bomb who someday would explode and splatter them all with neurotic garbage. Logan had shown her the minutes of those meetings.

Today was payback. She was so excited that she arrived at the courthouse two hours before their scheduled hearing. Suzie Rikkers paced the sidewalk and smoked so many cigarettes she felt like she had eaten an ashtray for breakfast. Her only regret was that Logan had insisted on handling the argument himself. Which was not good, but not too bad. Logan had his own reasons for hating Marcus. She glanced at her watch, sighed with relief that the hands had finally crawled into place, tossed her last cigarette into the gutter, and headed inside. Maybe hers wouldn't be the hand wielding the knife, but at least she'd be there to watch the blood flow.

Marcus walked to the end of the seventh-floor corridor and pressed the buzzer. When the latch clicked, he pushed through and entered the new chambers of Federal District Judge

Gladys Nicols. The outer office was large and well-appointed. The receptionist's desk was staffed by a compact man in a gray suit and silver-white beard. Most federal judges used retired highway patrolmen for receptionist-guards. All were armed.

"Marcus Glenwood to see Jenny Hail. She's expecting me."

"Marcus, hi, good of you to stop by." The judge's chief clerk was just as he remembered, a petite bundle of intelligent energy. "How are you?"

"Fine."

"You look, well, better."

"I am."

"Come on, I'll give you the ten-cent tour." Her stride was as quick as her talk, and in three minutes they had completed a circuit through the conference room, library, secretary's space, a smaller conference area, and two back offices for aides. The federal judge's private chambers sported thick-pile carpet, the latest journals and books, new desks, finely framed prints, fresh wallpaper.

"Quite a change."

"Tell me about it," she said, leading him past the closed door to the judge's inner sanctum. "Her new second aide is a Yalie."

Federal judges tended to attract the

cream of new lawyers. "Don't worry about it. Judge Nicols would be a fool to let you go. Which she most definitely is not."

Jenny led him back to the reception chamber. Eyes bright as a robin's egg and almost as blue examined him. "How about you, are you ready for today's hearing?"

He was not certain why this conversation was taking place in front of the receptionist, but he was the visitor here, and she was definitely calling the shots. "I think so. It's just the filing of preliminary motions."

Jenny glanced at the guard, who was observing all with a careful calm. She said, "That's not what I hear."

"Which is?"

"You know who's handling this case for New Horizons?"

"I haven't received official notice, but I assumed it would be one of Randall Walker's lackeys."

She shook her head. "Guess again."

"So tell me."

"Your old firm." Another glance at the patrolman. "Your old nemesis."

"Logan Kendall?" His heart squeezed. "You're joking."

"If you go look out the window, the black widow herself might still be wearing a furrow in the sidewalk."

"Logan's brought Suzie Rikkers with him?" Marcus hoped his smile looked more genuine than it felt. "What a pair."

"Word has it they have filed just one pretrial motion."

"I was wondering why the magistrate's hearing was arranged for just two days after I filed." But there was something he was missing here. He stared at the patrolman, was met with an utterly blank gaze. Then it hit him. "They're going for immediate dismissal."

"We think so."

His thoughts spun while this retired patrolman watched him like a hawk. Marcus went over and offered his hand. "I don't believe we've met. Marcus Glenwood."

"Jim Bell. Nice to meet you, sir. The judge and Jenny here have had some good things to say about you."

Marcus glanced back at Jenny, caught the tiny nod. Wondered what it meant. "That's nice."

Jenny said, "They're also going to request sanctions be leveled against you. They want to bury you." She waited, and when he did not react, she demanded, "Are you ready for this?"

His thoughts turned to the three boxes Kirsten had delivered two evenings ago.

He had been halfway down the drive this morning before turning back and dumping them in the trunk. At the time he could not figure out why. "I think so."

"Marcus," Jenny hesitated, then chose her way forward with great care. "You could make an unofficial request for postponement. Give yourself more time to prepare."

"It's not necessary."

"Are you certain? You really can't afford —"

"We have to do what we can for Gloria Hall. You know the name?"

Jenny glanced at the patrolman before replying, "I'm not sure."

"She's gone missing. We are accusing New Horizons of being involved. The case is our only hope of pressuring them to give her up. It's that simple. I can't wait. Not a single day."

When Jenny said nothing more, he started for the door. "I have to get some things from the trunk."

The judge's new chambers were at the end of a long hall, the only door along its entire length. Marcus resisted the urge to sprint down the corridor. He still had time. Everything was fine. He took the elevator to the lower level, and went out the back exit. He walked to the car and leaned upon the trunk. Somewhere overhead a bird chirped. Even that sounded calamitous.

He was not ready for this. None of it. Not for the pressures of a high-stakes court case, nor going up against his old nemesis, nor Suzie Rikkers. And especially not for having people as good and fine as the Halls depend on him. Marcus took a couple of hard breaths and resisted the urge to pound the trunk in helpless rage. The gift of sympathy from someone he admired as much as Judge Gladys Nicols made it even worse. Jenny Hail would never have brought up this matter except at the request of her boss. The evident pity behind Nicols' move hit hard.

Marcus used his fists to push himself upright. He stared into a sky of impossible blue, wishing there were some way to dive straight up. Lose himself in that endless depth, just swim away from this world and all its impossible woes.

Jenny and the patrolman stood together by the window at the back of the reception area, engrossed in the scene below. Jenny said, "You were right."

"The judge was the one who said Marcus would refuse to postpone," Jim Bell responded. "I just agreed with her."

"Okay, you were both right."

Jim Bell shrugged his unconcern. "But

you were right to ask."

Jenny stared down at the man leaning over the trunk of his car. "Is he ill?"

"Absolutely." The patrolman had the ability to claim any place he chose as his own, sturdy and rooted as a mountain. "Fellow's got a heart torn right in two. If he wasn't the kind of man the judge says he is, what he's been through would have killed him stone dead."

Jenny glanced at Bell. In the short time they had worked together, she was coming to consider him a friend. "What was it like, being a highway patrolman?"

"Lonely. Takes a special kind of man to drive down country roads in the middle of the night looking for trouble." His beard was pierced by a quick little grin. "The crazy kind."

Jenny turned back to the window. Marcus was inspecting the sky now, and appeared to be having trouble finding breath. "He sure looks ill to me."

"I've seen it before." Jim Bell's voice held the quiet matter-of-factness of one who had seen almost everything. "Any random act of kindness is like a bullet to the chest."

"Why is that?"

"Because it makes him want to feel. And all he's got inside is more hurt than he can handle." He turned to her then, placid gray eyes blank as a steel wall. "The judge is right to worry. I've had men under my command get hit hard like that. Most spend the rest of their lives looking for the right place to crash and burn."

She turned from all he kept hidden inside that gaze, and watched Marcus struggle to fit a box under each arm. "I wonder if he'll make it."

"I reckon we'll find out soon enough." He walked away from the window, clearly having seen enough. "Shame the judge will be the one who has to shoot him down."

FIFTEEN

The magistrate's chambers were a smaller version of the judge's but without the security. A case in federal district court first had to appear before a federal magistrate. This lower-level judge had the power to dismiss the case, rule on all nondispositive measures, even try it under certain provisions. Located on the third floor, these offices were as close as most federal cases ever came to a courtroom. For the few that measured up, the magistrate was then responsible for arranging the preparation of motions and setting the trial date.

Marcus arrived burdened by a bulky gym bag and two square boxes normally used for holding legal files. Suzie Rikkers turned and watched his entry. Logan Kendall did not. He was busy making time with the magistrate, talking about the Carolina Panthers' recent loss. Though he had the body of a little Napoleon, Logan possessed the profile of a tight end — bony, determined, and fierce. Only a frustrated ballcarrier could put that much enthusiasm into something so nonessential.

"Hello, Marcus." Magistrate Judge Bill Willoughby was a portly man with the distant, austere bearing of a priest. He offered his hand without rising. "How are you?"

"Fine, sir."

"Take a seat there, please. Of course you know Ms. Rikkers and Logan here."

"I read somewhere the Panthers' former linebacker got himself arrested again." Logan pointedly ignored the man now seated to his left. "Must still be trying to find himself, or whatever it was that made him run away in the first place. Crazy, if you ask me. They ought to make him do a little hard time."

Suzie Rikkers' suit was of standard legal-issue blue and not well-cut. It gaped about her hyper-thin frame. The flimsy hand-tied bow at Suzie's neck looked clownish, as if she had knotted it in a desperate attempt to keep her shoulders from slipping through the neck of her blouse. Logan was as dapper as ever. "Hello, Suzie. Logan."

Suzie said nothing. Logan made do with, "Marcus," but did not turn from his jovial monologue. "Problem with guys like that, they don't know how tough it is in the real world. Give him a season as a plumber's assistant, take away the Rolls and the women, you'd see how hard he'd start pushing for the goal line."

"Yes, certainly. Now let's move on." Judge Willoughby might have the look of a genteel Southern spirit, but he possessed more than thirty years' experience on the bench. Feuds between lawyers were not unknown, but they were certainly unwelcome. "We had a request from Justice Nicols for her chief clerk to sit in on these proceedings. As they are new to this level of the courts, we thought it was a fair request. But only if both parties agree."

"No objections, Your Honor," Marcus responded.

Logan actually smirked. "Fine with us, Your Honor." Clearly the more witnesses to the upcoming roast, the better.

"All right." He turned to his court recorder. "See if Miss Hail is ready to join us."

Jenny Hail entered and gave the room an oblique smile before seating herself to the back and left of Judge Willoughby's desk. The magistrate went on. "Mr. Kendall, you requested this meeting. As I told you on the phone, such a rapid pretrial hearing is not the norm. Mr. Glenwood, you have every right to request a postponement."

"Thank you, Your Honor, but I have no objections."

"Very well." To Logan, "I assume we are here to discuss the defense's pretrial motions."

"We wish to lodge only one, Your Honor." Logan handed the judge a slender file, paused as Suzie handed a copy to Marcus, then said, "We move that the complaint be dismissed forthwith, and Mr. Glenwood's license to practice law be revoked."

The judge's demeanor turned severe. "Licensing is an issue for the state bar, not a federal hearing. As you well know."

Logan held his ground. "With respect, Your Honor, we feel this matter is absurdly frivolous. A recommendation from you would carry substantial weight when we bring this matter up before the bar." Logan turned toward Marcus for the first time. "Which we intend to do as soon as this case is thrown out."

"I see." The judge looked from one attorney to the other, then opened the folder and adjusted his glasses. "All right. I'm listening."

"A young woman by the name of Gloria Hall has gone missing. Marcus Glenwood has taken advantage of two extremely distraught parents. His intentions are blatantly obvious. He seeks to focus public attention his way by besmirching the good name of one of our state's most respected corporate citizens."

The judge read swiftly, flicking the pages. "What are the facts here?"

"That's the problem, Your Honor. There aren't any facts to back up the plaintiff's claim. Glenwood has accused my client of orchestrating a kidnapping. The whole thing is absurd."

A quick glance at Marcus. "The plaintiff accuses New Horizons Incorporated of being behind an abduction?"

"Not the plaintiff, Your Honor," Logan responded. "I don't think Gloria Hall's parents have anything to do with this claim. This is something Glenwood dreamed up on his own."

Judge Willoughby glanced at Logan over the top of his reading glasses. "So what precisely *is* the complaint?"

"Glenwood has accused New Horizons Incorporated of kidnapping an American citizen. In China of all places. China, Your Honor. Nine thousand miles from here."

When the judge's gaze turned his way, Marcus offered, "Gloria Hall was investigating labor practices at a notorious facility in China known simply as Factory 101. This group operates in conjunction with New Horizons."

Logan snapped, "That is a ridiculous and unsubstantiated claim!"

"One moment." Willoughby motioned with his head. "Continue."

Marcus went on. "Gloria Hall has been researching New Horizons labor abuses for almost two years, in conjunction with a master's thesis she is writing at Georgetown University. Unfortunately, she drew too close to the truth at this point, and was abducted."

Logan retorted, "Your Honor, this is an outlandish concoction of bald-faced lies!"

Willoughby flipped a page. "You're saying New Horizons has no connection to this" — he back-paged, searched — "Factory 101?"

Logan's response was instantaneous. "None whatsoever, Your Honor. We categorically deny any involvement in the factory, and state that there is no basis whatsoever for bringing a case against us."

"I see." He examined the last page, flipped it over to ensure he had missed nothing. "So you are offering nothing further in the way of pretrial motions — depositions, motions on evidence, disclosures?"

"We offer none because none is required. There is no case here. Nothing on which a case can be based." Another swift glance at Marcus. "We therefore request an immediate decision on our motion to dismiss. And we are charging Glenwood with frivolous miscarriage under Rule Eleven."

Even though he knew it was coming, the statement jolted Marcus hard. Rule Eleven was one of the bugaboos of every trial lawyer's world, a statute whereby Marcus could be fined for all New Horizons' legal fees resulting from the action, plus substantial penalties. A finding against him under Rule Eleven would also be grounds for action by the state bar association. He could lose his license to practice law.

"Very serious allegations," Judge Willoughby agreed. "All right, Mr. Glenwood. I'm listening."

"Thank you, Your Honor." Marcus rose and fumbled with the top of his first box. "I submit as pretrial evidence the following items."

Using his own chair and two empty ones by the side wall, Marcus laid out three pairs of shoes and three very bright outfits. "These items belong to the line of sports clothing New Horizons markets under the name Teen Gear."

"Your Honor," Logan protested, "this is merely a game of smoke and mirrors —"

"Mr. Glenwood granted you the courtesy of listening in silence," Judge Willoughby retorted. "I suggest you do the same."

"Thank you, Your Honor." Marcus flipped the top off the second box, came up with two bulky files. He passed one to the judge and the second to Logan. He stood at the side of the judge's desk and watched his old adversary open the file. And saw Logan's jaw drop. He turned back to the judge, noted the man had observed Logan's reaction. "These internal company documents show that New Horizons has placed orders for over two million units of each of these shoes and outfits, contracting directly with Factory 101 in Guangzhou, China."

Logan collected himself as best he could. "This is inadmissible evidence, Your Honor. It cannot be considered."

Judge Willoughby glared across his desk. "It seems to me that you had every opportunity to make motions on evidence earlier."

"But Your Honor, these are confidential —"

"Be quiet." To Marcus, "Proceed, Counsel."

"If you will turn to the next section, you will see that these very same Teen Gear items were the centerpiece of the company's ad campaigns for the past three years; they are dated there in the top-left-hand corner. You will note that these ads used as models several top sports stars, including this year's NBA most-valuable-player award winner. In all these pictures, they are promoting the Teen Gear products originating from Factory 101."

Marcus granted a moment for all this to sink in, then concluded. "This constitutes incontrovertible evidence that there is, and has been for a minimum of three years, a direct connection between New Horizons and the Chinese factory in question."

Logan's voice sounded choked. "I demand to know where you got your hands on confidential corporate information."

Marcus remained silent. He fervently wished to ask Kirsten Stanstead that very same question.

The judge slapped the folder closed, his features a choleric red. "Is it your practice to lie to federal magistrates, Mr. Kendall?"

"Your Honor, please, this is all news to me."

"Is it." The judge's gaze sought to peel back the man's skin. "Is it, indeed."

Logan glanced at the file in his lap. "I respectfully request time to prepare a rebuttal."

"Motion denied," Willoughby snapped.

"Your Honor . . ." A single glance was enough to reveal that further entreaties were pointless. "I object to opposing counsel's possession of confidential company documents."

"Overruled."

Marcus unzipped the gym bag and delved inside. He came up with a sheaf of folders, one set for the judge and another for his opposition. "Your Honor, these are my motions for evidence, disclosure, and witnesses respectively."

"Fine." Willoughby settled a proprietary hand over the pile, and announced to Logan, "You are hereby granted three days to respond."

"Three days!" Logan's shriek half-pulled him from his chair. "Your Honor, that is utterly —"

"You demanded a swift pretrial hearing," Willoughby said, his gaze as hard as his voice. "You got it. Three days."

SIXTEEN

Logan Kendall stalked the length of the conference room at Kedrick and Walker. Walls on either side of him were floor-to-ceiling glass. The inner glass overlooked the reception area. The outer wall looked out to the Research Triangle Park, which from this viewpoint appeared as virgin green. Logan saw none of it. He paced along the inner glass wall, roaring blindly, seeing none of the fearful glances cast from outside. The reception area was packed. Every eye was upon them. Every single one.

Logan could not have cared less. "How could you have done this?"

"It was a terrible mistake." Randall Walker occupied the hot seat, the middle station on the table's opposite side. "I offer my most heartfelt apologies."

"Like that's going to change a thing now." Logan turned and shouted, "What possessed you to instigate such a totally asinine maneuver? And at my expense?"

"It was a mistake."

"It was more than that, buster! It was an absolute total shambles!"

"Because of me."

"I've got half a mind to bring suit against you for false representation. We're talking my reputation here!" Logan reached the end of the room and punched the oiled wood paneling. Turned and stalked again. Suzie Rikkers was the only other person in the room. She sat at the far end of the table and tried not to flinch every time he glanced her way, every time he paced in her direction. "I sat there and told the magistrate exactly what you told me. You know what I said?"

"That New Horizons and Factory 101 had no connection whatsoever." Randall Walker appeared painfully contrite. His coat was off, his collar unbuttoned, his tie down two notches. "A terrible error in judgment. I freely admit it."

"You instructed me to go in there and grind Glenwood to dust. Fine. No problem." Logan paced the chamber as he would a boxing ring. It was good Randall remained so remorseful. Otherwise the man would have long since been knocked over the ropes. "Only you give him a gun, load the ammo, aim it for him, and . . ."

Logan halted. Midstride, midbreath. Just stopped.

"It was absolutely the worst judgment call of my entire professional career." Randall extracted a handkerchief from his jacket pocket and mopped his brow. "Terrible."

Through the fog of his rage, Logan saw his surroundings for the first time. He checked the way Randall was seated, the open curtains, the watching throng. And understood.

"As a result, I have held you up for public ridicule," Randall went on. "It was a calculated risk. One that backfired horribly."

Logan's rage drained away. He nodded. Public ridicule demanded public contrition. Which Randall had skillfully arranged. This was not a conference room. It was a stage. Logan was *expected* to rant and rage. Word would get out, both of how he cowed the big man, and how Randall then begged him to stay on. All on Randall's terms. Word had to spread. A young partner from another firm blows in and publicly demolishes Randall Walker? Within the Carolina legal fraternity, this was headline news. Word would get back to Judge Willoughby. Logan's standing would be restored. Blame would fall upon Randall Walker.

Which meant there was a purpose behind this carefully orchestrated performance.

Logan inspected Randall, took in the dramatic precision of his expression, the carefully disheveled appearance, the crumpled handkerchief, the abject tone, the contrite way he said, "What a chaotic mess I've made."

Logan stalked around the table and pulled out a chair next to the man himself. Moved in close. Knees almost touching. And said simply, "All right. The show's over."

Randall jerked back as far as his chair would allow. "I beg your pardon?"

"You heard me." Logan settled one foot behind Randall's chair leg, locking it in tight. He felt Randall try to push away, saw the uncertainty flash across those polished features. Spotted the instant Randall realized he had lost control. Felt the first bit of pleasure since the debacle in the magistrate's office. "Question one: Did you arrange this to get me off the case?"

Randall sighed his acceptance of the new situation. "Absolutely not."

Logan felt the eyes still on him. Good. This was now his aria. The rest had just been the warm-up. "You hired me to go after Marcus. Does that still stand?"

"Most definitely." Randall's voice had lost its abject tone. And his expression had altered. Logan realized it was the first time the man was treating him not as a tool, but as an equal. "That is our express goal."

"All right. Here's how it's going to work." Logan moved closer still, until his knees struck the corners of Randall's chair. "From now on you are going to walk the straight and narrow with me. Clear so far?"

"Yes."

"Good." There was no need for volume. Nor a need to laden this ultimatum with doom. Logan had his own theatrical tools, honed before hundreds of juries and hostile witnesses. "You are going to supply us, your defense team, with everything we need to prepare and win this case. Starting with the absolute truth."

"Yes." Randall tried to push his chair away. "All right."

Logan halted the motion by setting his hand upon Randall's armrest. "And you are going to present to me one of the senior board members of New Horizons. Not just some PR dodo. Somebody who has full signatory powers."

Randall stilled. "That is not going to be possible."

"Why not?"

"The board is meeting in Geneva."

It was Logan's turn to back up a fraction. "Geneva, as in Switzerland?"

Randall gave a tight nod, then chose his words carefully. "The international division of New Horizons is incorporated in Switzerland. They oversee all twenty-nine foreign operations from there. Once each year, the entire board gathers in Geneva for a detailed overview."

"When are they returning to this country?"

Randall met Logan's gaze square on for the first time since he had drawn himself up close. "They are in Switzerland."

The conversation between Randall Walker and Hamper Caisse, which began immediately after Logan's departure, did not go well. "What do you mean, you didn't find anything?"

"That's not what I said." The little gray man droned so softly and subtly it was easy to believe he had nothing to hide, nothing whatever to do with anything evil. "I'm telling you there is nothing to find. Nothing."

Only today Randall was not willing to slide under the man's quiet spell. "Well, is that a fact."

"That's what you pay me to deal in. Facts."

The wrath and the frustration Randall had been forced to absorb from Logan emerged now in heaving breaths and thumping rage. "Then I guess we can all just wrap ourselves up in our warm fuzzy blankets and nestle down deep in our beds. 'Cause Hamper Caisse has gone out and made the world safe for democracy."

This was clearly not the tone Hamper Caisse was used to hearing. He had a lifetime's reputation for being the best. The man nobody saw. "We're not on the same wavelength here."

"Buster, we're not even on the same planet. Do you know what just happened to me? Well, sir, I'll tell you. I've just endured the worst day of my entire professional career." The power of his ire lifted Randall from his padded leather chair. "That lawyer you called no-account, the one you claimed couldn't find his own front door without a guide dog and a compass, remember him?"

"Marcus Glenwood, sure."

"The very one. He marches into the federal magistrate's chambers armed with nothing but what that little spiky-headed blond gave him. You know who I'm talking about, sure you do."

"I was the one who told you Kirsten was making the trip down. But —"

"Wait, now, you just hold on! It gets way better." Randall knew his voice was loud enough to echo down the outside corridor and ring the marble tiles of the reception-room floor. Which perversely made him feel the best he had felt all day.

He had already endured a public shaming, the worst since he had hung up his law degree in an office so tiny he and a broom couldn't have fitted in there together. Randall Walker had come a long way in his climb to the top of the legal dunghill. And the top was where he intended to stay.

He took a breath big enough to carry the shout one notch higher. The effort crouched him down over his polished walnut desk. The red-hued reflection that stared up at him was not a pretty sight. "So, does that no-'count lawyer roll over and play dead like you predicted? Noooo sir! Not him! He uses the machete that spiky-headed girl handed him, the one you said she didn't have, and he proceeds to disembowel my lawyers!"

"That can't be."

"Don't you tell me that! You didn't have to sit in my conference room and listen to how our attorney got skinned alive!"

"No." A hint of nerves entered that drab voice. The first Randall had ever detected. "I mean the information must have come from somewhere else."

"You want to tell me where? Gloria's momma?" The shouts served a second purpose, in that others would now know someone else had been responsible for

Randall's debacle. It wasn't much, but it was all he had. "Then why didn't the woman give it to the first lawyer? The one we could control! Or maybe you think this Glenwood managed to sift through three years of confidential in-house corporate memos and ferreted this out himself?"

"No. You're right. It had to be the roommate." A pause. "He was armed with confidential memoranda dating back three years?"

"Longer." Randall collapsed into his chair. His heart felt like it was going to explode.

"Maybe she put the information in her trunk earlier. You know, before our first search."

"You want to take that risk? Worry maybe she's got another trick up her sleeve we don't even know she's got?"

"But I'm telling you that place of hers was *clean*." For the little man, it was a desperate plea. "Not only that, I've been listening to her conversations ever since she got back up here. And I'm telling you Kirsten Stanstead is clueless. She's a spoiled rich kid putting in her time with a Washington charity. She talks about guys. She talks about who's been invited to what cocktail party. She talks about *Cosmo* articles and —"

"We're missing something here."

"I don't see how. I've got every room of the house wired. And now her car's bugged."

"No, that's not what I meant." Randall Walker pulled out his handkerchief, grimaced at the need to use it a second time in one afternoon, mopped his face. The problem was he didn't know what he meant either. "Get back in there and look again."

"All right." Resigned now. "But it'll be riskier now that she's back."

"You said yourself she puts in time with that charity. Do it then. Tomorrow. Tear the place apart. Look for trapdoors, hidden safes."

"I already have."

"Then look again." Randall swiped his face again. "My gut tells me we're missing something major."

Oathell was down to the county lockup. Again. There to bail out his younger brother, Darren. Again. Darren had called him at ten minutes past the midnight hour and begged him to come get him out. Again. Darren didn't dare call their momma. Darren knew his momma wouldn't pay any mind to his pleas of innocence. She'd thrash him and trash him. Kick him out of the house. Been promising it ever since Darren hit that man in the bar and broke every bone in his face. Didn't matter that the man had come at Darren with a bottle in one hand and a chair leg in the other. Darren had no business being in that bar in the first place. One more time in trouble, their momma had warned Darren, just one, and the boy wouldn't have a home to come home to. Which was why Darren had woken him up. Again.

But Oathell had a soft spot for the boy, always had. And there'd been something in Darren's voice, something other than the panic of being held by the Rocky Mount police. Or at least Oathell wanted to believe there was.

The county lockup was attached to the back of the central police station. Which, like everything else bought and paid for with tax dollars in Rocky Mount, stood on the Nash County side of the Tar River. It didn't matter that 60 percent of the town's population lived east of the river. No. The only things you could buy on the Edgecombe County side of Rocky Mount were burgers and booze. The biggest grossing Hardees in the whole United States was located two blocks from Oathell's home — a statistic that Hardees managed to bury deep.

The lockup was grim as grim could be,

a series of metal cages with no interior walls, none at all. Just big old cages built inside what had been a tobacco warehouse. The building's north wall still bore the old name, SMITH BROTHERS AUCTIONEERS, SINCE 1887. The din, even inside the police-station waiting room, was just plain awful. Oathell leaned his head on the brick wall behind his bench and pretended to a patience he did not feel. Almost all the people in uniform were white, almost all the people waiting in that decrepit hole were black.

Darren was not a bad boy. Oathell truly believed that. Otherwise he would have given up on his younger brother a long time ago. The problem was that Darren wasn't smart enough or ambitious enough to get what Darren wanted, which was out.

Oathell turned his head, and straightened in alarm. For who should walk through the police station's front doors but Deacon Wilbur. And with him was that grim-faced white lawyer Glenwood. They walked straight over and sat down before Oathell could even manage to get his jaw shut up proper.

The reverend asked, "How you doing, son?"

"Okay." Oathell glanced back toward the doors, expecting to see his momma come storming through any minute now.

"She doesn't know we're here," Deacon said, understanding him perfectly.

Oathell relaxed a fraction. "How'd you find out about this mess?"

"Friend on the force." Deacon sighed long and hard. "Don't know why I didn't call your house. Not sure I did right there."

"Don't tell her nothing. Not a thing." Oathell looked over to where the white man sat on the reverend's other side. Weird. Guy was dressed for Raleigh downtown in a nice suit and silk tie. In a Rocky Mount jail. At two o'clock in the morning. "What you doing here, man?"

Deacon answered for him, "Marcus is here because I asked him to come. My friend said Darren might be accused of something he didn't do."

"They haven't told me a thing. I been sitting here over an hour and I still don't know nothing." Oathell was too tired and too angry to try for nice as he asked the white lawyer, "What you so dressed up for?"

Marcus rose to his feet. "Sometimes a suit helps to get things moving. You know who's in charge here?"

"That man with his gut hanging over his belt. Sergeant Richards."

Marcus studied the policeman, who in

230

turn was pretending he had not noticed any change in the waiting room, although every other cop in the place had been casting wary glances in Marcus' direction. Marcus asked, "Is there anything about your brother I ought to know before I talk to the officer?"

Something in the way the man spoke, soft yet strong, distant yet right there with him. Not talking from the mountaintop like a lot of the white managers at IBM. No. This white lawyer was all right here, right now. Just like on the fishing boat. Nothing superior about this man. So Oathell was able to say, "Darren is about the biggest man you'll ever meet."

"Stands close on six foot fourteen," the pastor agreed. "And strong. Played ball until his knee gave out, when was that, his junior year in high school?"

"Naw, it was his senior year." To Marcus, "Darren's never gone looking for trouble in his life. He's a good man. Real good. But he knows how to fight and he don't take nothing from nobody. That's a problem 'round these parts."

"And he stutters," Deacon said.

"Yeah, but he's so quiet most people don't know how bad he talks."

"All right." Marcus walked over and said to the man by the desk, "I'd like to speak with my client, please."

Sergeant Richards was known to be the Piedmont's ugliest man, and dumb enough to take pride in the fact. Oathell watched the pockmarked face shift around, the dull brown eyes widen as though he were finally spotting this white man. "Your client?"

"Darren Wilbur."

The smirk poked up one puffy cheek. "The Wilbur boy's got himself a fancy-pants lawyer, huh." He dropped his eyes to the papers in his hand. "Well, he's gonna need one."

"What are the charges?"

"Armed robbery."

Oathell gasped and would have launched off the bench, except for Deacon's reaching over and placing one hand on his leg. Steady.

Even so, the sergeant looked Oathell's way. And grinned. His teeth were as brown as his eyes. "Yeah, he came screaming and shouting his way into the 7-Eleven over by the highway. Waving this big old pistol around, looks like a cannon in the videotape."

Marcus nodded, giving the statement calm thought. "You caught the whole thing on tape?"

"Sure did."

"And Darren's face is clearly visible?"

"Naw, the boy's so tall he stepped

outta the shadows and just sorta loomed over that poor girl at the counter. Scared her to death, having him wave that cannon —"

"And the video has him screaming and shouting at her, isn't that what you said?"

"Foulest language I ever heard." Another smirk in Oathell's direction. "Judge is gonna love it."

"I'm sure the judge will," Marcus replied, still very calm. "Especially once I put Darren on the stand and let the jury hear how bad his stutter is."

The man shifted around fast enough for his belly to bounce off his belt. "What's that?"

"Didn't your arresting officer mention that fact? Or maybe he didn't even bother to notice. All he wanted was a big black man to collar and close the case."

"That boy has a stutter?"

"Why don't we bring him out," Marcus replied, "and let the *man* speak for himself."

Richards weighed twice what Marcus did, him with the beefy red arms sticking out of his short-sleeved shirt, the knuckles on his hands scarred and twitching. But all he said was, "Jimbo, run on back and bring out that Wilbur boy."

"Sure, Sarge."

All eyes were on the pair now, and everybody in the room heard Richards say, "I heard about you. You're that Glenwood fellow."

"That's right."

"Sure." The smirk again. "Word's gotten 'round about you. How you done got your tail whipped over Raleigh way. So you figure you can move in here, start playing your big-city games, is that it?"

Marcus said nothing.

"Yeah, that's what I thought." Richards gave a wet chuckle. "I give you about a week."

Darren appeared in the doorway leading back to the pens, wearing a T-shirt so tight his muscles looked carved onto the cotton itself. The cuffs on his hands glinted like pure evil, enough to have Oathell wishing he had a gun. Instead, he swallowed down the rage, rose, and walked over, all calm on the outside.

"O-Oathell, y-you g-g-g-g . . ." Darren swallowed and tried again, but like always when he was excited, the words just wouldn't come.

"It's okay, little brother." Silly thing to be saying to a man towering up there near the ceiling. But Darren was his little brother and always would be. "Everything's fine."

"B-b-but I d-d-d-didn't d-d-d . . ." The effort to shape that short little word twisted his head up and to one side.

"I know you didn't. Just hang on, man. We got us some help this time."

Marcus said, "Screaming and shouting, isn't that what you said, Sergeant?"

The sergeant snarled, "Jimbo, take off those cuffs."

"I assume you're going to be dropping all charges," Marcus said.

The policeman's face was a choleric red. "Don't you go assuming a thing, city boy. Not even how long we're gonna let you hang around these parts."

Marcus raised one hand, motioning Oathell and his brother and the reverend out of there. Oathell didn't need a second invitation. He grabbed his brother's arm, like holding on to warm granite, and pulled him forward. "Let's go, Darren."

Marcus said to the sergeant, "Nice to know I can count on the local police to do their job."

"Sure can, city boy." The sneer was pure wicked. "Any time you need an escort outta town, you give me a holler."

SEVENTEEN

A northeast wind blew in with the dawn, lacking its customary burden of cold hard rain. Marcus stepped out onto the veranda and breathed in the Atlantic's salt-laden gift. Although the ocean lay a hundred and fifty miles farther east, the cry of gulls seemed to mingle with the cardinals and jays. A third breath, and he sensed that summer was now gone. The humid sweltering heat might return for a day, causing the earth to shimmer in abject apology for the discomfort it caused. But from now on the day's heat would come as a visitor, not reign as king.

By nine-thirty the house was a hive of activity. Deacon Wilbur was completing the kitchen trim and cabinets. Darren had arrived with him, and been set to sanding the sweeping banister and oak stairs leading to the second floor. The sanding machine with its high-pitched whine was like a toy in the young man's massive hands. Another painter, a friend of Deacon's with the worst overbite Marcus had ever seen, was hauling tarps upstairs to drape and paint the hall and guest bedroom. Deacon had reserved the master suite for himself later that same afternoon. There was a new air to the work, a sense of haste Marcus had not noticed before. One that suggested the job was nearing completion.

By ten Marcus had met with four new clients. Two were from the church. Two had driven over from Princeville, a place of dark hovels and deep despair since the previous year's floods. Although his conference room and office were essentially ready, the doors were not hung and the furniture remained stacked in the garage. Netty fielded calls and ran the fort from her front room while Marcus held his preliminary interviews in the kitchen. If any of his clients minded discussing legal problems while seated at a breakfast table with Deacon perched on a ladder ten feet down the hall, they kept it to themselves.

Just before eleven Netty stuck her head in the doorway. "Call for you."

Marcus was wrapping up work with partners in a produce cooperative being threatened by a supermarket chain. "Take a message."

"It's the Stanstead woman."

Marcus was already up and moving for the door. He passed Netty fast enough to ignore her smirk and the remark, "I hear she's right fetching."

Marcus went to his corner cubbyhole and picked up the phone. "Kirsten?"

"I have the lawyer's name."

"Excuse me?"

"You asked me to find a D.C. lawyer who worked with China. I have a name."

"Oh." He marveled at his own disappointment. "Right."

"His name is Ashley Granger. I've called and he's in the office all day." A pause. "I also have some more files ready for you."

"Great." He was struck by a thought so sudden he could not help smiling. "I'll come up this afternoon and pick them up."

"What?"

"I need to meet this Granger face-to-face." Forging on before she could formulate a refusal. "I'll stop by Richmond on the way. So it'll be late by the time I see Granger. I'll call and ask if he can fit me in at the close of business. How about meeting me for dinner afterward?"

"I . . ." The pause was so long Marcus had already accepted the turndown. Then a small voice said, "I'll try to rearrange something and be here."

Marcus hung up the phone, then stood staring out the window, seeing only light. A voice behind him said, "So we're off to the big city again, are we?"

He nodded, as much to a jay's laughing call as the question.

On the best of days the journey to Richmond took just over two hours, the journey from there to Washington two hours more. The weather and the traffic were both with him, the afternoon beautiful and the roads quiet. Just over the Virginia border, Marcus spotted his first autumn foliage. A copse of sycamore and elm, hidden eleven months of the year within a larger grove of pine and scrub, shouted defiant joy at their sudden independence. He slowed and gave them silent homage, then continued with good memories for companions.

Autumn had been his grandmother's season. She was in truth a perennial, a woman who managed in all seasons, no matter how harsh or dry. But autumn was when she most thrived. Strange how a woman housebound by age and poverty and a crippled husband could so dearly love life. But she had. Especially in the cool dry months before winter's onslaught.

It began when the first wild berries ripened. The house smelled of cinnamon and clove and molasses and equally dark Caribbean rum and baking. Maude Glenwood did not drink liquor, but she was not averse to using it as a spice. She made all manner of berry pies with graham-cracker or sugar-cookie crusts, and sold them at the Farmers' Market. She had a name as a pie maker, as she did for being sparse with words. Marcus could recall dawn-lit journeys into Raleigh, where all the pies would be sold before the first customer arrived, taken by other farmers carting produce. On such September days they made the trip and returned before the sun cleared the treetops, and never said a single word between them.

With the changing of the leaves, Maude started on her faces. She was very particular about her artistic elements. From an entire bushel of leaves Maude might elect to use a dozen. She would glue together the coppery hues, using cardboard for a backing, with elm for a beard and acorns for eyes and bone-white birch bark for teeth. Pressed dogwood blossoms made hats for the ladies. Woven straw caps for the men. The faces sold almost as fast as the pies. Through his grandmother's nimble fingers, Marcus lived and breathed and feasted upon autumn's awesome splendor.

His grandfather had finally passed away the October of Marcus' first year of law school. The night Marcus arrived home for the funeral, he had watched his grandmother bake the entire night before the service. The two best pies, one of blackberry and one of brown sugar and apple, had been set upon the shelf over her husband's empty seat by the back sash window. They had still been there when Marcus departed four days later. Maude Glenwood saw no need to explain the pies. Marcus felt no need to ask.

The people who had come for his grandfather's funeral were mostly farmers and church friends, eastern folk who valued silence more than words. There had also been a remarkable number of black people in the congregation, a startling fact in a county where there was little social mingling between the races, especially in church or in grief. Marcus recalled the funeral as a quiet and watchful time, one he had spent wondering if somewhere in Maude's own silence she was glad to be rid of the burden.

The last night before his return to Pennsylvania, as they sat on the veranda and listened to the crickets and the owls, his grandmother had said the house would be overquiet without her two fine men. For Maude Glenwood it was quite a speech. Five weeks later she passed away in her sleep, departing as silently as she had lived. The day after that second funeral, Marcus returned to the cemetery and blanketed her grave with the last of autumn's finery.

Marshall Taub's office was located in a Richmond strip mall between a pool hall and Bubba's Barbecue Palace. Marcus walked in, passed through the empty receptionist's office, and knocked on the inner door. "Mr. Taub?"

The voice was familiar, yet crisper and far more alert. And wary. "Who wants to know?"

"My name is Marcus Glenwood." The back office was marginally neater than the man's home, and smelled far less nasty. "I'm an attorney in Rocky Mount."

Marshall Taub wore a frayed white shirt, no tie, and suspenders. He squinted and asked, "Have we met?"

Marcus hesitated only an instant. "I don't do much business in Richmond."

"You look familiar."

"We spoke on the phone. I called you at home."

"Oh. Right." Clearly he was accustomed to forgetting what happened after he left the office. "What brings you up this way?"

"Mind if I sit down?"

"Sure, take a load off. Sorry about the

mess. Secretary's on a long lunch break."
A trace of a smile. "Like about eight
months now."

"I know what you mean." The chair
back creaked in a threatening manner, so
Marcus kept his weight well forward. The
carpet was lime green shag, the desk a
metallic tan that matched the filing cabinets. "I make do with a part-timer."

Rheumy eyes that would have better
suited a man twice his age gave Marcus a
swift inspection. "Funny, I figured you
for a partner in some corporate-law outfit."

"I was, until about eight months ago."

"Which one?"

"Knowles, Barbour and Bradshaw."

Eyebrows jiggled. "Musta been nice.
What happened, they pass you over for a
partnership?"

"Something like that." Outside the back
window a Budweiser truck unloaded
crates into the pool hall next door. "I'm
entering suit in federal court against New
Horizons."

Marshall Taub leaned back until he was
jammed up tight against the wall. "You
don't say."

"We have reason to believe they had a
hand in kidnapping a woman researching
illegal labor practices."

"Wouldn't surprise me one bit." No

hesitation there. "Not that they would engage in improper labor practices, or that they'd kidnap somebody who got in the way of the next almighty dollar. What was she, a union activist?"

"No. Just an academic."

"Doesn't matter. If she stood between them and profit, they'd clean her clock."

"I read the transcript of your own case."

"Buried me in appellate court." The voice turned gravelly. "Worst thing I ever did was take that case."

"I'd like you to testify. I'm going to try to build a case on past practice." This meant attempting to bolster his case by showing how the company's previous actions formed a consistent pattern. "It's a long shot, but the best I have."

"No problem." The eyes glimmered with a trace of old life. "Love to tell my tale to another jury."

"I imagine the defense will bring up . . ." Marcus hesitated, then trod delicately. "All the unsavory details about you that they can."

"Hey, it's not like I've got a lot left to lose." He brought his chair forward and leaned over his desk. "Speaking of which, you better be ready. They'll do their dead-level best to roast you over a hot fire."

Marcus rose to his feet. "I don't have much left to lose either."

Marshall Taub grinned for the first time. "Sounds like you might be the right man for the job."

EIGHTEEN

Ashley Granger, the attorney referred by
Kirsten Stanstead, occupied a small suite of
offices on M Street, just down from the
Washington Marriott — distinctly downtown but very much a medium-priced
spread. A series of Chinese prints hung on
the walls, a hand-woven Oriental carpet
marked the waiting area, a vase and two lacquered bowls rested on an end table.
Marcus gave his name to the secretary-
receptionist, scouted the cramped outer office, and took Granger's independence as a
good sign. Here was someone who had
carved out a niche and succeeded well
enough to remain his own man, but not so
well as to move into the lofty suites occupied by lobbyists and allies of the mega-
corporations. In another life, it was the kind
of station he would have liked for himself.

"Mr. Glenwood? Ashley Granger. Why
don't we step inside." Ashley Granger
was tall and had probably once been
slender. But the desk and city living had
padded his frame. His wavy hair was thinning but still more coppery than gray, and

his face held to the freckled imprint of the little boy. His gray eyes were level and his manner direct. Even before he had settled in behind his desk, he demanded, "What can I do for you?"

"I'm bringing a civil case against a North Carolina company and an affiliated factory in mainland China, not far from Hong Kong."

"Is this factory located in a Special Territory?"

Marcus tried to be just as direct. "I have no idea what that is."

"Special Territories are Chinese versions of free-trade zones. Special laws, special dispensations. A lot of foreign joint ventures choose to locate there because the flow of capital is less restricted." Ashley Granger's speech held a slight Southern edge. His attitude was both comfortable and briskly big-city. "Even have different court systems for handling disputes."

"I don't know for certain, but I doubt this factory is located in a Special Territory." Marcus scanned the office walls until his eye was caught by the twin framed diplomas. "You attended Wake Forest."

"Undergraduate and graduate both. They gave me a free ride and I wasn't about to argue with that."

"Don't blame you. I chose Duke and Penn for the exact same reason." Marcus inspected the man, wished he knew whom to trust. And how far. "How did a Wake Forest grad wind up practicing the Chinese branch of international corporate law?"

"My parents were missionaries over there. Taiwan first, then Hong Kong, then the Chinese population in Singapore and Malaysia." Words spoken so often they did not occupy much of his mind. His gaze remained alert, measuring. "Mind if I ask how you got my name?"

"A young lady based here and working with a D.C. charity suggested you. How she found you, I don't know."

"I do some pro bono work for some of the local groups. Maybe there's a connection."

"Asia Rights Watch?"

"Some."

"Do you know a Mr. Dee Gautam?"

Granger held Marcus' card up for a more careful inspection. "For a local Rocky Mount attorney, you get around, Mr. Glenwood."

Marcus had to ask, "Did you ever meet a woman by the name of Gloria Hall?"

He noted a flicker of something down deep, there and gone in an instant. Despite his boyish looks, Ashley Granger played his cards close and well. "Might have. I meet a lot of people in this game."

"I heard more or less the same response from Dee Gautam."

"Probably because it's true. There's a big gray area in pro bono work, Mr. Glenwood. Sometimes it's hard to tell exactly what falls under attorney-client privilege." A longer inspection. "You do much pro bono work yourself, Mr. Glenwood?"

"Some." Clearly the man wanted more, so he continued. "Until eighteen months ago, I headed a Raleigh group trying to reinstate the policy in all the major firms."

"Now that's interesting." Granger reached for his yellow pad, pulled a pen from his shirt pocket. "Got someone down there who could confirm this?"

Marcus started to ask why it was important, decided to let the man lead on. "Charlie Hayes is a retired federal appellate judge. Gladys Nicols was a former local judge, she's now been raised to the federal district bench. We three headed up the program."

Granger nodded twice, as though agreeing with some internal voice, then launched straight ahead. "Business in China, Mr. Glenwood, has nothing near the same transparency as you find under U.S. law. The Chinese do not have as well-developed a legal system or commercial system. You have to look at business relations in China with a certain degree of skepticism. In the United States you have rule of law, you have regulatory bodies, you have precedent, you have an existing legal structure. China is the Wild West by comparison. They don't have a standardized process under which their rapid commercialization is taking place. The result is a haphazard body of law and regulation, one based more on the preference of people in power than on the rights of average citizens. The little people are squeezed hard, but they have no voice, no legal recourse, no democratic means of affecting policy. The people in power just cruise along. This is particularly true of companies not directly in the spotlight. Smaller companies, including many international joint ventures, operate in a netherworld, beyond the pale of what we would consider normal constraints of law and regulation. These legal vacuums are being sought out and exploited by the wrong kind of U.S. company."

Marcus heard him out, understanding little beyond a single fact. "I think I need to trust you fully."

Granger smiled thinly. "Big mistake."

"I have a more serious problem than what I just said. Do you know New Horizons Incorporated?"

"The name, sure."

"Have you ever represented them?"

"Not a chance. Look around you, Mr. Glenwood."

"Call me Marcus."

"I work with the small-fry. Companies like New Horizons go for the higher-priced spread. There's a group called the China Trade Council, they exist to service the needs of companies that size. The council charges a quarter mil a year to join the elite, but its members have access to the top guys on both sides of the ocean. People like New Horizons press their case at levels I can't reach. We don't operate in the same spheres."

"Gloria Hall was apparently kidnapped while researching labor abuses at a Chinese factory. One allegedly operated jointly by New Horizons, called Factory 101, located in something called the Guangzhou Industrial Compound." Marcus waited for a response, and when none came, said, "If this was a United States–based situation, I would press for criminal proceedings."

"It's not the United States," Granger replied flatly. "You contact the boys over at State?"

"And the FBI. All we know is they are making inquiries through their embassy."

"Which will get you precisely zip. You know about the Vice President's upcoming visit to China?"

"Yes."

"Their primary concern is trade. The guys with the fat wallets are not interested in backing an administration that focuses on human rights. Or even on missing Americans. Those who bankroll the election campaigns want free trade, open borders, hands off everything to do with making money."

Marcus asked, "So what do I do?"

"Find out who is responsible for that factory. Determine who is the top local man. Remember what I said: Business in China is all about who holds power. See if pressure can be applied directly to the top dog."

"Can you do that?"

Granger rose to his feet, offered his hand. "Give me a few days."

It was dark and well past the worst of rush hour by the time Marcus entered Georgetown. He snagged a parking space several blocks from the house on P Street. He walked through a misting rain as cars drove by slowly, tires whispering on the wet asphalt. Lights were softened by the rain, the sidewalk and the street and the houses transformed into an unfinished painting. He saw no one and enjoyed the moment's solitude.

Kirsten opened the door before he could knock. There was no pleasure in her greeting, and scant welcome. "Something's come up. I've been called back to the office."

Disappointment was becoming a familiar response to this woman. "I was looking forward to a nice evening."

The only consolation she offered was an absence of anger. She pushed open the door, said, "I've made us a salad. It's all the time I have."

Marcus followed her retreat through the house. Every light in the kitchen was on. The place was neat as a model home. Two plates were set on the kitchen counter, two stools drawn up at right angles, water glasses, no smell of food. Just bread and cheese and a bowl of lettuce. He glanced to where Kirsten stood hugging her middle, ready to accept his irritation. So he just smiled and offered, "Looks great."

Over dinner he related his meeting with Ashley Granger. She toyed with her food, avoided his gaze, said almost nothing. He finally ran to the end of his tale, made his first question as casual as he could. "How did you come across Ashley's work?"

"From Gloria's papers."

"Is there much more I haven't seen?"

Her gaze rose from the countertop to dance over the ceiling and the corners of the room. "No. Not much at all."

"When can I have the rest? I need anything that would help tie New Horizons into an actual collaboration with the Chinese —"

"You never told me how you met your wife."

He stared at her and the flitting gaze. "Excuse me?"

"I was just wondering." Her tone sounded light, but her features were taut as stretched hide. "You don't have to tell me if you don't want."

"No, no, it's fine." Speaking words he scarcely heard himself, searching for what she seemed determined to keep hidden. "I met Carol when I was finishing my law studies up north. She was everything I had never known or had, as alien to me as if she'd been raised on Mars. Rich, old-family rich. So settled in their wealth and their power they acted as though it was their right to be happy and well and strong and in control."

Somehow his words melted her. He did not know what it was he said that could have caused such a reaction, but he liked seeing the tension and the barriers dissolve. So he kept on, though the act of speaking raked his heart with razored spikes. "I think we both knew from the beginning it was a mistake. At least, I'd like to think now that I had the wisdom to see what I was doing, but chose not to accept it. It's a lot better than accepting that I was blind and dumb all along. She was happy with the status quo, and expected me to fit the mold shaped by her father and her uncles and every other man she'd been close to. Socially active, opera, golf, donations to the right charities, house on the right street, vacation home here, apartment there. Working for her daddy's companies, sitting on boards because her family held controlling interests in the companies, wielding power without ever raising my voice."

He smiled at his own folly, and found strength in the way Kirsten twisted her mouth in time to his own. It was like looking in a mirror and seeing his own pain reflected in her beautiful face and pale lips and shattered turquoise gaze. "Only I hate the opera and I never liked golf. I was hungry and felt like the only way I could ever be the person she needed was to fight my own way to the top. Which was crazy, I know. Any money I earned would be new money, any power tainted by my ambition and my hard work."

Marcus stopped, astonished at his confession. It was the most he had spoken about himself in over a year and a half, the first time he had ever consciously shaped the ribbons of thought that laced the early hours of almost every day. He had to turn away from all he had said, all he had shown to himself with unaccustomed clarity. The only way he knew was to ask, "How did you wind up here?"

"I was at Georgetown studying law." She struggled with herself, tried to pull the taut mask back into place. But the words came almost of their own volition. "My parents were killed in a car accident. I told you that already."

"I'm so sorry, Kirsten."

"They were the greatest parents anybody ever had. When they died, I fell apart." A big breath. "If it wasn't for Gloria I don't know what I would have done. She looked after me, helped me sell the family place up in Boston. I was an only child. I couldn't ever go back. The funeral was bad enough. The very thought of packing up their stuff . . ."

"I understand."

"She helped me find this place, pick up the pieces, start over. I never went back to law school. It all seemed, I don't know, something from another life. Gloria knew about a charity that needed help. She got me up and going in the morning. Day after day. She wouldn't let me stop. Wouldn't let me lie around and mope."

"She sounds like a great person."

Kirsten's effort to draw the world back under tight control rocked her entire body. Back and forth, struggling to quell the talk and the emotions. Marcus resisted the urge to reach over, halt her struggle and her movement by holding her close. Then it was over, the openness a myth as fragile as steam. "This is not about me, Marcus."

He had no choice but to nod.

"I've been between men for a very long time. Which is exactly how I intend things to stay." She rose and gathered plates and filled the air with brisk clatter. "And you really should be leaving."

"Can you tell me something about Gary Loh?"

The question froze her solid. "Who?"

"Gloria's boyfriend. You didn't know him?"

"I'm not sure." Her motions were jerky, as forced as her words. "She might have mentioned something."

"I need whatever you can give —"

"I told you I'll get it to you as soon as I can. But it's not much." The plates were slammed down hard. "And you have to go. Now."

The phone call woke Randall Walker an hour after midnight. The gray voice said simply, "You were right."

"Call me back in five minutes." Randall hung up the phone and slipped from his bed. His wife stirred, but did not roll over. With clients all over the globe, late-night interruptions were common. Randall walked to his bathroom, washed his face, regretted the third scotch he had drunk that night. And the fourth. His reflection looked more than tired. It looked old. And very worried.

He took the second call in his study. "I'm listening."

"You were right all along." Hamper Caisse sounded as worried as Randall had ever heard. "That Stanstead woman has another file."

Perhaps it was the hour, but it took Randall a moment to recognize the cold hand that gripped his gut as fear. "Tell me."

"She had dinner with Glenwood at her house. She told him there was more information. Not a lot, but some."

"You searched her place." It was not a question.

"And her office. Top to bottom. Nothing."

"Then she's got it hidden." He sighed, wishing it was over, cursing the compilation of stupidities that had landed him in this situation. "This could be bad."

"She said it isn't much."

"We can't take a chance she was lying."

"What do you want me to do?"

"Stay on her. Try for an intercept. Something to lead us to where she's got things stowed."

"I could, well, stop her."

"And risk letting the press find whatever she's got hidden, and blow the horn even louder?" He emitted a puff of breath that fluttered his flaccid cheeks. "I'll get to work on something at this end."

Randall hung up the phone, rose, and headed for the bottle on the wet bar. He didn't want another drink, but he needed it. He could already taste the burning smoke as it settled down and filled the hollow spaces inside him. Or at least numbed them enough to let sleep return.

NINETEEN

Marcus' weekend was given over to an exhaustive review of evidence and pleadings. His only time away from the growing clutter in his office was church on Sunday, and that was merely a two-hour review from further afield. By Monday evening he was so tired the stairs threatened to defeat him. He stripped and collapsed into bed, his final thoughts of a soft-edged blond woman and the mystery of why she so desperately wanted to be harsh.

He awoke to sunlight and voices and rumbles from downstairs. The nightmare was nothing more than a vague murmur at the back of his mind, like memories told by a stranger. The light was not the muted horizontal of dawn, but strong and closer to directly overhead. He glanced at his watch, and swiveled his feet to the floor. The dial read half past ten.

He dressed hurriedly and started down the stairs still knotting his tie, only to be halted midway by the sight of Oathell and Darren hauling his conference table through the front door. Marcus had picked it up at the same auction as the law books. In a previous life it had graced a formal dining room and seated twelve most comfortably. Marcus watched as Oathell snagged the carpet and almost tumbled.

"You watch where you put those big feet of yours!" A matchstick of a woman climbed into view carrying a lamp in each hand. Marcus recognized her as Fay Wilbur, Deacon's wife. "You mess up this floor and you're gonna be catching my business, you hear?"

"Yes, Aunt Fay." Oathell's normal scorn was nowhere to be found. And for good reason. Deacon Wilbur's wife looked ready to hammer him with either lamp. "It's heavy, is all."

"Hmph. You don't watch your step, I'll give you heavy. I'll give you so much heavy you'll need all the angels in heaven just to carry that load."

Deacon Wilbur grunted his way through the open door, carrying what was to become Marcus' office chair. He glanced up to where Marcus stood, then looked away. But the one glance was enough.

Fay Wilbur swung around and showed Marcus a face like an angry washboard. "Just how long did you aim on living in this mess of a half-finished house?"

Marcus pulled his tie free and draped it over the edge of the banister. "Just until your husband gave the trim a final coat."

"Deacon's done. He's been done." She glared at the silk tie like she would a dead snake. "You aim on leaving your mess hanging there?"

Marcus whipped the tie free. "No ma'am."

"That's good. 'Cause I'm too old and too angry to be picking up your messes." She eased the lamps to the floor, straightened up, and set knobby fists on her hips. With the squinty eyes and the jutting chin and tight frown, the arms looked cocked like two triggers. "Now you listen up. I don't do windows, you hear what I'm saying?"

Marcus knew better than to argue. "Loud and clear."

"Then you best be remembering as good as you're hearing." She paused long enough to watch the three men hustle back through the door. They were all sweating and puffing hard. "Y'all get a move on, now. We got lots to do 'round here."

Marcus called out, "I'll be right there to help you."

"No you ain't gonna do no such thing. You got yourself some lawyering to tend to. What you think brought me over here, my health? I got five children and fourteen grandchildren and a growing church making all the messes I'll *ever* need. I don't need to take on yours. No sir. Only reason I'm here is on account of my husband not knowing when it's time to stop painting and start finishing."

"Excuse me." Netty appeared in the side doorway. She said to Marcus, "Randall Walker is on his way out."

"Randall Walker is coming here?"

"Any minute now. I was just going to have Oathell go up and wake you." Her tone was apologetic. "I thought you'd want to see him."

"You thought right."

"He said it was extremely important. And urgent."

"It's fine, Netty."

"There, you see now?" Fay Wilbur had listened all she cared to. "You get on to your lawyering, you leave this shifting about to Deacon and the boys."

Marcus said to no one in particular, "I need a cup of coffee."

"Pot's been cooking up all morning. Oughtta be just about right. Dropped an eggshell in it for flavor, just like your granddaddy liked it."

Marcus stared at the wizened woman. "You knew my grandparents?"

"That's for another time." One bony finger rose in the air between them. "Right now I got just one more thing to say to you. I'll come back 'round from time to time to help clean and give this place a woman's touch. Can't say when, can't even say how often. I'll come when I can. But on one condition." The finger moved in closer. "Don't you ever bring no outside messes inside this house. You do and I'll quit 'fore I get started. You hear me?"

"Yes ma'am." Marcus watched her heft the lamps and stump away.

His secretary gave him a satisfied smile and said, "About time somebody brought you in line."

Marcus walked to the kitchen and was halfway through his first cup of coffee when Deacon huffed his way through the back door. "Marcus, I can't tell you how sorry —"

"It's fine."

"No it ain't. Fay's not like this often, but when she is, there's just no stopping her."

"It's better than fine. You want a coffee?"

Clearly this was not the reaction Deacon had expected. "Better not."

"I was going to try to get Charlie Hayes and the Halls together and take them to a pig picking today. You want to join us?"

The old man's eyes lit up. "Law, I do surely love a country pig picking."

"See if Oathell and his brother will join us. I need to thank them for all this."

"No, Oathell's got to get on to his office and Darren's got some piecework he's picked up for this afternoon. That's why we're hurrying." The concerned expression returned. "But all this commotion, and in your house while you were still upstairs —"

"It's better than fine," Marcus assured him. "It's a gift."

Marcus was on the phone with Austin Hall when his secretary showed Randall Walker into his newly appointed office. Randall did a slow sweep of the room as Marcus finished up with, "So you'll pick up Judge Hayes and meet us here in an hour? Thank you, Professor, that's great. Good-bye."

Randall watched him set down the phone and said, "That wouldn't happen to be old Charlie Hayes, now, would it? I thought he was dead."

Randall Walker stood waiting to be recognized and ushered into a chair. But because of Randall's lofty probing to discover if Charlie had spoken of their conversation, Marcus tossed his manners aside with his pen. "What do you want, Randall?"

The smile vanished. "And I suppose the Professor refers to Dr. Austin Hall."

Marcus leaned back in his chair, liking the way it creaked and settled under his weight, and waited.

"Quite a nice spread you've got yourself here." Randall gave the room another slow inspection. "Lot nicer than I expected, I got to admit."

Marcus had to agree. The room was spacious and lit by a brass chandelier that once held gas lamps. Tall sash windows spilled late-morning light. A grand sycamore and the oldest dogwood he had ever seen stood lookout. The oak flooring shone ruddy and ancient. His desk was battered old solid mahogany that reeked of Fay Wilbur's application of linseed oil. The air was redolent with the odors of a newly completed house. It was a good place to work and live, and Randall Walker's presence was a bane on this new start. Marcus repeated quietly, "What do you want?"

Randall accepted the question as the only invitation he would receive, and slid into the hard-backed chair opposite Marcus. "I came out here to make your day."

Marcus settled his hands across his

middle and tried to ease the knot of sudden tension.

"No. Scratch that. Make your entire year, is more like it." Randall offered his full-wattage beam, the one that had melted the hearts of a thousand female jurors. "You know our firm."

"I know of it."

" 'Course you do. Retired governor, two senators, Congressman Hodges, all partners. Nationwide reputation. Why, we're even thinking of opening an office in London, England."

Marcus realized the man had paused because he expected a response. "Long way from Rocky Mount."

"Now you're talking." If anything, the smile broadened. "How'd you like to run that office for a couple of years. Leave all this mess and baggage behind."

"Are you offering me a job?"

"More than that, son. More than that. I'm offering you a *future*. A chance to start over. We've been watching you. Saw how you almost collapsed, watched you recover. Not many men could come back from what you've faced." The smile was gone, the mask now showing deep concern. "You're a strong man, Marcus. A good man. We want you on our team."

Marcus reached for his pen, his hands suddenly restless. Listening to words

267

about his past slip from between those lips filled him with a homicidal urge. "I'm honored."

"Well, you oughtta be." The benign smile returned. "Yes sir, honored is the absolute right response."

Marcus studied his opponent. Randall Walker's suit was navy mohair, his shoes handmade. His hair was as precisely cut and fitted to his head as his smile. The skin of his cheeks and neck flowed over his starched collar. "What's behind the offer?"

"That's simple enough." Randall was not the least bit shaken by Marcus' query. "The legal world is full of, I'll scratch your back, you scratch mine. Successful lawyers learn early and well to do one another favors. But you know all this, don't you. 'Course you do. Life its own self is built on finding how everybody wins."

"You want me to throw the Hall case."

"Well, now, it's hard to tell sometimes just how good a job a lawyer's done." The smile tightened, a thin line cut across pasty features. "You can always blame a negative verdict on the judge or the jury. Or the wind."

Marcus nodded slowly, as though taking it all in. Finally he said, "Release the girl and we drop all charges."

The smile slipped away unnoticed.

"You can't be serious."

"Deadly."

"Son, we're talking a lifetime career opportunity here."

Marcus leaned across the desk. "I want Gloria Hall."

"Do you now." The words hardened. "Shame I don't have the first idea what you're talking about."

Marcus met the man and his glutinous gaze head-on. "Then we don't have anything to discuss. Do we."

"If I wasn't the gentleman I am, I'd say something about your landing in over your head."

"Thanks for stopping by, Randall."

"Well." The man rose to his feet. "Glad I had one final chance to meet you, Marcus." He tapped the desk lightly. "Don't bother to get up, I can show myself out." Another tap. "You just go on sitting there. Enjoy the place just as long as you possibly can."

They left Rocky Mount just after midday, heading east. Marcus drove. Austin Hall sat beside him. Charlie Hayes and Deacon Wilbur took the backseat and argued over directions with the good-natured banter of old friends. Occasionally Marcus glanced over to see if the dispute was bothering his client. Austin remained silent and still in the manner of the stiffly bereaved.

There was a reason to be cautious with directions, as their destination had no name and shifted location every second or third autumn. Marcus left the highway for a county road, and that for a long thin strip that cut an asphalt swath through tobacco fields and time-washed farmhouses. The journey became a withdrawal from worry and the world for all save Austin Hall.

They knew they were drawing near when their car joined a convoy. Most of the other vehicles were pickups with rifles in the rear window and kids and dogs jumbled in the back. Leathery arms rose in languid salute to other mud-spattered pilgrims. Everybody was headed in the same direction.

The parking lot was a newly plowed field. Close up to the road sparkled a few Buicks and Cadillacs, their owners not wanting to muddy up a citified shine. Marcus followed the pickups down a red-clay track and stopped by an ancient tobacco barn. A long-forgotten painting advertised Redman chewing tobacco in letters washed of all color. Below that, just beside the door, was an almost invisible ad for Burma Shave.

Charlie Hayes was talking as they

walked the hard-beaten clay path and joined the swift-moving line. "Back there used to be the Columbia Road."

"Naw, Judge," Deacon corrected. "You got that wrong. That road led down to New Bern."

Charlie looked affronted. "You saying you know this region better than me?"

Deacon's grin creased his face worse than the field they had just crossed. "Reckon I am."

Charlie turned to the man in coveralls in front of them. "Mister, you know this area?"

"Cropped 'baccy not five miles north since I could walk."

"Then set this gentleman straight on where this road is headed."

"Like to, but I cain't."

"Why's that?"

" 'Cause he's right and you're wrong." The man aimed a brown stream and a well-chewed plug at the stained paint can by the door. "Can't make it no plainer than that."

"Well, I'll be . . ." Charlie threatened to toss his cane away. "Never thought I'd live to see the day I'd stand sandwiched between such ignorance."

Argument was halted by the line moving them inside. The barn's interior was just slightly cooler than a blast furnace. The air was thick and cloying with the smells of tobacco and sweat and pork. Two men worked a tall brick oven; one tended the wood-chip fire and the other turned a huge iron handle. Through the cast-iron door Marcus could see three entire hogs roasting and dripping fat. A third man used a razor-edged machete to carve off hunks that fell onto a wooden spatula he gripped in his other hand. He cut and caught and turned and deposited the steaming pork onto a paper plate, then wheeled back. Marcus set down two twenties for the four plates, one price for all they could eat. No one lingered long inside the barn.

Out back the air seemed springtime fresh. Trestle tables stretched out in long lines, with plastic barrels of beans and slaw and potato salad and iced drinks marching down the center aisle. While the others loaded their plates and claimed a table, Marcus went over to where two women operated a fryer and returned with a basket of hush puppies. Deacon led them in prayer, then they dug in.

Their table garnered more than its share of glances. There were many groups made up of blacks and whites and Native Americans, but none where one of the black men wore a suit and vest and gold fob. Attention soon turned elsewhere and they were left alone to feel as welcome as they cared. For a moment on this balmy autumn day, in a restaurant walled by ripened tobacco and ceilinged in endless blue, the farmers sat united in tired satisfaction. Another growing season was ended. The auctioneers and tobacco buyers were in town to bid and pay. In the warehouses and back rooms, where experts rolled gold-leaf panatelas and sampled the crop's flavor, word was spread of where this year's pig picking would be held. If any health inspector happened to be among the crowd, he showed the good sense to feast in silence.

Marcus waited until the others had finished to say to Austin Hall, "I asked Charlie along because I'm hoping he will help me with this trial. He already is in an unofficial capacity. Do you mind if we talk a little business?"

"I have no secrets from Deacon," Austin replied.

"It's a measure of the man who's talking," Deacon offered, "that he actually means what he says."

"We need to make a decision here. I'm sorry Alma couldn't join us, but this can't wait."

"She couldn't get out of the faculty meeting. She told me to make the decision for us both."

Deacon gave the man a gentle smile. "Then miracles do indeed abide in this land."

Austin replied with a look of woeful openness. "We can't thank you enough."

"Ain't no need to say anything."

"Yes there is. Alma and I, we were so moved, you can't imagine." Austin turned his gaze toward Marcus and explained, "The church is helping us put together the ransom."

"Just being there for a friend in need, is all." Deacon took a breath. "Since we're talking about this, there's one more thing that needs saying. A lot of the money came from Kirsten Stanstead."

Austin's control threatened to crumple. "What?"

"She figured if she went to you direct, you'd say no. But the only reason she didn't give the whole amount was because I wouldn't let her. There's others at the church who wanted to help. And Fay said to tell you we got people praying 'round the clock, gonna keep at it till your girl's been brought home."

Austin's struggle for control needed outside help. Marcus used his most clinical tone to demand, "So you've decided to go ahead and pay the ransom?"

"I don't see what choice we have." Austin managed a ragged breath. "The police and the FBI are against it, but what have they done for us? They've spoken with the embassy. The embassy has written a letter to the Chinese authorities."

"More than that," Marcus countered.

"Not enough!" A few heads turned their way. Austin lowered his voice. "Not enough. They haven't got a thing to report. All we hear is how they don't understand what Gloria was doing in China. Over and over the same words."

"That's natural enough." Charlie Hayes spoke up for the first time. "They're government employees. Government employees learn early on the most important part of their job is making sure blame gets stuck to somebody else's hide."

Marcus said, "As your attorney, I cannot officially advise you on the payment of ransom. Unofficially, I would urge you to inform the police the moment the transfer of funds is made."

"Gloria said no police."

Charlie said, "It's good advice, Dr. Hall. I'd take it if I were you."

Because Austin's gaze remained on the old man, Marcus said, "Charlie and I have worked together on more cases than I care to count. He's been a friend since I started practicing, and my best source of advice since he retired from the federal bench. He's still a member of the bar and knows federal court procedure from the inside out."

"Then I suppose," the professor said, "you'd best call me Austin."

"It'd be a pleasure, sir."

"We also need to discuss timing," Marcus went on. A soft breeze touched the surrounding plants, most of them well over seven feet tall and cropped of all but the highest leaves. These whispered and clattered amidst an orchestra of birdsong and buzzing insects and quiet conversation. The other tables granted them privacy in the manner of country-born. "I've received a call from the judge's aide. The defense has requested a meeting for tomorrow, and another for the day after."

"So?"

"My guess is they're going to ask for an immediate trial, giving us almost no time to collect depositions and evidence."

Charlie broke in. "Normally this works in the defense's favor, since it keeps the plaintiff from preparing fully. Or fishing for new leads."

"But we don't have much of a case," Marcus went on. "And to be honest, I don't think more time will help us. We want to make some noise. Nothing more."

Austin rolled that around in his analytical mind, and came up with "The payment."

"Exactly. If you are going ahead with the transfer of these funds, do you want to give it more time? I have no idea whether time pressure will work in our favor or against us."

"Do it." Austin did not hesitate an instant. "Do it now. No waiting. We do everything possible, soon as possible." His face was as stern as Marcus had ever seen. "Hit them just as hard as you can."

"Most lawyers don't have the guts to tell their clients the good, the bad, and the ugly." Logan's opening remarks were not standard fare for either of his guests, and it showed on their faces. He didn't care. He was less than twenty-four hours from his next in-chambers meeting with Judge Nicols, and the case was already a bad taste in his mouth. "That's not my problem. Randall, you took me on with the express purpose of burying this guy Glenwood. Fine. You tell me there is no connection between New Horizons and the Chinese factory. So I go in armed for bear. What happens? Marcus gets up in front of the magistrate and proves there *is* a connection. And now you're in here to tell me the connection is tenuous at best.

I'm not sure I should believe that, Randall."

Randall Walker sat there and took it because he had to. He was the one who had requested this meeting, and for some reason had brought Logan's senior partner in for backup. Two cronies of the old power structure, polished and easy, their meanness hidden down deep. But Logan knew it was there. He had seen them both in action. The only way to handle these guys was by holding hard to the offensive.

Logan was ready when Randall started in with "I need you —"

"Wait, Randall. Just wait, okay? This meeting is not about what you need. I'm the one going head-to-head in front of Judge Nicols tomorrow. Big meeting. And I've still got a lot of questions that need answering. Such as, where did Glenwood get that information he showed the magistrate?"

"I don't know. I wish I did."

"Could it have come from your office?"

"Absolutely not."

"You're not setting me up as a patsy, are you, Randall?"

He reddened, but held to the even tone. "I want you to win this case."

"All right. So play ball with me."

"I've brought the chief North Carolina

accountant and the two vice presidents of the Rocky Mount distribution facility."

"Hang on here. I'm smelling more than furniture polish in the air. Two low-level VPs with no knowledge of the international markets? Who are you kidding, Randall? Where are the board members?"

"I told you. They're all in Switzerland."

"Can I talk to them by phone?"

"No." Randall turned to Logan's senior partner for emphasis. "No way."

Logan waited, giving his boss a chance to back him up. The older attorney remained stone-faced. Logan sighed. "Okay. Right now I need everything you can give me to build us a fire wall. You tell me there's not just an arm's length between these two companies, but a nine-thousand-mile gap. Is that correct?"

"Precisely."

"I need proof, Randall. You've heard that word before, I assume."

The senior partner shook his head and said mildly, "Logan."

But he would not be stopped. "Proof is what we're after, Randall. Proof that I can wave in front of the judge's nose."

"It's right next door."

"Then what are we waiting for?"

The senior partner and Randall did not move. Randall said, "I want to make a request."

Logan glanced from one to the other. "What, you two had a strategy session and forgot to invite the defending attorney? Guys, in case it's slipped your tiny minds, my good name is the one on the line here."

"Logan, Randall merely said —"

"It's all right." But Randall's expression did not back up his words. One glance was enough for Logan to know it was not all right at all. Randall was watching him cautiously, measuring vigilantly. Logan knew he was proving to be more of a handful than Randall had ever anticipated. Which was good. Because Glenwood was threatening to present the exact same risk. Randall went on, "New Horizons has an extensive trade relationship with Factory 101 in China. But we don't want you to admit this tomorrow."

Logan gaped at the two older men. "You're both certifiably insane."

"Not at all."

"Tomorrow is the next-to-last meeting in-chambers before we go to trial!"

"We have to determine," Randall went on, pressing down hard on each word, "exactly how much Marcus knows."

The senior partner spoke, "We realize this is a lot to ask."

"What's this *we* business? Who's side are you on?"

"We're all on the same side." The senior partner patted his head of burnished silver, adding contentedly, "Randall Walker is offering to grant us a significant portion of the New Horizons corporate account. An account you would personally manage."

Logan settled back in his chair. "All right. I'm listening."

Randall said, "New Horizons' relationship with Factory 101 is a critical part of their overall import business. One we would prefer not to have exposed to the light of an American courtroom. So we need you to hold back and see if Marcus Glenwood has managed to come up with the impossible."

Logan mulled that over, then demanded, "So just how much trade do they do with these Chinese guys?"

On the ride back after the pig picking, Deacon sat up front because Austin insisted. A glance in the rearview mirror was enough to reveal the reason why: Austin spent the journey locked upon the view out the side window, eyes blind and face weary in the way of one whose sleep was stolen. The mood in the car remained thoughtful and quiet until Marcus turned back onto the state road and reentered familiar territory. Then Deacon eased himself about, until he was leaning against the door and able to watch Marcus and Charlie both. "Did you ever know Marcus' granddaddy, Mr. Charlie?"

"No, can't say I ever had the favor."

"Old Mr. Horace was a fine man. Real fine. Helped build our church, in a manner of speaking."

Marcus quickly glanced over. "What?"

"Those fields out between the cemetery and the rise, they once belonged to Mr. Horace. They were deeded to him in a settlement. Back when I was just starting out my days at the pulpit, lightning struck the old church. Least, that's what we figured it was. Big storm passed late one night. Next morning we didn't have nothing but ashes. That church was built by freed slaves with the first money they earned. Lots of wailing by their grandchildren and great-grandchildren the day after that storm. Didn't have nothing left but a bell and four cornerstones. Lost it all."

"Hard blow," Charlie offered.

"Marcus' granddaddy came by that very same day, deeded the land over to us. Said he had no use for bottom land, he wasn't no farmer and never would be. Shame to let good tobacco land go to waste."

"I never knew any of this," Marcus said.

"We farmed that land and sold the crop and built the new church. Yes, Mr. Horace was a fine man. And my, but he could talk." The memory caused Deacon to smile. "Talk the hind leg off a dead mule. Talk all day and all night."

Charlie asked, "Marcus, your granddaddy was a tobacco auctioneer, do I recall that straight?"

"Until his stroke." But Marcus was caught by the memory of an old man who, once settled by his wife into the corner rocker, neither moved nor spoke. Marcus' grandfather had watched his growing-up years and never uttered a sound. For a born talker, it must have been an assignment in hell itself.

The car was silenced and sobered by passing the red-brick sign announcing the entrance to the New Horizons complex. One corner remained broken and scarred where Marcus had clipped it. A team was busy erecting a burnished copper shield on top of the brick, one bearing the star-and-rainbow logo and embossed with the world-famous command to GET IN GEAR. They took the downward-sloping curve through the forest, reentered the light where the road flattened and revealed the church. Marcus studied the surrounding fields with new interest. "Hard to believe all this started with them wanting to move the cemetery."

Deacon shifted impatiently. "Wasn't the cemetery and it didn't start there."

Marcus started to say how he was speaking of his own involvement. But he sensed something more than just casual conversation in Deacon's tone. "What do you mean?"

The old man was long in responding. They were approaching Marcus' street before he finally said, "Some things are harder to talk about than others. Dark spots you wish never happened, shadows you can't never wash off."

"You don't have to tell me anything you don't want to."

He might as well not have spoken. "Cropping the tobacco we raised on the land your granddaddy gave us, the collections we gathered, it was enough to put up the walls and get in the windows. But we were short almost two thousand dollars. Winter was coming, and the man wouldn't roof the building till he got paid. Back then it was Baker Mills on the hill behind our place, not New Horizons."

"Old man Baker was a piece of work," Charlie offered.

"Evil man," Deacon muttered, his voice as tight as his gaze. "Carried the dark 'round with him. Grass died where he stepped."

"I had him appear in my courtroom a couple of times," Charlie went on. "Felt like ordering the bailiff to wash the place down with lye after he left."

Marcus pulled up in front of his house, cut the motor, turned so he could study Deacon, who went on, "Old man Baker came by my house. Said how he'd give us the two thousand, and five hundred more for two stained-glass windows. But he wanted use of the church all winter, every Friday and Saturday night. I asked him what for. He gave me a grin I will carry with me to the grave and said, 'Far as you're concerned, it's just a few friends looking for a place to have a good time.' "

"They were gambling," Charlie suggested.

"That and more," Deacon replied darkly. "A whole mess more."

Charlie struck his knee with the flat of one hand. "I heard tales of their wild ways. Probably got run off someplace by the law, were looking for somewhere that wouldn't get raided."

"They fouled our church for a whole winter. Shot out both the stained-glass windows soon as we got them in. We didn't ever replace them neither, not till we had money of our own." Deacon breathed heavy, shook his head. "Come May and planting season I went by old man Baker's house. Took the elders with me, couldn't make that journey on my own. Told him we were starting a weekend Bible school, and he was gonna have to find some other place to meet. Old man Baker said maybe we'd find use for two thousand dollars more. No sir, I told him, the time for sinning was done. He gave me that same old death's-head grin of his, and said how it'd be a shame to have to burn the place down again."

The look Deacon gave Marcus was full of hard-earned knowledge. "Only one way to handle men like that. Got to stand up, stand strong, fight the good fight."

TWENTY

Wednesday morning Marcus sat in one corner of Federal District Judge Gladys Nicols' outer office. He was relegated to a straight-backed chair because the defense team, seven in number, had arrived ahead of him. They clustered around the sofa and side chairs in the far corner and raked him with angry glances. The only greeting he received was from Jim Bell, the retired patrolman on receptionist duty, who approached them every half hour to apologize for the judge's being so late. They had been kept waiting almost two hours, but Marcus was too preoccupied to give either the defense team or the time much notice.

He sat and turned the pages of his dispositive motions, and pondered the mysteries the morning had revealed. Some of his questions were even about the trial.

"Morning, Marcus."

He slapped the file shut and rose to his feet. "Logan."

The man standing before him had a dancer's body and a butcher's face.

Logan Kendall's forehead formed a broad shelf with which he liked to bull his way through the opposition. From a distance Logan looked ruggedly handsome, the image heightened by his smooth voice and tailored suits and flashy ties. Up close it was possible to see the scar tissue under his eyes and where his nose had been surgically rebuilt.

Logan offered a smirk instead of his hand. "Nice to know you've recovered enough to join the walking wounded."

"I'm busy."

"Yeah, I noticed you over here all by yourself, still trying to cobble together a case." Logan jerked about, the move shockingly swift. This was another of his little traits, revealing his boxer's speed in lightning motions. Especially when standing in his opponent's space. He pointed to the sole woman on his dark-suited team. "Of course you remember Suzie."

Marcus ignored her irate glare. "What do you want, Logan?"

"Just thought I'd give you one last chance to drop out with your skin still intact." He kept his tone light and low, so that the receptionist could hear nothing but a faint lyrical drone. "You know Suzie's just dying to finish the job she started during your last court appearance."

"I'd be happy to drop the case, and I told Randall Walker exactly how and when."

Logan blinked. "You talked to Randall?"

It was Marcus' turn to softly chant, "Looks to me like there's a communication problem between client and counsel."

Logan recovered as best he could. "I assume he didn't pass it on because your offer was utterly without merit. Just like your case."

"Nice talking with you, Logan." As his opponent was turning away, Marcus was struck by a sudden thought, and asked, "What does the term *lao gai* mean to you?"

Logan's step did not falter. "I'm not here to play word games, Marcus. I'm here to nail your hide to the wall."

Instead of returning to his seat, Marcus walked to the window. The mist had burned off to reveal a sun-splashed day. The federal courthouse was a relatively new encroachment into what was known as Old Raleigh. The region east of the governor's mansion was a hodgepodge formed by decades of tragic decline. From his perch on the seventh floor, Marcus could see four Victorian-era manors, a muffler shop, a restaurant specializing in grits and grease, and two drunks arguing over a bottle. He stood there thinking of the last time he had himself heard that strange-sounding term: *lao gai.*

Ashley Granger, the Washington lawyer, had called that morning. "I expected to get your office machine."

"My office is in my home."

"Sorry it's taken so long. And sorry to have called you so early. But I just got woken up by someone who could finally tell me something worth passing on." A pause, then the further excuse that "It's late afternoon over there in China."

"You don't need to apologize. Give me a second to pour another cup of coffee and grab a pen."

When he returned, Ashley began. "Factory 101."

"Yes."

"Sometimes what is not said is as important as what you actually hear. You follow?"

"I'm not sure."

"I faxed and e-mailed some contacts I have in the Hong Kong and Guangzhou regions. They instantly cut all connections, like they'd vanished from the face of the earth. I called some others. Soon as they heard who was on the line, they hung up. Even before I asked my first question, they were gone."

"Something big must be happening there."

"You're partly right but mostly wrong. An occupational hazard when dealing with China. It's not what's happening that stops people talking."

"But who is behind it," Marcus guessed.

"See, you're learning. Monday I finally hired a local lawyer. I didn't need a lawyer, you understand. I needed to purchase information. This particular lawyer is middling honest. All their local business derives from one central source, and they learn to bend and shape the meaning of honesty around what this central source tells them is that day's flavor."

"I'm not sure my clients will approve payment to a Chinese counsel at this time," Marcus warned.

"We'll cross that bridge when we get to it. By this point I wanted to find out what had everybody in a lather. For that I needed a local source."

"Is that risky for you?"

"I'll find out my next trip over. Right now, I can officially confirm that Factory 101 is definitely a *lao gai* prison."

"Just like Dee Gautam said."

"Yeah, that little weasel was right again. 'Course, he wouldn't give me the time of day when I asked. Hates dealing in rumors, old Dee does. Told me to get involved and dig for myself. Which I did." Ashley Granger was clearly enjoying himself. "You ever heard of a place called Daolin?"

"I don't think so."

"Doesn't matter. The thing is, *lao gai* are located all over the country. Local governments use them as a dumping ground for troublemakers."

"If they're so commonplace, why wouldn't people talk to you?"

"Exactly. Daolin is the answer, or part of it. It's a farming community north of Guangzhou. The local population rioted there twice in the past two years. This is big stuff. The farmers were the backbone of Mao's revolution. For years they've been chafing under the double burden of artificially low prices and Communist Party corruption. The local party buys all their crop at prices set by Beijing. These same local officials demand bribes for everything — seeds, tools, use of communal machinery, birth certificates, travel permits. The corruption keeps getting worse, the prices stay the same."

"So they rioted," Marcus said. "So?"

"So the national party knows it's sitting on a powder keg. They ordered the local militia to come down hard. And guess where all those poor joes wound up."

"Factory 101." He breathed. "Who runs it?"

"Now that's an interesting question. About as interesting as whether or not they're in cahoots with New Horizons. And the answer to both is: I don't know. But I'm digging."

Marcus found himself thinking of a little brown man with impossibly merry eyes. "Think maybe Dee Gautam might know?"

"Can't hurt to give him another shout."

Marcus hesitated, then found he had to ask. "Do you know what happened to his arms and thumbs?"

The response came swiftly. "Never had the courage to ask, don't know if he'd say. Bet it hurt, though."

Marcus swallowed on the thought of Gloria Hall. "A lot."

When the lawyers finally were permitted to file in, Judge Nicols greeted them with, "I apologize for making you people wait. But there are certain bureaucratic hoops a new federal judge must jump through."

They were seated in Judge Gladys Nicols' new private chambers. The office was a full thirty feet long, her desk at the far end and flanked by the state and national flags. The judge was dressed in a formal gray suit that solidified her bulk. From his lone chair by the window, Marcus thought Judge Nicols held the bearing of someone with decades on the federal bench, rather than preparing for her first trial. To the right of her chair sat her chief clerk, Jenny Hail. To her left was seated the court reporter, steno machine at the ready.

Many Raleigh trial lawyers loathed Gladys Nicols. It was common rumor among the courtroom vultures that her appointment had come about because she was the right sex and the right color at the right time. Marcus had been before her on numerous occasions, and knew her to be a harsh tactician who brooked no malingering or grandstanding. She was often sharp-tongued and detested people who sought to instruct her on the law. She was known as mean, snippish, nasty, wickedly bad-tempered. Marcus had long since decided it was the result of having to deal with white Southern lawyers whose every word and gesture dripped with a desire to see this black female judge slapped into place.

Judge Gladys Nicols was a product of poor farming parents. By dint of driving ambition and scalpel-sharp intelligence she had lifted herself to the heights of

UNC undergrad and Harvard law. She had returned to the South specifically because she wanted to make a name for herself as a Southern judge. Marcus knew this because she had told him. She made no bones about her ambition. She wanted to stand as a beacon for other young black women. She taught two classes each semester, one in judicial procedure at Duke Law School and the other in civil rights history to Carolina undergrads. She was tough as nails, and if she had a heart of gold she hid it very well.

Logan offered as sincere a smile as his battered features could manage. "May I offer my congratulations on your recent appointment."

"Thank you." She waited through the chorus of approval from Logan's minions, then glanced at her watch and said, "We can adjourn this until after lunch or forge straight ahead."

"We're ready to proceed, Your Honor," Logan responded.

When the judge's gaze turned his way, Marcus handed her a slim file. "This is our list of requested subpoenas for New Horizons corporate officials."

The strong features registered surprise. "How many are there?"

"Thirty-six. I realize this is more than the norm —"

"By a factor of ten."

"Yes, Your Honor. But there are extenuating circumstances. All of the New Horizons board members and senior executives hold joint United States–Swiss residency status."

That pulled her up short. "All of them?"

"Every one."

Logan could hold himself back no longer. "That's perfectly reasonable, Your Honor. New Horizons derives almost 40 percent of total revenue from its international operations. A number of these subsidiaries are incorporated in Switzerland." He paused for a baleful glare at Marcus. "We continue to object to these proceedings, Your Honor. There has been no connection whatsoever drawn between the plaintiff's allegations and my clients. We therefore move for a summary dismissal."

Judge Nicols wore gold-rimmed reading glasses, which she lowered and stared over as she would a rifle scope. "No connection to the plaintiff's allegations."

"That is correct, Your Honor."

"I seem to recall hearing how you told the magistrate there was no connection between your client and the Chinese *factory*."

Logan coughed, shuffled his feet. "That happened to be the best of my knowledge at the time, Your Honor."

The dark gaze continued to hold him. "But now you concur that there exists a relationship between New Horizons and this" — she paused to check her notes — "Factory 101."

"Yes, Your Honor. A *business* relationship. They make, we buy. Nothing more." A swift glance in Marcus' direction. "Nothing so preposterous as what the plaintiff's counsel has tried to suggest."

Judge Nicols turned her attention to Marcus, who countered. "We intend to prove the relationship extends far beyond mere trade agreements, Your Honor. And that New Horizons and Factory 101 did indeed collude to make Gloria Hall and her dangerous investigation vanish. The documents and depositions we have requested will prove this connection."

The judge's gun-barrel gaze swiveled back to Logan, who sneered. "These motions are nothing more than a fishing expedition, Your Honor. Mr. Glenwood doesn't have a thing to offer at this stage, so he wants to go dig through my client's records to try to come up with some dirt."

"It seems to me our meeting before the magistrate documented the first level of proof," Marcus countered.

"Of what," Logan shot back. "Of sales between a Chinese factory and a U.S. company? Not to mention the fact, Your Honor, that the plaintiff's evidence consisted of confidential corporate documents. I feel we have a right to know how he got his hands on them."

Judge Nicols demanded, "Are you so moving?"

Logan's wince showed he had been fearing that question. Marcus understood why. To say yes meant proceeding beyond the frivolous-claim dismissal. To say no meant putting all his eggs in one basket a second time. Which he could not risk doing. "Yes, Your Honor," he reluctantly allowed. "We move to question the propriety of these documents. Are there employees illegally involved? Has the plaintiff been in contact with hostile unions?"

"Absolutely not," Marcus responded.

"Your Honor, we have a videotape of Mr. Glenwood presenting himself at corporate headquarters, claiming to be an attorney representing an unnamed union!"

Marcus shot back, "Does your videotape also show how company employees demolished my vehicle and threatened my life?"

This time Logan's pain was theatrical. "Your Honor, this is typical of the kind of case this man is trying to bring against us, full of absurd allegations and bald-faced lies."

"Mr. Glenwood?"

"I wanted to see their reaction. One of the allegations we will prove is a pattern of violent past practices. I wanted to view this for myself."

She stared at Marcus. Hard. "You went to New Horizons with the intention of deliberately provoking them?"

"I did."

"Why?"

"I had not decided whether to take the case. I wanted to see if New Horizons reacted in a manner that would suggest they were capable of kidnapping and severely abusing a young woman."

"Your Honor, I object! This is just more fiction cooked up by a man desperate for publicity!"

"All right, Mr. Kendall."

"This is trial by slander, Your Honor."

"That's enough, Mr. Kendall. I am turning down your motion to dismiss." She picked up her pen. "Being new to the job, I find my docket is almost entirely free. I understand the defense is requesting a speedy trial?"

"It's the only way to halt the plaintiff's ludicrous plans to drag my client through the mud."

"I said that was enough." Mild this time, aware the defense was smarting from the news that the case was headed for the public eye. Her glare was now directed at Marcus, as was the sterner tone. "Mr. Glenwood, this is for the record. I am concerned to see you here, taking up the court's time with such a matter, acting on your own. Are you sure you are up for this?"

"I think so, Your Honor."

"Well, I have my doubts. I am very familiar with your background. While I might offer you sympathy outside this courtroom, in these chambers I am bound to uphold the law and the rights of everyone involved." She leaned across her desk. "So I want you to think very hard about taking on this matter. I would hate to be forced to declare you incompetent."

Marcus ignored the round-eyed glances among the defense team as best he could. "So would I, Your Honor."

"If you violate the rules of this court, I will sanction you heavily. If you mishandle the litigants' rights and claims in any way, I will personally see that your license comes up for review." She let that sink in a moment, then leaned back and said, "The defense has requested we move forward with this. I agree. Final pretrial hearings will take place tomorrow morning at nine. Trial is set to begin next week. You people are dismissed."

Marcus made his way slowly toward the door, allowing the defense team to draw well ahead. At the doorway he turned and said quietly, "Thank you very much, Judge."

Gladys Nicols did not look up from her writing. "Now what do you suppose has got the defense in such an all-fired hurry?"

"I was just asking myself the same thing."

The judge could very well have been speaking to herself. "Must be something mighty big, whatever it is."

Marcus nodded and shut the door behind him.

TWENTY-ONE

The telephone call came in the middle of that same afternoon. Marcus bolted from the house, shouting to Netty words he scarcely heard himself as he raced for the car. He hit ninety miles per hour on the Raleigh highway, and made it to the Halls' subdivision in record time. He parked down the road, as the drive and the street in front of their house were already blocked by gray government sedans.

Alma Hall answered the door, tight-lipped and grim. "Thank the heavens above."

"You haven't said anything?"

"Not a word. But if you'd taken much longer, blood would've flowed."

"Don't let them goad you, Alma."

"I'm trying." She led him inside. "Goodness knows, I'm trying just as hard as I know how."

Marcus entered the living room and walked straight over to Austin. He said simply, "Hold on."

Austin rose with the others. His expression was as tight as his houndstooth necktie. "That man there says they're going to arrest me."

"Wonderful." Marcus rounded on a roomful of cold gazes. "What a lovely picture that would make for the six o'clock news. Respected members of the black community are jailed for sending money to their missing daughter."

The man closest to him had features sharp as his voice. "This is a private meeting."

Alma Hall said, "This man is Marcus Glenwood. He is our attorney. And he is a *lot* more welcome in this house than you are."

"I'd like to see some identification, please." Marcus pulled a pad and pen from his jacket. "From everyone."

There were two FBI agents from the Raleigh office, a State Bureau man, a sheriff's deputy in plainclothes, and an assistant prosecutor from the district attorney's office. Marcus took his time over the IDs, giving everyone a breather, gently asserting control. "All right. What's this about pressing charges?"

"We were informed that a ransom had been paid." The prosecutor, Wayde Barrett, possessed the aggressive attitude of someone who bullied for pleasure. "That is a felony."

"It's strictly a nuisance charge." Marcus

addressed the FBI agents. "I can't believe you would be a party to this sham."

"Aw, these fellows got roped in the same as me." The deputy sheriff had the long flat drawl of the Carolina coastal plains. He dangled a white Stetson from the fingers of one hand. "Somebody called the office, said they were making a major arrest, and we needed to be part of the action." He turned to the silent gray-suited men. "Ain't that right."

This only increased the prosecutor's ire. "Funding a felonious crime is a serious offense!"

"This is absolute rubbish," Marcus told the room.

"Why don't we all take a load off," the deputy suggested.

All did, save the prosecutor, which left him looking like a soapbox orator. "You could lose your license to practice law for this!"

The deputy had a long neck with skin so loose it hung like a chicken's craw over his collar. But his eyes were sharp as ice-blue blades, and there was not an ounce of fat on his six-foot frame. He spoke to Marcus as though they were the only people in the room. "You're that feller who moved back over to his granddaddy's place in Rocky Mount."

"That's right."

He hitched up one trouser leg, revealing a lizard skin boot. "You as big a trouble-maker as they been saying?"

"Absolutely," Marcus replied. "Who is they?"

"Aw, you know how talk goes 'round in these parts." The deputy leaned forward, offered a hard-callused hand. "Amos Culpepper."

"Nice to meet you." The man's grip was like iron. "Is that why they sent you, to warn me?"

"I'm not in the warning business, Mr. Glenwood. One thing I'm not looking forward to when the sheriff retires next spring and I take over is dealing with folks who'd like to tell me my business."

"I had a local businessman bring a man by my house the other night. A man who rammed my car when I visited New Horizons. The pair threatened me." Marcus' voice grated in his own ears. "I didn't like it either."

Exasperated at being ignored, the prosecutor snapped, "How about we talk about something that matters!"

The deputy disregarded him entirely. He asked Marcus, "You file a complaint?"

"There was nothing substantive said or done. But the threat was there."

"You got names?"

"The spokesman was Hank Atterly. He called the muscle Lonnie."

The prosecutor flopped down on the sofa opposite Marcus and fumed, "This is absurd."

"Know Hank well. The other name doesn't ring a bell." The deputy swished his tongue about like someone searching for a chaw that wasn't there. "You get a good look at that other fellow?"

"Lean, reddish gray crew cut, big nasty pickup, redneck accent." Marcus heard the wreck and the threat anew. "There was a second man at the New Horizons attack. He was heavyset and balding. I only saw him for an instant in my rearview mirror before he broke the back windshield with a baseball bat."

The prosecutor demanded, "Can we get back to the business at hand?"

The deputy showed him a cold eye. "I don't know what your business is, bub. Mine is fighting crime." Back to Marcus. "Lots of local families eat food bought with New Horizons paychecks. Looks to me like you'd stay healthy longer if you didn't blow smoke straight in their faces."

"I plan to steer clear of them, don't worry." Marcus turned to the prosecutor. "My guess is you're out here without your superior's authorization. This is a harassment charge that could clearly backfire on you."

The prosecutor sneered. "Word is, you've got no cause to be telling anybody the finer points of law, Glenwood."

Marcus let that one pass, something that came much easier these days. "All we want is to bring the Halls' daughter home. You should be helping us, not making threats."

"Don't try and tell me my job!" The prosecutor had one of those faces that reddened easily. "There's nothing to keep me from charging you as well!"

"On what grounds?"

The prosecutor searched his associates' faces, found no support. He huffed to his feet, snapped, "You'll be hearing from my office, Glenwood." When the front door slammed, everyone in the room breathed easier.

The two fibbies rose, and the elder said, "We should have a report from the embassy in Beijing sometime next week."

Alma's ire had drained away, leaving her voice flat and tired. "You think it will do any good?"

The agents exchanged glances. "In all honesty, I don't hold out much hope." When they arrived at the front door, the agent went on, "We've ordered a full-time watch on the account that received your payment. If the Hong Kong authorities do their job, we should be able to track who withdraws the funds."

Amos Culpepper waited until the agents had departed before saying to Alma and Austin, "I've heard talk of this prosecutor fellow. None of it good. I'm sorry you folks had to go through this." To Marcus, "He's ambitious and he's dumb. Makes him open to the wrong kind of offer. You need anything, you let me know."

In the void left by Culpepper's departure, Marcus offered the only hope he could. "We have the final hearing in the judge's chambers tomorrow. There shouldn't be any surprises, but I'll call when I get back and let you know."

Randall Walker was well aware that the greatest power was often the most secretive. Which was one reason he had eventually left the bench. Randall's finest thrill in earlier days had come from looking down on the defendant and declaring sentence. But that power had been limited by law and the public spotlight, and in time it had grown stale.

He had studied Machiavelli for years, knew his writings well enough to quote entire passages as though they were his own original thoughts. There was a man who understood where real power resided. Let others lay claim to the throne or boardroom or television lights. Sooner or later they would find their roles threatened, and the public eye too constrictive. They would then turn to him. And each time it happened, his reach grew wider. Once this New Horizons case was over, Randall's power would span continents and national boundaries, reach across the great divide of history and national interests. All Randall had to do was win. And win big.

Which made his reaction to the detective's report even more surprising. Hamper Caisse called just as he was leaving for dinner with a client, and announced, "Stanstead's vanished. I had a man on her, trying for an intercept. He lost her."

Randall felt almost none of the expected gall and ire. Instead, as he waved for his wife to go on out to the car and grant him privacy, what he felt most at that particular moment was anticipation. "And how, pray tell, did he manage that?"

"He says she was on to him. I've used him before, the man's a pro. He says she left home and went to work, carried nothing but her purse. He broke into her car, found nothing. Not a file, not a toothbrush. She came out of the charity office around four, went into a local café, never came out. A half hour went by, then he goes in, she's not there."

"She's on her way down here." Randall had never before resorted to violence. Never had a genuine reason. But he'd always wondered what it would be like to confront a threat that required a physical response. Now that the moment had arrived, he found himself tasting an almost erotic thrill. "And she's got more information for Glenwood."

"Maybe."

"No maybes about this one." Time for a decision. And action. He had heard stories about what Hamper Caisse would do if asked. Having such power at his beck and call left him slightly breathless. "All right. Leave that and come down. Tonight. I need you here."

"You want me to track the girl in Rocky Mount?"

"I very much doubt," Randall replied, "you'll have the time."

Marcus sat on his porch and watched the day fade. He wore a ragged sweatshirt and cutoffs and a sheen of drying sweat. His ears still rang from the mower he had bought off a neighbor for twenty-five dollars. The muffler had long since rusted away, and it roared like a weary machine of war. By the time he finished the two back acres, he was convinced he had overpaid.

The autumn twilight tarried longer than Marcus felt was natural. Streetlights glowed in faint mimicry of the sky's final colors. Trees and neighboring houses gradually faded to dark etchings of their former selves. The air smelled of cut grass and smoke from backyard grills, and rang with the clamor of children playing in the street.

A small, thin shadow separated itself from the nearest tree, and an alien yet familiar voice said, "Your home looks most inviting, Mr. Glenwood. May I join you?"

Marcus rose to his feet, lifted by the sudden, unnerving jolt. He recalled a blank hallway in Washington, and solid steel doors leading into a whitewashed world of silent terrors. "Is that Dee Gautam?"

"Remarkable, Mr. Glenwood. Most remarkable." The slender shadow approached and took on form, beginning with his smile. "You continue to surprise me. First I think you are nothing more than some American lawyer visiting our offices like another person would travel to the zoo. I look at you and I think, here is someone very comfortable in his living room with wall-to-wall carpet and big-screen television. Too comfortable to

311

worry about strangers suffering someplace very far away."

The steps did not creak as he climbed to the veranda. Dee Gautam stood smiling up at Marcus. "Then I hear that this strange American lawyer does not turn from a case he cannot win. No. He asks many questions and finds surprising answers. So I decide to come and see if he will listen to my warning, and I discover that this strange American lawyer lives alone in a neighborhood where almost all others are black."

"Warn me about what?"

"May I sit down, Mr. Glenwood?"

"Sorry, of course, you surprised me, showing up like this." He pulled over a second hickory rocker and set it so he could face the man square on. "You said something about —"

"Why do you choose to live here, Mr. Glenwood?"

Marcus seated himself, decided to let Dee Gautam chart the conversation's course. For now. "My grandfather built this place for his wife. Back then the area was different."

His visitor was so small he sat as a child would in the straight-backed rocker, sliding up to the edge so his feet could push against the floor. The chair drummed lightly over the uneven boards.

"Still I am not understanding, Mr. Glenwood. Why are you choosing to live in this place?"

Beyond the reach of the porch light, darkness gathered and conquered. "Would you like something to drink?"

"Thank you, no. I am not able to stay very long."

"My grandparents raised me. When they died, I kept the place. I'd come out here and work a little, but not enough. After an . . . accident, I decided to come back here to live. I've been restoring it ever since."

Gautam's hands reached out to settle upon the chair arms. In the half-light the pitted scars seemed to run the entire way through his wrists. "Please excuse me for the repetition, Mr. Glenwood, but I am trying so hard to understand. Why are you choosing to come back here?"

"You mean why do I live in what has become a black neighborhood?" When the little man simply rocked back and forth, using the chair and his entire body to nod, Marcus went on, "Some people resent my living here. Especially the young men who don't have work. You see them gathered on some of the porches. They watch cars with white drivers, and give me this look like, well, like I don't belong and never will."

The nightly chorus rose so gradually it was only when he paused to sort through jumbled thoughts that he heard it at all. "But there are a few people who have made me feel more than welcome. Deacon Wilbur, my secretary, a few others. They . . . understand."

"They accept your pain and your loss."

Marcus found himself unwilling to meet the man's gaze. "You've been checking up on me."

"That is what makes a home, I feel. Finding a place and a people who accept you as you are." The rocker drummed quietly for a moment. "This Deacon Wilbur, I have heard the name before. He is Gloria's pastor, yes?"

"You told me you didn't know Gloria Hall."

"No, Mr. Glenwood, I said I meet many people. Which I do." Dark eyes glittered yellow and alien in the porch light. "Look at it from my side, please. A stranger comes in and asks many questions. Many *sensitive* questions. Questions that, if answered to the wrong person, could hurt others who are helpless. You understand me?"

Marcus leaned forward. "Is there a direct tie-in between Factory 101 and New Horizons?"

"Rumors, Mr. Glenwood. Nothing

more than rumors." A pause filled by the cry of an owl. "Almost nothing. Gloria once told me she knew how to obtain proof. But if she indeed found this, I do not know."

"Was she kidnapped?"

"This also I have tried to discover. Tried and failed. There is no information coming from Factory 101. None."

"Who is in charge?"

Dee Gautam stopped rocking. "Ah. Yes. The most dangerous question of all."

"Dangerous how?"

"People are trying very hard to keep this answer a mystery. I smell danger for those who search." The smile was gone entirely. "I have a very good nose for danger, Mr. Glenwood."

"Ashley Granger is trying to identify the owner."

"Indeed I am speaking to Mr. Granger. He is a good man and must also take heed." Dee Gautam rose to his feet. "You are a good man as well, Mr. Glenwood. I am here to be telling you to take great care."

Marcus rose and followed the little man back across the veranda. "I've already met the New Horizons goons."

As he descended the stairs, the light caught the top of Dee Gautam's head, shining through his few remaining tendrils of hair and exposing the scalp beneath. For the first time Marcus noticed two long white scars running in parallel almost from ear to ear.

"Sometimes a person can focus upon the snarling dog and miss the bear farther back." Dee Gautam fitted comfortably into the night. "Beware the bear, Mr. Glenwood. It will eat you whole."

TWENTY-TWO

The final pretrial hearing on Thursday proceeded pretty much according to his expectations. Marcus struggled to remain tightly involved. The dark-suited defense lawyers clustered like opposing chess pieces set in intricate balance to his lonely knight. They raised the issue of dismissal, accusing him once more of making a frivolous claim. He neither objected nor spoke, for his mind remained fastened upon the morning's earlier mysteries.

That morning he had gone running in the dark, fleeing the whispers that awaited the moment he had opened his eyes — the ones that said, You have no case. As he wound his way homeward through a biting chill mist, a blond head stepped into the streetlight's glare, an apparition of false dawn and promises unfulfilled. Kirsten motioned back to the files piled by his front door. In a flat voice she had simply said, "I'll bring what I can when it's ready. You don't need to call me again." All Marcus could think to say was, "Don't leave!" Kirsten had not even turned around, just said over her shoulder, "I've driven all night, I'm tired, and all I want to hear from you is good-bye." But Marcus would not let go. His puffing breath had mingled with the pre-dawn mist as he had rushed over and stopped her car door from closing. "Is it me," he had demanded, "and if so couldn't you at least let me apologize?" Kirsten had bitten down hard on what-ever she had been about to say, wrenched her door shut, and driven away.

Marcus sat now before the judge's desk, and could not help but reflect on how, until recently, simply living from day to day had been enough. Waking before dawn, following a steady routine, at-tending to what small legal matters chance brought his way — these were ac-complishments enough. But now there was this case, and people relied on him once more. He found this only added fuel to his predawn inferno. He loathed the prospect of adding to his burden of unful-filled obligations.

"Marcus?" Judge Nicols' voice forced him back to the here and now. "Do you intend on joining us today?"

He turned to Logan. The words rose unbidden from his own internal depths. "Release the woman."

The quiet demand caught the entire

chamber by surprise. Logan scoffed. "Are you talking to me? Because that doesn't sound —"

"Tell the Chinese factory to release Gloria Hall. That's all we want. Bring her home and all this will vanish." He turned to the judge. "That offer is for the record."

"Your Honor, this is the most ludicrous accusation I have ever heard."

"There is no intended accusation at all, Your Honor. Free Gloria Hall and all charges will be dropped."

But Logan was striving too hard for the advantage to listen. "Your Honor, this merely confirms our contention that the plaintiffs are bringing a nuisance suit. Glenwood must be severely punished."

She turned slowly, as though reluctant to show Marcus her thoughts. "Well?"

Marcus nodded acceptance. The game was so rigidly set that no such maneuvering was possible. No one could see beyond the next move, when battle would officially be joined. "We have received none of the requested corporate documents from New Horizons, Your Honor."

Logan was ready. "That is because they do not exist."

"Your Honor, we have shown to the magistrate and yourself photocopied documents on corporate letterhead —"

"Which we claim to be false, Your Honor. Clearly this Miss Hall copied the New Horizons logo and drew up these documents herself. It is a well-known ploy of unions trying to smear a company's name. No doubt she learned it from the same cronies who are backing this frivolous suit. New Horizons has placed a few scattered orders with Factory 101. Nothing more."

Obtaining the original documents was critical. What case Marcus had was based upon the disputed documents. The court did not generally admit photocopies as evidence. The law required confirmation that what Marcus possessed was bona fide. Marcus reached for his briefcase. "Your Honor, I have an affidavit from the customs house at the Wilmington docks."

Logan exploded. "This was not included in his list of evidence!"

"If you supplied what we had requested it would not have been needed." There was no need to mention that Kirsten had only brought the documents that very morning. Marcus kept his eyes on the judge. "The affidavit states that New Horizons has cleared hundreds of container-loads of Chinese-produced clothes. And that this has been a practice followed over several years. I therefore request that the court grant us exceptional permission to submit all our photocopied documents as bona fide evidence."

The judge's features tightened around the edges. She scanned the affidavit, said, "So ruled."

Logan could not let that one go. "Objection, Your Honor, you —"

"Mr. Kendall, I do not approve of such shenanigans any more than the magistrate." Her voice was cold and hard as dark iron. "Try anything like that in my courtroom and I'll hold you in contempt." She looked back to Marcus. "Anything else?"

"Yes there is. We have received no response to any of our subpoenas of corporate board members. None of them was available to grant testimony."

"Well, Mr. Logan? Of the — how many subpoenas did you issue, Mr. Glenwood?"

"Thirty-six, Your Honor."

"Of the thirty-six requested depositions, how many officers are available to give testimony?"

Logan cleared his throat. "The two senior vice presidents of the local distribution company, Your Honor."

"I don't see those titles on this list."

"Neither hold board-level positions, Your Honor," Marcus said. "They would therefore know next to nothing about the

Chinese partnership."

"We deny that such a partnership exists!"

Judge Nicols extended the sheet of names to Logan. "Where are all these people?"

"Out of the country, Your Honor. This trial coincides with the annual corporate meeting in Switzerland."

Marcus said, "I hereby request the court's intervention in having the State Department order embassy officials in Bern to take depositions of all these corporate officers."

"So ruled." Judge Nicols slapped the file shut. "Nothing further? All right. We begin jury selection bright and early Monday morning."

As usual Marcus lingered and allowed time for the defense to depart ahead of him, discussing the weather with the judge's receptionist-guard. Jim Bell had a countryman's corded strength and a gentleman's beard, white and cropped tight to his face. He sat on the narrow chair as he would a saddle, solid and very erect. With the directness of one born in the eastern flatlands, where people spoke sparingly and straight, he dropped the issue of a possible early frost to say, "I lost a daughter two days before her tenth birthday. Like to have killed me and the wife both. Been nineteen years and the wound hasn't healed yet."

For an instant Marcus supposed the man was speaking of his own accident, and the pain was like someone having dropped his heart onto a red-hot skillet. Then he breathed and pushed away the pain, knowing he had to be mistaken. No one who had suffered thus would ever willingly blindside another so afflicted.

No, the guard had to be speaking of Gloria. "You've been following the Hall case?"

"I listen, and the others around here have been talking."

"Every day we don't hear anything more, I find myself hoping a little less."

The bearded man nodded agreement. "Handled a few kidnappings in my day. Not many. The first few weeks were always make or break."

"You were a highway patrolman?"

"Thirty-one years. Some nights I still dream of the open road." His smile was surprisingly gentle. "How's the Hall family holding out?"

"About like you'd expect. Worried sick. Not sleeping well. Everything is a crisis." Which brought to mind the recent confrontation at their house. "Do you know an assistant DA by the name of Wayde Barrett?"

"He's whipped through here a few times."

"What's your impression of him?"

"If I found him on my shoe, I'd use a long twig to scrape him off." The easy tone did not alter. "I hear tell the man can be bought."

"Is that a fact?"

"No sir. But it's a rumor I've heard more than once."

Marcus turned toward the door. "I appreciate that bit of news."

"Don't mention it, Mr. Glenwood. You take care, now."

Marcus' thoughts remained a jumble of unsorted pieces as he came out of the judge's chambers. The long hallway leading back to the elevators was empty, which was hardly surprising, for Judge Nicols occupied that entire side of the building. Another judge's suite opened from the hall's other end. Opposite the elevators was a marble-tiled foyer with a fountain that no longer worked. Opening off this were two federal courtrooms. Marcus was walking down the long empty hallway when someone turned in from the foyer and approached him. The man was small and gray and nondescript. He carried a file like a manila shield over his middle. His footfalls were as soft as dead air.

Marcus nodded a greeting as they passed. The man gave a little smile, and just as he came level with Marcus, he struck.

The blow was too powerful to have come from such a small man. Marcus felt as though the fist reached in through his gut, probing for his heart. He collapsed over the arm in a convulsion of agony and escaping breath.

The man was ready for this. He held Marcus upright and slammed him backward. But instead of striking the wall, Marcus fell through a door.

Hands were there to catch him. Three pairs of hands. They dragged him fully into the bathroom. The little gray man kicked inside the briefcase Marcus had dropped. "Watch the door."

Marcus focused enough to realize the three men wore masks of nylon mesh. The little gray man stepped forward and slammed his fist a second time into Marcus' belly. Marcus doubled over in dry heaves. Air was impossible to find. His lungs burned worse than his gut.

A hand gripped his hair, plucking his head upward. A wad of material was crammed into his mouth. Marcus gagged, fought the arms that held him. He still could not find enough air.

"Stand him up."

The hands lifted him upright. Marcus blinked through swimming tears. His breath whistled through his nostrils.

A toneless voice said, "Here's the thing. I could just tell you to drop the case, and right now you'd agree to just about anything. Look at me, Mr. Glenwood."

The man's voice was as gray as everything else about him. Marcus blinked hard. The image came and went. His whole body quaked with pain and the effort to find air.

"But I don't want you to agree now and forget. Because if you do, I'll have to come back. And if I come back, I'll kill you. Nod if you understand me."

Marcus nodded. The man's voice was as empty as a waiting grave. Marcus nodded again.

"Good. Even so, I need to make sure you don't forget me and this warning, Mr. Glenwood. It's the last warning you're going to get." He took a step back. "Hold out his arm."

Marcus' eyes shot fully open as his left arm was pulled out tight from his body. The images became sharply focused — a rail-thin man with mud-spattered boots gripped his left wrist and hung on tight. Another unseen man with layers of lard over hard muscle held him in a headlock, hugging his body up so close that Marcus could scarcely move, much less put up a struggle. A shorter pudgy man stood with his palm flat on the door, keeping out all hope. Through the pair of masks that were visible, Marcus could see two men grinning hugely. With their features mashed and yellowed, they looked like gargoyles made flesh.

But the little man did not smile. Marcus saw him clearly now as he reached into his jacket and brought out what appeared to be a bulky black pen. A jerk of his wrist, and he flicked it into a slender black rod. With the swift motions of long practice he reached for the other end, gripped it with both hands, and sent it in a swinging arc down upon Marcus' left forearm.

His scream was absorbed by the padding in his mouth. He heard the bone crack from inside his body. The four arms dropped him, and he fell, taking his weight on the broken bone. The agony was a bright white fire that exploded in his brain. He screamed again.

The gray shadow bent over him. "Don't forget what I told you, Mr. Glenwood. Make this case go away."

A mud-splattered boot moved in close enough for Marcus to see it through his pain. A narrow country voice rasped, "I still say he oughtta die." The boot reared back, and crashed mercifully into the side of his head. Marcus dove wholeheartedly into the waiting darkness.

TWENTY-THREE

Consciousness came and went like the moon peeking through wind-chased clouds. Twice the nightmare tried to capture him, or at least twice that he recalled. Marcus held for a time to the notion that Dee Gautam had arrived. The little man bore a solemn expression as he said, "You did not listen to my warning." Marcus wanted to reply, "I listened but not well enough." Yet the effort of framing those words threatened to split his skull. Soon he was off once more, traversing a scattered realm of dreams. Or perhaps he had never left there in the first place.

The first time he came fully awake, it was to pure astonishment. For there beside his bed sat Kirsten Stanstead, and as he opened his eyes she even tried to smile. "How are you?"

Right then he was so poorly he feared a hard nod would dislodge his skull. His mouth tasted truly foul. His tongue seemed glued to the roof of his mouth with some gummy industrial sealant. He worked his jaw, and his lips parted reluctantly.

"Thirsty?" She reached to the side table and fitted a straw into his mouth. Marcus drew and felt his whole being absorb the cool liquid. He groaned with the pleasure, then moaned a second time from the pain in his head from the sound.

"I offered to spell Alma so she could rest." Kirsten held the cup until she was sure he had finished drinking. "The police called last night to say you'd been hurt."

Her blond head came and went within his field of vision, and he realized it was her movements that were jerky, not his sight. "I should call the doctor, but there's something I need . . ."

For a moment Marcus was not certain whether he had drifted off again, passed smoothly back into the province of apparitions and fantasy. Then he heard her draw a ragged breath and realized he was still there. And was glad for it, though holding his thoughts together and his eyes even half-open was hard indeed.

"I've made such a mess of this. Of everything. I couldn't help Gloria, and now I've failed again with you."

It finally filtered through his groggy veil of pain that Kirsten was apologizing to him. For what, he felt he should know, or at least hear and understand. But the words came and went like the sound of waves crashing one against the other, making a gentle musical cadence in time to his labored breathing. Then she stopped talking, and he knew she awaited some kind of response. "You are truly sorry?"

"Oh, yes. I'd do anything to make it up to you."

His head pounded in rhythm to his arm. His stomach and lower chest felt raked raw. "Fine. Go ask the nurse for something for my pain." Marcus allowed his eyes to close. "Then come back and hold my good hand."

His second awakening was to a crowded room. Marcus found that alertness came without such pain this time, which he took to be a good sign. Two women were there by his bed, both in white coats. Alma Hall stood by the window, and beside her was a tall gangly man in a uniform. The man looked vaguely familiar, but the effort of searching for his identity was too great just then.

Without asking, the older of the two white-coated women fitted the straw into his mouth. "Can you talk?"

"Yes." His voice sounded rusty and disused.

"I'm Doctor Teller. You've had a clean

break of your left forearm, what appears to be a mild concussion, and around your middle there's bruising of a sort I haven't seen before."

The man by the window cleared his throat. "I have, ma'am. Mr. Glenwood was most likely worked over by somebody wearing knuckle-dusters."

Marcus' stomach convulsed slightly at the pain and the memory. The doctor set the cup back on his side table and continued. "We've done a scan and there appears to be no skull fracture. Does it hurt to move your head?"

"Yes."

She pulled a penlight from her pocket. "Follow the light, please." She watched his eyes track. "Any blurred vision? Dancing colors?"

"No."

"Good. Tell the nurse if that changes." She motioned to the uniform. "The deputy here wants to ask you some questions. Feel up to it?"

"Yes. What time is it?"

"Nine o'clock Saturday morning." To the deputy, "Keep it short."

But after the doctor had departed, it was Alma who moved around to seat herself by the bed. She reached down and came up with a thermos. Before she had unscrewed the top, Marcus was already salivating from the aroma.

"I've boiled this for six hours before I put it through the sieve." Marcus watched her fill the cup with a golden liquid thick as syrup. "Can't imagine we lost too many vitamins."

Marcus sucked so hard the chicken soup squirted hot and sharp to the back of his throat. He kept it up, sighing noisily for air, until the cup was drained. Alma poured a second cup and held it for him, smiling tired and sad all the while.

He shook his head to the offer of a third cup. "Thank you."

"You don't have to thank me for anything. Not ever." She screwed the top back on. "I'll leave this right here for whenever you want more."

The deputy shifted his weight, causing the leather of his gunbelt to squeak noisily. Marcus turned his gaze back toward the window.

"Amos Culpepper. We met at the Halls'."

"I remember."

"You see who did this?"

"One of them. The others wore masks."

"Tell me about it."

Marcus did so, pausing often to allow the pain in his head to subside. The arm ached no matter what he did, but each word had to be squeezed through his pounding skull. By the time he was finished he was sweating hard.

"So you think two of the men were the same as those over at New Horizons."

"Yes." He shut his eyes, and saw again the mud-spattered boots. "Can't be sure."

"Think I'll mosey on over, see what I can stir up." Amos started for the door. "When you're moving around I'd like you to look at some pictures."

"All right."

He opened the door, then paused another time. "You aim on dropping this case?"

"No."

The deputy nodded once, up and down, very slow. "Good." His eyes tracked over to Alma. "Ma'am." Then he was gone.

Alma waited until the door sighed closed to turn back and start in. "Marcus . . ."

But he could hold to the room no longer. He closed his eyes and went spinning away.

Marcus awoke to a fuller sense of alertness. With the wisdom of the ailing, he knew it would not last. Even so, he was grateful for this assurance that his faculties were not damaged. What was more, the thunder in his head had lessened somewhat. He was able to turn without agony and see Austin Hall seated there beside him, dark eyes glittering in the light from the window.

"Like some more soup?"

"Please." Marcus moved one limb at a time, saving the weighty cast on his left arm for last. "But first help me to the bathroom."

He had to lean heavily on the older man, who took his weight without complaint. When Marcus returned he rested a moment on the edge of the bed, though it hurt his head to do so. He wanted to revel in his mobility a moment longer.

Austin took it as a sign, and handed him the steaming mug without a straw. "How's the head?"

"Better." The soup was divine, almost a distillation of good health. "You don't have to sit here."

"I wanted to." Austin finished that subject off cleanly by holding out a plastic pill cup. "The nurse said you were to take these when you woke up."

Marcus did so, not minding the prospect of more drugged fogginess now that he knew it would pass. Then, because they were both thinking of her, he said, "Tell me something about Gloria."

Austin seemed to have expected the question. Or perhaps it was just that his thoughts remained centered upon this subject. All his thoughts, all his energy. "She hates math." The late-afternoon light was golden and warm and glinted off the man's tie. Sitting weekend duty in a sickroom and the man's top button was still closed, the tie still tight. "She has a great mind for strategy and none whatsoever for numbers. Three rows needing addition sends her screaming from the room."

Marcus sipped at his mug. "Strategy."

"She's brilliant at chess. Learned the game before she started school." The smile was a swift shadow. "Beat me the first time on her ninth birthday. I was astonished, I can tell you."

Marcus felt that it all meant something. Or it should. But the mental struggle was too much. "She looked so happy in that photograph."

"Gloria is all or nothing. And all the time. One hundred percent happy, one hundred percent angry, or sad, or excited, whatever. She dives into her emotions like she does all of life. She is a good student when it suits her, and terrible when her mind is elsewhere."

"How was she just before she left for China?"

"Like the walking dead. Utterly and completely miserable. She had been absolutely despondent for months. Morose and weepy and quarrelsome. Kirsten was the only one who kept her on an even keel. The two of them had been close for years, but they grew closer than sisters. Ever since she and that Loh boy broke up, Gloria had been teetering on the verge of a breakdown."

Marcus set down his cup. "Who?"

"Gary Loh. Brilliant kid. Medical student. Strong in the church."

"You approved of him."

"He changed Gloria's life around. Before, well, Gloria went through a wild stage her first year at Georgetown."

A lethargic fog began to take hold of Marcus' limbs. "So I heard."

"Who from?"

"Oathell." He swung his legs up and onto the bed, eased his head onto the welcoming pillow.

"Yeah, she broke that boy's heart. But Gary was good for her and Oathell couldn't keep up, and that's the truth from her own daddy. She and Gary made a fine-looking couple. Real fine."

The warm languor seeped into his bones and traveled up his body. "But they split up. Why?"

"Gloria wouldn't say a thing. One moment she and Gary were planning to get married. The next, nothing. We didn't hear anything for over a month. Then she came home for Thanksgiving and spent the entire time locked in her room sobbing. Like to have broken Alma's heart, especially when she wouldn't tell us what was wrong."

His mind could not hold a train of thought. It flittered about, landing where it would. "How did she get so interested in New Horizons?"

Austin seemed to find nothing odd in the sudden shift. "I doubt there's a single family in our church without some tales about that company. All of them bad."

Marcus murmured, "You?"

"Ask Alma sometime about her nephew, the one who worked for the unions."

Marcus wanted to ask more, but the talk left him. His final awareness was of a strong dark face watching as he slid into sleep and away.

He awoke late in the night. It was only in the midst of this silence that he recognized the noises that had occupied the rooms and hallway outside his door. Marcus reached for the phone and dialed a number from memory. When Charlie Hayes answered, Marcus asked, "What time is it?"

"I know you must be sick. Calling me in the middle of the night, waking me up so you can find out the time." There came a rustling sound, then, "It's just gone one. There. You satisfied?"

"I was thinking about one of the stories you told me. About that case when you got so excited in your closing argument you fell over the railing and landed in the jury's lap."

"I won that case, by the way. Guess the folks figured if I was that excited I had to be telling the truth." A pause. "How are you, son?"

"Better."

"I came by twice, but you just snored through my visits. Libby brought me one time, Deacon the other. Made Libby cry to see you lying there with your head all bashed in."

Marcus fingered the bandage over his left temple. "Tell her I'm fine."

"That why you called, to remind me about some foolishness from forty years back?"

"No." A single breath, then the commitment. "Jury selection is scheduled to start on Monday."

"Been pondering that myself."

"I can't handle it alone."

"Recognized that fact the moment I laid eyes on you."

"I don't want to postpone the trial, Charlie. It means they win, at least for the moment. And every day counts."

"You can go ahead and ask, son. I won't turn you down."

"That means a lot," he said, taking an easier breath. "Good night."

Marcus was alone when he awoke the next morning. After breakfast he showered and shaved, finding great consolation in his isolated mobility. The doctor came soon after, inspected him carefully, and declared him free to go. "But I want you to watch for signs of internal bleeding."

"I will." His belly was a rainbow of dark and violent hues. It was not a time for a cavalier attitude.

"And if your vision should start blurring or the headaches worsen, call me immediately. Otherwise I want to check you over in a week's time."

"Thank you, Doctor."

As the doctor departed, Kirsten stepped inside. "You're up."

"I'm more than that. I'm free to go." Marcus wanted to ask why she had been apologizing earlier, but not at the cost of that small sad smile she gifted him. "You look very nice."

And she did, standing there in the doorway in her floral-patterned skirt and dark blouse and hair so blond it held

340

highlights of fine morning mist where the sun touched. He even liked her uncertain air and the way her purse strap was wound tightly through her fingers.

"Alma and Austin are downstairs. We wanted to check in on our way to church."

Though his body ached and he doubted he would have the energy to go the full round, he found the prospect pleasing. "Is there room for me?"

Clearly this had already been discussed. "I could drive you in your car, if you like. The deputy brought it over from the courthouse."

"That would be great." He rose slowly, ashamed of the need to test each joint in turn. Then he was glad of it, for she walked over and fitted herself to his side. Almost as if she belonged.

The drive out of Raleigh was under clouds so low they almost grazed the eastern hills. Their leaden color was scarcely lighter than the asphalt. Marcus cracked his window and let the warm, humid air wash away the hospital's bitter tang.

Kirsten followed Alma and Austin out of town. She waited until they hit the four-lane U.S. 64 to say, "I want to help you."

"That's good. I need all the help I can get."

"I mean with the case."

"I know what you mean, Kirsten. And I'm grateful. Really." Her expression showed she needed more convincing. "We're going up against an army. They had seven lawyers in the meetings with Judge Nicols. I need help with the prep work. A lot."

"I thought after what I told you in the hospital, you wouldn't want to have anything to do with me."

Marcus knew he would have to ask her to repeat herself, and sooner rather than later. But her tone had the somber openness of the confessional, and right then his greatest desire was to give back in kind. "I never wanted to take this case."

"I know."

"Not because I couldn't win it. Because I was afraid of letting the Halls down." He settled his head onto the backrest, easing deeper into the cushions, letting the seat take all his weight. "I guess you've heard about the accident with my family."

"Alma told me. I'm so sorry."

"I never went back to my old house. Neither did Carol, my ex-wife. I hired a mover and some friend of Carol's supervised. Except for my clothes, I haven't unpacked any of the boxes. I couldn't risk accidentally coming across something that belonged to one of the kids."

"I could do that if you like."

The offer meant so much he had to confess, "I never wanted anyone to rely on me for anything important, not ever again. I've been too good at letting people down."

"Alma said the accident wasn't your fault."

Marcus sighed and made do with, "I always saw my grandparents' place as my last refuge. Somewhere I could go and take only what was comfortable." He paused, then concluded, "It's not the first time life has proven me wrong."

To her credit, Kirsten did not respond. She held to her silence as she drove into the church parking lot. Only after she cut the motor did she say, "Alma and Austin both think you are the only one who can bring Gloria home. Deacon Wilbur feels the same."

The words weighed heavily upon his entire being. Marcus opened his door and started the distressing process of unlimbering, only to be halted by a featherlight touch on his arm. He turned back to meet a gaze far keener than the day's light. Kirsten said, "I think they are absolutely right."

★ ★ ★

The church gleamed white beneath the slate-colored sky. The neighboring hillside was dotted with autumn colors, startling in their brilliance when all else loomed dark and gray. The building on the summit seemed washed to an ashen sullenness, as though mortally offended by Marcus' arrival.

The congregation had always been pleasant in their welcome, gracing his arrival with genuine smiles and warm handshakes. Today the customary was not sufficient, however. Marcus was met by a charge of faces and greetings and softly spoken questions. Alma and Austin could not even make it to where he stood, for too many others moved in and claimed him as their own. Everyone seemed intent upon calling him by name. There was much laying on of hands as they ushered him inside and settled him down. Even then they still surrounded him, reaching over to pat his shoulders, arms, hands. The attention left him wounded and grateful both.

He sat by himself, Kirsten across the aisle with Alma and Austin. People stood all around him, their singing a shout of impossible harmonies. Impossible that so many voices could find so many different ways of joining together. He felt sorely alone and yet glad of it, as though the two sides of his conflicting nature were both exposed and comfortable in this noisy yet hallowed place. Here he was, both the man who sought to remove himself from the world and the man who loved to do battle. The man who scorned the fray and the one who lived for the formal jousting of courtroom wars. The man who was newly wounded and the one who could not deny that he was healing still.

Marcus found the world returning to focus, and he realized that Deacon Wilbur was walking toward the center of the stage. The audience hummed approval. Clearly this was an unexpected gift. Marcus had not heard the old man preach before.

Deacon reached forward and took hold of the podium. He did not merely stand. He gripped the wood and leaned out, scowling, fierce as a bird of prey. Through his fatigue, Marcus struggled to listen.

"You're out there, running life's race. The pressure is constant, the pace relentless. Is it so? Let me hear how hard it is for you folks outside these sacred doors." Deacon Wilbur waited through the calls and the clapping, scowling and squinting, forcing those who watched to watch themselves. "Tell me, brothers. Are you tired? Speak your mind, sisters. Do you lose sight of the finishing line?"

He remained utterly unmoved by the clamor he was raising. He shouted to be heard. "Do you feel like you're not going anywhere, you just stay busy running? Is an easy breath hard to find? Has the struggle left you wounded?"

A woman in the second row, big and made bigger by a bright scarf wrapped around her middle like a second skirt, wriggled by those blocking her way and danced into the central aisle. She shook from her head to her feet, her hands up and waving, the words a chant of startling beauty. "Hard, oh yes, Jesus, so hard, so hard!"

Deacon Wilbur remained unfazed. Only his glistening face suggested he was moved by the message. "Then the problem is, brothers and sisters, you are running alone."

Marcus was not aware he had risen to his feet until he noticed that Deacon had become easier to see. "Brothers and sisters, just because you're busy doesn't mean you're moving in the right direction. No. Can I have me an amen?"

The crowd sang its chant of accord.

"You're not drawing closer to the goal just on account of you're making good time. No. The task here isn't to be busy.

No. The world is full of the lost and alone, filling every crack in the mask they use to hide an empty heart with *busy*. Look around, see the desperate people shouting words they don't want to hear. Just filling the world with busy, yeah, filling the void with everything they can."

Deacon Wilbur was a man transformed, fierce and authoritative now, as though the cloak of age had been kicked aside. The old pastor's face shone like it was coated with a fine sheen of oil. "Listen to me now, brothers and sisters. Listen good. Your very lives depend on this. Are you listening to me now?" When they shouted their attention, he said, "All right. Here's the truth revealed. You've got to do your work for a higher cause. You've got to take your steps for something more than yourself. You've got to draw that next breath with something greater than your own selfish desires in mind. Can I have me an amen!"

The church rocked to the shouted response. Dozens more clustered and danced along the central aisle.

"Then you know what happens? You will rise up on *eagle's* wings. Shout me an amen, brothers and sisters! You will run and *never* stumble. Let the Lord hear your joy!"

"Hallelujah!"

"You will strive and not grow weary, no. Sing your praise to the Lord!"

When the tumult quietened, the old man went on, "You got to work for something bigger, something finer, something eternal. You got to cross that great divide to make your work matter. You got to march over the bridge set in place by perfect sacrifice. The bridge God built for you and you alone."

The upheaval grew more intense, the chants a song that carried no set tune, but swept like a lyrical wind through the church. "The bridge across the great divide, oh yes, it is the infinite gift. The *holy* gift. Yeah. And there is only one thing you can do to give it meaning, you hear what I am saying? You must accept this gift. You must aim your walk. No matter how scared you might be, looking down over the sides and seeing that chasm open up, yes, the one that looks dark as eternal night, the one that whispers words of death. Keep your eyes focused on the other side, the place where light dwells in all things. The place where you are welcome. Yes. The one place you can call home."

Rising fatigue forced Marcus back into his seat. The weariness swelled until the words no longer mattered. Only the welcome they contained stayed with him.

And that was more than enough. He looked around him, his gaze met by such open friendliness he wanted to weep. He found himself thinking of Dee Gautam's words, about how home was the place that accepted him. Marcus found himself adding new words of his own. Perhaps home was the place that accepted him because of his needs. Not in spite of his lacks and failings; *because* of them. Then he shook his head a fraction. No. That would be too much to ask. Except perhaps for a single moment now and then, in a time out of time, one touched by the divine. Such as here and now.

TWENTY-FOUR

Monday morning brought no physical improvement whatsoever. Marcus' body and mind both seemed stubbornly set against the day. His head pounded, his arm and gut ached, shaving was a chore, even the shower found tender places to probe. His tie defeated him entirely. As he descended the stairs, a burdensome weight remained upon his heart. He knew the reason for his concern, and was helpless in the face of it all. Today marked the beginning of the most hopeless trial of his entire career. He was wounded in body and mind and spirit. He felt lonelier than he had since the funeral eighteen months earlier. And he was sorely afraid of letting everyone down. Again.

As he entered the front hallway, footsteps clumped across the veranda. His entire frame seized up as shadows drifted by the narrow front windows. He saw with vivid clarity the gray attacker, heard the warning so loud it took a moment to realize the doorbell had rung. Marcus forced his muscles to unlock. He was fairly certain that if the gray man returned, he would not pause to ring the front bell.

Deacon Wilbur was positively dwarfed by the young man beside him. "Morning, Marcus. How are you feeling?"

"Fair." He sketched a smile to the young man. "Hello, Darren."

"The church elders met last night. We've decided to ask Darren here to keep an eye on you."

The previous fear was still too vivid for Marcus to refuse outright. "It's a good thought, Reverend. But I can't afford to hire more staff."

Deacon Wilbur demonstrated his ability to frown with his entire face. "Who said anything about you paying? Matter of fact, I don't recall ever seeing a bill for protecting our cemetery."

"That was nothing."

"Don't you say that. Don't you even think it, not for an instant."

The conversation was halted by the sight of four vehicles pulling in behind Deacon's truck — Kirsten in one car, followed by Austin and Alma Hall in another, then a sheriff's patrol car, and finally a Jeep Grand Cherokee painted Carolina blue.

The first voice he heard was that of Boomer Hayes. "Marcus! If I didn't see you standing there in your own front door, I'd guess folks were gathering for your funeral!"

"You just hush up and take this." Libby Hayes was quieter only by degree. "Charlie, get back here and carry this coffee cake."

Amos Culpepper was the first to the stairs. "Good to see you up and about, Marcus. Hello, Reverend." He nodded to the young man who towered almost a full head above the deputy. "I know you."

"This is Darren Wilbur," Marcus said. "He was rousted last week by the local police."

The deputy kept a cool eye on the young man, who had turned to sullen stone. "Rousted."

"Charged with the 7-Eleven robbery. He had witnesses who placed him on the other side of the river. Not to mention that the clerk says abuse was shouted at him and Darren has a stutter, and the clerk made no mention of any. But the officer in charge refused to listen. He needed a warm body. Darren is big enough to scare him."

The deputy sheriff observed the young man for a long moment, then asked, "Do you vouch for him, Marcus?"

"I do."

"Then I'll see if we can't talk some sense into the arresting officer."

"Marcus!" Boomer Hayes led the crowd up the veranda steps. "I hope you're hungry, 'cause Libby's been up since dawn making all kinds of good smells."

"Cultured Southern ladies are taught at an early age that food is the answer to whatever ails you." Libby wore a pants and sweater outfit of sharp blue. "Land sakes, Marcus, the side of your head looks all bashed in."

"You should see his gut," Charlie said, doing his sideways climb up the stairs. "Morning, Reverend."

"Hello, Judge. How're you this fine day?"

"Partial to sleep. Libby made enough racket to wake the dead."

"Momma always said food tastes better if you bang the pans." Libby gave Darren a slow up-and-down. "They surely do grow folks big down east."

"Darren here is offering to keep watch over Marcus," Deacon said. "There's a little apartment back of the kitchen, got its own sitting room and all. He'll be fine."

The news met with such a chorus of approval that Marcus felt his own objections swept away. Amos said, "I better be off, Marcus. Just wanted to see how you were doing."

"Not so fast." Charlie hefted his

platter. "We need all the help we can get here."

"We got us cheese-grits soufflé," Boomer agreed. "Sausage-and-eggs casserole. Spoon bread. Sweet-potato pie. Coffee cake with pecans from my own tree. And scratch biscuits with smoked country ham."

"Marcus, stop cluttering up the door," Charlie ordered. "Go do something useful like putting on a fresh pot of coffee."

"All rise. The Seventh District Court of the United States is now in session. Judge Nicols presiding."

Marcus' multiple pains protested loudly as he stood, yet he did not mind at all. Alongside the throbbing in his head and gut, closer to him still than the arm plastered and aching, was the laughter he had heard that morning in his kitchen. Boomer Hayes had never in his entire life met a stranger, and not even Alma Hall could hold on to her pretrial nerves. Marcus had sat and eaten until his belly felt bruised inside as well as out, and marveled at his home's momentary change of atmosphere.

"Be seated." In her dark robes and high-backed leather chair, Gladys Nicols looked impossibly solid and as regal as a queen. Her features appeared even more sharply defined than usual as she inspected Marcus long and hard. "Counsel are requested to approach the bench."

The courtroom was an elegant walnut-paneled theater. Attendance was free, participation outrageously expensive. For the losers the cost was everything they had, pride and freedom included. Only the United States flag was mounted behind the judge, as the state flag did not belong in a federal court. A carved wooden Great Seal of the United States was set in the wall above the judge's head. The seal and the flag were the courtroom's only adornments. The result was a chamber both grand and uncompromisingly stern. The tables, jury box, witness stand, judge's high bench, and the recorder's station and public seats were the same polished walnut as the walls. A rich and impressive seat of law, or a very public morgue for the mourning of shattered ambitions — it all depended on who won.

The judge's bench rested high upon its carpeted platform, ringed by lower stations for the reporter and two clerks and the witness stand. The court reporter started to rise as Marcus and the others approached, but was waved away. Up close, Judge Nicols was so somber as to appear ageless. "Marcus, are you up for this?"

"Yes, thank you, Your Honor."

"I'm willing to grant a continuance if you want."

"Every day counts here, Your Honor." Because of his throbbing head, Marcus found it easier to swing his entire body toward Logan. "Have your client release Gloria Hall and we will immediately drop all charges."

Logan pulled his gaze from the head bruise extending beyond the borders of Marcus' bandage. "Your Honor, I find the implied accusation offensive in the extreme."

But Judge Nicols was not done with Marcus. "I had my clerk speak with the hospital staff. They doubt your ability to handle the rigors of trial work so soon."

Charlie moved in closer. "I'll be taking care of jury selection, Your Honor."

Gladys Nicols unbent enough to offer a small smile. "How are you, Mr. Hayes?"

"Raring to go, Your Honor."

"All right. Marcus, if you need to retire early, say the word."

"I'll be fine, Your Honor. But thank you."

He held to his stoic denial only as long as it took to return to the plaintiff's table. As Judge Nicols greeted the prospective jurors, Marcus palmed a tablet from his jacket pocket. He could do nothing about

356

the palsied shake to his hand, however, and was grateful when Alma took the carafe from him and filled the glass. Charlie watched from Marcus' other side and commented, "You're in a bad way."

Austin was seated to the right of Alma, the closest person to the jury box. "The man should be lying down."

Marcus set down his glass and touched his forehead. His fingers came away damp. He said to Charlie, "You're on your own today."

"Don't you worry, son. I've prepped more juries than you've had hot meals."

The pill settled the pain and the courtroom into a soft, dull drone. Marcus sat and pretended to observe as Charlie went through the jury questionnaires. Nothing registered, save for the fact that little mattered, since the case's outcome was already decided. It was all for show, and Charlie could handle that just fine.

Mercifully, the judge called it a day before the pill wore off. Marcus listened to her instructions as he would the buzzing of an insect, then rose and found himself mildly surprised to find the four of them joined by Darren and Kirsten. He was glad to discover his legs could carry him to the elevator. There the judge's receptionist was standing with the building's security detail, all retired police, all wanting to ask how he was. Marcus let Charlie speak for him, wishing he could curl up right there on the floor.

Tuesday started better and faded more slowly. In the time between awakening and coming downstairs, Marcus took great comfort in the quiet sounds of someone else moving around his house. Darren drove him into Raleigh as though he had been doing it for years, silent and very watchful.

At midmorning, when pain and fatigue threatened, he slipped a pill from his pocket and waited while Charlie poured him a glass of water. The old man murmured, "They're stacking the jury."

"I know."

"They're turning the jury box the color of fresh mayonnaise." Both teams were granted eight peremptory strikes. Logan had used six, Charlie one. Judge Nicols had excused four others. The one black person among the five jurors chosen thus far was a dentist, also the only professional among the group. Marcus knew the defense had let this one stand because medical personnel were notorious for loathing big payouts.

"Why didn't you strike the dentist?"

"Can't rightly say. Just had a hunch about him is all." Charlie motioned toward the rows of potential jurors behind them. "Wish I knew what to look for in this bunch."

Marcus started to say it hardly mattered, since the case was bound to be dismissed long before the jury retired. Charlie went on, "The next five prospects are white. I could strike them all, then —"

"Don't bother with that." Marcus pointed vaguely with his water glass. "Nicols will hardly take kindly to the defense using race as a selection tool. Let's not lower ourselves to their level."

"Can't see how that matters if we wind up with a jury that's firm against us." Charlie wore a poplin suit and a bright yellow bow tie. This close he smelled slightly of camphor and hair oil. The eyes behind his thick lenses swam with intelligent concern. "Bound to be some whites in that bunch who'd love to give an intelligent black troublemaker her comeuppance."

Marcus swallowed his pill. "Charlie, listen to me."

"Not to mention the work the defense team must have put into studying the jurors' profiles. Look at that bunch, like vultures in drag. Bet they've got some whoop-de-do jury consultants prying through those folks' garbage —"

"Forget them." Marcus felt his will and

focus fading. "Find out which ones are churchgoers."

Charlie Hayes seemed to have difficulty getting Marcus into the right frame of his bifocals. "Shouldn't be too hard, seeing as how we're sitting on the buckle of the Bible Belt," Charlie replied. "But in case you haven't noticed, most every church I've set foot into has its share of racists. Ain't saying it's right. Just saying it's so."

Marcus lacked any will to argue. "Just the same."

"Mr. Hayes," Judge Nicols interrupted. "Any question for prospective juror seventeen?"

Marcus watched Charlie rise and begin his jocular probing. His poplin suit had been bought for a much younger man, and tended to flap on Charlie's aging frame. But the jurors apparently did not mind, for they watched Charlie's creaking dance with a smile. Marcus wholeheartedly agreed. Charlie Hayes pranced and waved and flittered like a poplin butterfly.

"Is the door locked? All right. Everybody pay attention." Logan surveyed the group crammed into his office — seven lawyers, two paralegals, two in-house jury consultants, three secretaries. As senior associate, Suzie Rikkers claimed the most comfortable visitor's chair. The others squeezed into whatever space they could find. Five remained standing. All wore sullen expressions and the bored air of people wasting their time.

"I know what you're thinking. The trial is a sham, the plaintiff has no case, and you're all there for padding." Logan noted the nods around the room. Even the most junior associate felt the senselessness of their presence. And he knew what they all expected next — the partner in charge would now give a pep talk: how this was crucial courtroom experience, how they needed to watch and learn, ask questions, anticipate, get ready for their own big day.

"Well, up to now that's been exactly right. Dan Fussell, our senior partner, actually stopped me yesterday in the hallway and asked if we couldn't use a couple more associates in there." He waited long enough to see the surprise filter through the boredom. Here was something new, a partner actually telling them the truth. "Obviously our client has given the senior partner a blank check. Since I refused to take on anyone else, my guess is he'll bill you all at partners' hourly rates. I know I would."

Logan stood and turned to the window behind his desk. The descending sun shone through a horizon-level slit in the clouds, and painted the world ocher and rose and gold. At least here was space and clarity. Logan continued, "Dan has bought the client's line. He assumes this is a nuisance claim. He accepts that New Horizons has no formal tie to the Chinese factory. The vanished girl has nothing whatsoever to do with New Horizons. And we're off for a walk in the park."

He turned back, and this time all eyes were on him. "As far as Dan is concerned, that's exactly what we're thinking too. You don't discuss this with anyone not in this room, not even your own secretary. You need a letter typed, do it yourself. Don't open your mouth to anyone around here except the people in this room. We can't afford the risk of this getting back to the client. New Horizons has announced that they are granting us a bigger slice of the corporate pie, and we don't want anything to disturb this new relationship. Are we clear so far?"

This time the nods were sharp assents. He had their full attention. "All right. I've got a strong gut feeling that the company is leading us right off the cliff."

The room took a single breath. Suzie asked in her patented whine, "You really think they kidnapped that girl?"

"I think it doesn't matter. I think they're hiding something. Something big.

Whether it's about Gloria Hall or Factory 101 or something else entirely doesn't make any difference. What we can't afford any longer is to simply go where they direct."

He clenched the leather backrest of his chair with both fists, and leaned as he would over prize-ring ropes. "We're going to prepare for the worst. Suzie, get a team together. Assume Marcus is going to hit the jury with past practices. Prepare arguments for the judge."

"Right. But —"

"No buts." A quick glance around the room. "From now on, we work on the assumption that our client is not our friend. Clear?" When their assent came, he continued, "Two people start digging through New Horizons' court records. I want to know every time they have even sneezed within a hundred feet of a courthouse. Volunteers? Fine. You and you."

All notepads were out now, all pens in use. "Two more start prepping for defense. Okay, you two. Every time Marcus comes up with something, you prepare a counterattack. We meet every day a half hour after court adjourns for strategy sessions. I'll have sandwiches brought in. Weekends and evening activities are hereby canceled for the duration. Any questions?"

They looked around, the unasked question on everyone's face. Finally Suzie blurted out, "Do you think New Horizons had Marcus beaten?"

Logan replied with a growl. "Get to work."

TWENTY-FIVE

On Wednesday Marcus awoke with enough clarity for his arm to ache more than his head. He greeted the nightmare's lingering dread not as he would a friend, but at least as a sign that things were returning to normal. By the time he had showered and dressed, he could hear sounds rising from downstairs. Marcus entered the kitchen to find Kirsten and Darren cowed and silent at the table, while Fay Wilbur clattered about the stove and grumbled angrily to herself. She rounded on him the instant he appeared. "Well? What you staring at?"

"Good morning, Mrs. Wilbur. Nice to see you again."

"This ain't some good-time show. Get on over there and sit yourself down." She turned back to the skillet and muttered as she would a curse, "You look like a three-egg man to me."

"All I normally take is toast and coffee."

"Hmph. Probably why you got yourself messed up. Didn't have no strength. Anybody with the sense God gave a little blind mole knows you gotta start your day with a full belly." She whipped plates in front of Kirsten and Darren. Kirsten gawked at her two eggs and bacon and sausage and three biscuits and grits and ham hock, then directed a horror-stricken appeal at Marcus. Fay Wilbur caught the glance out of the corner of her eye and demanded, "What're you staring at him for? He can't tell you a thing worth knowing 'cept you gotta eat it all before you rise up."

Soon as she turned back to the stove, however, quick as a flash Darren picked up Kirsten's plate and shoveled a goodly portion onto his own. She responded with a sigh of pure gratitude.

Marcus asked Kirsten, "What brings you over so early?"

"Starvation, most likely," Fay Wilbur rattled the biscuit tray. "Girl's all skin and bones and eyes. Even her hair looks peaked."

Kirsten replied, "Netty called this morning. Her son had a bad night. She asked me to handle the office."

"Hush up, now, you got all day to do your lawyering." Fay Wilbur slapped a plate down in front of Marcus. "Right now what I'm hearing is folks not using their forks fast enough."

After breakfast Marcus waddled his way

to the front door. Kirsten wore a mildly astonished look. Only Darren was smiling. As he pushed open the door, Darren spoke for the first time that day. "D-don't see how Deacon stays so th-thin."

Marcus asked Kirsten, "Have you found anything more in Gloria's research materials?"

"Maybe." The enigmatic wariness returned to her features. "I'm not sure."

Marcus glanced at his watch. There were questions to be asked, but not now. "I need whatever there is."

"I brought the rest of her stuff with me." Their gazes no longer met. "I'll start on it tonight."

"Can I help?"

"Gloria wouldn't want a stranger going through her personal things." The reply sounded practiced. "I can do it faster by myself."

Marcus carried his suspicions with him to the car and out of town. Just as they hit the highway, with Darren driving, Marcus' mobile phone rang. "Glenwood."

"It's Ashley Granger here, sport, calling from Washington. How're you doing?"

"Fine."

"That's not what I hear. Old Dee tells me somebody got you good."

Marcus stared at the day ahead. "How did Dee Gautam hear about that?"

"Been asking myself the same question. Only found one answer. Because he thinks what you're chasing is important enough to watch, and watch closely. How does that grab you?"

Marcus replied truthfully, "I've got a load of questions and no answers this morning."

"You and me both." Ashley sounded impossibly cheerful. "You dropping this case?"

"Not a chance."

"That's the spirit. I'm still trying to track down who's the top dog at your Factory 101. Lots of people are taking offense. I've even earned a couple of warnings from Dee himself."

Marcus hugged his bandaged arm. "You watch yourself."

"I'm not taking any chances. But I called to tell you I might be closing in on some answers."

"Anything you can give me now?"

"No, I don't like dealing in rumors. But I'll tell you this much. If what I'm thinking proves to be true, you might have more of a case than you think." Ashley's voice rang with the excitement of the hunt. "If I were you, I'd start treating this like something maybe I won't win, but at least I might take down to the wire."

Marcus cut the connection, and sat surrounded by the traffic and the mysteries.

"Mr. G-Glenwood."

"Call me Marcus."

"Somebody's d-dogging us."

The words snapped him into focus. "What?"

"T-three cars b-back." Darren's hands made fists the size of mallets as he watched the road and rearview mirror both. "W-white pickup."

Marcus swiveled, searched, felt his gut protest as he sighted the dirty truck. Swiftly he searched his pockets and came up with the deputy's card. He punched in the number.

"Sheriff's department."

"Patch me through to Amos Culpepper, please."

"Who is this?"

"Marcus Glenwood. Deputy Culpepper told me to do this."

"Hold one." There were a number of pops and hissing silences, then, "Go ahead."

The rich twang said, "Marcus?"

"I'm being followed by one of the pickups that attacked me at New Horizons."

Through the static of a radio patch, the deputy's voice tightened. "Where are you?"

"Highway 64, traveling west, about

twenty miles outside Raleigh." He rose in his seat. "Hang on, they're veering off. They just took the Zebulon exit."

"Means they're listening in to police band. Not a good sign. Where are you headed?"

His heart seemed to hammer louder now that the truck had been replaced by an unseen threat. "Federal courthouse."

"I'll meet you there." Anger grated over the airwaves. "Somebody's about to get me riled."

By ten o'clock the jury had been fully selected and Judge Nicols was well into her introductory lecture on procedural dos and don'ts. Marcus glanced at Charlie Hayes, saw his slackened features and vacant gaze. Marcus realized that the old man assumed his role was over, and that he missed the courtroom fray like a drowning man would the very air.

Marcus leaned over close and murmured, "I want you to make the opening statement."

A cattle prod applied to the man's nether regions would not have provoked a stronger reaction. Even so, the old man's voice kept to a courtroom whisper. "I don't have the first idea of what to say."

"Then that puts us in about the same fix." Marcus grinned for the first time since his visit to the hospital. It felt like he was awakening muscles given over to permanent slumber. "I also want you to handle the first few witnesses."

Charlie's head bobbed like a bird searching the heavens as he fitted Marcus into focus. "We talking strategy here?"

"Maybe." Marcus decided he owed the old man a fuller slice of the truth. "A lawyer in Washington thinks he might have something that will turn this case around."

"So you want me to start off, then if we need to change course it'll come more natural." Charlie did not need to ponder long. "I can live with that."

"Good."

" 'Course, my experience is, most times these last-minute reprieves hold off like smoke on the horizon."

"Then we don't have a case, and it doesn't matter one way or the other, long as we build up some publicity." Marcus proceeded to tell him what the opening statement needed to contain. It did not take long.

Judge Nicols broke in. "All right, Mr. Glenwood. Counsel for the plaintiff may proceed."

"I'll be taking that role, Your Honor." Charlie Hayes fumbled slightly as he plucked his cane from the railing.

Alarmed that he might have overstrained the old man's heart, Marcus started to protest that he should do it after all. But Charlie threw him a quick wink, scarcely more than a twitch. Marcus settled back, ready for the show.

Charlie leaned heavily on the cane as he moved in front of the jury box. "My name is Charlie Hayes and I am seventy-seven years old. I had the honor of practicing law in this fine state for nigh on fifty years. A lot of that time was spent sitting right up there where Judge Nicols is now. I retired, oh, it must be going on nine years back." He paused to adjust his weight on the cane. "I was ready to go. I'd loved serving my state and my country, but the time had come for me to step aside and spend more time with my family. Then the lawyer you see seated over there, Marcus Glenwood is his name, he came by and told me about this situation. And I knew that I had to find it in me to try one more case. And I'll tell you why. The reason is very simple, ladies and gentlemen of the jury: Never in all my born days have I come up against anything quite so vile and treacherous as what has brought us together here today."

Logan was on his feet in a flash. "Objection!"

"Overruled. Counsel is granted leeway

in opening remarks."

Charlie had used the interruption to move over and lean on the podium. It was a sturdy walnut stand set now to face the jury box. Charlie took a wheezy breath, then continued. "Now, I could run us through this and that, but I'm old enough to know you'll be sitting there through it all thinking, This is just lawyer talk. He's paid to say what he's saying. Am I right there, folks?"

Marcus watched as a few jurors rewarded him with smiles, even a couple of nods. They were a mixed group about whom he knew almost nothing. The defense had made judicious use of their strikes, holding the number of blacks down to the dentist and two older women. All the six white males, one of whom was jury foreman, bore the mark of hard work and the outdoors — scarcely the type to show sympathy for a black female activist. The three white women had the appearance of senior staffers, severe in bearing and alert. All Marcus knew for certain was that the final seven choices attended church every Sunday. Until Ashley's call, it had seemed to be enough.

"So I'm not going to hold you here for hours on end, showing off what's left of my voice," Charlie went on. "The evidence and the witnesses will speak for themselves."

Charlie let the podium do for a crutch and pointed toward the defense with his cane. "Right down there is New Horizons Incorporated and their bunch of fancy-suited lawyers. One of the biggest textile companies in the world. Sports, fashion, shoes, the works. Almost two billion dollars in sales. Everybody knows 'em. I imagine some of you have kids wearing their clothes. They've got the splashiest ads, the hottest music, the biggest names in sports today. But what those ads don't tell you is how New Horizons clothes are stained with innocent blood."

"Objection!"

"Sustained. The jury is instructed to ignore that remark. Mr. Hayes, watch yourself."

"Yes indeed, Your Honor. Thank you." Charlie thumped his cane upon the floor. "I said I'd keep this short, and I'm a man of my word. All I need to tell you now is that by the time we're done here, you're going to have a very different picture of New Horizons Incorporated. One that leads you not just to believe — no, but to know that they have kidnapped and abused and held against her will a young local woman named Gloria Hall. I do sincerely thank you."

Charlie limped back to his seat before either the defense or the judge recovered from their surprise.

"That's it?" Logan Kendall rose to his feet. "That's all they have?"

Judge Nicols demanded, "Mr. Hayes, are you done?"

"I am indeed, Your Honor." Charlie fished out a handkerchief and wiped his face. "And may I say, a more attentive jury I've never had the pleasure of addressing."

"Your Honor, this is absurd!" Logan stopped halfway to the bench. "The plaintiff has not connected the company in any way to this woman's disappearance!"

Judge Nicols lowered her head in a warning glare. "Is that the defense's opening statement?"

Logan caught himself. "No, Your Honor. Defense waives its opening statement, but reserves the right to claim it later." He retreated to his table, muttering just loud enough for the jury to hear, "If the trial actually manages to last that long."

"Very well." Judge Nicols turned to the jury. "The defense will not address you now, but may do so later on. This will probably take place before they call their own witnesses."

Logan remained standing. "Your Honor, once again we move to dismiss this case. The plaintiff's opening statement shows this whole thing to be nothing more than a sham."

"No, I am going to allow it to continue. For now." Her gaze was hard and searching. "Mr. Glenwood, Mr. Hayes, you have your work cut out for you." She banged her gavel. "Court is adjourned until nine o'clock tomorrow morning."

Thursday's dawn found Marcus already at work. The sunrise was filtered through his two favorite trees, the sycamore tall and looming, the dogwood gnarled and thick-limbed as a Florida oak. Marcus sat at his desk and wrestled with strategy. An hour or so later, Darren slipped a breakfast plate and a fresh cup of coffee in front of him, then left without saying a word.

When Marcus emerged from the house it was to find Amos Culpepper standing with Darren next to an unmarked car. The two were in the process of shaking hands, a sight that warmed Marcus as much as breakfast.

Amos said in greeting, "Looks like we've managed to clear up that misunderstanding with the local police."

Marcus stowed his load of papers in the

Jeep. "This is very good news."

"My visits over at New Horizons haven't done much but ruffle a few feathers. They claim they don't have a single Lonnie on staff, and they've never heard of anybody fitting the description of your gray attacker. Felt the need to deny that before I even finished my description." He squinted down the street as he asked, "What'd you think of the New Horizons reception area?"

"Very cold, very New York."

"Seems kinda strange how they need to have two armed bruisers guarding a textile company's front office."

"They've got a lot of celebrities coming and going over there."

"Maybe so." Amos started toward his car. "Thought I'd ride along with you, hang back a ways, see if that pickup makes another appearance."

The drive was uneventful. Amos walked him to the courthouse door and handed him over to Jim Bell, the judge's receptionist. The retired patrolman clearly took the attack on Marcus during his watch very seriously.

Charlie was there and waiting for him, making quiet conversation with Alma Hall. "Austin teaches class this morning," Alma said in greeting. "He wanted to come but I told him to go on to school."

"Whatever you two feel is best." Marcus turned to Charlie. "We need to talk."

Charlie reached over and patted Alma's arm. "You remember what I told you, now."

Marcus led him over to the empty jury box. "What were you saying?"

"Not a thing you need to worry over. She's scared, she's not sleeping, she's got strategies that'd wake a plucked goose. I heard her out and then told her to trust you."

"When did all this happen?"

"Last night and again this morning. Fine-looking young lady they got staying with them, by the way." The man sounded ten years younger and had a kick to his heels. "I assume you know who I mean. Blond, slender, smart as a whip, most remarkable eyes I ever did see."

"It's a shame she won't give me the time of day."

"Now that's strange, seeing how she fair hung on every word I said about you."

Marcus could not tell if the old man was joking, so he handed over the folder and said, "I've gone through and made a list of today's and tomorrow's witnesses. You have one key question for each witness. Take your time, establish each one carefully, hammer that one point home as much as you like."

Charlie scanned the morning's work and surmised, "Past practice."

"Exactly." Past practice was a legal jungle, with hundreds of rulings on either side. "Hopefully the judge will allow us at least to suggest this was not an isolated case."

"The defense will be all over this with bazookas."

"I know. Can you handle that?"

"I'm feeling a mite peckish this morning. Wouldn't mind taking a bite or two out of a fancy-suited lawyer." He closed the folder. "You think they did this to young Gloria Hall?"

"I'm more convinced with every passing day."

"Then vile and treacherous don't even begin to describe them." Charlie nodded to where the bailiff was holding open the door to the judge's chambers. "Let's get to work."

Charlie followed the order and the strategy with a veteran's ease. Marcus sat and rested and grew stronger, and marveled at the old man's ability. Charlie Hayes limped badly, his dentures clicked occasionally, his eyesight was mostly absent. But he remained a master in the courtroom. His timing rivaled that of a Shakespearean actor. The jury followed his every move.

The first witness was a local labor expert. Charlie walked him through his testimony on the textile industry's employment structure, detailing how textile companies preferred economically struggling regions because they hired large numbers of low-skilled workers. Such areas paid premiums to have the companies come, offering grants in the form of free land and tax subsidies and low-cost loans. Charlie paused at that moment, then slipped in the question Marcus had intentionally not raised at deposition. "If such companies don't require highly skilled workers, wouldn't it be easier for them to leave?"

The expert's surprise was evident. "Leave?"

"Sure, just pick up sticks and walk away. Go somewhere else willing to bribe them, soon as they've got trouble on their hands."

"Objection." The word did not come from Logan Kendall, but rather from one of the firm's young associates. "Irrelevant."

"Sustained."

"No further questions." Charlie headed back. "Your witness."

"No questions at this time, Your Honor."

Charlie scanned the sheet Marcus held out for him, said, "Plaintiff calls Weldon Smith."

Smith was the director of industrial development for eastern North Carolina. Charlie had him describe the difficulties in attracting a company to invest in Edgecombe County. The man was only too eager to explain how important New Horizons was to the local economy. Thirty-nine hundred jobs. New national headquarters. Great free publicity for a depressed area. Tax revenue. Boost to local businesses. New incoming suppliers.

"You mentioned taxes earned from the company." Charlie limped over to where Marcus had a page ready. "Do you have any idea how much in taxes New Horizons has paid?"

"How could I? That's none of my concern."

"I submit that it is very much your concern, since you arranged a ten-year tax exemption, and have offered them a further ten-year exemption for this new expansion of theirs." Charlie headed toward the witness stand. "They haven't paid one plug nickel in state taxes, now, have they?"

"Objection, Your Honor, this case is supposedly about some incident at a Chinese factory. It has nothing to do with local tax records."

"Sustained."

Charlie pressed on, "Is it not also true that the New Horizons group has been a headache from day one, and there are currently five outstanding legal actions the state has itself brought against the company?"

"Objection!"

"Sustained."

"No further questions."

"Defense, your witness."

A young associate rose to his feet. "Your Honor, I cannot ask questions of the witness since the plaintiff has failed to show any connection to the case we are here to try!"

"The witness may stand down." Judge Nicols gestured to both tables. "Counsel approach the bench."

Marcus stayed where he was, and noted how Logan glanced his way before doing the same. The young associate went forward to argue with Charlie. Marcus found tight satisfaction in the fact that Logan was planning strategy as well, matching him move for move. If Marcus was holding back, so was he. It meant Logan was treating the case seriously. This was the best sign of all.

Friday continued in the same vein, with

Charlie questioning and the same young associate defending. Judge Nicols allowed evidence on the issue of past practice, but with stern reservations: She might withdraw support if Marcus did not supply proof of a connection with the Chinese factory.

A local pastor testified to New Horizons' maltreatment of migrant Hispanic workers. A young labor activist described the difficulties she had faced trying to organize an in-house union; her car had been bombed, her sympathizers ferreted out and fired. On cross-examination, however, she was forced to admit that she had no concrete proof to tie the company to these misdeeds.

An aging union VP was brought to the stand after vigorous objections by the defense. The New Horizons factory he had attempted to organize, located outside Tulsa, had been using Mexican immigrants and paying them half the promised salary. They had been housed in unsanitary conditions, forced into debt by buying from a company store, fired at whim, paid no overtime, harassed, and abused. Objections continued to rain down.

That afternoon Charlie called both available company vice presidents to the stand. His tone was quietly mocking as he had first one and then the other go down the entire list of board members and senior directors, asking only where each one was. The answers were all the same. Geneva, Switzerland. Charlie asked how much responsibility either man had for overseas factories. The answer was the same from both: none.

In cross-examination, the young associate asked about ties to Factory 101. Both men had been well-schooled. They described how the North Carolina distribution center accepted goods from twenty-seven different countries. Was China among them? Of course, since China was the world's largest producer of finished textiles outside of the United States. Every major company in the business imported from China. Twice Charlie asked Marcus quietly if he should re-address the issue that neither man had anything to do with international operations. Marcus declined with a shake of his head. Either Ashley came up with the goods, or the case was almost done.

His day's greatest delight came after the court had adjourned, in the form of a man of mismatched parts. His bulbous head was fitted to a scrawny neck and a potbelly. His checked jacket and yellow pants seemed selected to mock a frame he disliked too much to clothe well. "Mr.

Glenwood, I'm Floyd Sneede with the *Raleigh News and Observer*."

Marcus noticed Boomer Hayes waiting by the rear doors, then returned his attention to the reporter. "Yes."

" 'Vile and treacherous.' Isn't that how Mr. Hayes described New Horizons in his opening statement?"

"You'll have to ask Charlie, but I believe that's correct."

"The lawyers for New Horizons told me they'd sue the paper if I wrote that you were attacked by somebody associated with the company."

It was the opening Marcus had hoped for. "I guess you'd better pay attention, then. Your newspaper wouldn't want to offend a big advertiser like that."

The barb bit deep. "You're saying they were involved?"

"Absolutely. I was told to drop the case or they'd be back to kill me."

The pen scribbled busily. "You want to give me a quote about the case?"

"New Horizons has made its name through exploitation. They exploit the nation's kids by suggesting that if they buy New Horizons' overpriced products, the kids will all become sports superheroes. New Horizons makes these same products in factories that exploit and abuse workers in truly horrible conditions. A young local woman by the name of Gloria Hall set out to expose their pattern of corruption and degradation. They kidnapped Ms. Hall to silence her."

The man's grin was as misshapen as the rest of him. "You sure you want me to quote you?"

"If you want a real quote, go speak to the girl's parents. They'll blister the paint off the newsroom walls." Marcus excused himself and walked over to where Boomer stood in a jacket and silk tie of Carolina blue. "What are you doing here?"

"Daddy sure is something, ain't he?" Boomer's tone was as low and respectful as he could get it. "Seventy-eight next month and not pulling a single punch."

"You came to watch him try a case?"

"Partly. Wanted to tell you the old man's been spending some time with the doctors. Hasn't said a word to anybody, but Libby knows a nurse over at the hospital." Boomer tried hard for brisk, almost succeeded. "Word is, Pop's got cancer."

Marcus felt the day rocked on its axis. "You're joking."

"Wish I was." Boomer's grin had escaped him, leaving his features puffy and very worried. "The nurse says it ain't too serious, whatever that means for somebody carting around his weight of years.

He's supposed to start treatment next week, but he put it off for this case."

Marcus turned back to where Charlie and Alma were giving the reporter an earful. "He hasn't told me a thing."

"Naw, that'd be his way. But Libby and I thought you'd want to know. She said to tell you that since he started working with you on this, the old Charlie was back again. Said she hadn't seen much of him since your accident. Says it's another reason we've got to be grateful. If I were you, though, I'd keep this under my hat. Won't do a bit of good to let on you know."

"No," Marcus agreed, "I don't suppose it would."

Boomer pointed with his chin to where Charlie was helping Alma sit back down as the reporter left. The old man took the chair beside her and draped one arm around her shoulders. "What's he doing now?"

"Just seeing to his job," Marcus said quietly. "Comforting the wounded and offering hope to the lost."

TWENTY-SIX

All of Saturday was given over to a hospital visit. Marcus was prodded and questioned and blooded and scanned, and finally pronounced fit enough to depart.

Sunday morning was metallic in its sunny frost. Tall trees sheltering the road to church were graced with autumn finery. Though the sun seemed intent on bearing down hard by afternoon, there was a comfort in the chill and a rightness to the day.

Ashley Granger called at dusk. "Hope you don't mind getting good news on Sunday evening."

"You've got to be kidding." Marcus carried the cordless phone into his office. "It's either now or no case. We're down to the wire."

"Not anymore. I've got good news and I've got great news. The good news first. The Factory 101 compound is run by none other than General Zhao Ren-Fan himself."

"First you need to spell that name," Marcus replied. "Then you need to tell me who he is."

"I'll fax you the details later. Zhao is none other than the top dog of the Guangdong military region."

"Sorry. I'm still lost." But growing excited nonetheless.

"Provincial power in China is split between the local Communist Party and the People's Liberation Army. They're supposed to operate as one, but that almost never happens. The conflict is growing steadily these days. The top power holder in each province operates freely and openly. And in the Guangdong region, it's the military. Has been ever since Tiananmen Square, when General Zhao's troops were in the thick of things."

"So the guy has power."

"In China, there's no difference between *business* power and *political* power. Power is power. The military operates its own businesses, factories, international licenses. Foreign firms who're looking for clout in the local markets don't just accept the need for high-level partners. They seek them out. They hunt them down. The best mark of success in China for a start-up company is the local partner's standing."

"And this general's got the clout?"

"In Guangzhou, there's probably nobody with more. Not only that, he's got a hold on power in Beijing. He's a member of the military command, has access to the top party hierarchy. He's a voice to be reckoned with."

"And the factory?"

"Right. Now, run what we know so far through your mind. The top general is openly responsible for savage acts, first in Tiananmen Square, then putting down the rioting farmers. He owns a compound outside the central city, and in this compound he's got a plant that operates as a commercial *lao gai,* a factory prison where political troublemakers are held without trial or right of appeal."

Marcus was too tense to sit. He paced the room, searching, finally confessing, "I'm still caught in a serious crunch here. I've got to find something to tie all this directly to New Horizons."

"Well now, there's something interesting on that front as well. Your fax machine on?"

"Yes."

"Wait and watch, my man. Wait and watch." As the machine lit up and started purring, Ashley went on. "Two things. First, I've been getting some strong-arm pressure from the U.S. side as well. Somebody in Washington is turning up the heat on this trial."

Marcus plucked up the first page, read

swiftly, could only manage, "Oh man, oh man."

"Second, I got a call from Dee this afternoon. Told him what I'm telling you. The man didn't seem at all surprised. More like pleased that I'd finally tracked this down." When Marcus did not respond, he demanded more loudly, "You hearing me over there?"

Marcus picked up the second sheet, and felt his heart rate surge until listening was almost impossible. "Yes."

"You better be. Dee told me to have you subpoena a guy from the Swiss embassy. I'm faxing you his name with the rest of this stuff. Last page. Dee said to tell you to be prepared just in case. In case of what, he wouldn't say. That little brown elf does love his secrets."

Marcus pulled the third sheet from the machine before it was ready, fraying the edge. "I don't believe this."

It was the response Ashley had been waiting for. "It's good, isn't it."

"This," Marcus said feverishly, "is pure solid gold."

Randall Walker could not find a parking space along the club's great front oval, which only intensified his bad mood. He had been pressing the board since the renovation for the oval to be reserved for senior members, a suggestion they had chosen to ignore. Which meant that when he arrived late for a function, such as now, he was forced to park back near the tennis courts and walk. Randall Walker despised anything that detracted from a grand entrance.

But his smile was in place and his worries masked by the time he passed beneath the Grecian portico and entered the ceremonial foyer. Randall had been one of the movers and shakers behind the club's renovation, joining with other like-minded kingmakers who said it was time Raleigh declared itself to be the power it was. The original clubhouse had served three generations and had possessed about as much majesty as a pair of house slippers. Under pressure from Randall and his cronies, the architect originally assigned the renovation had been fired. A new one had been brought in from Chicago, and plans drawn up for a mansion on the hill. Members had been assessed thirty-five thousand dollars each, annual dues were raised fivefold, new members were charged a hefty fifty-thousand-dollar initiation fee, and those of long standing who could not afford the payments were urged to leave. The resulting battle had been well worth it in Randall's eyes, for now the club did not just impress, it overpowered. One hundred and ten thousand square feet of rooms. Two hundred and eleven Persian carpets. Forty-six crystal chandeliers. Halls thirty-two feet wide. Six bars. Five restaurants, two in the golf pavilion. If only they had listened to him about parking around the great oval.

Randall adjusted the lapels of his dinner jacket and smoothed what remained of his hair. He could do nothing about his age, and he had long since decided to ignore the bulging legacy of poor diet and no exercise. Southern gentlemen did not need to age into lean greyhounds. They ruled by a code all their own. His tailor was chosen for his ability to lie with cloth and needle. He liked young women who were as generous with their praise as he was with his diamonds. So long as both parties knew and neither minded, what did it matter?

Randall patted a back, shook a hand, moved like a ballet star making the night's grand entrance. He spotted his prey, held back, chose his moment well. It was only when people began moving toward the next salon and the evening meal that he allowed the crowd to steer him toward the pair. "George, Weldon, my but don't you boys look the stuff tonight."

"Randall, where have you been hiding?"

The governor's top aide was compact and smiled with all the warmth of a jolly Japanese ice sculpture. "We got you a seat at our table or somebody's gonna be looking for another job tomorrow."

"No, can't stay. Can't stay. Got another dinner to attend." Randall massaged the second man's arm, the industrial-development director for eastern North Carolina. "Hear you took quite a beating there on the stand, Weldon."

"Old Weldon can take care of himself," the aide claimed. "Right, son?"

"They didn't lay a glove on me." The man had the face of a dedicated drinker who was two glasses over his customary limit. "We just danced a little tango, is all."

"Maybe so, but I got word that the New Horizons folk are worried. And the newspaper story this morning didn't help matters one bit."

The smiles disappeared. Randall found no resistance as he drew the pair aside. "Got me a call from Switzerland this morning. Woke me from the nicest dream. Been sweating ever since." He paused for dramatic effect, then delivered the bomb. "New Horizons is thinking about pulling out of North Carolina."

"They can't be serious," the aide scoffed. "One little piece like that isn't

394

cause for panic."

"Front page below the fold isn't what I call little. And they see this as a possible trend."

"Trend my left haunch. The reporter was looking for mud. That lawyer fellow and the girl's momma gave him some. End of story."

"There's gonna be more mud, long as that case drags on." Randall let a little of the steel show through. "New Horizons has done it before, gentlemen. You know it as well as I do. They'll pull up stakes and be gone tomorrow. This isn't some kind of distant warning I'm talking about here. This is nothing but the dead-solid truth. New Horizons is already putting out feelers to other states and making contingency plans."

"I can't believe this." The industrial director's flush had deepened. "I sweated blood to get them in there."

"This would be a terrible loss, coming in the face of next year's election," the governor's aide fretted.

A man nervously approached the aide. "Excuse me, George, but you're supposed to be seated up at the front."

"I'm going to be a few more minutes here."

"But you're —"

George silenced him with a single look.

"You go ahead and start, hear what I'm saying?"

When they were alone once more, George said to Randall, "You didn't show up here just to spread gloom and doom."

"There's only one way I can see to stanch this flow of adverse publicity," Randall replied. "And that's to put a stop to this harassment suit."

"Hard to do," the aide said, "seeing as how we're dealing with a federal case that's already in front of a jury. The judge is newly appointed, so even if Nicols is as ambitious as they say, she won't be hungry for the next step. Not yet."

George's level of awareness surprised Randall, but he decided now was the time to use it, not question it. "I've got me a couple of ideas."

The two men heard him out in silence. George accepted the suggestions with a single nod and the words, "I'll see what we can do."

"Whatever it is, it needs to happen fast."

"I told you I'd look into things, Randall."

He ignored the tone, and gave in to his curiosity. "Nice to know you folks over in the governor's mansion are keeping such a close eye on things."

"Don't have much choice," the aide responded, his gaze sharp and biting. "Not when the governor receives a Saturday-evening call from the White House. Somebody up in Washington asking about a little local nuisance case over the week-end, that's enough to light the warning fires, wouldn't you say?"

"Absolutely," Randall agreed solemnly.

"You wouldn't happen to know how this thing has reached all the way to Pennsylvania Avenue, now, would you, Randall?"

"No idea whatsoever," he replied, hiding his pleasure with all his might.

TWENTY-SEVEN

Marcus arrived at his courtroom table to find a manila folder waiting for him. His heart surged lightly at the familiar writing, only to ebb when he saw that Kirsten had left no note. He tried hard to be pleased at the thin pile of minor explosions in the form of further photocopied documents. Alma watched him riffle through the stack, and waited until he reached the last page to say, "Marcus, we have to talk."

He sighed and shut the folder. "I know we do."

"Austin tells me I should let you be. But there are things we need to know."

Marcus nodded acceptance. "I'll try to make it by your place tonight."

The tense set to her shoulders eased somewhat. "Thank you."

"Where is Kirsten? I haven't heard from her in days."

Despite the courtroom and the week to come, Alma had to smile. "Now, that's a curious thing. The lady spent all weekend going through the papers you see there and doing a dance around the phone.

One step forward, another step back. Never did work up the nerve, though what's holding her back I could not say."

He had to ask, "You think she wanted to call me?"

Alma gave the low chuckle of one saddened yet vastly amused. "That is the only foolish thing I have ever heard you say."

Charlie saved him by huffing up. "Sorry, folks, the old bones didn't want to obey me today. You're looking lovely as ever, Alma."

The bailiff entered through the judge's door and announced, "All rise."

Marcus said in a soft aside, "I'll be handling the questioning today."

Charlie rewarded him with a grand smile. "You heard from that Washington lawyer feller?"

"Last night."

"He supplied us with the goods?"

"The best I've ever seen."

Charlie sighed and lowered himself down into his chair as Judge Nicols settled herself. "I always did love fireworks and things that go bang."

As Judge Nicols bid the jury a polite good morning and inquired about their weekend, Marcus whispered, "I'm going to request a new witness be subpoenaed. If she grants it, you need to run out and phone this number." He handed over a slip of paper. "Tell him to expedite the papers."

Charlie noticed the area code. "Washington."

"The process server should be standing outside the guy's office at this very moment."

Judge Nicols turned toward their table and demanded, "Mr. Glenwood, are you ready to proceed?"

Marcus rose slowly, noting that the judge's eyebrows lifted in response. Logan stiffened ever so slightly in his seat. Marcus said, "Permission to approach the bench."

"Granted."

It was Logan who walked forward to represent the defense. Marcus did not need to glance over to know Logan was as keenly taut as he. "Your Honor, there has been unnecessary foot-dragging by the State Department with regard to our request for depositions from the New Horizons board members. Not even the first of these has taken place."

"I object to both the tone and the content of this accusation, Your Honor," Logan shot back. "The plaintiff's counsel is taking what is a normal business situation, the annual general meeting of the company's international divisions, and turning it into something sinister. Or trying to. Of course these depositions take time. These are busy men."

"And this is an urgent matter, one that our embassy officials have clearly put on the back burner." Marcus handed over the document containing the name supplied by Ashley Granger. "I have identified the man at State who is responsible for such matters. Grey Hadley is acting assistant director of the division of consular affairs. He is scheduled to be leaving the country the day after tomorrow. I hereby request a subpoena be issued immediately, so that we may have him testify prior to his departure."

"Your Honor, this is preposterous!" Logan leaned both fists on the corner of the judge's bench. "We've acted in good faith here, despite the fact that this is a case built out of thin air. Right over there are two senior vice presidents —"

"Of the North Carolina distribution center," Marcus added. "Who have nothing whatsoever to do with international activities."

"— who have already sacrificed a full week of their time just to be here and show the company flag."

"They cannot answer for anything to do with the company's ties to Factory 101, Your Honor. Which is all we are after.

One single person who has the power to sign off on international activities."

"Excuse me, Your Honor, but can't you see the plaintiff's strategy here? They're trying to bring another chess piece into play. They conceal what they can. They shuffle the pieces around to confuse the viewer. When things get tight, they move in another piece. They distract your attention. They frighten you. They threaten with more smoke and mirrors. No doubt when this is over they'll refile their claims, set up groundless appeals, tie up the courts with prevarication."

Judge Nicols observed Logan Kendall with an onyx mask. "Are you just about done?"

Logan backed off a fraction. "Yes, Your Honor."

She turned back to her inspection of the records, then handed them to the aide poised by her chair. "So moved. Have an affidavit drawn up immediately."

"Thank you, Your Honor. I took the liberty of doing so this morning." Marcus waited as she inspected the new pages, and he decided there would be no better time than this. "I have one other name I'd like to add to my original list, and for similar reasons." He handed over the second document. "Hans Klein, of the Swiss embassy in Washington."

She passed on it before Logan could frame a response. "So moved. Anything else?"

"No, Your Honor."

"Very well. Call your next witness."

Marcus walked back to his table, knowing that it was not just his imagination that the courtroom air was now singed with compacted energy. "Plaintiff calls Marshall Taub to the stand."

It was Logan who reached behind him, taking the file an assistant had ready to hand over. Several of the jurors moved slightly forward in their chairs. There was no change to the routine, except now it was the lawyer with the bruised and bandaged face and one arm in a sling who stood. All the same, the jury knew that the trial had taken a different tone.

To his lasting credit, Marshall Taub was not only sober, he was presentable. Nothing could be done about the Richmond lawyer's pasty features or the broken blood vessels across his nose and cheeks. But his dark suit was neatly pressed, his hand steady as it reached for the Bible, his voice resonant and firm as he swore to tell nothing but the truth.

Marcus started off slow and easy, going over the more successful aspects of Taub's career — his partnership with one of Virginia's oldest firms, his holding of office in the state bar association. The defense remained silent throughout. Marcus then asked, "You are involved in a long-running dispute with New Horizons, are you not?"

"Objection!" Logan vaulted from his chair. "Permission to approach the bench."

This time it was Marcus who followed Logan's march to the judge's stand. His opponent was ready. It was no longer a skirmish.

Logan launched directly into attack. "Your Honor, this is one Pandora's box you definitely do not want to allow them to open."

Marcus did not hide his intentions at all. "As Charlie Hayes indicated last week, Your Honor, we are establishing a pattern of past practice. New Horizons has a long history of such unsavory activities."

"This is totally irrelevant, Your Honor."

"Wherever New Horizons has set up operations, litigation has followed. They have left a trail wide as the Mississippi and just as murky."

Logan looked directly at him for the first time that day. "Very cute. Did your colleague come up with that one?"

"A little less histrionics, Mr. Glenwood," Judge Nicols agreed.

Logan took that as his cue. "There is no similarity of action, Your Honor. On the one hand you have labor relations at U.S. facilities. On the other you have a *Chinese* factory with no established connection to my client."

Marcus felt a singular thrill. Logan knew, or at least he suspected, that more was to come.

Logan kept his eye on the judge. "These other cases have been litigated and resolved, Your Honor, usually in the company's favor. And I might add that most of these cases have been underwritten by labor. These are classic union tactics, Your Honor. Throw mud at the company until they agree to whatever the union is demanding. Personally, I wonder whether the unions are financing this case as well."

"Your Honor, I object to these baseless insinuations."

But Logan was not finished. "Do you want to litigate on the issue at hand, Your Honor? Or do you want to litigate the past? It is patently unfair to give such extraneous information to the jury. We've got to stick to the facts here. And the facts are, the plaintiff has no case. There is nothing to tie my North Carolina clients to some problem nine thousand miles away."

Judge Nicols hesitated a long moment. Then, "I am going to allow this. But, Mr. Glenwood, I must warn you once more. A stronger tie must be shown."

"Thank you, Your Honor," Marcus said, turning away before either Logan or the judge could see what his adrenaline rush threatened to reveal. He did not have a tie, but at least Ashley had handed him some rope.

Through the rest of that morning and much of the afternoon, Marcus led the Richmond lawyer through his own research into New Horizons' activities. A ream of court records was submitted as evidence, with Charlie Hayes passing out summaries to the jurors. Charlie greeted the jurors with silent nods, showing that even a retired federal judge was not above waiting on them. It was an unexpected boon, the old man working as a willing assistant, and one that did not go unnoticed by the defense. Logan watched with frowning intent as Charlie rose time after time, but could find no reason to object.

New Horizons' pattern unfolded like a great and intricate fan. The company was shown to have a history of moving into an area and barely skirting the law. Taub described how he had been involved in a case he had first won, then watched as the New Horizons lawyers buried it with appeals. Marcus did not go further at that moment. Logan would first wield his knife and draw blood, there was no question of that. Then Marcus would try to stitch up the wound.

They moved on from the Richmond trial itself to patterns in other cases, the number of which totaled just over four dozen. Migrant-worker abuses, failure to pay overtime, minimum-wage violations, collective-bargaining problems, environmental infractions, assault and battery of union organizers, bribery of local officials.

Logan was up and out of his seat before Marcus could frame the words "No further questions." Logan approached the witness stand with a predatory stalk. "Mr. Taub, let's go back to some of the unfounded accusations you just leveled against my client. You seem so aware of everything. Would you be able to tell the jury precisely how many of the aforementioned cases were actually won by the plaintiffs involved?"

"New Horizons has very good lawyers."

"That's not what I asked. Answer the question, Mr. Taub. How many were won by the accusers?"

"My own, for a starter."

"Your own, yes, we'll come back to

your case in just a moment. But how many of the others have been resolved in favor of the plaintiffs. It's not a difficult question. Try and give us a straight answer this time."

"The straight answer is that whenever the lower courts found for the plaintiff, the company tied up the decision in appeal."

"That is not the answer, Mr. Taub. That is not the answer. Your Honor, I ask that you instruct the witness to pay attention."

"You are an attorney, Mr. Taub," Judge Nicols admonished. "You know the procedure here on cross."

"Yes, Your Honor." Marshall Taub turned back to the defense attorney with an expression that was both weary and resigned. But his voice remained rock-steady. "I would imagine very few."

"None at all is the correct answer, Mr. Taub. None at all. An interesting fact to escape your attention when you and the plaintiff's lawyer were so intent on sullying my client's good name. Not one of these cases has been resolved against my client. None. Zero. Zip." Logan waited a moment, then added, "Do you have any idea how the number of cases against New Horizons compares with those brought against other companies its size?"

"No."

"Interesting how this second vital statistic has been missed as well. But you are aware, are you not, that there is a steady rise in litigation aimed at big American businesses, as hungry lawyers and greedy plaintiffs seek to profit from nuisance cases like this one?"

"Objection, Your Honor."

"Sustained. The jury is instructed to disregard those comments."

Logan stepped away, distancing himself from the jury box and the fray. From the room's far end he asked, "You have had some problems of your own, haven't you, Mr. Taub."

"Yes." The man straightened his shoulders, though it cost him. He kept his voice strong, though it cost him more. "I have."

"Indeed you have. Many problems." Logan moved back to his table, accepted the paper handed him by Suzie Rikkers. "You were fired from your law firm, were you not?"

"I resigned."

"They found you incompetent in your duties, is that not correct?"

"I resigned," he repeated, looking at nothing.

"You declared personal bankruptcy, not once but twice. Is that not also correct?"

"Yes."

"And you have been disciplined by the state bar on two separate occasions," Logan's voice rose in surprised incredulity. "For showing up drunk in court?"

Marshall Taub remained stoic, unbowed. "Yes."

"Do you feel that leaves you in any position whatsoever to criticize my client, or to taint its reputation?"

"Objection!"

"I withdraw the remarks," Logan said, retreating to his table. "No further questions."

Marcus rose and slowly approached the stand. The shameful pain was etched deep on Taub's unhealthy features. Marcus could offer nothing by way of comfort, except a single slow nod. The Richmond attorney had stood up well. "Mr. Taub, about the case you brought against New Horizons. How did the lower court find in that trial?"

"They found the company guilty on all counts, and awarded my clients seven million dollars."

"Guilty on all counts," Marcus replied slowly. "And how long ago was that?"

"Six years ago."

"What has happened since then?"

"The company's attorneys have appealed, and attached to the appeal more than forty different motions. I devoted all my time to arguing these motions. Fighting this case cost my partnership almost nine hundred thousand dollars." His voice was toneless, his gaze aimed at all his past errors. "Finally they told me to either quit the case or quit the firm. I resigned. I put everything I had into fighting the case. I lost my family. I lost everything."

"Do you have any idea how many other cases have resulted in such an avalanche of appeals?"

"I have been in direct contact with nine other lawyers, all of whom won in lower courts. None has received a single penny in compensation. Four have —"

"Objection!"

"I withdraw the question." Marcus returned to his table, embittered by the exchange. "No further questions, Your Honor."

"The witness is excused. Court is adjourned until nine o'clock tomorrow morning." Judge Nicols paused for a moment before rising, long enough to issue Marcus a stern but silent warning. He gave her nothing but grimness in return. Charlie had requested fireworks. Fireworks there would be.

The sky was dark by the time Darren drove into the Halls' development. The

411

houses were so new they shone in the streetlights. Most, however, were adorned with whimsical Victorian flairs. Corner windows bowed around cupolas with high-paneled roofs. Porches were graced with intricate latticework. Light streamed out from almost every window he saw, gold and welcoming. Marcus found his tired mind wishing the unseen dwellers well, hoping they would never know the vagaries of unforeseen tragedy, yet suspecting even this fine scene withheld secrets of fear and need and woe.

As they pulled into the driveway, Alma Hall was already shutting the front door and buttoning her sweater. Marcus took this as a bad sign, and wished he had more energy to deal with the coming onslaught.

But the woman offered her own tired smile in greeting. "Austin's fallen asleep on the living-room sofa. It's the first real rest he's had in weeks. Do you mind if we talk out here?"

"Not at all."

"The poor man is wound up so tight I'm afraid he's going to snap." She leaned down and said through the open car window, "Hello, Darren."

"M-Mrs. Hall."

Marcus asked, "How are you?"

"Oh, I'm about the same as Austin,

only I hide it better." Another attempted smile flickered beneath the streetlight. "It was good to see you perform up there today. But that poor Mr. Taub."

"Is that what you wanted to see me about?"

"No. Will you take a turn with me?" Alma waited until they had left the driveway and entered the sea of night to reveal her nerves. "I want to know when you're going to show that videotape of them hurting my little girl."

"Probably never, Alma. I can't." Most cases held some evidence or angle of attack that the client felt was crucial but that, from a legal perspective, was a ticking bomb. The difficulty was in making the logic of court procedure shine clearly through his client's emotional storm. Marcus held to a gentle tone as he explained, "The issue is what the court calls establishing a chain of possession."

"I don't care about that!"

"You should, Alma. This is vital. We have to authenticate the evidence by showing exactly where the tape was made and how it came to be in our hands. The defense knows about the tape, it's listed as evidence and they have a copy. They can very easily exclude it because there is no way to tie it to the Chinese factory."

They entered the next island of streetlight. Alma clutched the front of her sweater with both hands, bunching it tightly across her middle. The yellow light turned her features waxy and translucent. Her eyes were dark and wide as nightmare pits.

When she said nothing, Marcus continued, "We are treading a very thin line here. Remember, our focus is on gaining publicity and finding out what happened to Gloria."

The cry seemed wrenched from the very night. "Then show them that tape! Let the world see what those fiends have done to my child!"

Marcus halted between the lights, where the dark offered this proud woman a private space. "We can't do that, Alma. All it shows is a badly beaten young woman in a concrete cell. There is nothing to tie it anywhere, not even to China. The defense *wants* us to show the tape. Why? Because they can then say we have based our entire case on something that is patently flimsy. Unless we have something to demonstrate there is a direct causal link between New Horizons and the making of that tape, we cannot show it. We cannot."

When Alma remained silent, Marcus draped his good arm over her shoulders. Her entire body trembled from the impact of sobs she did not wish to release. They stood at the border of the nearest street-light, while overhead leaves of a neighboring oak rustled like yellow parchment. When she finally took a deep breath and regained her composure, Marcus steered her around and started back up the street.

Her words were as quiet as the night. "All last night I was remembering times from Gloria's growing-up years. Austin and I have been involved in civil rights since before we were married. Austin marched three times with Reverend King. I was heavily involved in local politics and education. Austin used to call us foot soldiers in the battle for civil rights. I helped manage the campaign of the first black man elected to the United States Congress from this state. Gloria was eleven at the time. She loved it from the start, worked day in and day out, stuffing envelopes or passing out leaflets or putting up posters. She was a born activist."

"She sounds like a very fine woman," Marcus said, liking Alma immensely, imagining what it must have been like to grow up in such a household with these two people as beacons. And challenges.

The woman's tone deepened with worry. "I lay there all last night, remembering these things and praying the good Lord would give me a sign. Something to show my baby was all right. That she wasn't . . ."

Marcus could do nothing but hold her shoulders tightly and slow to match her broken pace. "You might both want to come to court tomorrow. Hopefully we're going to spring a little surprise."

Planning for the next day gave Alma a reason to recover. "Austin and I are taking time off work. Neither of us is doing anything save worry. The schools understand. We're on sabbatical until after the trial."

He could think of a dozen reasons why this was not a good idea. But it was their decision, and nothing would be gained by arguing. As they turned down the driveway he looked at the house and searched the windows. "Is Kirsten around?"

Sad humor tinged her words. "The lady took off the instant she heard you were stopping by."

"Any idea why she hates me so?"

The chuckle became clearer in her voice. "Kirsten doesn't dislike you, honey. She's torn, is all."

"By what?"

"Now, that I can't say. I've known her for years, ever since she and Gloria started living together at Georgetown. I thought I knew her as well as I do anyone, but I've found myself learning something new these past few days. This girl is mighty comfortable with her mysteries."

His mind flitted like a moth about a flame. "Strange how they lived together all that time and Kirsten never met Gloria's boyfriend."

"I don't know where you got that idea." Alma slid from his arm and started wearily up her front steps. "She introduced them."

The news planted Marcus firmly. "What?"

"Gary Loh did volunteer work at the foundation where Kirsten works." Alma seemed to labor at opening the door, she was that tired.

"Which foundation was that?"

"The Far East Mission Board." She stepped inside. "I'll tell Kirsten you asked about her. Good night, Marcus."

TWENTY-EIGHT

When they arrived back home, Marcus was still worrying over possible reasons why Kirsten would have lied to him about knowing Gloria's boyfriend. Which was why it took him a moment to realize there was a strange little camper parked alongside his garage. The camper was one of the humped sort made back in the fifties, a little metal mole pulled by what appeared to be a vintage Chevrolet painted with rust and years of grime. He and Darren exchanged a questioning look, then climbed from the Jeep.

A man as strange as the vehicles was found crouched in a corner of Marcus' front veranda. The porch light cast him as a mummy who muttered and flittered about, rising now to inspect the framework around Marcus' front door. He was of an indeterminate age, certainly over fifty, yet whether also over a hundred it was impossible to say. His skin was stretched tight over a hairless skull, his eyes black as coal, his mouth mobile, and his speech angrily musical. He glanced up at the sound of their approach, then returned to his grumbling inspection of the side window.

Marcus climbed the front steps and asked, "Can I help you?"

"Dee Gautam," the man snapped back. "He say you need gardener."

"I'm sorry, I haven't heard anything —"

Angrily the man pointed with what appeared to be a black pencil wedded to a thin cord. "You just open door."

Another glance at the tall black man beside him, then Marcus did as he was bid. "Dee Gautam sent you?"

"Gautam, yes. What I say." He took his angry muttering inside with him, scurrying through the front hall like a two-legged ferret. He paused long enough to snap back at where they stood, "Lights, lights!"

Marcus switched on the overheads. He and Darren followed him from the front hallway into the conference room, and from there into Marcus' office. When the man started toward Marcus' desk, a contrivance strapped to his belt gave off an irate squeal. The man shouted in an unknown tongue and stepped closer. The apparatus was about the size of a portable tape player and attached to the other end of the black cord. The man's features grew triumphant as he pointed his black pencil at the lamp on Marcus' desk, the squeal constant and high-pitched. He bent, searched, and pulled something away. He then marched back to where Marcus stood and thrust his hand forward, as though he were holding a live locust and not what appeared to be a metal button.

"Dee Gautam very right," the man exclaimed. "You need gardener bad."

Marcus reached for the tiny button, turned it over, watched it glint evil and secret in the light. Two tiny wires sprouted like hairs from the side.

"Here, Dee say, you take." The man shoved a wrinkled envelope into Marcus' numb fingers, then took his apparatus and his muttering from the room.

Darren stared down at the thing in Marcus' palm and asked, "Is th-that what I th-think it is?"

Marcus replied in soft wonder, "Somebody's bugged my house."

Darren turned to stare back at the open doorway, and said, "Who is th-this D-Dee fellow?"

"A friend. Here, take this." Marcus handed over the bug and opened the envelope. What he found inside granted him the day's final stupefaction.

From his secretary's office there arose another high-pitched squeal and a second shout of triumph.

Darren said, "You s-sure g-got yourself s-some strange friends."

The only person Marcus managed to locate before departing the next morning was the Washington process server, and that was merely to say, "Be ready for the next set of papers." His request to Alma for Kirsten to telephone when she woke up netted nothing. He then called the two numbers for Dee Gautam and received the same recording at both; a flat female voice said nothing except "Leave a message." He declined.

Marcus finally reached Ashley on his way into Raleigh. "I tried to call you last night."

"Been out hunting and pecking." The man's voice sounded heavy with fatigue. "Not much to report, but I'm still digging."

"I appreciate the effort, but I have to tell you, I don't know how much money there's going to be to go around. What the Halls had in ready capital, they spent on the ransom."

"Don't worry about that just now. First let's fight us a case. We'll haggle about filthy lucre when the battle's done."

The comment was as curious as the morning light, a hazy mixture of fog and blue sky that turned the entire world a shade of pewter. "I don't recall meeting many attorneys who aren't worried about having their bills paid."

"Well, you're new to this game, so let me share with you a simple truth." The man took a noisy slurp of something, and sighed the words, "This work is addictive."

"What work is that?"

"Fighting the good fight. Working for those who don't have a voice. You just wait, old son. Something tells me you'll have trouble going back to the same old, same old."

Marcus mulled that over for a stretch of silver-tinted roadway, then said, "I heard from Dee Gautam last night."

Beside him Darren shot over a single glance, before returning his full attention to the road ahead. Ashley said over the phone, "Yeah, he said he was gonna be sending you something he'd uncovered."

"The documents are incredible. I tried to call him last night and again this morning, but he's not around."

"Dee has the ability to turn into a ghost when it suits him. Leave a message at the office. Sooner or later they'll track him down."

"I don't think I can wait."

There was a long pause. "Is what he sent helpful?"

Marcus had to confess, "It might just turn this whole case around."

"Then I'd be careful, if I were you. You know what they say about overtight inspections of a gift horse. Dee Gautam has his ways, most of which are mysterious to the point of paranoia. But he's a good man to have in your corner."

Upon his arrival in the courtroom Marcus greeted Austin and Alma, then said, "Kirsten never called me back."

The glance between them held much humor, buried deep but there just the same. Alma said, "I can't do much more than pass on your messages."

He nodded acceptance and turned to find Charlie beaming. "What are you grinning at?"

"Aw, nothing much. Just nice to see you waking up to the world again."

Marcus ignored the harrumph of a laugh rising from Alma on his other side. "I need you to call the Swiss embassy. Ask for Hans Klein. He's a deputy in their commercial section. Lay on the charm. Tell him he's being subpoenaed for a case. We need him to testify as soon as possible."

"You want me to make this sound urgent?"

"Urgent and vital. But be nice. We

need him on our side. Once you've spoken with Klein, call the process server. You spoke with him yesterday. Tell him to go ahead and serve the papers. He already has them, and is waiting for your call."

"This Klein fellow is likely to want to know what it's about."

"Tell him it has to do with a missing woman, not in Switzerland, but his testimony could determine whether the girl lives or dies." Marcus fought back the rising tension. So much riding on a single thread. "Do your best. He has to come, Charlie. But I'd like him to come willingly. As soon as you know when he can appear, get back here and tell me."

As Charlie rose and slipped from the room, Judge Nicols turned from her customary greeting to the jury and said, "All right, Mr. Glenwood, you may call your next witness."

"Thank you, Your Honor. The plaintiff calls Grey Hadley to the stand."

The man who pushed through the swinging gate was bespectacled, slender, fiftyish, and very angry. He glared at Marcus before making his way up to the waiting bailiff. He gave his oath and sat stiffly in the witness chair, irate and looking for a target.

Marcus had no choice but to move into

range. "Mr. Hadley, you are acting assistant director for consular affairs within the U.S. State Department, is that correct?"

"Yes." The man was a coiled snake, eager to strike. "And may I say that this subpoena could not have come at a worse moment. As you may know, we have a serious economic crisis brewing in Latin America, and I am due at a high-level conference in Brazil tomorrow morning."

"Then we must endeavor to complete your testimony today," Marcus replied equably.

"That is not good enough." He turned to the judge. "I don't have a day to give to this trial. I don't have time to be here at all. I have position papers to prepare for Congressmen Williams and Jeffers, who are traveling down with me. This is absolutely vital work, critical to our nation's interests."

Marcus was grateful for the judge's patience, as the man's tirade showed the jury that Marcus was up against a hostile witness. Judge Nicols responded with the same quiet tone as Marcus. "The court is well aware of your pressing situation, which was why we agreed to subpoena you without delay. We require your testimony prior to your departure."

"Really, judge, this is not —"

She hardened her gaze a fraction. "I would advise you, Mr. Hadley, to refrain from further protests, as they are only wasting the court's time." When the man chose wisely not to argue, she continued. "You may proceed, Mr. Glenwood."

"Thank you, Your Honor." Marcus stayed well back from the stand, placing the entire jury box between himself and the witness. "Speaking of position papers, Mr. Hadley, were you not responsible for the preliminary organization of the President's visit to China five years ago?"

"Objection!" Logan leapt up. "Your Honor, this is in no way tied to the stated purpose of the subpoena. May I remind the court that the plaintiff was to ask about depositions of New Horizons officers!"

Marcus said to the judge, "If you will just permit a few questions, Your Honor, all will become clear."

"All right, I'll allow it," she responded, the reservations clear in her tone. "Objection overruled, for the moment."

Marcus asked, "Do you need the question repeated?"

"No. I — I don't recall."

Marcus hefted the documents sent by Ashley Granger. "Did you not prepare an overview for the President specifically related to Chinese factories that were pirating U.S. goods? Such a document, sent directly to the White House, does not seem to be something a person in your position could afford to forget."

"Maybe. I'm not sure." The man's anger was fading fast. "I do a lot of position papers."

"The plaintiff offers as documentary evidence this very paper, addressed to the White House and signed by the witness." Marcus passed it to the court reporter, who numbered it and handed it to the judge.

Logan remained on his feet. "Your Honor, I must protest."

"Overruled. Proceed, Mr. Glenwood."

Marcus handed the witness a second copy. "Mr. Hadley, I ask you to turn with me to the top of page eleven. There you will find mentioned Factory 101 within the military-owned complex operated by one Zhao Ren-Fan, and located between Hong Kong and the city of Guangzhou."

"Objection! This is not pertinent to this case, Your Honor."

"I think I should be the one to decide what is and is not pertinent, Mr. Kendall."

"Of course, Your Honor, but —"

"Wouldn't you say that was my choice, Mr. Kendall?"

"Certainly, I merely —"

"Then why don't you sit down and let us get on with this." To Marcus, "Proceed, counselor."

"There at the top of page eleven, Mr. Hadley. Would you please read for the court what you say about Factory 101?"

"I don't — I'm not certain this . . ."

"Do you not state here, in a document you prepared for the President of the United States, that Factory 101 is one of the worst pirates operating within the textile industry? Do you not state that in black and white, Mr. Hadley?"

"I may have," he muttered, now seeking to bury his face in the document. "There were several dozen such papers prepared by my subordinates. I can't recall them all, often I just sign them."

"But it is your signature there at the bottom of the document, is it not?"

"It appears to be, yes."

"All right. Let's go to the second paragraph on that page. The one where you describe how, because the factory is owned and operated by a high military official, this very same General Zhao Ren-Fan, it has been protected from closure. But New Horizons, a company that has been a major contributor to the President's own campaign, had lodged an official complaint. Do you not state this, Mr. Hadley?"

"I told you, it was probably prepared for my signature by —"

"Do you not also state that New Horizons claims to be losing as much as seventy million dollars annually through Factory 101 selling copies of its product, copies so good only an expert can tell the difference?"

"Objection!" Logan's voice was bitterly furious. "This is ridiculous, Your Honor. As I said before, counsel is attempting to submit evidence that is clearly in violation of the rules of relevance."

Marcus was locked and loaded. "Your Honor, I submit that the State Department has been intentionally dragging its feet over these depositions. The reason for this is clear. They are concerned about being implicated in the collusion between New Horizons and Factory 101."

"*What* collusion?" Logan almost shouted the words. "The plaintiff hasn't proven a thing!"

But all that was about to change. Marcus walked back to his table, picked up the next set of papers and said, "Your Honor, I wish to submit as evidence documents that I feel will demonstrate beyond a shadow of doubt that the New Horizons board fled the country to avoid answering questions related to how they had established a joint venture with Factory 101 in order to bring an end to the pirating. And that the State Department has been collaborating with the board to mask this."

Hadley shouted, "That's absurd!"

"Your Honor!" Logan's face bore the strain of battle. "This has absolutely no foundation whatsoever! Counsel is intent on tainting this jury with lies and baseless allegations!"

"All right, calm down!" Judge Nicols had the ability to strike with the softness of a velvet-covered fist. "There will be no further histrionics in this courtroom, do I make myself clear?"

Hadley mistook the resulting silence as an opportunity. "This is crazy. We haven't got a thing to hide."

She glared down. Hard. "You just hush up." Then to Marcus, "This had better be good."

"I submit that they have a very great deal to hide, Your Honor. And for very good reason." Marcus approached the bench, handed over the document. He waited as Judge Nicols read, and watched her features harden. Only then did he pass on a second copy to Logan. In the ensuing silence he noticed Charlie standing by the central aisle. He walked over, saw the old man mouth the word "Friday." He nodded his agreement,

430

turned back to the courtroom.

"All right, Mr. Glenwood. I am allowing this as evidence."

"Objection." Logan's voice was as weak as the hand holding the papers. "This has no bearing on the case, Your Honor."

"Overruled. Proceed, Mr. Glenwood."

Marcus handed the witness a copy of the document. The man was clearly reluctant to take hold. "Would you state for the jury the nature of this document?"

"I — this is confidential, you shouldn't —"

"Does it not contain a list of the business leaders who traveled with the President to China on that trip five years ago?" Marcus waited through the silence, letting it settle and squeeze. "Answer the question, Mr. Hadley."

"It appears . . . Yes."

"All right. There are two names marked halfway down. Would you please tell the jury what those names are?"

The witness mumbled an inaudible response, which was fine with Marcus, for it gave him a reason to trumpet, "Do they not belong to one Mr. James Southerland, chief executive officer, and Frank Clinedale, assistant chairman of the board, of New Horizons Incorporated? Does this not suggest that these men went to China to solve the pirating problem once and for all? Did they not decide then and there that it would be better to establish a joint venture and share profits, rather than risk years of further lost revenue? Answer the question, Mr. Hadley. Has the State Department not been reluctant to supply these depositions precisely because they are terrified of this coming out?"

"No." The man had sweated a stain the entire way around his collar. "That's not it at all. I don't know anything about this. Nothing."

"Fine." Judge Nicols cracked the word like a whip. "In that case, the State Department will have no objection to supplying this court with those depositions immediately. And State is hereby sanctioned to the tune of ten thousand dollars per day for every day the depositions do not arrive. And you, sir, are hereby ordered to remain in Raleigh and on call to this court until the depositions arrive."

"Judge, I can't, I'm scheduled to fly —"

"You are so ordered," she snarled. "I would be delighted to find you accommodations in the local holding pen if necessary."

TWENTY-NINE

Logan Kendall's fury carried him through a battery of protests, mostly from females, all of them rising in tone and temper as he marched on. He did not run, but his stride was such that few could have caught him without jogging, which was hard to do within the staid confines of Randall Walker's law firm. The complaints that followed him had alerted Randall's secretary, who was in the process of rising and moving to block the door when he appeared. Logan said nothing, just looked at her, his raging glower enough to halt her in midstride. Which was good, for he had no desire to release what he contained upon anyone other than the man himself.

But he had no choice, for when he opened the door and stormed the inner sanctum, he found Randall seated at the coffee table with a silver-haired couple. Logan held Randall with his gaze, and said simply, "Get them out of here."

"Really, Logan," Randall drawled, trying for a light tone. "There are better ways to get my attention than —"

"Glenwood came up with yet another surprise," Logan snarled. "You and I are going to have it out — right here, right now. This is your last warning."

Randall seemed to deflate, all the bonhomie and superiority flowing out with his sigh. He looked at his secretary crowding into the doorway behind Logan and said, "Perhaps you'd be so good as to show my guests down to Sandra's office."

The two silver heads turned as one. The male client had the cultured tone of trust funds and genteel afternoon teas. "Really, Randall. This won't do."

"I'm sorry, Stanley. Truly I am." Randall struggled to his feet. "But we have an ongoing crisis here that I cannot entrust to anyone else." When the two had left, Randall returned heavily to the sofa. "Have a seat."

Logan remained firmly planted where he was. "Marcus Glenwood came up with documents that tie New Horizons to official complaints rising all the way to the White House, Randall. The White House."

The older man's gaze seemed to go vacant. "Oh my."

"The judge has slapped a ten-thousand-dollar-per-day penalty on the State Department until the depositions are received. She has put off further testimony until Friday, at Marcus' request. He could have asked her to tango and she'd probably have agreed. She didn't even notice when I waived my right to cross-examine the witness."

"Yes," Randall said quietly to the empty space before his eyes. "I imagine Judge Nicols was rather irate."

"Is that all you've got to say?" Logan had a sudden urge to lift the coffee table and send it crashing down upon this pompous balloon in a three-piece suit. "Do you have any idea what you've done?"

"I can only imagine —"

"No! If you did, you'd find some hole to crawl into and die!" Logan shouted the last word so loudly it seemed to stretch his throat out of shape. Not that he cared. "I fought my way out of South Baltimore, made it to the top of my law-school class, worked hundred-hour weeks, made partner, and for what? So some slimeball like you could come by and set me up for Marcus Glenwood to use as target practice?"

Randall drew his gaze upward, focused with effort, and waved vaguely at the chair opposite him. "Please sit down, Logan."

Logan reared back and kicked the chair so hard it catapulted over the coffee table and cracked the wall paneling. The sound reverberated like thunder. Beyond the closed door, voices rose in strident concern. Logan lowered his face until it was inches from Randall's, a fear of litigation the only thing that kept him from tearing the man limb from limb. "My reputation was on the line here, and what happens? My *client* puts me in the position of lying before the court *again!* And this time in front of a sitting jury!"

"Logan, you have —"

"If Nicols gets it into her skull that I've been intentionally holding back, she'll have me disbarred!" He wiped the spittle from his chin with a shaky hand. "I'm walking. I'm off the case. I'm calling the paper and making a public proclamation. I'm telling everyone who'll listen how I've come into evidence that makes me suspect that my client has not only been lying, but they might actually be guilty. And then I'm suing you, Randall. I'm going to have you stripped down to your sorry silk shorts and kicked right out on the street."

Randall slowly shook his head, defeated not by Logan but by whatever it was graying his cheeks. "You're not going anywhere."

"Watch me."

"Believe me, Logan. This is the case

you've always dreamed of." But there was no pleasure to the announcement. Only defeat. And worry. "I'm sorry to say."

Logan realized his chest was hurting. And his foot from kicking the chair. "I'm listening."

"We told you nothing because there was nothing Marcus could know." Randall's voice had the sound of reeds rattling in the wind, toneless and weary. "We used your ignorance like a firewall. One that could only be breached by Marcus having information he could not logically possess."

"But he did, Randall. He did."

"Yes." Accepting the news aged him further still. "And what he doesn't have yet, he will soon. He must. He's gone too far not to come up with it all."

"I'm not convinced of anything except you're a lying dog." But the wind had left Logan's sails, and he knew his voice revealed it. "And I'm still planning to walk and sue unless you can convince me otherwise."

Randall did not seem to hear him. "Marcus is going to hit the core issue, and at the rate he's digging it won't take much longer. When that happens, you and your career are both going to be catapulted into instant stardom."

Logan backed up three paces, leaned

upon the corner of Randall's desk, and crossed his arms. "I want it all. Everything, right down to the final word."

Randall made a vague effort at flattening his vest against his hollowed chest, and said simply, "Get ready for the surprise of your life."

THIRTY

Marcus spent Wednesday and Thursday tending to legal matters that had been left abandoned since the trial began. Charlie Hayes arrived and remarked over the strange man gardening in October, then set to work beside him. Marcus waited for a call from Kirsten and ached mildly at her continued absence. Questions about Gary Loh and other secrets came and went like shadows beneath windswept trees. Even so, at times he felt ready to let the mysteries lie unresolved, if only he could have her nearer in body and spirit.

The *News and Observer* made much of Tuesday's courtroom disclosure, and on Thursday morning Marcus fielded calls from both the *Washington Post* and the *Atlanta Constitution*. It took the Richmond paper until that afternoon, and the Charlotte paper did not call until he was preparing to leave for dinner. He answered with patient thoroughness, going through all he was able to substantiate by public testimony. Yes, New Horizons had undisclosed international subsidiaries. Yes, it appeared that there was some hiding of profit from the tax authorities. Yes, they were reviewing allegations that the company operated offshore sweatshops. Yes, there were indeed other cases that detailed how the company used underage, underpaid workers in Southeast Asia and exposed employees to cancer-causing materials. Yes, he had written documents to back up these claims. No, he could not make any comment with regard to the missing woman, but they were welcome to call and interview her parents.

Thursday evening he dined in with Charlie and Boomer and Libby Hayes and their eldest son, back from Wake Forest for a long weekend. They ate in the formal dining room off Spode dinnerwear custom-made with an angry Carolina ram's head delicately painted upon every plate, saucer, cup, and bowl. Boomer made much of Marcus' new housemate, a man whose name Marcus did not even know, who continued to sweep each room of the house daily for bugs of the metallic species. Charlie laughed much and ate little. Marcus realized that none of them wished to disturb the fragile evening's tranquillity with anything so onerous as the truth about Charlie's illness. Marcus marveled at their easy laughter, the friendship, and the tight bonds of a family facing something so painful they could not even bring themselves to discuss it. Instead, they showered Charlie with every possible opportunity to laugh, to quarrel, to shine. Marcus found himself with little to say, he was so caught up in observing a spirit he had assumed was lost and gone forever.

Friday morning came too soon, and on the drive into Raleigh and court Marcus found himself so worried he called Charlie at home. "I'm thinking I should have walked Klein through his testimony after all."

"Who?"

"You know perfectly well who I mean. Hans Klein. The man from the Swiss embassy."

"This is a good sign," Charlie said, not bothering to hide his chortle. "Fretting over what you can't change. Means you're beginning to treat this like a real trial."

"I'm serious."

"So am I, son. But it don't make this any less funny. You didn't contact this Klein fellow because you didn't want him to realize what you were planning. Which means you are legally covered for changing direction. Just because he sounded like an underdone kid to me on the phone don't change matters one whit."

Marcus found himself unable to let go that easily. "I've always treated this trial seriously, and you know it."

"Maybe so." Charlie's merriment rang softly, like chimes covered and muffled by tangled vines of age. "But now you're treating it like a case you just might win."

"Plaintiff calls Hans Klein to the stand."

The witness was everything Marcus had feared since Charlie described their conversation — young, eager, passionately energetic. Defense would have a field day. Marcus had no choice but to proceed. "You are assistant commercial attaché at the Swiss embassy in Washington, D.C., are you not?"

"Yes sir." At least the man's English was good. Heavily accented, but very understandable. "For five years now. I go back to Bern in seven months. I wish I could stay. I like your country —"

Judge Nicols broke in. "Restrict yourself just to answering the questions, please." But her gaze remained fastened upon the defense table, a slight frown creasing her forehead. Marcus understood perfectly, but refrained from turning around and staring yet again. He had noticed Logan's appearance as well. The man looked positively gray, as though stricken by some ailment with a poor prognosis.

"Yes, judge, sorry." Klein could not have been more than twenty-eight or -nine, and probably had never been in a courtroom before. Certainly not an American one. He repeated for Marcus, "I am here since five years."

"And during that time, have you ever been involved in depositions requested by courts in this country involving witnesses residing in Switzerland?"

"Oh, yes, many times."

"Can you tell the court how long such depositions take?"

"It depends. Sometimes many weeks, other times just days."

"These often involve banking disputes, do they not?"

"Banking, companies, crimes, Holocaust victims, insurance issues, sometimes divorces and children." He shrugged apologetically. "Many things."

"All right." Marcus decided he had trod that ground long enough. He lifted a page from his table, walked over, and handed it to the judge's assistant. "Plaintiff requests this be submitted as newly discovered evidence."

Judge Nicols accepted the paper from the recorder, asked, "Is this German?"

"Yes, Your Honor."

"Objection."

Marcus took this as an excuse to turn and stare. Logan seemed to have difficulty rising from his table. His face held the sheen of a wax dummy as he went on, "Your Honor, no way should this have been sprung on us like this. No way."

"It is newly discovered evidence," Marcus repeated mildly. "It is crucial that we determine its validity through the testimony of this witness."

Nicols studied the document. "Do you know what this is?"

"I believe so, Your Honor."

"And you are certain it pertains to this case?"

"If it is indeed what I think, absolutely, Your Honor. Without the slightest doubt. It is critical."

"Very well. But I am warning you, Mr. Glenwood. If this is not as vital as you claim, I will come down very hard on you."

"Thank you, Your Honor." Marcus walked to the defense table, gave Logan a copy of the paper, and saw that up close the man looked even worse. He turned to the witness stand, where Hans Klein was watching the exchange with wide-eyed wonder. Marcus passed over a third copy and asked, "Could you please tell the court the nature of this document, Mr. Klein?"

It took the man only an instant to recognize and state, "These are Swiss articles of incorporation."

"Objection!" Logan marshaled what powers he had left. "Your Honor, I move for a mistrial. For the second time in a row, the plaintiff has brought forward a surprise witness for one supposed purpose and then hit us with something else entirely."

"This evidence could not possibly have been known at the time of filing these charges, Your Honor," Marcus replied. But his gut was telling him that Logan knew. "As I said, it is newly discovered."

"Your Honor, the days of the legal gunslinger are long gone." But Logan's protests rang hollow. "From the beginning, this entire case has not been about the truth. Let me remind you, Your Honor, this case is about the disappearance of a woman. What evidence has the plaintiff shown in this regard? None. What does this witness have to do with the case's central issue? Nothing."

Marcus cast a swift glance at the judge. She was watching Logan with that same small frown. Marcus gave a mental nod of agreement. During the past twenty-four hours, Logan had come to know what they were still seeking to discover. And it had rocked him to his very core.

"It is a sanctionable offense to bring forward a witness and elicit testimony that should have been disclosed to us beforehand," Logan continued. "This deserves the severest punishment, Your Honor, because the plaintiff's counsel has falsely manipulated the court."

"Your request is denied," Nicols said quietly.

"Then I move to have this evidence struck from the record."

"Motion denied."

"I then move for a mistrial on the basis that such ambushing evidence should never be permitted."

"Overruled."

"I request you issue limiting instructions to the jury."

"Denied." She waited a long moment. "Are you done? Very well. Proceed, Mr. Glenwood."

"Thank you, Your Honor." Marcus returned to the witness box. "Mr. Klein, you say this paper is an official governmental document?"

"Yes. The words at the top, they are the formal name of the Canton of Geneva."

"Geneva," Marcus repeated. "That is where the request for depositions of the

New Horizons board members has been sent, is it not?"

"I am sorry, I don't —"

"Never mind, Mr. Klein. Back to the document. Can you tell me what exactly it says?"

"Yes, of course." He read swiftly and translated, "These photocopies are of the incorporation of a joint venture between New Horizons and a certain Factory 101 —"

Logan had to pitch his voice to be heard over the rising swell of noise from the court observers. "Objection! Your Honor, the witness said it himself. These are not original documents!"

Marcus hefted further documents from his table and replied, "Request permission to approach the bench."

"Very well."

When Marcus was close enough to see the beaded sweat on Logan's forehead, Logan hissed, "Interesting how you waited to this point to request confidentiality."

"All right, enough. Go ahead, Mr. Glenwood."

"Your Honor, these documents have been unearthed not in Switzerland but in Beijing." He gave a verbatim recital of what Dee Gautam had scrawled in his cover note, and hoped the judge would not request further information, because he had none. "A quasi-governmental body exists there whose sole purpose is to extract special 'foreign operating taxes' from international ventures. That is why you see that strange stamp in the top-right corner." He offered his other documents. "I wish to offer these as further evidence, Your Honor. They are the corporate documents of the Swiss partner, a shell company established by New Horizons Incorporated just to hold this joint venture."

"I object," Logan said, but weakly. "This is further trial by ambush."

"It has taken us this long to unearth these documents, Your Honor. As I said, it is all newly discovered evidence."

"I am going to allow it," Nicols said.

"Your Honor —"

She stopped Logan with one black-robed arm. "Proceed, Mr. Glenwood."

Marcus returned to the witness stand and walked the witness carefully through all the documents, concluding with, "So what we have here are official documents lodged with the federal government in Bern. These documents state that a Swiss subsidiary of New Horizons is now the forty-nine-percent owner of Factory 101 in Guangzhou, China. The Chinese signatory, representing the controlling interest in the joint venture, is a certain Zhao Ren-Fan. And that payment for New Horizons' share was made in the form of equipment and sales contracts."

"Yes," Hans Klein emphatically agreed. "All is stated exactly so."

Marcus decided to risk one further question. "Can you tell the court why New Horizons would choose to go this route and incorporate in Switzerland rather than in the United States?"

"Objection. Requires conjecture on the part of the witness!"

"I submit this witness is an expert in this field, Your Honor," Marcus responded, "and can reply from a wealth of experience."

Judge Nicols leaned over her desk and asked the young man, "Do you fully understand the nature of this question?"

"Oh yes, judge."

"Very well, you may respond. But only to the exact question."

Marcus repeated, "Why would the company choose to incorporate in Switzerland?"

"Usually there are only two reasons," the man replied brightly. "Because our taxes are very low and all corporate records are held as secret documents — they are not shared with anyone in the company's home country, not even the tax authorities. Not by us, I mean. What they choose to do themselves is their business."

"No further questions." Marcus retreated from the witness and the one question he could not ask: How did the young man know Dee Gautam?

Logan gathered his forces and fought back. "Mr. Klein, what you have in front of you are photocopied documents, is that not correct?"

"Yes."

"Have you ever seen these documents before this morning?"

"No."

"Can you guarantee their authenticity?"

"No, well, perhaps, but it is hard, you see —"

"Could these documents not be forged, Mr. Klein?"

"It is hardly likely, because —"

"Yes or no, Mr. Klein: Could these documents be forged?"

"Yes, of course, anything is possible."

"Yes, of course, they *could* be forgeries." Head down, Logan tracked his way toward the jury box, as though intent on ramming home the fact. "How much business background do you have, Mr. Klein?"

"I am a graduate of the Bern School of Diplomacy, a part of the University —"

"A diplomacy school. So you are a civil servant. A federal bureaucrat. With no actual experience in business whatsoever. Is that correct?"

The young man's eager demeanor was swiftly fading. "I went straight from school into our foreign service."

"Do you know anything whatsoever about New Horizons' operations in North Carolina, Mr. Klein? Are you aware they employ four thousand people in this state, most of them in one of the poorest areas in the Southeast United States, and are in fact the largest employer in the region?"

"I'm sorry, I don't —"

"Are you aware of the charitable activities this company undertakes on behalf of young people playing organized sports nationwide?"

"I have seen their advertisements," he responded lamely.

"Their advertisements. How nice. Is it not true, Mr. Klein, that all you really know about this company is this one document, shown to you by the plaintiff, possibly forged, given to you for whatever motive the plaintiff might have dreamed up?"

"I . . . Yes, I suppose —"

"No further questions, Your Honor." Logan wheeled about and stalked by Marcus' table. As he passed he landed a single flaming glance, a swift warning shot across the bow. Marcus understood perfectly. Logan was bloodied, but far from beaten. This was only the first round.

THIRTY-ONE

"You've made a total shambles of this from the beginning." The silver-maned gentleman at the head of the table glared down at Randall. "Which I suppose should come as a surprise to no one present."

"The cameras aren't rolling, Sidney, and the press isn't here." Randall played at a nonchalance he did not feel. "You can stuff that censure back in your pocket."

"Now look here!" Before being forced into retirement, the chairman of the China Trade Council had run a seventeen-billion-dollar corporation. He was used to people jumping when he barked. Randall's slow drawl left him bilious. "I don't take that from anybody, especially not some gun-for-hire, two-bit shyster like you!"

"Calm down, Sidney." This from the deputy chairman, himself the former chief executive of a Fortune 50 company. "This is getting us nowhere in a hurry."

The opulent suite of Washington offices would have better suited a private club than a firm of lobbyists. But this was no common lobbying group, and the men gathered here were not mere mortals. The table was ringed by nineteen retired executives, all white, all over sixty, whose retirement packages had all exceeded twenty-five million dollars.

The China Trade Council had started life as a quasi-official arm of the International Chamber of Commerce. It had soon come to the council's attention, however, that it could operate far more effectively if it were independent. And secretive. Its chieftans included the top executives of over three dozen of the largest corporations in the United States. Membership in the council cost them 250,000 dollars per year. The board itself was selected on the basis of contacts within the current administration. Members of the council's board accompanied the President on trade missions, attended top-level Commerce Department strategy sessions, represented American industry before the Senate Foreign Relations Committee, slept in the Lincoln bedroom. As far as Randall Walker was concerned, these men had held power for so long it had rusted along with their brains.

The council's chairman attempted to rein in his rage. "I told those bozos at New Horizons they were making a mistake to entrust you with something this explosive."

"What would you expect," grumbled another board member. "Coming from a company that sells glow-in-the-dark tennis shoes."

"And pays a million bucks a year to some yahoo because he can jump," sneered the deputy.

Randall ignored the jibes because he was concentrating on another sound, the only one he could clearly hear. The China Trade Council's boardroom table was ringed by the noise of sharpening knives. "New Horizons pays their dues the same as you. They appoint their representative, the same as your own companies. That representative happens to be me. As per our rights as a council member, we are requesting your help."

"Help that should have been requested weeks ago! Back before this lawsuit became a public brawl!"

The deputy turned his placating tone on Randall. "You know how we hate publicity. Especially when the Vice President has a trade mission in the pipeline."

Randall smiled, and wished he could reach over and strangle the man. "I find it absolutely amazing how everybody at this table has such perfect hindsight."

The chairman barked, "I told you from

the beginning to destroy the Hall girl's files."

Randall sighed. "And just exactly when was that supposed to happen? Back when we didn't know there were any files, or after we realized she must have locked them in a safety deposit box?"

"Now you listen —"

But Randall wasn't done. "Hamper Caisse searched the Stanstead girl's car, house, office, bathroom, basement — not once, but three different times. Everyone in this room knows Caisse is the best in the business. That's why we use him. Caisse said there was nothing. I believed him."

"And look how wrong you were!"

"Yes." Randall's mind remained split between two fantasies. One was of carving out the chairman's tongue with a dull spoon. The other was of a frosty glass filled to the rim with crushed ice and single-malt scotch. He could not tell which one appealed the most just then. "We were all wrong. Remember the meeting we had soon after this broke, gentlemen? I'll be happy to draw out the minutes to refresh your memories. First we arranged for an attorney we tamed to tell the Halls they had no case. When that didn't work, we agreed that sooner or later this thing was bound to come out.

Then the Halls selected a lawyer so utterly incompetent the case was lost before it was started."

Randall felt suddenly weary, both of this battle and the overall war. It had all seemed so simple then. "It was a unanimous decision, gentlemen. We all agreed. The Halls were not going to drop this case. A lawyer would be hired. The Halls would pursue their case. And going after the Halls themselves would only heighten the risk of everything coming out in the press. We couldn't bribe them, we couldn't threaten them. We had to find a weak link. Glenwood was perfect."

"Perfect!" The chairman's face had turned a remarkable shade of puce. "The man is threatening to derail our trade mission! One of our most senior contacts has privately informed us that China is considering the closure of all American subsidiaries and cutting off further negotiations with all U.S. companies! We stand to lose hundreds of millions of dollars in new business! You call this perfect?"

It was the deputy who responded. "As soon as the facts began to emerge, we tried to stop this Glenwood. Caisse was sent in. And others."

"Yes, and I can now see where the problem lay all along!" The chairman stabbed a trembling finger at Randall.

"You didn't have the guts to finish things off cleanly!"

Randall had to release at least one small chuckle. "And you do?"

"Absolutely! And furthermore, we've got the intelligence to see this as the utter shambles it is!"

"On the contrary, Sidney." Randall decided he had had enough. "You're so dumb you could get lost in a round room."

The chairman catapulted out of his chair. "Get him out of here!"

"Sidney, calm —"

"You're fired! I'm getting your boss on the phone and personally taking control of this myself!"

"Oh, now we're in for a treat." Randall picked up his briefcase and graced the room with a grand smile. He had a villa on the Amalfi Coast he had visited only once, and two bank accounts in Switzerland stuffed to overflowing. It was time to taste the good life. As Randall gazed down at the eighteen other faces, he found himself wondering what had possessed him to want to join them in the first place. "I advise all of you to head for the nearest bunker."

When the phone rang, Marcus first thought it was part of a dream. His heart pounded in time to the jangling tone, and his eyes opened to a dark scarcely less vacant than the tomb. A vague yellowish light spilled through his window, enough to guide his hand to the phone. He lifted the receiver and squinted at the clock dial. It was four in the morning. "Hello?"

"Good, you are awake. This is very good."

Marcus recognized the voice of Dee Gautam. "You can't be serious."

"Good to be awake and receiving good news. Sometimes the clock is an enemy to be conquered, yes?"

Marcus swung his legs to the floor, searched for the lamp switch, squinted at the sudden brilliance. "What news?"

"You are having pencil and paper?"

"Hang on. Yes, all right, go ahead."

"A certain Hao Lin wishes to speak with you." The merry voice spelled the name. "She is in detention at the INS center outside Washington. You know the term, INS?"

"Immigration and Naturalization Service. But what —"

"They hold her. Here is the detention number they have given to Hao Lin." He read off the code. "Call today. See her now. Before she is moved and lost again. Hurry." Dee Gautam cut the connection.

Marcus sat holding the receiver until he

became resigned to the end of his slumber. He rose and padded for the bathroom, glad of one thing only: At least this night he had beaten the nightmare to the punch.

He went for a run in the dark, reveling in his brief solitude. He had not realized how much the constant presence of others weighed upon him. Even the ache in his arm felt like a healing pulse.

The night was black and starless, the clouds glinting dully with light reflected from the town below. Rocky Mount had the look of a place too weary to recover with only one brief night's rest. He headed toward the river, took the bridge, and passed through the deserted downtown streets. The previous year's floods had merely added new scars to more ancient signs of neglect. Tobacco barns, their windows black and toothless, sported wall signs of long-forgotten companies. Marcus ran and reflected upon how this was the perfect breeding ground for injustice, how inevitable it was for New Horizons to come and suck up what good remained within this tired old town.

He returned and showered and ate, waiting until eight o'clock to call Ashley. Marcus greeted the lawyer with, "This has the makings of a great tale, how one attorney wakes another on a Saturday morning about a case that probably won't earn either of them a nickel."

Ashley croaked, "I'm supposed to find something funny about this?"

"Dee Gautam woke me at four."

"Call me back in five minutes."

Marcus waited ten, then redialed. Ashley answered, "I assume the elf did not want to know how you were resting."

"He says there's a potential witness who can't wait. A certain Hao Lin held at the INS detention center somewhere near Washington. I'm sorry, he didn't give me any more address than that."

"I know the INS holding pen." There was no longer any sleepiness to Ashley's tone. "You want me to get a deposition."

"Yes. Soon as I hear from you that this person is genuine and has something to offer, I'll go ahead and request the judge serve papers to have her brought down."

"Fine. Good. Listen, I was hoping to contact you this weekend. There's something pretty amazing that I'm catching wind of. Do you want the rumors now or the facts in another day or so?"

Marcus pondered, then decided, "I'll stick with the facts. I don't know if I could handle anything else right now."

Marcus set down the phone in time to the chime of his front doorbell. Darren appeared in the back hall and stood watching as he opened the door only to find himself confronting a stranger with a tense look and a cast-off smile. "Marcus Glenwood?"

"Yes."

"Great." He handed over a bulky packet and turned for the stairs. "Have a nice day."

Marcus was still standing in his doorway reading the pages when his phone rang once more. Reluctantly he walked back to his office and picked up the receiver. "Glenwood."

"Marcus, this is Jim Bell. I hope I'm not disturbing you."

"Not at all." For a federal judge's guard-receptionist to call him on the weekend during a trial was definitely one for the books. "What can I do for you?"

"Judge Nicols doesn't know anything about this call." The words had a rehearsed quality. "I'm not gonna say a thing to her, and you probably shouldn't either."

Marcus searched for his chair, said slowly, "Okay."

"Last night the judge was approached by Senator Stern. He told her the White House is looking for a new independent U.S. prosecutor. Something about issues being raised by the Senate Ethics Committee. He asked if she'd like the position."

Marcus breathed tightly. "She said yes."

"Right. Also yesterday Jenny Hail was called by the governor's office. A district judgeship has come available over in Winston-Salem. They're considering Jenny for the position. You know how close those two are."

Marcus hefted the newly arrived document. "I've just been served with a subpoena. A grievance has been filed against me with the state bar. It's related to a case I was involved in, oh, it must be five years ago." He flipped the pages, confirmed, "Yes, here it is, five years. It accuses me of turning a man whose will I drew up against his surviving heirs." Marcus dropped the pages to his desk. "Charlie Hayes would call this a hanging offense, since if I'm convicted I would lose my license to practice law."

"Interesting how all this came up together."

"You said it."

"Well, see you on Monday."

"Right. And thanks, Jim. A lot." Marcus hung up, trying hard not to read too much into what he had just learned.

But Ashley Granger did not call back

that day, nor did Marcus receive any answer except a taped message when he phoned both Ashley's office and his home. Marcus held to patience through a steady stream of work, finally giving in to exhaustion just after eight. As he lay waiting for sleep to come, he decided the day seemed altogether incomplete.

As usual, his sleep was shattered before dawn. This time, however, he opened his eyes and searched for what remained just beyond the reach of his senses. He peered into the darkness, but found no reason for fear. Instead, his room seemed disturbed by the beat of disembodied wings.

Marcus sat up in bed and tried to listen beyond the night's sibilant hush. The chamber did not hold to the feel of his nightly trauma. Instead he sensed a different presence, neither good nor hostile, merely watchful. As though he was on trial himself, and the night was asking, Are you worthy? Marcus sat there until dawn, helpless to do more than hope the verdict would come down in his favor.

Monday morning dawned with a mocking beauty, a false clarity to the sky and the road ahead. Marcus did not see the lie revealed until Darren was pulling into the courthouse parking lot, and he finally had an answer to his repeated telephone calls to Ashley Granger's office.

Afterward it seemed that even before he heard the anguished voice, even before he detected the weeping in the background, even before Ashley's secretary sobbed out the news on the car phone, he knew. Marcus sat and heard the keening words, and loathed the absence of rain and gray and universal mourning.

He was all the way down the courtroom's central aisle before he realized he had passed Kirsten. He turned and greeted her with a solemn nod, and the thought that at this moment, her gaze of broken gemstone was completely appropriate. Here at least was one who shared his sorrow, even though she did not know it yet. Marcus moved to his table, said to Alma and Austin, "Do you still have the video?"

Something either in his eyes or in his tone stilled their questions. Alma said simply, "Yes."

"The original?"

"In our safety deposit box," Austin replied.

He turned to Charlie. "Find us an expert. Have it cleaned up, make Gloria as visible as possible."

Charlie nodded. "What's the matter, son?"

The bailiff chose that moment to announce, "All rise."

Marcus remained standing as the others seated themselves, isolated by more than his stance as the court was called into session. He waited until Judge Nicols turned his way to announce, "Your Honor, it is my forlorn duty to announce that an attorney assisting me with this case, Mr. Ashley Granger of Washington, D.C., was murdered on Saturday."

"No!" Kirsten's wail wrenched Marcus where he stood, but he did not turn around.

Logan catapulted to his feet. "Your Honor!"

"Mr. Glenwood, I see you are distraught," Judge Nicols began. "But —"

"Your Honor, Ashley Granger was brutally murdered while driving to take a deposition related to this very case."

"Your Honor! I move for a mistrial!"

"Hush up, the pair of you!" Nicols hammered her gavel so powerfully even Kirsten's second protest collapsed to weeping. "Mr. Glenwood! You are in serious breach of court discipline here!"

"Your Honor, counsel for the plaintiff has biased the jury with these utterly unfounded accusations!" Logan started forward. "I demand you declare a mistrial!"

The hand holding the gavel shook threateningly. "You get back to your table, sir. Mr. Glenwood, plant yourself in that chair." Only when they were both seated did she lower the arm and the gavel. "This will not happen. Not ever again, not in my courtroom, no matter what the supposed reason. Is that clear?" She glared at them until both attorneys nodded their acceptance. "All right. Mr. Kendall, your motion is dismissed. Mr. Glenwood, I see you are bereft. I am sorry. That is all I can say."

"Your Honor, Ashley Granger was going to take a deposition from one Hao Lin, who is being held in the INS detention center outside Washington." Kirsten's sobs tore at him, as if she were weeping the tears he could not himself afford to shed. "I request the court's permission to attend Mr. Granger's memorial service this afternoon, then proceed to depose the witness and if necessary return with her."

Logan was having none of it. "Your Honor, this is nothing more than yet another blatant —"

"I will not warn you again," Nicols snapped, holding Logan in his seat by strength of will alone. "I am this close to severely sanctioning you for misleading the court and intentionally withholding critical evidence. Do not try my patience at this point, Mr. Kendall. I am warning you." She turned back to Marcus. "Very well. Have the papers drawn up. You may use my secretary." She banged the gavel. "Court is adjourned until Wednesday morning."

At the bailiff's call, Marcus rose with the others, wishing there were some way to have the court remain there, standing in homage to the loss of a truly good man.

At least Kirsten mourned Ashley's passage. The preparations and the drive to the airport and the flight were punctuated by her sorrow. She did not seem aware that on occasion her eyes leaked a scattering of tears. Marcus waited until they were in a taxi headed for the Washington church to ask the first of what would have to be a multitude of questions. "The last time we talked, Ashley said he was chasing something critical to the case. Do you have any idea what that might have been?"

She was too far gone to even pretend anymore. "No. All I know is that about two weeks before she left, Gloria became so excited about something, I thought she was going to have a heart attack."

"Before she left for China?"

Her nod was little more than a shiver. "She wouldn't tell me what it was. Something so big it could mean everything, that was all she told me. It could make it all worthwhile."

"Make what worthwhile?" Marcus demanded. "Her research? Her trip?"

But the question only renewed her tears. "I begged her not to go. I pleaded with her. I told her I couldn't do what she wanted. All she said was, 'If I fail, then it will all have been for nothing.' " Kirsten seemed unable even to draw a decent breath, leaving the words tattered. "Now another person has died. And I can't help feeling it's because I didn't get it right."

Marcus assumed she was talking about Gloria, and said only, "You don't know she's gone." When Kirsten's tears continued, he could not bring himself to say anything more.

The memorial was in one of the great landmarks of downtown Washington, a church of stone and lofty dimensions. It had to be, for the crowd was astonishing. Whatever else Ashley Granger might have been, he was certainly well-liked, and by a vast assortment of people. Blacks and Asians and Hispanics and Indians and whites all mingled and shared the pallor of the truly grieving. Marcus settled Kirsten into a pew toward the rear, for the church was full and growing cramped.

He gave his own seat to a woman weeping jewels and genuine tears, and moved to the back wall. There were people in corporate-style suits and others in baggy jeans and sweats, polished shoes and work boots, all burdened with unexpected sorrow.

As the minister completed his greeting and led them in the first hymn, a diminutive figure walked up and said, "It is good to see you, Marcus Glenwood. Though the reason is not good, no, not good at all."

Marcus stared at Dee Gautam, the little figure swallowed in a dark suit two sizes too big, or perhaps too big for the size of the man this day. "I can't believe this has happened."

"This is the problem with our lot and our life." Dee Gautam surveyed the crowd, nodded to someone Marcus did not see. "We are witness to the bitter fragility of life on earth."

Marcus asked because the sorrow he carried demanded it, "Is Gloria Hall dead as well?"

Dee stared at him with eyes deep and liquid. "I do not deal in rumors, Mr. Glenwood. You must try to avoid this as well. Rumors are a sea you can drown in."

The similarity to his own last conversation with Ashley only pushed the sorrow deeper. "Is she?"

Slowly Dee Gautam shook his head in refusal. "This day we bury Ashley Granger, a good man and a friend. That is enough for now, Mr. Glenwood. The day can only hold so many tears."

The little man turned and walked away, leaving Marcus open to the thrust of unassailable fact. The gathering condemned him with both its numbers and its grief. Marcus stood at the church's back wall, aware that were he the one laid out in the bronze coffin there in the central aisle, his own passage would go unnoticed and unmourned. He would simply depart and be gone, a leaf plucked by winter's bleak hand and tossed away, overlooked and unsung. A loss to none but his own forgotten dreams.

The pastor started to speak, his words both a dirge and a personal conviction. Marcus heard about a man he had hardly known and now never would. A man whose tenets ran so deep they were rarely expressed, and then only in the barest of words. History was full of such men, the pastor lamented, while the present knew only their lack. Ashley Granger had lived the Samaritan's challenge, turning his back to no man. He died, yes, yet still he lived. The pastor did not shout this news triumphantly, nor even strive to convince anyone. Instead, his voice beat steady and determined as a drum. Ashley Granger lives on because he must. He enters the wedding feast and is taken to the very first table, greeted there by the bridegroom himself. Marcus stood and listened and understood very little save for his own lack of accomplishment.

Afterward he stood by the bottom stair, watching the throng drift out slowly. The mourners seemed reluctant to give this good man such a paltry sum of time. Marcus stood and realized that something had happened to him in that service. What it was, he did not know, for genuine awareness remained below the level of words. Yet he knew, and felt the resulting energy there in his gut. He was taking something away from this tragic confrontation, something so potent it would require days and perhaps weeks to understand. For now, all he could do was resolve not to let his weakness dominate. He would do his best to keep Ashley Granger's parting gift from fading into yet one more toneless memory.

The resolve hardened his gaze and his voice as Kirsten walked slowly toward him. "You knew Ashley?"

She was unable to lie. "We dated for a while. After Gloria started going out with

Gary. But I wasn't ready . . . It didn't work out."

He accepted the admission with a single nod. "I want you to stay up here in Washington."

The direct command was enough to focus her gaze. Marcus continued, "Ashley was investigating something. I have no idea what it was, only that it was important enough to turn our case around. I want you to find out what it was."

She gave the barest nod of acceptance. "I'll try."

"No more trying, Kirsten. No more avoidance. You will do it. And fast. I can only give you tomorrow." He did not care how it sounded. The time for velvet wordplay was over. "I'll speak with Dee, ask him to have you watched and make sure you're safe."

"Who?"

"It doesn't matter. The day after tomorrow, you need to be ready to travel to Raleigh with a new witness. I won't know any more until tomorrow night at the earliest."

"But —"

"Let me finish. Whether you decide to stay in Raleigh is your choice. But if you do, I expect to find a change staying with you."

Something sparked within her violet

eyes, a gleam that left him with a sudden urge to draw her near, hold her so tight she could feel the hollowness at the center of his own chest. The desire only hardened his tone. "Up to now, you've done nothing but try your best to run away. No more, Kirsten. If you stay in Raleigh, I want you to do so with answers and a will to fight. A determination to see this case through to the very end."

He turned and left her there, not looking back, not needing to. He was not turning from Kirsten, but rather from all that had been before. The path leading forward was lined with mourners and with grief, as it should be.

THIRTY-TWO

The following evening Darren met him at the Raleigh airport with the news, "C-Charlie Hayes, he's b-been calling all the t-time."

"Does he have the video ready?"

Darren handed Marcus the cellular phone as they passed into the night. "Sounded t-that way t-to me."

But Marcus did not call. He needed time to sort through everything he had learned at the detention center. He kneaded his neck, leaned back, closed his eyes. Charlie could wait. They would go into court the next morning with whatever they had.

They were midway to Rocky Mount before he picked up the phone, and then it was to call his secretary, not Charlie. The familiar voice with its strange mixture of humor, good sense, and constant tragedy said, "Well, hello stranger."

"How are you, Netty?"

"Can't complain. Well, I could. But it never helps, so I won't bother. Things have been jumping around the office."

"New business?"

"Some. Nothing that can't wait. People coming in know you're tied up with this trial — shoot, the whole world does. No, most of the calls have been from the press."

That pushed him up straight. "You don't say."

"Charlie Hayes has been having himself a field day. Talking to the *New York Times* reporter almost gave the man hives, he got so worked up. He was interviewed by PBS and a couple of the local television stations."

"This could be a very good thing," Marcus said, wishing he could feel more hope for the missing woman.

"Kirsten there with you?"

"No." Marcus noted his own disappointment at the unspoken news that she had not called. "She's looking into something up in Washington."

"Pity. Alma's been asking about her. I'll miss her, too. She was a big help last week."

"Kirsten helped you?"

"Almost every day. Jay's been going through one of his bad spells. She was seeing to things around the office. That girl is a good worker, hon'. Solid as they come."

"I didn't know."

"Now that's a curious thing." The humor was back full force. "She made me promise not to tell you, wouldn't arrive till after you left, had to be gone before you came home. I guess them big-city ladies got ways we country folk won't never understand."

"I guess," Marcus agreed idly, and took a long moment to decide there was no profit in studying that course. "Can you do something for me tonight?"

"What, now?"

"Soon as possible."

"I suppose so."

"I need you to come by the office, get the last couple of New Horizons annual reports. I'll have them ready for you. Go to one of those late-night photo places, have them make copies of all the executives' pictures. Make one set big as they can. Then fifteen eight-by-tens of each."

As they pulled into the driveway, Marcus was immensely gratified to see Dee's gardener leave his shabby trailer and make his bowlegged way toward them. He said into the phone, "We've just gotten home. Come on by any time."

The gardener opened his door and announced, "Dee Gautam say, it all done. Lady, she come."

Marcus felt the cloud of worry he had been carrying begin to coalesce into action. "He found us an interpreter?"

The ancient face screwed up tight. "I just say that, yes?"

"Good. Right. When does she arrive?"

"You say tomorrow, she come tomorrow." The man huffed his way around and started off, muttering a chanted curse.

Marcus called, "Wait." He picked up the shopping bag and slid from the Jeep. He walked over to the little man and held it out. "This is for you."

The man seemed not to believe there was any good reason to reach for the bag. "You not pay. Dee Gautam pay."

"This isn't payment. It's a gift. Take it. Please."

Reluctantly the wizened figure accepted the package, and drew the first of two items into the streetlight. The man breathed a quiet *Eeeeya*. He unfolded the sweater, cable-knit merino wool, green and chased with suede along the shoulders and the elbows. Marcus was vastly relieved that the store's smallest size apparently would fit him well, and said quietly, "There's something more."

Slowly the man returned to the bag, drew out a pair of deerskin gloves, yellow as butter and soft as an autumn sunrise. Marcus said simply, "It looks to be a cold winter for gardening."

The man's gaze rose in glittering wonder. "Why you do this?"

Marcus still could not find a way to express what he was feeling, except to say, "Sometimes words alone are almost a lie."

The man nodded slowly, then returned to the inspection of his gifts. Marcus asked, "What is your name?"

The gardener took a long time answering. "Long time ago, I was Chung. Since then, many names. Many places, many names."

Marcus settled a hand upon a small shoulder, hard as wind-carved rock. "Thank you, Chung." When the man did not respond, Marcus turned and went inside.

Marcus slept little and woke hard. His dawn nightmare was the same, yet longer and more feral, trapping him and gnawing at him like some flesh-eating critter of the dark hours. He awoke gasping and drenched from the effort of freeing himself. He arose and ate a solitary breakfast, then turned to the task of preparing for what would no doubt be a long and wearying grind.

When Marcus entered the courtroom on Wednesday morning, Charlie Hayes was there to greet him. Alma and Austin had not yet arrived. Before Charlie could start in, Marcus said, "Kirsten is arriving with a new witness. Darren went to the airport to collect them. They should be arriving any minute now. With an interpreter. I need you to be downstairs to greet them and walk the witness through the process. Wait in the coffee shop for further word."

Behind his glasses, Charlie did a slow blink. "An interpreter."

"That's right. The witness's name is Hao Lin. She's Chinese. And terrified. We're bringing her straight from the INS detention center outside Washington. She was caught with a boatload trying to sneak into Chesapeake Bay."

Charlie's body might have slowed with age, but his mind was as swift as ever. "This why you told me to go ahead with the video enhancement?"

"Yes."

"Did you know what the witness would tell us?"

"I guessed as much."

"You guessed it." Charlie gave his head a slow shake. "You sure had a lot riding on that guess."

"I knew it had to be something big for them to murder Ashley over it." When Charlie started to turn toward the defense table, Marcus continued, "I'm pretty sure Logan doesn't know anything about that."

"That witch he's riding with looks vile enough."

Marcus glanced over, found Suzie Rikkers glaring back. "Maybe. But not Logan. Being driven and ambitious doesn't make a man an accomplice to murder." Marcus ignored Suzie's baleful stare and rose to greet Alma Hall. "I need you to help us with something."

"Just say the word." Tired but steady.

"I'm going to speak with the judge. When I turn toward you, go find Charlie in the coffee shop and bring them in."

Marcus swiftly outlined what he wanted from Charlie. He was still heads down when the bailiff ordered the courtroom to rise. It was only when Marcus reseated himself that he noticed the continued murmur from behind, and turned to find himself facing a packed courtroom.

Charlie said, "You hear about the press?"

"Netty told me you'd fielded some calls."

"Calls and cameras and microphones galore. Had myself a time." Charlie rose from his seat. "I'll go wait for the witness downstairs, take them for a cup of coffee."

"Have them ready to ride within the

hour," Marcus said, and rose to address Judge Nicols. "Your Honor, I ask to approach the bench."

"Your honor, we wish to present the video to the jury as evidence."

Although the tape had been included as part of Marcus' original evidence, clearly Judge Nicols had not expected him to request a jury showing. But Logan had. Before the judge had recovered, he launched into, "We hereby lodge an objection as to the authenticity of this evidence, Your Honor."

She turned sternly toward Logan. Marcus refrained from turning as well, for Suzie Rikkers was standing on Logan's other side, glaring at him. From this range he could almost feel the scalding heat. He kept his eyes fastened on the judge as Logan continued, "We don't know who produced this tape, Your Honor. We don't know where it came from. So the first issue is one of reliability. You can't tell from looking at it who the speaker is. With today's computerized manipulation techniques, it could be a voice-over, a different person entirely."

Judge Nicols cast a swift glance at Marcus, but was drawn back by Logan's insistent attack. "There is also the question of the purpose for which this video was made, Your Honor. It could all be part of an elaborate hoax. We have witnesses who will testify to the fact that Gloria Hall had a long history of activism and troublemaking. She apparently held a grudge against the Chinese regime. She had her own agenda. This could be something she cooked up entirely for dramatic effect. The risk of prejudice outweighs any probative value."

Logan paused as the judge turned to Marcus, both of them apparently expecting him to respond. But Marcus would say nothing until the defense had fired off everything they had. Arguing at this point would only reveal his hand.

"One last point, Your Honor," Logan went on. "Counsel for the plaintiff wishes to submit this video only to inflame the jury. He remains intent upon inciting prejudice against my client. We therefore move for its exclusion from evidence."

When Marcus still remained silent, Judge Nicols decided, "Reluctantly I must agree with the defense. Unless you can establish its authenticity and demonstrate a valid purpose behind its being shown, I must exclude the tape."

Marcus turned and nodded toward Alma, who instantly rose and left the courtroom. "We have a witness who can do precisely that, Your Honor."

The judge's eyebrows lifted. "This is the result of your requested deposition?"

"It is, Your Honor. Her name is Hao Lin."

"She can authenticate this video?"

"And establish not only who made it, but the purpose as well."

Logan started in, "Your Honor, I protest —"

"No, Mr. Kendall. I heard you out. Plaintiff has the right to demonstrate validity. I will reserve my final ruling on the tape until after I have heard this testimony. Proceed, Mr. Glenwood."

"The Plaintiff calls Miss Hao Lin to the stand."

The INS officer who accompanied her forward only magnified the woman's frailty. Hao Lin was just twenty-eight, but she bore the weary legacy of much hardship. She carried herself like a woman hoary with a wealth of winters. The entire courtroom watched mesmerized as the officer released the woman's shackles. The bailiff clearly had no experience administering the oath through an interpreter, and had to be instructed by the judge to administer the oath a second time to the interpreter herself, who identified herself as a lecturer in Cantonese and Mandarin at Georgetown University and a licensed United Nations interpreter. Marcus gave silent thanks for the thoroughness of Dee Gautam.

Marcus decided it was best to start with the worst, and hope to at least partially disarm the defense. "Miss Hao, how exactly did you arrive in this country?"

Her response was a singing whisper, more a sigh than a true voice, and carried with it all the calamity of this age. By contrast, the interpreter's voice sounded almost harsh. "I came by boat."

"Was this a legal transport?"

"No."

"So you were a refugee on an illegal vessel."

"Yes."

"Where did you board the vessel, Miss Hao?"

"Macao."

"How much did you pay for the journey?"

"Twenty-five thousand dollars."

"Did you have these funds?"

"No. I signed a paper promising to work for these people for ten years."

"So you agreed to ten years of what amounts to bonded servitude in order to come to this country." He cast swift glances all around. Judge Nicols and the jury were clearly riveted by her words.

Logan was scribbling madly. Suzie blistered the air between them with her gaze. "Do you know what work you would be doing here?"

"No. It didn't matter. Anything would be better than what I left behind."

Marcus moved slowly until he stood at the far edge of the jury box. Hao Lin wore a neat cotton top, patterned with flowers and dancing figures, that most likely had once belonged to a schoolgirl. Her jeans were bound about her middle with rope, and folded over to fit her tiny waist. She seemed swallowed up by the hard witness chair. "Please tell the jury what exactly you were leaving behind in China, Miss Hao."

The voice diminished further still, until the interpreter's translation sounded almost a shout. "For six years I was a political detainee, held in the *lao gai* prison of Factory 101."

Judge Nicols hammered long and hard to silence the resulting uproar. Her voice was one notch below a snarl as she lectured the crowded room, "Listen up! This is not a theater. What you have up here is not for your entertainment. This is a court of law. I expect you to show proper decorum, or be expelled. Now, is that clear?" When she was greeted with silence, she nodded to Marcus. "Proceed."

"You were at Factory 101 in Guang-dong Province for six years," Marcus repeated. "Were you ever given a trial?"

"No, a hearing in front of a Party tribunal. Nothing more. I did not even learn how long my sentence was until I had worked there for seven months."

"Did you have a right of appeal?"

The question caused a series of back-and-forth discourses between the interpreter and the witness, who clearly had no idea what Marcus meant. Her face showed utter bafflement. Marcus caught sight of Judge Nicols watching the girl with pity. Finally the interpreter answered simply, "No."

"No trial, no right of appeal. What was your supposed crime?"

"I was arrested while protesting the anniversary of Tiananmen Square."

Marcus walked over to the other side of the room, distancing himself from what was about to come. He asked, "Did you ever see Gloria Hall at the factory?"

"Yes." The reply came instantly. Much of the response was drowned out and had to be repeated. "The black American who spoke no Chinese. She worked on my line."

Marcus took a photograph from his table, which meant he had to view the Halls' stricken features up close. He showed the photograph to the witness. "Is this the woman?"

The witness looked long, very long, then replied to the photograph, "The same girl, but she did not look like this."

"How was she different?"

"She was badly beaten."

A low moan rose from the Halls. Judge Nicols looked over but did not speak. Marcus chose not to turn around, letting the jury stare for him. "Can you tell us about conditions at the factory, Miss Hao?"

"Horrible. We were chained to our machines. I glued the soles onto shoes. This American woman operated a steam press. The presses were the hardest work. We were fed gruel and beaten if we did not meet our daily quota." The tiny chanting voice was dreadful in its simple clarity. "We slept in a dormitory, a long hall of concrete benches. We worked every day."

"What did Gloria Hall work on?"

"Clothes. Bright colors. For children, I think."

"We offer as evidence a New Horizons label." He handed over the slip of cloth. "Do you recognize this?"

She shuddered as she took it. "I sewed this for three years before I made shoes. The shoes had the same logo."

Marcus walked back to his bench for

the next picture. "Plaintiff offers as evidence a photograph of the man whose name appears upon the incorporation records of the joint venture between Factory 101 and New Horizons Incorporated."

"Granted."

Marcus handed the photograph to the witness. "Can you tell me who this is?"

The woman drew back, refusing to take the picture, even to touch it. Her face showed total revulsion. "Zhao Ren-Fan. He owned the factory. He came and walked around and left."

"Who ran the factory in his absence?"

"His son. A bad man. Very bad. And another man. He was more evil than the son."

Marcus took the sheaf of photographs prepared by his secretary. "Plaintiff offers as evidence photographs of the New Horizons board and senior officers."

Logan vaulted to his feet. "Objection! Unsubstantiated, inflammatory, unproven!"

"Overruled. You may cross later. Proceed."

"Miss Hao, I would like you to examine these very carefully. Tell me if you have seen any of these men before." Marcus held his breath as she went through the sheaf, for there had been no chance to prepare. Only to hear that white men had been there with the general.

She handed two back. "These only."

"You saw these two men at the factory?"

The courtroom erupted. She winced as the judge pounded for order. "Yes. Several times."

Marcus read the names off the back, "We identify these as photographs of James Southerland, chief executive officer, and Frank Clinedale, assistant chairman of the board, of New Horizons."

Logan had to shout to be heard over the tumult. "Objection!"

"Silence! Mr. Kendall, I told you to wait your turn." She glared out over the court, but said simply, "Proceed."

"Miss Hao, let us move on to one day several weeks ago. You saw the two Chinese men who operated the factory in Zhao Ren-Fan's absence unchain Gloria Hall from her steam press."

"Yes."

"Where did they take her?"

"To the room."

He wished he could prevent Alma and Austin from hearing this, but he knew there was no way. "What room is that?"

"The room. The punishment room." The woman's features were hollowed to the core. Her gaze was lifeless. "The room."

"How do you know what went on there?"

"Everybody knew. The room had a window so all could watch."

"The punishment room had a window overlooking the factory floor, is that what you are telling us?"

"Yes."

"How far were you from this window, Miss Hao?"

"Five machines."

"So that would be no more than fifty feet, is that correct?"

There was a swift discourse, then, "Less."

"So they took Gloria into the room. What was she doing?"

"Crying. Everybody cried."

"Did you see what happened in there?"

"Yes. All must watch."

"Please tell the court what you saw, Miss Hao."

"They brought in a camera and made a tape."

"A videotape?"

"Yes. They make her read off a sheet of paper. I watched carefully because I had not seen anything like this."

"Was General Zhao taking part?"

"No. The general had not been to the factory in over a month. Longer."

"So his son made the tape." Marcus

turned toward his table. He had to at least try and show the Halls what this cost him. Both parents looked stricken to the point of numbness, which was not altogether a bad thing. He asked quietly, "What happened then, Miss Hao?"

"They took the American girl down the stairs."

"Where did the stairs lead, Miss Hao?"

She had the decency to stare sadly at the parents and say nothing.

Marcus waited a long moment. The air itself held a choking breath. "Miss Hao, where did the stairs lead?"

"Nobody knows." The woman's voice blew through the court like breath of the final winter. "Nobody ever came back."

"No!" It was not Alma who shrieked, but Austin. The man toppled from his chair and would have collapsed in his attempt to rise had Charlie and Alma not been there to catch him. *"No!"*

Judge Nicols was on her feet as well. "Court is recessed until one o'clock."

THIRTY-THREE

"Your witness, Mr. Logan."

"Thank you, Your Honor." Logan was slow in rising, not out of fear, but rather from caution. He faced a new opponent. He sought to strike the killing blow. "Let me understand what you told the plaintiff's lawyer, Miss Hao. That *is* your real name?"

"Hao Lin. Yes."

Marcus struggled to concentrate fully. But it was difficult. His mind felt clawed by the morning's testimony and Austin's collapse. Not to mention the news that Kirsten had given him during the break.

Charlie was off comforting Austin the best he could. Marcus sat with Alma, who had insisted on returning to the courtroom. One of them had to be there, she said over and over, not for themselves but for Gloria. Marcus had sent Kirsten off on another assignment, one that could not wait. Not after he had received the information she carried.

Marcus remained caught not only by the news, but by the way Kirsten had delivered it. Alma and Austin had been broken by the morning, and the scars were fresh upon Alma's drawn features. Kirsten, however, had neither wept nor withdrawn. She had kept her gaze fastened upon him, as though his example was what kept her intact. She had delivered her news in a steady voice, turning so that she could not see Gloria's parents huddled with Charlie. She had watched him digest the news, and accepted his instructions with the silent steadiness of a pro.

Marcus willed himself to turn away from the memory of that beautifully intent gaze, and watched Logan begin his stalking dance. "All right, Miss Hao. What you want the jury to believe is that you just happened to be held in this factory in China. Then you escaped. Then you got on a boat. Then you crossed the ocean — wait, excuse me, you crossed *two* oceans. Because you would have first passed over the Pacific, then somehow gotten over here to the Atlantic. And then you wound up in little old Raleigh, North Carolina. Now is that right, Miss Hao? Have I stated that correctly?"

"I was released. Not escaped. But all else is correct."

"You were released."

"Yes. I served the full six years, then they let me go."

"Then you just happened to find a boat heading to America."

"No. The boat master found me. They like to take *lao gai* prisoners. They know we will pay anything to leave China."

Logan kept his distance from the witness stand. He did not approach, did not threaten. He moved cautiously, lightly. His tone was mild, almost a singsong. "But you didn't have any money, did you?"

"No."

"So if you couldn't pay anything, you would *do* anything to get away from China."

"Yes. Anything."

She was so diminutive, so frail and weary and tragic, that Logan did not dare turn the jury against him by striking hard. He paced, but far away. He asked his questions in a voice almost as soft as her own. "You got into this country by not telling the truth, is that correct?"

"Yes."

"You had to lie to get in."

"I came without papers."

"But the ends justified the means, didn't they?"

"Yes."

"So you feel there are times when lying is justified, is that not true, Miss Hao?"

"Yes."

"You took an oath at the beginning of your testimony. Do you know what an oath is?"

"A promise."

"Exactly. A promise to tell the truth. But you have just said that you would do anything, *say* anything, to stay out of China. Even perjure yourself."

"I have told the truth."

"All right. Tell us a little more about your life back there. Are your parents still alive?"

"My mother only. She is a village doctor."

"What did you do before you were arrested, Miss Hao?"

"I was studying at Guangzhou University."

"What was your major, your field of study?"

She cast a bitter look over to where Logan stood on the courtroom's far side, the only real sign of life she had given since he had risen to his feet. "I studied law."

He hid his wince well. "How long were you at university?"

"Three and one-half years."

"Over three years at university," Logan said, moving gently back in her direction. "And yet you never studied English?" He caught her momentary hesitation, and moved in closer still. "Wasn't English a required part of the university curriculum, Miss Hao?"

She spoke for herself then, the accent very strong. "Understand little. No speak."

"So you *do* speak English. Did you not say you understood the oath to tell the truth?"

Hao Lin resumed speaking through the interpreter. "I never said I did not speak any English."

"Of course not." His smirk was for the jury. "You merely insisted upon the court's paying the expense of flying down an interpreter for you, when in truth what you really wanted was to give yourself a bit more time to think over the questions and frame your answers more carefully. Is that not correct?"

Marcus rose. "Objection. Belaboring the witness."

Judge Nicols hesitated, then shook her head. "Overruled. Witness is required to answer."

"No. I needed help understanding and speaking."

"One of the many great things about this country, Miss Hao, is how you are required to tell the truth up on the witness stand." Logan moved to where he could lean upon the railing of the jury box. "Tell us the truth, Ms. Hao. Did you not always want to come live in this country?"

"Yes. Some. Not like now."

"Isn't it also true that the Great Wall of China may have been built to keep foreigners out, but now it serves to keep its own citizens in?"

"I don't understand."

Logan asked his softest question yet. "What would happen if you were sent back to China, Miss Hao?"

She showed electric terror. "I must not go back. I can't."

"So you would do *anything* to stay."

"Yes. I said that."

"Sell your brother?"

"Yes. But I have none."

Soft as a velvet lash, he asked, "Sell your body?"

For the first time, she bowed her head. And did not respond.

Marcus readied for an objection if Logan pressed further, but he divorced himself from the question and her silent answer by crossing back to the courtroom's other side. From that distance Logan continued, "No matter how genuine your motives are, Miss Hao, no matter how badly you want to stay in this country, nothing justifies lying under oath in a court of law. *American* law. It is a serious matter." He turned back toward the stand. "So I ask you once again, Miss Hao, under oath: Would you not do or say anything to stay in this country?"

A voice like wind through broken reeds sighed, which the translator rendered as, "Yes. But I am telling the truth here."

Logan took a single step toward the witness. "Is it not true that this video is essential to your own case?"

"I don't understand."

Another step. "In order to remain in this country, you must show the INS that you face severe persecution in your home country. You claim to have been held for years in this so-called factory prison. Isn't this video the only evidence to uphold your claim?"

A tighter note entered her voice. "I have told the truth."

Logan took a third step. His prey was in sight. He moved in for the kill. "Isn't it true, Miss Hao, that you know how the game is played? Are you not aware that if you tell the jury everything the plaintiff's lawyer wants them to hear, he will then help you stay in this country?" He walked over and rested one hand upon the witness stand. "Hasn't he already offered to represent your own petition for asylum?"

The interpreter did not have time to

catch up before Hao Lin begged in English of her own, "I tell truth."

Logan turned away. "No further questions."

THIRTY-FOUR

The morning was formed by all the treasures of autumn, yet Marcus took no comfort in the viewing. He stared out the Jeep's side window as Darren drove him into town, seeing the magnificent fall cloak unfolding beneath a sky as deep as heaven's well. But his heart still ached from the night tremors, and his mind was busy with what lay ahead. It was a bilious mixture, and ridiculed the day's bequest. The air was so cold as to lift a silver-white veil from the fields and the forests, one that clung close and low to the earth. Trees rose from the mist as they would from a lowland of dragons and myths, some still green, others flaming beacons to the season's wonder. Marcus felt an overpowering urge to shut his eyes, either that or tell Darren to drive faster. His inability to drink nature's elixir shamed his grandmother's memory.

The nightmare had clenched him tight as a jealous woman's embrace, refusing to let him go, holding him under until he was sure he would drown, or perhaps merely wishing for a swifter demise. It whispered to him even now. Worse still was how it had occurred today of all days, when the world was waiting. Today, when the trial hung upon a silver thread, ready to be sent spinning like a mirrored top.

He realized he had to do something, just as they passed a trio of lakes bordering the highway. "See that picnic area up ahead. Pull in there for a second, will you?"

Darren either thought it was natural enough a request not to require comment, or not bearing enough importance. He slowed and turned, then turned again, finally coming to a halt with the Jeep's snout pointing back toward the highway, ready for any trouble and a quick departure. Marcus pried open his door and walked away.

The mist was heavier here, rising to his thighs and drifting in cold swaths as he moved. The graveled road was not hard to hold to, as pines and sycamores and wild fruit trees accompanied him to either side. Marcus walked out to where the loudest sound came from unseen ducks. They rested upon the mist-clad waters and chattered softly about this baffling day.

As he looked out over low-lying fog, the sun's lip cleared the horizon. The vista was instantly transformed from one world to the next, rising to a province of glory and gold. The trees' eastern faces shone a greeting of blondest adoration. The strengthening light must have reached to the lake's surface, for a few dozen mallards burst from the golden froth. The instant they cleared the fog, they metamorphosed from feathered beasts to miniature seraphim with flame-touched wings.

Marcus followed their flight eastward, wishing he felt something more than empty. He knew now why the nightmares were becoming steadily fiercer. He sought to take a turning in his battered and wounded life. But the wisdom brought no consolation, only hazards.

Marcus stared at the sky, empty now of celestial spirits and signs, and wished he knew how to pray. It would be good to have someone from whom he might either seek strength or at least beg a way forward.

The rear of the federal courthouse had a pillared alcove in one corner, a space set aside for the deputies standing courthouse duty. As Marcus exited the Jeep, a lone figure took the brick steps down from the alcove and started toward them. Marcus angled his approach to meet the retired patrolman.

Jim Bell said in greeting, "Feels cold

enough this morning to make you think maybe summer's been done in for good." The bearded receptionist granted Darren a friendly nod. "How you doing, son."

"Pretty g-good, Mr. B-Bell."

Bell waited until Darren moved ahead a few paces, then said quietly, "A man in my position, he hears some things if he has the notion."

"I'm listening."

The voice dropped another notch. "The judge and Jenny both got calls yesterday. Asking no-account questions about their possible appointments."

"Leaving no room for doubt that the calls are tied together," Marcus filled in for him. "And tied to this trial."

"The question is, what is so all-fired important that they'd both get this heads-up yesterday?"

"They'll find that out this morning," Marcus said. "The whole world will."

"All right, Mr. Glenwood." Judge Nicols had dispensed with the morning's formalities in record time. "You may call your next witness."

"Your Honor," Marcus announced, "I feel it is time the jury had an opportunity to meet Miss Gloria Hall, and let her speak for herself."

"Objection!" Logan had risen well before Marcus finished speaking. "Permission to approach the bench, Your Honor."

"Very well."

When they were in close, Marcus said, "I move that the video be admitted as evidence, Your Honor."

Logan retaliated with the swiftness of hard preparation. "Objection. The witness Hao Lin clearly stated she could not hear what was being said. It might be the one time Miss Hao, or whatever her name really is, told us the full truth the entire time she was on the stand."

"That was uncalled for."

Logan ignored him. "By Miss Hao's own testimony she heard nothing, Your Honor. All she could say was that she saw a video being made. And we stipulate that even this is highly questionable testimony. The witness repeatedly perjured herself."

"That is not true."

"She admitted under cross that she would say anything, do anything to stay in this country. This video was critical to her own case."

"That does not in any way make the witness a liar, Your Honor."

"No, but it certainly offers a motive." Logan did not let up, nor release his grip on the edge of the judge's bench. "Miss Hao has every reason to want this video to be true. It backs up her own request

505

for political asylum. She said as much herself."

Marcus countered, "Miss Hao showed herself to be both intelligent and reliable, Your Honor. Her testimony stands as a valid and direct tie-in between Gloria Hall, the factory, and this video."

Logan shook his head like a bull tossing flies. "This is inherently unreliable testimony, Your Honor. The woman was obviously lying to advance her own cause. We have shown this witness, someone the plaintiff actually brought from jail to testify, to be both a liar and a fraud."

Judge Nicols pondered a long moment. Marcus felt the air clog until he could not draw another free breath. Finally she decided, "I am going to credit the witness as having given this court a reliable testimony. You may enter the video as evidence."

Marcus fled before she could change her mind. The trek back across the floor was lengthened by having to stare into the afflicted gazes of Alma and Austin Hall. The previous day had cut deeply. Marcus forced his lungs to unlock. Today would scarcely be better. They had been warned, and they had insisted on remaining. There was nothing else he could do. "Plaintiff calls Maureen Folley to the stand."

The woman certainly lived up to the Charlie Hayes' description of the night before — short and stocky and possessing all the charm of a tenpenny nail. As she gave her name to the bailiff and affirmed the oath, she also revealed the flat, toneless voice of a big-city taxi dispatcher. Marcus sorted his handwritten notes, and gave Charlie a short nod. She was perfect.

Marcus rose to his feet and began. "Mrs. Folley, you are a full professor of visual arts at North Carolina State University, are you not?"

"Yes."

"And your specialty is digital imaging, is that not correct?"

"Yes."

"Objection!" Logan's alarm was clearly genuine. "Your Honor, plaintiff has been granted permission to show the video, not render it!"

Judge Nicols did not even permit Marcus to respond. "Overruled."

"Mrs. Folley, you have testified in a number of trials regarding the authenticity of videotapes, have you not?"

"Yes."

"What can you tell us about the video we are about to see?"

"That it is all of one piece. It has not been spliced." She turned to the jury and continued. "Amateur video recorders will scar a tape just like the grooves carved into a bullet exiting the barrel of a gun. This entire tape was shot by the same camera, and in one continuous session."

"Objection!" Logan pressed against his table, as though needing this barrier to keep himself from racing forward and grabbing Marcus by the neck. "This is unproven, unsubstantiated, theoretical!"

"Overruled. You will have your turn on cross. Proceed."

"Please continue, Mrs. Folley."

"I have done a microscopic search of the tape. As I said, the camera ran continuously. What you see was done in one take."

"Objection! It is just as possible that the tape was spliced together from a series of takes, just done on a machine that scarred it like a camera!"

Judge Nicols rounded on him. "I will not warn you again."

"But Your Honor, really, this is —"

"Sit." She held him fast with her gaze. "Proceed, Mr. Glenwood."

"Before we go further with this testimony, Your Honor, I'd like to show the original tape."

"Very well."

Marcus helped the bailiff roll forward the metal stand bearing four televisions, angled so that at least one screen was visible to everyone — judge and defense and jury and the packed audience chamber. A tape machine rested upon a shelf beneath the screens. Marcus walked back to his desk and took the videotape from its packet, his movements slow, making good theater of the process. When the bailiff had turned on the machine, Marcus inserted the tape and pushed the play button.

Gloria Hall reached across time and distance and spoke to the jury. Marcus listened and heard something new. The change was not merely because it was a public performance. It was the first time he had studied the tape since the previous day's testimony. He knew now that Gloria Hall's voice held the same dull weeping quality as Hao Lin's.

The realization added a deeper poignancy to her crude pattern of speech. Her almost invisible form remained silhouetted against the backdrop of overbright light. Marcus risked several glances at the jury, and saw many of them squinting hard, as though seeking to penetrate the light and study the woman more closely. Marcus turned back to the video and watched to its too-brief end.

He left the televisions where they were, creating a technical barrier in the middle of the floor. Alma's quiet weeping merely punctuated the moment's piercing quality. "Mrs. Folley, could you describe for the court what it means to digitally clean up a picture?"

"Objection! Your Honor, plaintiff intends to fabricate reality from what is merely theory."

"Overruled." Judge Nicols did not even glance his way. "Proceed."

"Do you require the question to be repeated, Mrs. Folley?"

"No." She addressed her response to the jury, showing her experience at courtroom testimony. She seemed utterly unfazed by the video, which was natural, as she had probably seen it a full hundred times by now. "Essentially, it is the same as taking an analog tape of old music and remastering it. The video is first digitized, and then rerendered through computer analysis. All ambient particles and, in this instance, unnecessary light are removed. The image is redrawn into tighter focus."

Marcus realized that the majority of the jury did not understand, and that it did not matter. "But this cleaned-up version is still the same, is it not?"

"The underlying image is identical to the original, yes. Just as it is when you remaster an old jazz recording to hear the sound better."

"All right. Your Honor, we would now

like to show the remastered version of this video."

"Objection!" Logan started across the floor.

But Nicols was having none of it. "Stay right where you are, Mr. Kendall."

"But Your Honor —"

"This court accepts the testimony as valid, and has decided to overrule your objection." The dark jaw jutted forward slightly. "I would advise you to reseat yourself. Now."

Logan expelled a vast sigh of fury as he retook his seat. Marcus used this moment, when all attention was elsewhere, to reach behind the back of his table and draw forth the blown-up photograph. He held the poster-size print backward as Charlie Hayes fumbled with the easel, so that all the jury saw was the white styrofoam backing. "Mrs. Folley, would you please set up the digital video machine?"

He stood there holding the unseen photograph as the ungainly woman with her flat face and voice retrieved her bulky briefcase from beside Marcus' chair. Charlie and he had cooked up the plan while discussing the witness the night before. As Marcus watched her feed in the wires and hook up the machine, however, he fretted that they had made a huge blunder. A more unemotional witness he had never sought to bend.

He waited until Mrs. Folley had completed her check and risen to her feet. She pointed at the central button in a vast array of dials and switches and said, "Push that and it will run."

"Thank you. Please, if you would return to the stand." Then he turned the photograph, and set the picture on the easel.

It was only as he turned back that he knew they had chosen wisely.

Mrs. Folley had not moved.

She stood staring at the photograph. It was the first time she had ever seen Gloria Hall anywhere except on the video. Her attention was rapt. The fact that her face revealed no emotion whatsoever did not matter. With her, the jury's attention was drawn to study a black woman in her midtwenties, poised upon the bottom step of a well-appointed house, dressed in a fashionable cocktail gown, her head thrown back and her eyes closed with the pleasure of laughing with all her body and mind and spirit. Marcus saw a number of the jury smile in return. They had no choice. Gloria's joy challenged one and all.

He said merely, "Mrs. Folley, could I please ask you to resume your seat upon the stand."

The woman moved in jerky stages, a puppet hung by knotted threads. It was only when she was reseated and searching her purse for a handkerchief that she sniffed. Once. But it was enough to draw all the jury back to her and away from Gloria, enough to reveal the tears streaming down her flat, hard face.

Marcus pushed the button.

This time Gloria was no longer hidden by lights. The image was vividly clear. The laughing young woman was gone. Her hair was so matted that one side of her head appeared shaved. A deep bruise painted one cheek with a nightmare bloom. Her lips were so puffed and misshapen that they snagged on each word. Her left ear was crusted with dried blood. She was battered to the point of being scarcely recognizable. The same, yet Gloria Hall no longer. The change, heightened by the poster standing alongside the television screen, brought such gasps from the jury that Austin Hall's own agonized moan was scarcely heard.

"Hello, Mother. Hello, Dad. I am fine. Everything is fine here. I am staying here awhile. I am working. I study hard. I am fine. I need money for my work. Send money now. Send money and I will be . . . fine. I am happy. Send money. I want to be left alone. But send money. A hundred thousand dollars. Send it to the Hong Kong branch of the Guangzhou Bank, account four-five-five-seven-two-two. I am happy. Send the money. Do it now."

Marcus waited a long moment after the screen went blank to turn off the machine. He turned and gave Gloria's parents a very long stare, as long as he dared, willing the jury to look with him. There was nothing more to be said. The realization that he was approaching the end of his line of witnesses left him neither jubilant nor drained. He was too depleted for anything except the realization that the case was no longer his. "No further questions."

Marcus returned to his seat. Logan and Suzie Rikkers rushed forward and plucked the photograph from the easel. They stowed both behind their own table, then pushed the television stand back out of view. Each time she passed, Suzie Rikkers raked Marcus with her furious gaze. In the moment's silence, Marcus finally understood why Logan kept bringing her forward, why the warning was being made. His rising fear was such that he did not even hear the questioning or the testimony, did not object once to Logan's furious tirade. He remained seated and staring at his hands, seeing only the horror that now lay revealed. When Logan finally reseated himself, Judge Nicols twice had to ask for Marcus to call his next witness.

Rising to his feet was the hardest point thus far in the case. Marcus said the words because he had no choice, because the pieces were laid out and the next move foreordained, "Plaintiff requests a special hearing in chambers."

THIRTY-FIVE

The hallway from the courtroom to the judge's private chambers was lined with old Norman Rockwell prints. The prints had followed Judge Nicols from one set of chambers to another. In her early days there had been a great deal of speculation about them — how they had been chosen to appease the white voters who might not like having a hyperintelligent, uppity black woman reigning over a courtroom. But those who knew Judge Nicols were certain she did it for herself alone.

Judge Nicols' conference room seated eighteen at an oval table and another dozen in leather chairs around the perimeter. She did not bother to shuck her robes, nor to wait until she had seated herself to say, "All right, Mr. Glenwood. Let's hear what this is all about."

Marcus found it harder to ignore Suzie Rikkers now that the presence behind her presence was known. "Your Honor, we feel that the case as it currently stands requires an expansion in the number of defendants."

Logan huffed his frustrated rage. The scalding that the video had given his case remained evident in his voice. "Your Honor, this is patently absurd. We have the two senior vice presidents of the North Carolina company currently present. This charge he's leveling against the board is ridiculous."

"I was speaking," Marcus replied quietly, "of General Zhao Ren-Fan."

The moment's silence was not all he had expected, nor was the shocked expression on Logan's face. Marcus turned and studied his opponent carefully, ignoring Suzie as best he could. Logan knew, Marcus finally decided. The stupefaction was good theater, but theater just the same. The defense knew.

But Logan merely said, "What?"

"General Zhao Ren-Fan," Marcus repeated quietly. "The man named in the corporate documents as head of the factory in China. The man our witness claimed was proprietor and chief operator of Factory 101."

Logan turned back to the judge. "This entire case is a travesty of federal jurisprudence. This latest absurdity only shows that Mr. Glenwood will go to any and all lengths to subvert the good name of my client." Logan tossed an exasperated glance at Marcus. "Just how is he planning to extend the court's jurisdiction to include someone situated more than nine thousand miles away?"

Marcus' trial sense clamored that none of this was the surprise Logan was pretending it to be. There was a carefully rehearsed quality to the man's shock and outrage. Marcus nodded once. It was all the confirmation he needed, all he would probably ever have, that he had finally arrived at the secret they had so viciously sought to hide.

"Your Honor, the last conversation I had with Ashley Granger, the Washington attorney who was murdered —"

"Here we go again," Logan blasted. "First of all, I have spoken with the Washington police, who categorically deny that the evidence they hold suggests wrongdoing of any sort. The man was killed in a tragic highway accident. Secondly, the plaintiff's counsel seeks to use this man's demise in all sorts of tangential ways, tying together an argument that holds nothing but hot air."

Marcus sprang what he was certain would be a surprise only to the judge. "Your Honor, two weeks ago General Zhao Ren-Fan took up the position of defense attaché to the Chinese embassy in Washington, D.C."

Judge Nicols' astonishment was undisguised. "He's here?"

"Right under the court's nose, Your Honor. This was the information Ashley Granger had uncovered the day he was killed." And what Gloria Hall had discovered, Marcus knew beyond a shadow of doubt, that had made her journey to China so urgent. She had known of this, all right. As did the defense.

"Your Honor!" Logan's voice demanded the judge's attention. "We object on a number of grounds. First of all, the information Glenwood used to present this joint venture as reality is anything but sound. His evidence was nothing more than a photocopy from a so-called Chinese government office nobody has ever heard of. It is not admissible evidence. And secondly, the concept of drawing a foreign diplomat to North Carolina on what is essentially a missing-persons case, and doing so on such highly questionable evidence, will make this court a laughing-stock."

The judge's eyes narrowed, but Marcus could not determine whether she shared his conviction that this was not news, for all she said was, "I am not laughing, Mr. Kendall."

"No, Your Honor, I did not wish to imply that you were." But Logan did not back down. "I merely wish to save Your

Honor the risk of being shamed by an adverse ruling on appeal."

"How kind of you."

Marcus wrested back control of the situation. "Your Honor, a corporation acts only through individuals. I merely want this case to include the people who were actually in charge of the decision that led to Gloria Hall's disappearance."

"You have proven none of this," Logan lashed back.

"On the contrary. We have shown through its past unscrupulous practices that the U.S. company is indeed capable of colluding to kidnap Gloria Hall, precisely because she was tracking down these practices and planned to bring them to light. And we have demonstrated that New Horizons specifically chose to work with Factory 101 because this Chinese group threatened the one thing they hold in greatest esteem, their profit."

"Your Honor, I protest. He continues to besmirch my client's good name with no basis whatsoever."

Glenwood pressed home. "Profit, Your Honor. That was the motive behind all of this. Profit and power. General Zhao joined in because he shared both a lust for profit and the power to hold and abuse these workers. There was a pattern and practice to *both* companies' actions, which was precisely why they were successful partners, and exactly why they were forced to do away with Gloria Hall."

Judge Nicols' gaze tightened. "Do away with her?"

"Kidnap and hold her against her will," Marcus amended, though he remained shattered by what he had finally admitted to himself.

"Your Honor, we object —"

"Enough." She used the flat of her palm as an effective gavel. "I accept the plaintiff's request as valid. The evidence supports his claim of extended jurisdiction over General Zhao as a necessary codefendant."

"We will appeal this ruling, Your Honor." Logan's hoarseness revealed the cost of his defeat.

"Appeal all you like. In the meantime, papers will be served on the Chinese embassy this very afternoon."

Logan clutched for another rope. "He will claim diplomatic immunity."

"That may well be so. But we can nonetheless subpoena the man and require him to stand before this court." Judge Nicols rose to her feet. "We will now adjourn until nine o'clock tomorrow. You gentlemen are dismissed."

The call came through at a quarter to

six the next morning. As Logan groped blindly for the phone, his bedmate moaned and rolled over. He complained, "This better be good."

"And you better be awake," growled the caller.

"One second." Logan recognized the voice instantly. As he slid from bed his current girlfriend called out another man's name. He glanced down, caught by the sudden decision that it was time to trade her in for a newer model. Four weeks was long enough for both of them.

Logan carried the cordless phone out of the bedroom and over to the hall window. Dawn remained a faint rumor on the horizon. He pressed the phone to his chest and took a series of steadying breaths. He was not hesitating in order to wake up. He had never been more awake in his entire life. He had been expecting this call, but still the sheer potential of what it meant left his heart hammering. Another breath, one more. He lifted the receiver again, hoping he could keep the tremor out of his voice. "All right. I'm listening."

The head of the China Trade Council said, "Whatever you want, Kendall. I have the board's full backing on this."

The caller held an admiral's gruffness, the bold commanding grip on power that reflected decades of leading a corporate army. Logan knew the man now. After the first call, Logan had ordered an associate to research the man's background. Up until the previous year, he had been chairman and chief executive officer of one of the nation's top fifty companies, a behemoth that was into everything from cars to home financing.

Logan responded, "The problem is the same as the first time we talked."

"Double your fees. Triple them for all I care." The man chose not to hear Logan. "Take this additional client and name your price."

"I appreciate your offer, sir. But accepting General Zhao as a second client may not be in New Horizons' best interests."

"Forget them!" The bark suggested Logan was treading on thin ice by even questioning the bid. "It's their fault we're in this mess to begin with!"

"Actually, sir, General Zhao —"

"New Horizons was the one that initiated the whole deal!" The chairman of the China Trade Council struggled to rein in his legendary temper. "Look, Kendall. I'm telling you how it is. You understand? Now name your price to include General Zhao as a client."

Logan knew the moment had arrived.

"I want to be named outside counsel."

"What?"

The fact that he had finally managed to throw the chairman gave him confidence. "Not just of the China Trade Council. Your former company has two subsidiaries in North Carolina. I want them too." When the chairman did not respond, he finished with a certainty he did not feel. "Take it or leave it."

To his astonishment, the chairman laughed. "You've been up nights planning this out, haven't you."

"I couldn't afford to give it that kind of time, sir. I have a case to win, remember?"

Another laugh. "All right. It's a deal."

"I want it in writing." This time the tremor could not be kept out of his voice.

"Sure you do. I'll have my people draw it up and courier it down to you today." The humor died, choked down to grating fury. "Just win this case, Kendall. And bury that Glenwood. Bury him deep. Right down to the center of the earth."

THIRTY-SIX

Marcus awoke to the deep black of some predawn hour, a time so vague and fretful even the poets of yore had forsaken the task of naming it. He was not sorry, though he had worked late and his need for sleep was as strong as a starving man's hunger. He decided against an early run. His mind had already tuned in to the day and the work ahead, so he made coffee and took it to his office. Papers were strewn across his desk and the next room's larger table. The night before they had seemed adequate. Now they flouted the truth of what had fueled his labors. Suzie Rikkers hid in the shadows, waiting for him to return to court, eager to pounce.

The phone crashed about the house, as though the machines were all triggered to shout alarm if ever used before dawn. A merry voice asked, "Do I not wake you again?"

"Dee Gautam," he said, and took comfort from naming the mystery. "No, this time I beat you."

The little man rewarded Marcus with a

high-pitched giggle, somewhere between the highest note of a pipe organ and a cackle. "Good, very good. You are learning to catch the worm, no?"

"Learning, but let's leave the worms out of it. What can I do for you?"

"I am calling to say that Chung must leave. He has much fear of the police."

"Maybe I can help him."

"Thank you, but no. His problems are all in the past, and his fears are of the kind that do not heal. You understand?"

Marcus picked up his mug, though the coffee was cold and he no longer wished to drink it. "All too well."

"Yes, you are learning much. It is a good thing and a bad thing, this gift of wisdom."

"The wisdom is fine," Marcus responded. "It's all the baggage I have problems with."

"We will speak of this another time, yes? For now, I am calling at this dark hour to say that today you must find another way to go to your court."

Marcus settled into his chair. "Run that one by me again."

"Your car will not be safe for the drive today, oh very much no. You may call this Chung's parting gift to his new friend." Dee Gautam hung up.

Marcus set down the receiver and spent

a long moment wondering at all the sharp-ended farewells the little man had been forced to make. Then he picked up the phone once more, but set it down again and rose to his feet. Darren would want to be awake when the sheriff's deputy arrived to discover the bomb attached to their car.

They departed for Raleigh in Amos Culpepper's official car. Darren was squeezed into the front passenger seat with his knees bumping against the dashboard computer, the radar gun, and the radio. He did not seem to mind at all. At Amos' suggestion Marcus had spread a towel over the backseat before settling in. With every bounce the low-sprung seat gave off an aroma of sweat and sickness and fear. Marcus listened to Amos give Darren a guided tour around the car's assorted toys, from the siren to the pump-action shotgun to the nightstick with its numerous dents and tooth marks. Marcus then drew out his cellular phone and spent twenty minutes talking strategy with Charlie Hayes. It was only when Darren hit the siren that Marcus felt obliged to explain why they were riding to work in a cop car.

Charlie heard him out, then demanded, "Did they find a bomb?"

"Attached to the starter motor. First place they looked. Said it was very professional."

"Well, hey, that makes everything all right, then, don't it. Long as you're getting blown up by somebody who knows his business."

"We're okay, Charlie."

"This time. How'd you find out about it, anyway?"

"Long story. I'll tell you later."

"If you live that long. You take care, son. I'm fine handling one witness at a time, but this is your trial, you hear what I'm saying? And it's a big one."

Scarcely had Marcus cut the connection when the phone rang again. As soon as he answered, Kirsten said in a rush, "We have to talk."

Marcus sighed his way deeper into the seat, hoping the scents would not linger. "No we don't."

Of everything that he could have said, this was clearly what she had least expected. "I don't understand. You said you had a lot of questions."

"Not anymore, Kirsten. All I need to know is: Are you holding out anything that could have an effect on this trial?"

"No." Solid and swift. "I've finished going through Gloria's things. There were some more papers about the shipments

from the Chinese factory, but that's all."
A moment's hesitation, then a much
smaller voice asked, "You don't care anymore, is that it?"

"No, not at all." Her evident pain invited more of a response than that. Marcus glanced at the front seat, but the two
men were deep into some quiet discussion
and paying him no mind. "Kirsten, we all
have our mysteries."

"I don't understand."

"How can I demand that you tell me
things when I have so much I don't want
to talk about myself?" An image of Suzie
Rikkers and her baleful glare drifted in
and out of focus. The only question for
Kirsten he had at the moment pertained
to Gary Loh, and even this was tainted by
what he would soon be facing. "So long
as you're not withholding evidence we
need for the trial, I'm out of bounds
asking you anything at all."

Marcus had a long moment of listening
to the overpowered engine's muted roar,
the dull murmurs from the front seat, the
hum of tires and wind. Then the same
small voice asked, "What if I want to tell
you things anyway?"

He felt his heart leap in his chest.
"That is another thing entirely. But it will
have to wait awhile. Today or tomorrow
the press is going to attack, and I want

you to handle them."

The voice sounded childlike in its surprise. "Me?"

"Charlie and I have to prepare for next week." As best they could, he amended silently. "You are to be the plaintiff's appointed spokeswoman. Are Alma and Austin there?"

"Downstairs waiting for me."

"Tell them what's going to happen. Ask them if they want to tell the world their story. If yes, then print up some flyers giving their address, telling the press where and when to meet for daily Q-and-A's. But if the Halls want their privacy, you need to arrange the meetings with the press downtown at the courthouse. The guards will let you in, we can arrange that."

"I'm pretty sure they'll want to be involved in this."

"Call Netty, ask her to help with the flyers. Print a lot of them. Inform the police. They'll need to station some people there at the house."

A long pause, then, "How can you be so sure about this?"

"You'll find out," Marcus replied, "very soon."

He cut the connection in time to hear Amos Culpepper say, "There's room in our department for a few solid fellows like yourself, Darren."

Darren's head swung in slow surprise. "I d-don't t-talk so good."

"Shoot. We got men out there on the road, they don't talk at all. You call them on the radio, they click one for yes, two for no. Only thing you ever hear. Lone Rangers, we call 'em. Get two of 'em chatting over the air, sounds like a party of grasshoppers." When Darren did not respond, Amos pulled the car up in front of the courthouse and said, "You think about it, get back to me anytime."

Marcus entered the courthouse to muted fanfare. Amos Culpepper had called ahead; Jim Bell was there with two other deputies, all wanting to know how he was, and how on earth he had discovered the bomb in time. A friend, Marcus said. And luck.

Jim Bell drew him over to one side and said, "My granny used to say there were people who lived a thin life. She meant they were just an inch or so away from death. I'd say that applies to you, Marcus."

"I'm trying to be careful."

"You need to do more than that. You need to be worried." He lowered his voice a notch. "You understand, the judge doesn't know I'm talking with you, and can't ever know."

Marcus studied the bearded man with his taut bearing and eyes that said one thing while his words said another. "I hear you."

He patted Marcus' arm, as though sealing a bargain. "The governor's aide is upstairs in the courtroom."

Marcus did not bother to search the faces. It would do no good. He was utterly unconnected politically and had no idea who to look for. He did nod to Kirsten, however, and was rewarded with a smile that he felt in his bones. It shielded him from the first sight of Suzie Rikkers' glare, and the foreboding of all that was yet to come. He dropped into his seat and addressed the Halls together. "Did Kirsten speak with you?"

Alma answered for them both. "We're going to shout this from the rooftops."

"That's your decision. Long as you both understand that you don't have to say a word."

Austin leaned over his wife, and said, "Yes, we most surely do."

Alma asked, "What's this I hear about a bomb?"

"The police are taking care of it right now. They say I should have my car back this evening."

"That's not good enough, Marcus. I'm going to speak with Deacon Wilbur at lunchtime."

"I doubt he can do much about this, Alma."

Her reply was cut short by the bailiff intoning, "All rise."

Judge Gladys Nicols went through her morning ritual of greeting the jury with one eye on the defense table and one somewhere toward the back of the courthouse. She did not seem particularly pleased by either sight. But all she said was, "Plaintiff may call the next witness."

Charlie rose to his feet and said, "Your Honor, at this time we'd like to call Professor Sara Seymour."

An older woman with a tightly seamed face approached the stand and was sworn in. Charlie took his time as he went through the routine of establishing her as an expert witness on modern-day China. Marcus listened and was pleased with his decision to have Charlie handle her. Sara Seymour held to the tedious monotone of someone who wished to be elsewhere. But Charlie's unfeigned interest not only drew her out, it helped to hold the jury's attention. Charlie knew nothing about Chinese power politics. Whatever she said, however cut-and-dried, he found fascinating. And so did the jury. Charlie drew from her the critical information — that in China, power was power. Business or government, money or politics, courtroom or backroom or military, there was little or no difference. The professor became gradually caught up in the process of teaching, and added a touch of academic energy to her explanation of how such a system utterly lacked any form of checks and balances. Why? Because the people who held political or military power used their might to gather business connections and property and licenses. For them, profit from bribery and the sale of corporate rights was merely an acceptable perk of holding high office. Since their tentacles stretched out in so many directions, any attempt at reform was hobbled by entrenched self-interests and greed. And because the process of reform was so hampered, the laws and the courts could not keep up with the rapid transformation of commerce and industry. Thus China's business environment was almost medieval in its approach to workers' rights. Charlie Hayes took his time and showed deep gratitude for anything the professor wished to say.

Throughout the testimony, Judge Nicols cast occasional brooding glances at the defense table, which was perhaps why Logan Kendall offered no objections to

Charlie's rambling discourse. When Charlie rested, Logan avoided meeting the judge's eyes as he rose and offered a halfhearted cross. He finished in record time, drawing from the professor the single admission that there was indeed a court system in China, with laws governing both commerce and crime. One that conceivably could be used to try a case such as this one.

Yet when Logan returned to his table, Judge Nicols merely excused the witness and continued her glaring inspection of the defense team. Every eye in the courtroom was drawn to the tableau, unchanged from the first day. Logan sat in the far-left chair, followed by Suzie Rikkers and three or four dark-suited associates. Behind them and next to the railing were the two New Horizons vice presidents. Two secretaries huddled next to them, flanked by boxes of documents and law books.

Judge Nicols allowed the moment to stretch until the jury was shifting uncomfortably and observers were exchanging glances and whispered queries. She finally turned to Marcus and said, "Well?"

Marcus rose slowly, trapped in the amber of his own imminent demise. He did not need to look toward Suzie Rikkers to know what was coming. And there was no way to stop it. None. "The plaintiff rests, Your Honor."

The judge merely nodded and turned back to the defense. Finally she said, "We seem to be missing a defendant, Mr. Kendall."

"Your Honor." Logan rose with the reluctance of an attorney who could neither anticipate nor control what was coming. "I have this morning received a letter from the Chinese embassy in Washington, D.C. The government of China has officially responded to your request."

"Have they, now." The tone was even more threatening for being so muted. "They have *officially* responded to my *request.*"

"The government of China takes great offense at this subpoena, Your Honor. They remind this court that General Zhao Ren-Fan is a man of immense power within their regime, a member of the military's central command. They refuse categorically to submit to such an affront."

"An affront." The murmur was scarcely audible.

"They declare your request contrary to international law and demand that it be withdrawn." The letter rattled in Logan's hand. "They warn that a serious diplomatic breach could result."

"Do they now." She held out one

black-robed arm. "May I see the letter, please."

She took a long moment to read the letter, then set it down and said to Logan, "All right. I'm listening."

"There is a serious jurisdiction issue here, Your Honor. This court does not hold authority over a *Chinese* owner of a *Chinese* factory." Logan stepped around the table and took a solid stance. He was practiced, he was ready, he was on the offensive. "Even if this court could assert jurisdiction, which I submit is impossible, the defense attaché to the Chinese embassy is not a necessary party to this case."

Judge Nicols picked up the letter once more, dividing her attention between the embassy's words and Logan's. The defense attorney continued, "Furthermore, we are already too far down the road in this case to add an additional defendant. We would have to declare a mistrial and start over."

"Would we," Judge Nicols murmured.

"Yes, Your Honor, we would. This case, were it to include a senior official of a foreign sovereign power, would be a matter for Congress or the State Department to resolve. Not this courtroom." Logan punched the air between himself and Marcus. "If this is what the plaintiff

wants, if he wants to turn this into a political trial, and if you think the court can
establish jurisdiction in this matter, fine.
Then we don't have a dog in this fight.
We move to dismiss."

Judge Nicols drew out the moment before quietly demanding, "Are you done?"

"Yes, Your Honor. We hereby move to
dismiss."

"Your motion is denied." She swung
her gaze toward her chief clerk, who
stood ready and waiting beside the court
reporter. "I hereby issue a bench warrant,
a writ of habeas corpus for General Zhao
Ren-Fan."

Logan took the news as he would a
hammer blow to the chest. "Your
Honor!"

"I hereby order the U.S. marshal to escort this man into court."

Logan struggled to recover. "He'll bolt,
Your Honor."

Her eyes swiveled back with the
smoothness of matched gun barrels. "Is
that a fact."

"Absolutely. He'll flee the country and
you'll be left with a huge political mess
on your hands."

"Fine. In that case, this court has no
choice but to protect the plaintiffs' interests in the event the jury finds in their
favor." She hefted the letter from the

Chinese embassy. "As their government has chosen to declare itself officially involved, and as this man is now recognized as a senior member of their government and is acting in an *official* capacity, I am hereby freezing all assets of the Chinese government now held by any and all United States financial institutions." She hammered once, not even trying to still the uproar, merely shifting her glare to some unseen point toward the back of the court and saying, "One final point, Mr. Logan. The defense is hereby *requested* to present to the court someone who holds the power to respond to questions about New Horizons' international activities. That sounds like a reasonable *request* to you, now, doesn't it?"

Logan replied weakly, "Yes, Your Honor."

"I'm so glad." Her smile was truly awful to observe. "Court is now adjourned until nine o'clock Monday morning."

As Marcus stood with the others, Alma used the moment of confusion to ask, "Did you know this was going to happen?"

"I assumed General Zhao would not show. And the judge would feel forced to respond."

Charlie almost shouted to be heard, "The Chinese government weighing in like that — now, that was a gift from on high."

Marcus nodded, both to show his agreement and to hide from the raking glare Suzie Rikkers gave as she passed. "Tell Kirsten to be ready for a siege."

THIRTY-SEVEN

On Saturday Marcus woke to the remarkable sensation that he had actually fought back against his predawn foes. He arose weak and shaking as usual, but holding to a shred of satisfaction. The loss seemed foreordained, as though there were but one outcome to the strife that scarred his every morning. But at least this day he had joined in battle.

Charlie arrived early, bringing breakfast in the form of baskets and casserole dishes and Libby's message that the best answer to any trouble on this earth was a good feed. Together they ate and studied the news.

The newspapers and the television were both full of their story: what the Chinese embassy said and what Washington said and what the judge was not saying. Photographs of Alma and Austin Hall figured prominently. Netty arrived and soon tired of the journalists' renewed telephone onslaught. She put a message on the answering machine saying that all queries should be directed to Kirsten Stanstead, and gave the Halls' number. Darren camped out on the front porch and scared away any who made it to the wilds of Rocky Mount. Marcus and Charlie hunkered down and plotted against the defense's coming attack.

They sat through the evening news in stunned amazement. CBS had it as the second story of the night. The newscaster began by saying what had begun as a tempest in a Carolina teapot was now brewing up the latest international crisis. They showed Kirsten standing beautiful and resolute. Her measured tones were in direct contrast to Alma Hall's furious tirade against New Horizons. They then showed the picture of Gloria Hall laughing on the stairway, followed by fifteen seconds of her bruised and battered face asking for money. They finally cut to the spokesman for the Chinese embassy saying his government would not stand for such outrage and was considering a large number of retaliatory measures. The Chinese official was not merely angry, he sounded downright evil.

Charlie had the good grace to wait until Netty had left and he was putting on his coat to finally say, "Suzie Rikkers is gonna come at you like a razor-backed hog."

Marcus could not help staring. "You've

known all along, haven't you."

"Didn't take much in the way of figuring. She represented your wife at the divorce, didn't she."

"It was more like representing my ex-mother-in-law."

Charlie shrugged his indifference to such nitpicking. "Logan's got more of a brain for strategy than I figured."

Marcus saw his old mentor out, then stood on the veranda as Charlie did his bandy-legged gait into the shadows. "You're a good friend, Charlie Hayes."

The old man wheeled about and made his way back up the stairs, as though he had been waiting for just such a chance to say, "I'll tell you what's the truth, Marcus. I'd have paid all my remaining years for what you've given me for free."

Marcus nodded. "It's turned into quite a case."

Charlie's gaze reached out of the night and gripped him hard. "Son, I wasn't talking about the case."

On Sunday Marcus awoke to sunlight and the chill of distant thunder. The nightmares had not come at all. Instead, they seemed to loom just over the horizon. Even while he slipped from bed and showered and breakfasted and prepared for church, he felt the brooding menace of what had not been.

The church's welcome enveloped him like the embrace of an old friend. Deacon Wilbur slipped back to say merely, "We'll be taking measures to see you stay safe." Marcus was too held by his own accompanying shadow to respond with more than a nod. He entered the church, and felt his entire body drink in the noise and the peace.

Impossible harmonies. Marcus remained surrounded by noise and peace both, protected and yet utterly exposed. The singing gave way to prayers, and still the congregation shouted responses and clapped and waved their hands. Marcus sat in quiet repose because he was a quiet man. The sounds and the words washed over him, settling him further into himself. All the times before, all the other visits to this church and all the realizations he had made and the comfort he had found, all had been building a foundation, preparing him for this descent into himself.

Marcus sat and felt the moment unfold. Calm and sheltered, exposed and vulnerable and suddenly terrified. And listening. Not to the noise around him, but to his own internal world. The noise outside crashed like waves upon his secret island, the colors and the people rising and dancing and sitting and filling the aisles like a tumultuous sea. He just sat. And in his quietly watchful state, he observed the shadow approach.

He wanted to run. Even before he knew what it was, he wanted to flee with every scrap of his being. He was not ready for this, and never would be. But still it came.

Then he felt what had become customary in the predawn hour. He was unable to move, to stand, even to breathe. Trapped in the amber of this lucid moment, he was both awake and more aware than ever before.

Sunday after Sunday he had been sitting there and listening and learning to listen better. Being quiet and letting the silence speak. Now he sat and watched the shadow congeal into his greatest terrors, and felt so betrayed he wanted to shriek and scream until his vocal cords were ripped from his own throat. But he could not even draw enough breath to moan.

The shadow that chilled his dawns formed with such clarity he could finally name what had haunted him for so long. The word coalesced in a place where neither the shade nor the name had any place entering, but had gained entry because of him. He stared into the void of his shattered life, and called the shadow by its name.

Death had not entered his world quietly, not the day it had stolen away the two beings he treasured more than life itself. That brilliant sunlit afternoon had been filled with radio music and the kids' chatter and his wife's cold argument. He could not recall now what they had been arguing about. Something important, as they almost never fought in front of the children. Probably his drinking. The argument and the cause all belonged to another life, one not yet shattered by death's hand.

Death entered the car that day with a noise so great it had robbed his world of light and meaning. His soul had died along with his children. Why had his body remained? What was so bad in his former life that he had to be continually punished by his children's absence?

There within the church the shadow formed more clearly still, gliding upon slippered feet. The shroud it carried wrapped him up so tightly that Marcus felt his hold on the church and the comforting noise slip away until he could scarcely hear anything save the frantic beating of his terrified heart. He sat there, trapped and helpless to do anything save observe the approach of his own eternal night.

His eyes were shut so tight his entire face felt clamped by the effort of keeping out the invader. Yet still it came. Marcus sat bowed over his knees and knew he was defeated. And lost.

Behind his clenched eyelids, Marcus stared into the darkness of his nightly battleground. His nightmare became not just a memory he could run from in the light of day. Here in his one weekly moment of peace, he was trapped within that which was as real as his loss. As real as his sorrow. As real as his own death.

He stood in the upstairs hall of their Raleigh home. The house he had never entered after that day, and yet to which he had been taken almost every night for a year and a half. He stood in the hall, lit by a light so bright it threatened to sear his eyeballs. Or perhaps it merely seemed so bright because the darkness into which he peered was hopelessly empty of light and all else. Yet though he could not see, he could hear, and from the sound he knew he stood in the doorway of his son's bedroom. From out of the darkness there came the sound of his son singing a soft little song about a bird and a ladybug and a little yellow butterfly. His son had been singing it that day, the day they had driven back from the beach. Singing as his father had driven him into the intersection. Singing as though trying to blot out the sound of his parents arguing. Singing with a voice gentle as summer rain.

Then his son stopped singing, and Marcus felt the remnants of his heart wrenched yet again by the sound of the loveliest voice in the entire universe calling out one tiny word.

"Daddy?"

He had no choice. It did not matter that he knew what was to come. His son called to him. He had to respond.

Marcus entered the doorway.

Instantly there was the same horrible flash to his right, the same moment of looking over to see the truck's polished metal grille catch the sunlight, and there in its reflection to see the face of approaching death. Then there was the sound of exploding metal and glass, and a scream cut off too quickly — one so high he could never tell if it was his wife or his daughter or his son who had made the sound. Perhaps all three. Or perhaps it was his own heart shrieking as the cords binding his life together were severed all at once.

The dream continued. He was back in the hallway, the blackness mocking him now. And again his son called out to his father. Only this time the little boy was crying and frightened by the nightmare Marcus was powerless to end. He leapt through the doorway again. And again he was struck by the truck, the demon, the carrier of death. The wrenching metal and the exploding glass and the single scream catapulted him back into the hallway.

Only this time it was not the hallway where he stood, helpless and straining as the little voice cried to him once more. Now he was in the aisle of the church, caught within the pain of living a nightmare that did not end, not even when he opened his eyes and saw Deacon Wilbur rushing toward him. The agony wrenched Marcus like a bullet to the heart. He fell to his knees, so numb from inner pain that he did not even feel the dozens of hands there to catch and hold him.

A voice too kind and too caring to ever appear in his nightmare world murmured, "It's all right, brother, it's all right. The Lord is here. He knows."

The sound only intensified his pain. He managed a single breath then, one that felt raked over the coals of eternal regret, one that gave him the power to scream his son's name. "Jason!"

"Yes, Lord, be here with this suffering

man. Call his name, God, let him hear you. Let his heart know your healing."

Marcus could respond only with the cry of his daughter's name, his precious "Jessica!"

"Dear Jesus, heal this broken spirit, be the salve to bind his wounds and heal his heart."

A hand gripped his hair so hard he could not burrow into the ground as he wished. He groaned, and felt as though all the earth groaned with him, crying with him and for him. Marcus wept, and felt a rightness that all those around him wept along, for the pressure of holding back a year and more's worth of tears was so great that all the world should have cried, and still there would be a surfeit of unshed sorrow.

THIRTY-EIGHT

The next morning Marcus arose still scalded by the public shedding of his mask. It mattered little that the nightmare had been but a whisper that morning, and he had slept until the sun's first traces were strong and clear over the eastern rooflines. He slipped into his sweats simply because it was his morning routine, though it seemed to him that a window mannequin had more life and would fill the clothes better.

When he stepped out the front door, he was greeted by soft footfalls and a pair of young and vaguely familiar faces. He walked down the steps and stood there in the quiet light of morning, trying to figure out where he had seen those dark faces before. Then he recalled the groups of teens clustered on several surrounding porches. Previously they had watched him pass, either in the car or on foot, missing nothing, saying less. No signal had ever been given that they even wished to acknowledge his existence as a neighbor, until now.

When he just stood there staring at

them, the taller one informed him, "Old Deacon says you ain't to go runnin' alone no more."

He could not help but show his surprise, which resulted in the sprouting of grins. Marcus asked, "You've been watching me?"

"And yo' house," the younger boy replied.

The taller one, a young man of perhaps eighteen with an Indian's chiseled features, said, "Why you think you got something to come home to at night, luck of the draw?"

"Trucks pulled up a coupla times and stopped," the other said. "We just walk over and give 'em the eye. They pulled away fast enough."

Marcus fished among the mass of sudden questions. "Why didn't anyone tell me?"

"We told Deacon," the older one replied. "Deacon says he told the sheriff. Guess they figured you got enough to worry about already."

Marcus felt a catch in his throat, as if a vestige of the previous day's sorrow were still hanging around. So he just nodded, and afterward was glad he had, for there in the predawn light he could not have found anything fitting to say.

The old town became filtered by the

comfort of not running alone. A heavy autumnal mist had fallen, squeezed from the stars that seemed reluctant to give way to the strengthening day. His footfalls swished along the narrow path leading across the field and toward the bridge, and the sound merged with birdsong and the panting tread of three men. He seemed to find some remarkable way to draw upon their youth and strength, for he had not run so easily in years.

When he finally pulled back in front of the house, the sun was up and caressing the old fired brick with a ruddy dusting of gold. He stared over the front lawn, a field now of prisms and tiny rainbows, and cherished this place anew. He then turned back to his running mates, puffing and grinning at how they had caught him out and joined his private time. Marcus asked, "What are your names?"

"Aaron."

"Orlando."

"I'm Marcus, in case anybody was wondering." He shook their hands in turn, wishing he could think of something to say, seeing in their eyes that they did not expect words. Or need them.

By the time he had showered and dressed, the deputy's car was pulled up in front. Marcus gripped his briefcase, then set it back down and stepped out to where Darren and the deputy were talking. "Morning, Amos."

"Marcus." His eyes showed a glimmer of deep-set humor. "See you've met Deacon's secret service."

"Darren, I forgot my briefcase. Would you mind getting it for me?" When the tall young man had departed, Marcus went on, "I can't thank you enough. For everything."

"I've known good folks and bad, Marcus. And the best kind of folks are those who give more than they take." He touched Marcus for the first time, settling his hand briefly on the lawyer's shoulder. "You just worry about winning this here case."

He heard the door slam behind him, and said, "Has Darren told you about his trouble?"

"Didn't need to."

"You know he can't go into police work with a record."

Amos gave a fraction of a nod. "Been meaning to speak with you about that. Think you can do something to wipe it clean?"

"The adolescent stuff is no problem, his records were sealed by the court when he turned eighteen." He heard the young man's approach, and said simply, "As to more recent events, I understand there's only one that matters."

"That's right," Amos said. "I checked."

"I could ask," Marcus said, nodding his thanks as he accepted the briefcase. "But I'm afraid my stock has sunk pretty low when it comes to calling in favors."

Amos had to grin. "I do believe you might be in for a surprise there." He said to Darren, "I'll follow you gents on in today."

"There's no need," Marcus protested.

This time Darren shared the sheriff's grin. Amos said, "You best prepare yourself for surprise number two."

He decided there was no need to dispel their good humor with further questions. As Darren slid the Jeep in behind the deputy's car, Marcus used his mobile to call the Halls. The phone rang so long he feared he had missed them. He was hard put not to smile when Kirsten answered somewhat breathlessly. The morning was so fine in its start he could almost pretend it was excitement over hoping the call was from him. "You did great handling the press."

"Wait, we were halfway to the car when the phone . . ." She took a long breath, then started over in a rush. "The police are here. Two cars. One has been parked here all weekend to keep back the crowd. Another is going to drive us in today. I got another call this morning: ABC wants me to come in for a live debate with someone from the defense team. I don't want to do it, Marcus."

"Then don't."

"But it might mean some big publicity."

"As much as we're getting already," Marcus replied, "I don't think one debate will matter much. Don't do anything you don't want to. Tell Alma and Austin I said the same applies to them."

"Yes. All right." A smaller voice, then, "When can we talk?"

The question was enough to give him the strength to admit one more time, "We're both carrying more than our share of secrets, Kirsten. You don't have to tell me anything you don't want to."

"I want," she said, the words almost musical. "A lot."

"All right." He had to stop and swallow. "There's something I need to ask you, then. The defense's first witness is a woman named — wait, I have it here." He opened his briefcase and shuffled the papers. "Stella something."

"Gladding. Stella Gladding."

"You know her?"

"We've never met, no. But Gloria talked about her."

"Okay, I need to know why the defense called her."

Kirsten's voice returned to the flat monotone of earlier days, but she did not flinch from the task. Marcus took notes through much of the journey, his mind strategizing as she talked. When she fell silent, he asked, "That all?"

"I think so. Is it bad?"

"The truth is, maybe. But as long as we know in advance, we can prepare."

"Marcus," she sighed, "when can we talk? I don't mean like this. I mean, really."

His heart replied first, with a fleeting image of what he was certain the coming week would hold. "It may need to wait until this is over." What he did not add was: If you still want to after what you're about to witness.

They arrived to find the federal courthouse under siege. Police roadblocks held back a packed placard-hoisting mob, the signs so jumbled together Marcus gathered one blurred impression of Tibet and fashion and children and China and trade and missionaries and human rights and several missing activists with Asian names. Amos put on his flashers and the police moved the barricade and waved them through. A dark-windowed limo was pulled up in the fire lane. Then he could see no more, for the press surged forward. Marcus emerged from the Jeep to camera flashes and klieg lights.

Jim Bell was there to usher him inside. The questions were a torrent of verbal rain, striking him from every side. He allowed the retired patrolman to burrow forward, saying nothing, astonished by it all.

Charlie Hayes awaited him just inside the doors. "You hear the news this morning?"

Marcus shook his head, stared out at the mayhem, struggled to accept what he had caused.

"The Chinese government issued a formal statement condemning the United States government for what they call a petty attempt at trade terrorism." When Marcus did not respond, the older man led him toward the elevator. Jim Bell continued to dog their footsteps. Charlie said, "Looks like you won yourself some publicity, son."

He waited until the doors shut to reply, "Let's just hope it works."

"If this don't, well . . ."

Marcus did not allow the unspoken to hang for long. "We need to talk strategy. I want you to handle this first witness."

Charlie turned away from the tumult. "Trouble?"

"Probably."

"All rise."

Judge Nicols swept in with the majesty of one born to wear royal robes. She seated herself and made a noble pretense of ignoring the packed hall by issuing her customary greeting to the jury. "Good morning. How is everyone?"

The foreman, a retired machinist with the reddened neck and face and arms of a dedicated outdoorsman said, "Good, Your Honor."

"Any particular reason I should know about?" She let the smile slip away as she turned to where Logan stood by the defense table. "Yes?"

"Your Honor, I have the pleasure of presenting General Zhao Ren-Fan."

Marcus turned with the rest of the packed hall. The man was stocky and not aging well. His face was pocked, his body chunky and sagging. Not even the finely cut dark suit could hide the general's hard battle against approaching winter. Zhao turned to meet Marcus' stare, and his face clenched up slightly around eyes black as Arctic night. No light was emitted from those eyes. No light, no hope, no message at all.

Even so, the dark eyes flickered once, then turned away. When Marcus swiveled back in his seat, he caught sight of the look shared by Alma and Austin Hall as together they glared at their daughter's nemesis.

The judge did not need to speak to silence the crowd. One sweeping glare sufficed. Nicols turned her attention back to Logan. The defense attorney continued, "The Chinese government wishes to state formally that they have nothing whatsoever to do with either this trial or this gentleman's presence. He is here of his own volition, at the behest of the China Trade Council. The council vehemently objects to this entire trial, Your Honor, and wishes to go on record that this is an extremely volatile matter, one that should be left to the federal government. We so move on their behalf."

"Your motion is noted and denied."

"Very well. In that case, Your Honor, the defense wishes to open its case with my postponed opening statement."

"Very well." Judge Nicols turned to the jury and explained, "As you may recall, the defense chose not to give an opening statement. I told you at the time that they might do this later, probably before calling their first witness." She turned back to Logan. "You may proceed."

Logan walked to the corner by the judge's entrance and picked up the portable podium. He carried it to the center point between the plaintiff's table and the witness stand, about twelve feet from the jury box. He leaned against it, and launched straight in. "Ladies and gentlemen of the jury, what we have here is a case within a case. Things have become infinitely more complicated, and your job is now much more difficult. But what you mustn't do, under any circumstances, is lose sight of where the burden of proof lies."

Logan Kendall was a consummate actor. The courtroom was the only stage he would ever see, the only one he desired. Nothing could be done about his boxer's face or his inborn aggressiveness. But he used them to his advantage, and had polished all to a hard shine. His hair was as perfect as his tan and his suit and his manicure. His tie was a two-hundred-dollar Brioni, his shoes hand-tailored calfskin. In an instant he could switch from hard and feisty to warm and welcoming. When he turned on his considerable Irish charm, a mere few moments in front of the jury was enough for them to want to believe him. They knew it was an act, but as with all fine performances, they really didn't care.

"This case is now vastly different from what it was in the beginning. And what we said earlier does not apply so clearly anymore. We have new defendants that the court in its wisdom has ordered us to include. But we are in this together, ladies and gentlemen. And together we are going to find out the truth. My job is to lead you through this process. You are judges of the facts. And though this has become far more global an issue, and far more complex, still I am certain that we are all up to the task of finding out just what these facts are. We are on a truth-seeking mission here. And when we are done, we are going to talk again. At that time, I hope we will have some hard facts upon which to base a valid judgment.

"The lawyers for the plaintiff have filled the air with some pretty outlandish contentions, suggesting that somehow my clients are at fault. Mind you, their accusations against my clients are preposterous. Their lawyers, ladies and gentlemen, are claiming that my clients have formed some amorphous ties to a mystery factory sitting on the other side of the world. And somehow this factory has secreted away a woman named Gloria Hall. It is vital that you remember this one fact, ladies and gentlemen, because there has been a lot of smoke blown in this trial. The one issue we are here to determine is: What, if any, responsibility do my clients have in the disappearance of this woman.

"One thing is certain. Up to now we have been watching a trial by ambush. The plaintiff's lawyers have repeatedly bent the rules of procedure by introducing new witnesses, new evidence, even new defendants. We have been so caught up in this widening series of attacks that we may have lost sight of what we are here for. But all that is over and done with. The plaintiff has rested — it's no surprise he's tired after all the stunts he's pulled. Now it's our turn.

"You hold me to my promise now," Logan said, winding down. "We are going to uphold the American system of justice. We're going to roll up our sleeves and look hard for the facts. And when you go home at night — and remember the judge's injunction not to discuss this case with anyone — as you sit there and you relax, you can rest assured that my team and I are going to continue our hunt for the truth."

Logan turned and walked back to the table, inspected his notes for a long moment of punctuation, then said, "The defense calls Ms. Stella Gladding."

The woman's skin was close to the same shade as the Chinese general's. But in her case the sallowness came from a very rough life. The suggestion of hard living was heightened by the voice that gave her name and took the oath. Stella Gladding sounded as though she had gargled that morning with bourbon and ashes.

"Ms. Gladding, you knew Gloria Hall well, is that not so?"

"Very. We roomed together our first two years at Georgetown."

"Would you please tell the court what she was like?"

"Wild."

"Gloria Hall was wild." Logan maintained his position at the podium, swiveling it so that it angled halfway between the witness stand and the jury, slid over just slightly enough that Marcus could not object that Logan was intentionally blocking his view of the witness. "Just how wild, Ms. Gladding?"

"Not only would she try anything," she replied, "she would do it twice."

"Objection," Charlie said, his voice bored, his slouched appearance suggesting that this woman was not worth getting riled over.

"Sustained." If anything, Judge Nicols responded in a tone flatter than Charlie's.

Alma shifted in her seat next to Marcus. He glanced over, knowing no warning was possible, no words sufficient. Even so, she nodded without looking his way. She would hold on. To her other side, Austin Hall might as well have been carved from some dark and sorrowful stone.

"Ms. Gladding, did Gloria Hall have any boyfriends?"

"A lot." She had been prepped well and dressed more carefully still. But no amount of professional makeup or dark-suited grooming could disguise that this was a woman who had seen much and done even more. "They changed from week to week." A quick little smirk. "Sometimes from hour to hour. Gloria was a real friendly girl."

Logan asked quietly, "Did Gloria use any drugs?"

"Absolutely."

"Alcohol?"

"All the time."

The questioning continued until Gloria Hall had been painted as a full-on party animal, studying little, hanging on to her place at Georgetown through luck and a strong memory. Charlie Hayes seemed to be asleep; Marcus watched because he felt at least one of them should show they cared. Logan's problem was that the longer the witness remained on the stand, the stronger grew the woman's bored carelessness. Her voice grew harsher, the answers tighter, as though she needed a

drink or a smoke or something stronger.
Badly.

Logan realized this, and as he walked
back to his table he said, "Defense requests a brief recess."

Judge Nicols was having none of it. She
shook her head, her eyes glued to the witness. "We'll finish with this witness first."

Logan had no choice but to say, "Your
witness."

Charlie rose from his slouched position,
his voice emerging before his legs were
fully under him. "Ms. Gladding, you say
you knew Gloria through your first two
years at Georgetown, is that right?"

"That's what I said."

"And just how long ago was that?"

"Four years."

He smiled, as though the answer
amused him. "You're sure it was four,
now?"

"I just said . . ." The eyes searched.
"No. Five."

"If my math is correct, Ms. Gladding,
it was more like six. Isn't that right."

"Five, six, fifteen, it doesn't matter. I
remember Gloria. Real well."

"Fine. That's just fine. It's just that,
well, a lot can change in five or six years,
wouldn't you say?"

"Maybe. But not Gloria."

"No?" Charlie limped his way over to

lean upon the corner of the jury box. "Ms. Gladding, could you enlighten me as to why you and Gloria Hall stopped rooming together?"

"I moved out."

"Is that a fact. My understanding was that Miss Hall was the one who did the moving."

The hand that rose to flick at her hair shook slightly. "Gloria started getting seriously weird. I couldn't take it."

"Weird." Charlie cast a glance at the jury, then limped over to the plaintiff's table and accepted the sheet of paper Marcus held. It contained a photocopied statement of court proceedings. But the witness did not know this. "Ms. Gladding, a careful inspection of Gloria Hall's university transcript shows that she underwent a marked transformation at the start of her junior year."

"I'll say."

"In fact, from that semester on, Gloria Hall's record shows that she earned almost straight A's for the remainder of her undergraduate career."

"She got into this crazy religious phase. It was worse than the guys. Always talking about God and stuff. Wanting me to come with her to church, treating it like an AA meeting. Had to go every night, like she was afraid of falling off the wagon otherwise."

Charlie kept up his slow nod long after Stella Gladding had stopped talking. "Are you aware that Gloria Hall went on to graduate from Georgetown with honors, and earned herself a full scholarship for her graduate studies?"

"At that price," the woman sneered. "Who cares?"

"And what, may I ask, was your standing at graduation?"

"Objection," Logan declared. "Irrelevant."

"Overruled. The witness is instructed to answer the question."

Stella Gladding flicked her head in careless irritation. "I flunked out my senior year."

Charlie made his way back to the table. "No further questions."

Most of the day was made up of such small combats. The defense attacked with one foray after another. Charlie countered with a few quick questions, gentle in tone, decisive in result. Yet Marcus watched as his case gradually unraveled before his eyes, knowing there was nothing he could do about it, knowing the worst was still to come. He did not need to look at the defense table to know Suzie Rikkers' eyes were upon him.

Logan's parade continued with a Washington, D.C. street cop who handled the beat around the Chinese embassy. He was followed by a security guard from the embassy's permanent detail, then a court-appointed D.C. lawyer, and finally a prison guard for the city's female lockup. All attested to the trouble they had experienced with Gloria Hall. In a space of fourteen months she had been arrested nine different times, on charges ranging from obstructing traffic to unlawful assembly to rioting to resisting arrest to causing mayhem while incarcerated. Charlie's cross-examination was focused solely upon showing that all charges had related to activities taking place around the Chinese embassy, or in conjunction with visiting Chinese dignitaries. The defense countered by showing that the charges had arisen from a variety of Chinese-related issues, everything from imprisoned dissidents and freeing Tibet to missing missionaries and trade. A picture slowly developed of an angry young woman determined to make as much trouble for China as possible. Any pretext would do, so long as China was the target.

The clock showed a few minutes past four when Logan stood and announced, "Your Honor, the defense requests that the jury be dismissed for the day, and that we be granted a moment to lodge a private motion."

Charlie leaned over and muttered, "Here it comes."

In chambers, Logan could scarcely bring himself to wait until Judge Nicols had settled behind her desk. "Your Honor, we wish to invoke the Best-Evidence Rule, and call Marcus Glenwood to the stand."

In a truly bleak moment, Marcus found the judge's shock mildly gratifying. "Come again?"

"Best evidence, Your Honor. It requires the plaintiff to present the original sources of all critical evidence."

Judge Nicols gathered herself and said peevishly, "Do not presume to instruct the court on points of jurisprudence, Mr. Logan."

"No, Your Honor." Logan remained utterly smooth, totally unfazed. It was superb strategy. He knew it, so did the judge. Flawless. The only reason he had permitted Suzie Rikkers to flaunt an open warning was because there was no way of derailing this train. "The plaintiff's lawyer has repeatedly stated that a critical source of his most vital evidence was a man we have never been allowed to question."

"No surprise there," Charlie Hayes drawled. "Seeing as how your boys did him in."

"I object to the tone and the statement, Your Honor." But Logan was too pleased with himself to be angry.

Judge Nicols switched her ire to the chamber's other side. "Mr. Hayes, another such outburst and I will have you removed from this court."

"Sorry, Your Honor." Charlie took a long moment adjusting his bifocals. "And I apologize to these people if I was mistaken."

Logan let that one slide by. "This attorney, Your Honor, Ashley Granger was his name. He apparently sourced any number of critical points for the plaintiff. We know that from the counsel's own repeated statements. We desperately need to get to the bottom of all this. Since Mr. Glenwood was the only person here who spoke directly with the deceased, we are more than justified in wanting him to give testimony."

Marcus could not help glancing over. Suzie Rikkers no longer glared in response. Instead, she stared at him with eyes slitted by a tiny smile that compressed her lips into an almost invisible line. The woman looked to be approaching ecstasy.

"Very well." Judge Nicols gave Marcus a searching, worried inspection. "Does counsel for the plaintiff wish further time to prepare?"

Charlie Hayes responded as Marcus had instructed, though the old man sounded almost bereaved. "No thank you, Your Honor."

"Mr. Kendall, this is a highly unorthodox move, one that will be held to the light of national publicity." She was trying to keep the concern from her voice, but not succeeding. "I expect you to conduct yourself in the most professional manner."

"Of course, Your Honor." Logan almost purred the words.

As Marcus rose and started for the door, Suzie Rikkers mouthed one word: Tomorrow.

THIRTY-NINE

Though the dusk was chill enough to bite his lungs, Marcus kept his window open for the entire journey home. He breathed the night in deep, trying to rid his lungs of courtroom dust. His left arm in its cast felt heavy and lumpish. His heart thudded slow and irregular. He was not mortally wounded yet, but the lesions were multiplying and their effect was telling.

Because of his position in the passenger seat, he heard the roar and recognized the coming angle of attack. Which gave him enough time to grip the edge of the car roof with his one good hand and shout, "Here they come!"

The roar turned into a night-driven behemoth that slammed into their right rear fender so hard the Jeep's tail end slewed clear off the road and started toward the highway's median ditch. But Marcus' shout had been enough warning for Darren to grip the wheel with shoulders tight, arms strong and ready. He worked the wheel and floored the motor so that it screamed and pushed them back onto the highway.

Marcus felt more than heard a rending of metal as they parted ways with their attacker. He risked a glance behind him, saw a heavy automobile with tinted windows, a Cadillac or Town Car or Marquis, then heard the motor whining and said, "Hang on!"

The hammer blow was less jarring this time, as Darren timed his swerve just right. The attacker caught the Jeep's tail and ripped the bumper free so that its bolts popped with the sound of gunfire and the silver rod went clanging off into the dark behind them. The car veered away to miss the falling debris, and Marcus heard the more powerful engine race up alongside. "Faster!"

"Can't!" Darren was hunched up over the wheel, as though squeezing it might press a trace of additional speed from the Jeep.

Marcus risked another glance, saw that the car's long nose was almost in line with their rear door. "Hit the brakes!"

Darren responded so fast he might have thought of the same thing at the very same moment. His leg muscles knotted like tree trunks as he used both feet to ram the brake into the floorboard. The Jeep screamed and shuddered violently, but remained upright. The enemy's car raced by and was enveloped in its own cloud of burning rubber.

The attackers sliced across the highway, moving sideways, blocking the way ahead. Marcus shouted, but Darren was already slapping the gearshift into reverse.

Marcus watched the car's window roll down. A long rod protruded and glinted dully in the headlights. He caught sight of a face behind the barrel, gray and cold as death.

Before he could cry a warning, another car raced up alongside and past them, a blur moving so fast all he saw was a sweep of roaring metal. It slammed into the attacker's side, shattering glass and knocking the car up on its two opposite wheels. The newcomer reversed almost to where Marcus and Darren sat in the halted Jeep. The engine roared a second time and squealed into attack mode. But the first car signaled retreat with a roar of its own, and burned rubber far down the highway.

The newcomer backed up close to Marcus' side, a nondescript Chevy of seventies vintage. A sharp and hungry face protruded from the window and called over, "You all right?"

"Fine." Marcus looked into the face, and seemed to find his answer before even framing the question. "Who are you?"

"Friend of Dee Gautam's! Follow us! Drive!" The window rolled back up, and the car sped away.

Darren rammed the pedal to the floor, drawing so close he almost grazed the Chevy's taillights.

When they pulled into Marcus' street, however, the car ahead did not slow, but rather did a swift U-turn and roared away. Marcus looked ahead and understood immediately. His house was ringed by flashing lights — fire and police and sheriff and an ambulance. Police officers held back what seemed to be dozens of people armed with television lights and flashing cameras. A second group formed another perimeter out in the road, one that parted and let them through. Marcus pushed open his door and rose so he stood balanced on the car's running board and breathed easy once more. His house was still standing.

He walked toward two uniformed figures squared off and bawling in each other's faces. One was Amos Culpepper, the other he recognized from his nighttime visit to the police station. Only then did he realize that Darren was no longer beside him.

The cop was taller than Amos by a good six inches and outweighed him by the tub of lard he had strapped to his middle. In the glare of police spotlights he looked pasty and pig-eyed, a degenerate sow carrying a full litter. Amos was drawn up close to his face, and not hiding a bit of his disgust. "You call this doing your duty?"

"We know all about this, Amos."

"I'm not talking about knowing. I'm talking about stopping. You know who's behind this same as me!"

"I'm the one who's walking these streets, not you. You boys spend all day driving around the country, dreaming your big schemes, popping by after we've done cleaned up the mess!" The cop's lips were flecked with spittle. "I'm telling you this lawyer pal of yours has got the whole town against him!"

Amos swept an angry arm out and around, missing the cop's chin by an inch. "Take a look around, buster. I heard the dispatcher same as you! You got sixteen distress calls warning you about what was coming down here! Don't look like no hate-filled population to me!" He took a single step forward. "And if my boys aren't showing up till after the mess is over, how come I beat you and the firemen here by a good five minutes!"

"Cause you're hovering 'round this place like a deranged vulture!"

"Good thing for us both, ain't it, seeing

as how you'd have been here in time to watch the embers cool! Seems to me it's about time you started doing your job and stopped leaving it to me!"

The cop did some arm waving of his own. "What, you want me to go out and arrest the whole city council? Glenwood has riled up the people who hold power in this town, Amos. You know that as well as I do."

"I know you've got one concerned citizen who's finally willing to stand up to those madmen over there on the hill!"

"Those madmen are putting food on the tables of half this town!"

"Don't give them the right to break the law, now, does it? Only reason we're in this mess is 'cause you and your kind spent too many years licking their boots!"

The cop made a quick jerk forward, but Amos merely narrowed his eyes, ready for anything. The cop backed down, and hated it. "You're out of your jurisdiction, Amos. Best you make tracks."

"I'm leaving when I know somebody's gonna protect this citizen against the enemies of the law floating about here like bugs 'round a light."

"Then you're gonna be here till they finish digging the grave you've just started on." The cop turned and shouldered past Marcus, not even seeing him in his rage.

"Come on boys, we're all done here."

"That's right, tuck your tails and run!" Amos shouted after him. "Head straight home, strip off those uniforms you're shaming, and burn 'em in your back-yard!"

The three cop cars wheeled through the crowd as though the people were not even there. Amos stood breathing hard and watching the path they had furrowed, then said to Marcus, "We'll get us some backup in here tonight. This thing is way outta hand."

"We were attacked on the highway home tonight," Marcus said, wanting it over and done with. Swiftly he sketched out what had happened.

Amos' vision cleared in the process, and he looked at Marcus with the power to see who was speaking. "You go on over and see to your house. I'll get the rest from Darren."

"Was anybody hurt?"

"Nobody was inside, far as I know." Amos walked away.

Deacon Wilbur moved up as soon as Marcus was alone. "Aaron and Orlando were over there watching. Saw the fellows pull up, watched 'em start the fire, called for help."

"Where was Netty?"

"She left an hour or so earlier." The

hand on his shoulder was concerned, strong. "You all right, brother?"

"I think so." Marcus started toward the house, and Deacon fell in beside him. A stain of soot curled around the side of the house. Up close the ground squished wet and soggy under his step. The stench of smoldering ash and the thought of how close he had come to losing the old place left him nauseated.

Deacon's hand returned to offer comfort. "Never seen the like. Had neighbors from all over out here, running around with buckets and hoses, like a circus without the horses."

Marcus halted when the side of the house came into view. "Oh no."

"I tell you, those old trees went off like a bomb. Whoosh. I was just driving up when the taller one caught. They had two choices, save the house or save the trees. I'd say they chose right."

The sycamore and dogwood that had graced his office window were now charred skeletons. The sycamore's top branches rose as high as the house and were as naked as old bones. Marcus could have wept at the sight.

"We'll get in there tomorrow soon as it's light and start cleaning up. Have the old place right in no time."

Marcus stared at the trees' remains,

and thought of the coming day. "I don't know if I can take much more."

The hand rose and fell one more time. "I know, son. I know."

FORTY

When Logan stood up the next morning, it was not to address Marcus, but rather to announce, "Defense calls Ron Nesbitt to the stand."

Judge Nicols showed a flash of anger at being surprised yet again. Marcus took no pleasure from the reprieve. Logan was merely drawing out the agony of waiting. Suzie Rikkers was no longer looking his way, but rather seemed to ignore the courtroom entirely, deeply involved in her notes.

Logan lost no time in establishing the witness's credentials. "Mr. Nesbitt, you are head of the Raleigh regional office of the Federal Bureau of Investigation, is that correct?"

"It is." In fact, Ron Nesbitt looked more like an accountant than a federal agent. He was prune-faced and balding, and had the nasal twang of a dedicated pencil pusher. "For the past nine years."

"Your business is catching criminals, is that not so?"

"Yes."

"Fine. When you have a case involving assault, such as the plaintiff has accused my clients of here, could you please tell the court where your investigations would begin?"

"With the body."

"The *body*." Logan gave the jury box a slow nod. Pay attention. "You have reviewed the evidence of this trial, have you not?"

"I have."

"And is there a body here, Mr. Nesbitt?"

"There is not."

Logan waited a moment, ready for the objection. But none came. Charlie was handling the witness, and for all intents and purposes appeared to be asleep. Marcus was busy staring at his hands, trying to hold down a queasy stomach. He wiped at one temple, rubbed the sweat between his fingers. Back and forth.

Logan continued, "How long have you personally spent studying this case, Mr. Nesbitt?"

A glare was cast at the defense table before he responded, "Two days."

"Two days. And how many active investigations is your office now handling?"

"Forty-seven."

"And how many of these have received two full days of your own time?"

"Not many. Five. Maybe six."

The plaintiff's silence made Logan bold. "And yet for reasons we all find somewhat confusing, you have been forced to give two full days to this case?"

"It's a political football. I had to prepare reports."

"So this case has become bothersome to your bosses in Washington?"

Another glare. "It certainly has."

"How would you rate the evidence in this trial, Mr. Nesbitt?"

"Scanty. We would not make an arrest on what has been presented."

Another long glance at the jury. "You would not."

"No." He addressed the jury directly. "As a matter of fact, if a subordinate of mine suggested such a tactic, I would feel obliged to submit an official rebuke."

Charlie sounded bored. "Objection."

"Overruled. The witness is instructed to restrict himself to answering the question."

Logan continued smoothly, "What is your experience of parents who report their children missing?"

"Happens all too often."

"What about well-intentioned parents who are genuinely concerned about their children's welfare?"

The witness followed Logan's example

and avoided looking toward the Halls. "As I said, it happens all too often."

"Why do they contact the FBI, Mr. Nesbitt?"

"Usually because the parents fear the child has been kidnapped."

"Is that generally the case?"

"No."

"How often is foul play actually a factor? One time out of a hundred?"

"Less."

"What in your experience is a more common scenario?"

"They are runaways." His words were made more brutal by the uncaring tone. He could just as well have been reading figures off a page. "They have problems at home. They fight with their parents or their boyfriends, and they run."

"Or because they have an agenda all their own?"

"Objection," Charlie intoned.

"Sustained."

"No further questions." Logan retreated, vastly satisfied.

Marcus took a deep breath in time with Charlie's rise. He wished he could ask his old friend to drag his questioning out for months.

"Going back to your earlier testimony, Mr. Nesbitt." Charlie limped over to lean heavily upon the podium. "Does a civil case require the same burden of proof as a criminal case?"

"No. Usually it requires less evidence."

"Thank you." Charlie turned away and started back to the plaintiff's table, clearly finished. Charlie's swiftness surprised everyone — the judge, Logan, the jury. The witness was in the act of rising as Charlie arrived back at the table, and raised one finger, as if a thought had suddenly occurred to him. Without turning around, he calmly asked, "Oh, by the way: What was your impression of the video?"

Logan vaulted upright. "Objection!"

Judge Nicols turned her surprise toward the opposing camp. "On what grounds?"

Logan had to search for a moment. "Calls for supposition, Your Honor."

Her gaze narrowed. "You have just led this witness down the primrose path, asking him to suppose what happened to *one* person based on his experience with others."

"He is an expert witness, Your Honor."

"And expert witnesses are presumed to have opinions pertaining to evidence in their domain, are they not?" Her voice dripped scorn. She waited until Logan had retreated into his chair, then turned to the witness and said, "Answer the question."

The dry demeanor was shaken. "I have not seen it."

Charlie showed astonishment. "You didn't see the video?"

"No."

Charlie shared his bewilderment with the judge, then the jury. "In that case, I would say the defense has been pretty selective in the evidence it showed you, wouldn't you agree?"

"Objection!"

Charlie settled into his seat. "No further questions."

The entire chamber seemed to shudder when Suzie Rikkers rose to her feet. She did so with the delicacy of a dancer, her fingernails tapping lightly upon the wooden table as she said, "Defense calls Marcus Glenwood to the stand."

Marcus heard first a murmur and then a roar. He could not tell which was his own fear and which was the chamber's reaction. Judge Nicols pounded her gavel for silence, but the sound was drowned out by the hammering in his chest. As Judge Nicols explained the coming process to the jury, Marcus walked forward, leaned hard against the railing around the witness box, and waited for the bailiff to approach. The man was a retired patrolman, one of the same breed as Jim

Bell, and he shared Marcus' distress as he administered the oath and told him to be seated.

"State your name and occupation for the record, please."

"Marcus Glenwood, attorney-at-law."

Suzie Rikkers reseated herself and did a very swift walk-through, establishing provenance for the critical documents and showing how Ashley Granger was the source for much of what tied the Chinese military and the general and New Horizons to the factory. Marcus scarcely heard his own answers, much less the questions themselves. Charlie objected only once, and on a minor matter, merely to issue a verbal warning that he was there and watching.

The silence, when it came, had the focused intensity of a laser. Suzie Rikkers rose to her feet a second time. She did not speak as she did a little swaying walk toward him. Marcus found himself unable to resist the unspoken command to watch her approach. It was what Suzie had been waiting for. Her own gaze was almost sensual, dark and liquid. Her hair was styled, her dark dress new and fitting snugly to her miniature frame. She wore a single strand of pearls, a tiny gold brooch, fresh lipstick. She was made up as carefully as she would be for a big date.

Suzie Rikkers snagged the podium, the hand halting her forward progress. "Mr. Glenwood," she sighed contentedly. "You were fired from your former position, is that correct?"

"Objection." Charlie seemed to have difficulty rising to his feet. "Your Honor, this witness was called to establish provenance only."

Suzie delayed turning to the judge long enough to give Marcus a single sloe-eyed look, smiling with all but her mouth. She knew, as did he, that Judge Nicols had no choice but to permit this line of inquiry. "Your Honor, the questions I intend to ask will demonstrate beyond any shadow of doubt that the witness has ulterior motives for bringing this case."

"This is neither the time for opening statements nor for closing arguments," Judge Nicols snapped.

"Perhaps not, Your Honor." Suzie Rikkers' whine held a new edge, one that drew her words out in small panting breaths. "But if the plaintiff's lawyer insists on interrupting my highly legitimate questioning with objections, I have no choice but to respond."

Judge Nicols opened her mouth to slap the woman down, then stopped herself. Suzie Rikkers was watching her with the same tiny grin she had bestowed on

589

Marcus. Begging the judge to come down heavily on the side of the plaintiff's counsel, granting the defense a basis upon which to lodge an appeal and call a mistrial. Judge Nicols' gaze narrowed, her dislike for Rikkers evident to all in the room. She had no choice but to say, "Proceed."

"Thank you, Your Honor." Suzie Rikkers turned with studied slowness. "Mr. Glenwood, you were fired, is that correct?"

"I resigned."

"You resigned. You were a partner with the firm of Knowles, Barbour and Bradshaw, is that not correct?"

"Yes."

"Is it normal for full partners to just up and quit?"

"No."

"Isn't it true, Mr. Glenwood, that you were brought before the firm's disciplinary board for incompetence?"

"Objection, Your Honor." This time Charlie did not try to rise. It would have slowed his cry an instant longer than necessary. "Those are confidential records that have not been called as evidence."

"I withdraw the question." The words carried a dreamy whine. "You left one of the largest firms in North Carolina on your own volition, is that what you want the court to believe?"

"That is what happened."

She started a slow, lithe pacing in front of the witness stand. "Who are you in partnership with now?"

"I operate my own practice."

"So you are by yourself."

"Yes."

"Where are you practicing?"

"In Rocky Mount."

"And where are your offices located?"

"In my home."

"So you left a prestigious partnership, a coveted position with a major national firm." She traced one newly lacquered fingernail along the railing's edge. "You started a practice in your house in a small regional town, you work all by yourself, and you expect the court to believe that you did this voluntarily?"

"Yes."

Her eyelids were languid, heavy, the look she gave him blankly ardent. "Why did you make this choice, Mr. Glenwood?"

"I was going through a difficult period. I wanted to scale back."

"For the moment, let's set aside just how far you've scaled back." This time the smile actually touched her lips. "I'd like to spend a moment discussing this difficult time of yours. It began with an accident, is that correct?"

His swallow was forced through a throat gripped by a terrible hand. "Yes."

"Objection. This is utterly irrelevant."

Suzie Rikkers did not bother to turn toward the judge. The pleasure was there in watching Marcus. Holding him with her gaze. "Not only is it relevant, Your Honor, it is critical to this case. Vital."

Judge Nicols' tone said she had no choice but to declare, "Overruled."

"You were in an accident, is that not correct?"

"Yes."

"You were traveling back from the coast."

"Yes."

"Your son was with you, was he not? What was his name?"

From the corner of his eye Marcus caught sight of two other smiles. One belonged to Logan Kendall, the other to General Zhao. The two dark-suited men sat close together, the pleasure on their faces shouting across the distance. "Jason."

"How old was he?"

"Three and a half." Laughter lucid as heaven's chimes sparkled in the dead courtroom air.

"Your daughter was there too. Her name was . . ."

"Jessica."

"And how old was she?"

"Sixteen months." Another sound, the gentle music of a contented child, tore the heart from his body, leaving him bleeding and exposed.

"Tragically, you lost both your children in this accident, did you not?"

The courtroom gasped a breath Marcus could not find for himself. "Yes."

She leaned closer still, blocking out all but her own presence. "The loss hurt you deeply, didn't it?"

"Yes."

"It was a terrible, painful blow, was it not?" The lilt given to her words by the tiny panting breaths erased her screeching whine almost entirely. "It shattered your life."

"Yes."

"You have a drinking problem, don't you, Mr. Glenwood?"

"No."

The fingernail returned to its slow tracing. "I must warn you, we have a number of witnesses who will testify to the contrary."

"I had a problem before the accident. Since then I have stopped drinking altogether."

"Have you?" Her snakelike whisper trapped him in an unwelcome intimacy. "As a result of this same accident, you also endured a difficult divorce."

"You should know," he said, the words strangled in his own ears.

A slow turn, an almost chanted, "Your Honor, please instruct the witness to answer the question."

Marcus did not wait for Judge Nicols to speak. "Yes. It was difficult."

"You lost your little boy, Jason. You lost Jessica, your daughter. You lost your wife. You lost your standing within the legal community. You could say, could you not, that the accident totally demolished your life."

Marcus found himself unable to answer. Hearing Suzie Rikkers speak his children's names left him desperate to reach across the railing and crush her neck between his hands.

Suzie Rikkers took a pause for breath, both hands out and reaching across the wooden railing. Her blood-red fingernails weaved and danced as if they were casting a spell. "Have you recovered from this accident and the losses you suffered?"

"As much as anyone can." Not caring that it was the wrong answer. Not caring how it sounded at all. Simply striving for control.

"I suggest that you have not recovered at all." Another intimate smile. "A lone attorney, working without support, bringing such a case as this to federal court — would you not say that was the act of someone who still has a long way to go to recover?"

"Objection!"

Suzie did not turn. Did not speak. She simply waited for the inevitable, "I am going to allow the question."

"No," Marcus replied, "I do not agree."

"Don't you." Her sigh was a small shiver of ecstasy. "How many clients do you now have?"

"Several dozen."

"Of these, how many are major corporate accounts?"

"None."

"And yet, before the accident, how many clients did you carry?"

"Several hundred."

"And how many of those were corporate accounts?"

"I don't recall exactly. About thirty."

"Thirty major clients, hundreds of cases." She gave him a little grimace, regretting the need to add a slight whining edge to her voice. The intimacy was giving way to the knife. "And now, almost nothing. Except this one case."

"I said I have other clients."

"Indeed you did. I'm sure they must be something." She moved to the podium.

"This case against New Horizons is your ticket back to the big time, is it not?"

"Objection."

Judge Nicols shook her head. Slowly. Almost in apology to Marcus. "Overruled."

"Let me rephrase the question." Sharper now, the whine that of a jagged-toothed saw. "You are trying to reestablish your reputation, are you not?"

"No."

"You are *desperate* to generate some publicity for yourself."

"No. That's not —"

"You have everything to gain and nothing to lose in this case. Is that not so, Mr. Glenwood?"

"I believe this case represents a genuine —"

"Starting over in a small town, operating out of your own house, starving for business, missing the big time. You had to come up with something so off-the-wall, so utterly outrageous, that the press would have no choice but to take notice!"

"No. That's not true."

"Is it not. Is it not." Her features twisted with the scarring of jaded lust. "Would it not be more truthful to say, Mr. Glenwood, that you have taken aim at a fine local corporation and trashed its good name for no other reason than to jump-start your own dismal career?"

"No." Knowing the weakness in his voice would sound like guilt, caring only that the end was now in sight. "That's not true."

"Isn't it." The sneer was acrid. "Isn't it."

"No."

"Well, I suppose then I am done here." She gripped the podium with a vulture's claw and forced herself around. "No further questions."

FORTY-ONE

When Marcus stepped from the car, he had difficulty mustering enough strength to get himself moving. The vague scent of ashes drifted about the car like the remnants of his own pyre. Darren walked over and gripped his arm. "You j-just come on."

When he saw the three women gathered on his veranda, Marcus could have wept with relief over having someone there to help vanquish the ghosts. Netty was the first to come forward, inspecting his face and then embracing him hard. "I'd like to roast the lot of them over a slow fire."

Alma was next, her arms as strong and solid as her frame and her concern. When she released him, it was to say, "I brought you some dinner."

"I'm sorry, Alma, I should never have taken this —"

"You hush up now." She tugged him up the steps. "You need something hot in your stomach."

Alma released him so that Kirsten could approach. Her concern was just as genuine as the others', her embrace as

598

natural. But her arms were sweet as honeyed wine, her fragrance drawn from a season of greater promise. Marcus closed his eyes and gave in to the thought that here he could finally rest.

They took him inside and put a plate in front of him. He ate because they watched him, though the only flavor in his mouth was dust and ashes.

They knew enough of hard times not to make the moment linger. Only Kirsten hung back after Netty and Alma moved toward the car. "I could stay if you like."

"I'll be asleep in five minutes." Though she stood ten feet from him now, he felt her arms around him still. "Thank you for coming."

"There's so much I'd like to tell you."

He had no will left to hold back. Thoughts formed and instantly tumbled out. "I couldn't say anymore what I'm asking for the trial and what I'm asking for myself."

She closed the distance between them and reached for his good arm. Only when she gripped his hand with both of hers did she say, "I thought if I stayed mad at you it would keep me from caring."

"You were right to try."

She shook her head, causing the flaxen crown to shimmer. "It didn't work."

He breathed, and felt his crushed soul

tasting a fragrance that was too good for this moment, too fine. He held it just the same, wishing there were some way to keep it always.

She seemed to understand, for her grip upon his hand tightened. "Do you think," she whispered, "two shattered hearts could join and make one whole?"

His entire inner world keened a sad yearning, but his willful tongue betrayed him. "I'd say it was more the making of a tragedy."

Even so, she did not let him go. "They say love can heal all wounds."

No, he wanted to say, that was merely the stuff of poetry and dreamers and a world far finer than this place. Here it was different. Here love pierced with a lance's thrust, killing not once but daily. But Marcus imprisoned the words behind a tightly clenched jaw.

Kirsten waited and held his hand until Alma's voice called faintly from the front lawn. Then, she touched his cheek with lips too soft and warm for his hard nature. She crossed the foyer, pushed open the door, and tripped down the steps into the night. Kirsten left him scarred not by her touch but rather by its absence.

When the cars had driven away, he reached up and with two fingers wiped at the spot, seeking to vanquish the flood of yearning. Only now did he miss what he had gone so long without.

Randall Walker passed through customs at the Raleigh-Durham airport with the ease of one who always traveled first-class. His houseman-driver was there to greet him and accept the baggage tags. Randall walked outside and stopped by the big Mercedes parked in the emergency zone. He stood beside the car and took in great drafts of the night air. It did not matter that the place stank of jet fuel and airport fumes. Behind those odors lurked the finest scent in all the known universe — the smell of home.

He did not realize how much he had missed Raleigh until this very moment. His villa on the Amalfi Coast was everything he had recalled from his one brief visit, a true Renaissance castle. His wife was ecstatic, still walking around in a dreamlike state, scarcely believing it was actually hers. But in truth he was not made for the easy life, no matter how sweet the wine nor how fine the Mediterranean light. He missed the fray, the battles, the danger. Power was nothing unless it was used.

His houseman came out toting his two alligator bags. "Have a good flight?"

"Long. Naples to London, London to

home." Home. How wonderful a word it was. How much Marcus Glenwood and this case had almost cost him.

The houseman shut the trunk, glanced over, and asked, "You all right, sir?"

"Fine." Randall Walker forced his limbs to unlock from the sudden burning fury.

"You've gone all white."

"I'm just tired, that's all." He let the houseman open his door, slid inside, tried to settle the churning rage. It had been like this, on and off, ever since his departure. Sudden furies that threatened to send him screaming about the villa, shattering everything and everyone in his path.

He had to come back. Had to be there for the kill. He pulled out his cellular phone and keyed in the number for Logan's home. When the man answered, Randall said simply, "I'm back."

"Where have you been?"

A wave of relief swept through him. Logan's tone was naturally impatient, demanding. Which meant the China Trade Council chairman had not gone through with his threat of public dismissal. James Southerland, the CEO of New Horizons, had assured Randall that he would personally handle the council chairman and his hair-trigger temper. Obviously Southerland was a man of his word.

Randall forced himself to ease back. He smiled at the ceiling over the backseat, then at the night outside. "Business in Italy. I hear it went well today in court."

"You should have been there." Logan's gloating voice rang like great Oriental gongs. "Suzie just plain tore that guy apart."

"You taped it?"

"Unofficially."

"I want a copy."

"Sure. No problem."

"Any problems with the general?"

"None. He hasn't spoken more than ten words to me since his arrival. The guy might as well be one of those big carved Chinese dogs."

Not according to Randall's other sources. In private, the general was a frenzied maniac, screaming for the blood of everyone who had trapped him within this Carolina courthouse. Which was what had brought the New Horizons chairman back to the United States, not the judge's so-called request. "When are you planning to have James Southerland testify?"

"Last thing tomorrow."

"You mind walking me through your strategy?"

Randall leaned back and listened to the trial attorney sketch out his plan of attack. Walker's mind expanded gradually, stretching and assuming the old familiar shape. He sighed, working the anger and the anxiety from his bones. Randall Walker was indeed home.

The next morning Marcus was relegated to the injury box, sitting and watching as Logan began an onslaught of witnesses. In swift succession the defense attorney led his people through their paces. He attacked hard and fast, moving in for the kill while Marcus was still flayed and wounded. Charlie handled the work like a pro, taking on the witnesses according to Marcus' written notes, striking back with what force he could muster.

Two workers were brought forward to counteract the plaintiff's accusations of New Horizons' mistreatment of employees. The personnel manager described their sensitivity program, given to all levels of management at all U.S. facilities. A black female VP from New York described her rise from the factory floor of their New Jersey plant, one that Charlie managed to reveal on cross had long since been closed and moved south. With each witness Logan drove home the company's excellent labor policies. Solid training schemes. Great working conditions. How well New Horizons treated their employees. Even in his drained state, Marcus could not help seeing that his case was evaporating. Logan was distancing himself and his clients from the accusations, drawing the jury farther and farther from the initial testimony.

The day's final witness came as no great surprise, since he had spent the entire day seated between Logan and Suzie Rikkers. As chairman and chief executive officer of New Horizons Incorporated, James Southerland was as polished and powerful as a man in his position was expected to be. Logan's opening question granted him an opportunity to apologize first to the jury and then to the judge for not being there throughout. But with a two-billion-dollar company to run and over two dozen foreign subsidiaries to manage, Southerland explained, making time for this case required a great deal of juggling. Nevertheless, he was here, and he wanted to set their minds straight on some very important matters about his fine company. Judge Nicols sat stone-faced as Logan respectfully walked the chairman through the company's vast array of subsidiaries. Photographs were shown, supposedly taken from the Factory 101 shop floor. The pictures showed well-lit, pleasant enough surroundings. The workers were clearly Asian. The gleaming machinery was all new and part of New Horizons' investment in this fine, upstanding partnership, the chairman declared, his tone as refined as his appearance. General Zhao unbent enough to offer his first reaction other than silent fury, smiling benignly as Southerland praised the partnership and the wonderful opportunities it offered their workers.

At Logan's request, Southerland explained why few employees knew where the products came from. The company's policy was for all their products to be treated as New Horizons' and not belonging to any particular factory. Some workers on the shop floor were resentful of products coming from foreign suppliers, he explained with an apologetic smile. The way the company handled this was, once a product entered their distribution center, to mark its origin only with a tiny inside tag, which was hidden by the packaging.

Charlie did his best on cross. He showed how each of the managers who had testified earlier had over a third of their total salary tied up in annual bonuses, which were given at the sole discretion of senior management. He then turned to the company's policy of employee screening, and asked Southerland to describe the extensive background checks given to all managers. Was it not true that they did this, Charlie demanded, because of all the complaints that had been lodged by earlier managers about company practices? When Logan's objection was upheld, Charlie changed his tack and asked if the company had ever had an independent audit of its overtime wage payments. That objection led to Charlie asking if the company were not currently under federal investigation for unfair labor practices.

Logan had not even bothered to sit down after his previous objection. "Your Honor, I must request you halt this line of questioning. In case everyone has forgotten, this trial is supposedly about a woman missing in China."

Judge Nicols glanced at Charlie, who wearily struggled to fend off the strain of an overlong day. "Mr. Hayes, I must agree."

Charlie allowed his shoulders to slump, speaking volumes to all who watched. "Plaintiff requests permission to recall this witness."

"Permission granted." Judge Nicols tried hard to keep the pity from showing. But she failed, and for Marcus her expression was the stamp of death to their case.

"Then for the moment we have no further questions." Charlie felt it too. He slid into his seat and murmured so quietly

Marcus could scarcely hear it himself, "Sorry, son."

"You did fine."

"Don't dress the wounded with lies, son. It doesn't help. They cleaned my clock, and we both know it." Charlie used the knuckles of both thumbs to squeeze the fatigue and the perspiration from his temples. "All I could do was give you a chance to get in there later and deliver a few blows of your own."

Marcus' gaze followed Logan's as the defense attorney rose and glanced at the wall clock. Marcus found it hard to believe it was only two-thirty. The day had already lasted the length of droughts and famines and plagues.

"We have just one more witness to call, Your Honor." Logan was striving to hold the exultation from his voice. Juries disliked attorneys who assumed they had won. "But we cannot bring her forward until tomorrow morning."

Judge Nicols bristled, "Are you now presuming to set the court's schedule?"

"Not us, Your Honor, but our witness." Logan's voice rang with quiet triumph. "As our final witness, we intend to call the Attorney General of the United States."

When Marcus reached for the phone

that evening, he felt as if he were hefting his corner of the continent. Seeking to avert the earth's natural course by shifting its axis several degrees. He dialed nonetheless, and said when the phone was answered, "Randall, this is Marcus Glenwood calling."

"As I live and breathe, it surely sounds like you." Randall Walker seemed positively joyous at the call. "I won't ask how you are, because I already know."

"I wanted to repeat my earlier offer."

"You're crushed, is how you are. Isn't that right? Dead and don't know it." The man's chuckle sounded wet, as though he were salivating at the prospect of a wonderful meal. "If you hush up a minute you can hear the hounds baying outside your door."

"Let Gloria Hall go and we'll make this all disappear."

"What, and ruin the show? After all the hard work you've done bringing this crowd together? The press and the television and a general all the way from China? And now the attorney general of these United States?" Each word was punctuated a little more sharply than the one before. "We can't disappoint all these fine folks, now, can we!"

"She's dead, isn't she." Marcus heard the dirge in his own voice. "That's why you didn't let her resurface when all this started. Gloria Hall is dead."

"I don't know what you're talking about. Have you tried the embassy?"

"It's the only reason you'd let this show drag on so long."

"In case you didn't notice, hoss, this ain't my show. This is *yours*. You're the one who's pulled the whole world in close, so they'll all have a bird's-eye view." The voice rasped with pent-up fury. "And now the whole world can watch you get skinned alive."

Marcus felt it necessary to say it all, speak the words in a litany of sorrow over having let more people down. "You can't release her because you don't have her anymore. You must have slipped up somehow. I'm sure you never intended to let this happen."

"I'll be held responsible for just one death, and that one is yours. And don't you think it's ending when the jury comes back and says to the world, 'We find for the defense on all counts.' No sir. That's when the fun starts. Right then and there, we're gonna stake you out and sharpen the knives."

Randall Walker had to stop and fight to breathe around a chest filled more with rage than air. "You ever heard of death by a thousand cuts? We'll take you apart one tiny piece at a time. First your career, then what's left of your good name, then every cent you have. We're suing you for a frivolous claim and charging you for all our legal fees. And we're gonna win. Yeah we are. Bankrupt you and take it all, right down to that fine fancy house you set so much store by. Already got me some good folks who'll take it off my hands. Good folks, yeah, the kind who *deserve* a place like that."

Marcus saw what was coming, and the realization struck like a stone-hard fist to his heart.

"New Horizons wants to turn it into a museum, people tramping through there looking at all the fine clothes they make, all the great stars who endorse their gear." Randall Walker laughed aloud. "When they came to me, you know what I said? I told them it was a great idea. Such a fine plan, once we bankrupt you and claim the old place for our own, they can have it for a dollar."

FORTY-TWO

United States Attorney General Samantha Paltroe had a round face creased by worry and power, and wore her dark suit with the dignity of a judge's robe. Both she and Judge Nicols greeted Logan Kendall's approach with the full-bore sternness of long judicial practice.

Logan began, "We are most grateful that you would take the time to join us today, Madame Attorney General. Could you perhaps begin by telling the court what you have been forced to postpone in order to be here?"

"A meeting with the director of Interpol with regard to organizing efforts in the international war against drugs," she responded in the deep bland drone made famous by hundreds of televised appearances. "A hearing before the Supreme Court, and attendance at a presidential cabinet meeting."

Logan let the moment hang for emphasis, then continued, "The plaintiff has made a lot of fuss about alleged labor violations in China. Even if these allegations were true, which we adamantly declare they are not, do you not have a number of punitive measures at your disposal to deal with such international matters?"

"At our *nation's* disposal," she corrected sternly.

"The nation's disposal. Of course." Not minding the correction. Not from this woman. Logan's manner was as meek as he could make it, given the global spotlight, the packed courtroom, the attention given to his every word. "What would some of these measures be?"

"Various diplomatic treaties outline possible sanctions, both trade and otherwise."

"Given your understanding of both the law and this specific situation, do you feel this case should have been brought to trial?"

"I do not."

"Do you feel General Zhao should have been forced to attend?"

"Under no circumstances whatsoever. His appearance is a serious embarrassment to both our nations. Not to mention the absolute chaos this court's freezing of Chinese financial assets has caused to trade and the international markets." She looked directly at General Zhao for the first time. "A situation for which I heartily apologize."

Logan paused long enough for the jury to turn and watch the general respond with a single jerky nod. Then, "Given your understanding of the case, Madame Attorney General, what is your impression of the allegations?"

"My opinion as both a former judge and federal prosecutor is that the plaintiff's lawyer is seriously confused." Her tone was coldly dismissive. "I understand from the newscasts that he has been through a rough time personally. It shows in how he has sought to try this case." The creased face pointed directly at Marcus. "He should seek help."

Logan turned to grant Marcus the same smile he had shown during Suzie Rikkers' questioning. "Confused."

"The United States Congress has instituted a series of trade laws dealing with unfair commercial practices overseas. Such issues are best dealt with through the International Labor Organization and the United Nations. This attempt to resolve such issues by filing a federal lawsuit for alleged false imprisonment abroad is utterly misguided."

"Is it now," Logan purred, then repeated for the jury's sake, "misguided."

"Absolutely." The attorney general turned to Judge Nicols and continued, "General Zhao is protected by diplomatic immunity. He is here strictly as a personal favor to the China Trade Council, which is as concerned as I am about the way this trial is jeopardizing both diplomatic and trade relations." Her voice took on a stronger edge. "With all due respect to this court, this trial is a serious breech of judicial boundaries, one that should be rectified immediately."

Logan spun about, marched to his table, accepted the paper offered by Suzie Rikkers. "Your Honor, based upon the expert advice of the United States attorney general, we hereby resubmit our motion to have this case immediately dismissed."

Judge Nicols accepted the paper and set it down unread. "First I will grant the plaintiff the right to cross."

"Your Honor —"

She showed her own steel. "Proceed or relinquish the witness, Mr. Logan."

Logan retreated, fuming. "No further questions."

Charlie started to rise, but Marcus settled a hand on his shoulder and held the old man down. He had arrived at the next distressing moment in a long line of painful junctures he would have given anything to avoid. He rose to his feet, dreading his next move, which was to turn and look at the jury. Their eyes reflected morbid curiosity in the walking dead. He nodded his acceptance, grateful for the sleeplessness that had left him numb from the brain down.

After confronting the jury, meeting the attorney general's overt hostility was a cakewalk. "Mrs. Paltroe," he began, stripping her of all titles, ignoring the stiffening of her spine, repeating it for emphasis. "Mrs. Paltroe, could you tell the court just precisely how you have utilized the powers of your office to assist us in returning this young woman to her home?"

Her reaction was etched with corrosive clarity. "I have yet to see evidence that suggests the woman is in fact being held against her will."

Marcus nodded slowly, moving nearer to the jury. Letting them inspect the damage up close. Hiding nothing. Not his fragility, not his two sleepless nights, not the pain he knew was there in his gaze. "Then perhaps you could tell us how much time you have spent actually obtaining the evidence upon which you reached this conclusion."

"It may have escaped your notice, Mr. Glenwood, but the world does not revolve around you." The gallery tittered, but the jury did not. They were too close, too aware of him and his wounds. "I have other affairs that command my attention."

"Other affairs," Marcus said, "that are, in your opinion, more important."

She hesitated for the first time. Sensing the trap. "Other affairs that are of national importance. Vital issues that will affect generations to come."

"Of course." He felt no need to engage this woman in battle. This close to the jury box, he could almost feel the waves of pitiful rejection. They were sorry for him, they felt for the Halls, but they were going to find for the defense. And Gloria Hall was dead. These facts he had spent his days and nights struggling to accept. The torment left him feeling as though he were dancing upon the stage of the damned. "Mrs. Paltroe, as you may or may not know, we have material this court has permitted us to enter as evidence that points to serious wrongdoing by the defendants. With respect, this hard evidence is not something that would hold the attention of Congress. The court's task is to determine who is *responsible*. Who is *guilty*. The political realm, Mrs. Paltroe, does not *want* to assign responsibility."

"Objection!" Logan pointed his silver pen at Marcus, but his face said he would have preferred to be holding a loaded gun. "Is that man asking a question or giving a lecture?"

Judge Nicols responded with a severity that managed to push through the fog of misery surrounding Marcus. "Mr. Glenwood permitted you to bring in a new witness yesterday without even objecting. Is that not true?"

"But Your Honor, our witness is —"

"I know who she is as well as anyone else in this court." She leaned both elbows on the bench. "Mr. Glenwood then permitted you to traipse this witness wherever you wished to go, including a personal insult against his professional abilities. And he did not offer a single objection throughout. I therefore suggest that you sit down and allow him to continue."

Marcus turned to face the judge and said quietly, "Thank you, Your Honor."

"Proceed, counsel."

"Yes ma'am." He turned back, and found a reluctant wariness in the attorney general's gaze. Hostile, still, but aware of him now as an opposing force. "Is it not against the basic rules of diplomacy to assign blame?"

"In some cases, perhaps. But not all."

"You *negotiate* a matter. You do not condemn. Is that also not correct?"

"In such areas as international affairs,

sometimes it is better to find a joint resolution."

"And in cases where such a resolution is not possible?" When he was answered by a longer hesitation, he took a step closer, and attacked. "This very administration, which included in its election manifesto a sharp criticism of Chinese human-rights abuses, now says nothing at all. Now that they are in office, trade has become the critical issue. Trade and campaign dollars. Anything so minor as the disappearance of a young woman has to be swept aside."

A flash of anger. "That is not true at all."

"I submit that it is in fact very true, Mrs. Paltroe. I submit that the hundreds of officials under your command have done absolutely nothing to determine what happened to Gloria Hall. Why? Precisely because they are terrified of what they might find."

"Objection!"

"Overruled."

Marcus retreated a single step. "As you yourself said, Mrs. Paltroe, the drug war is an international issue, is it not?"

"Yes."

"And yet when we have people selling heroin on our streets, we do not let them go, do we?"

"No." It was her turn to lean forward. "Not if they are selling on *our* streets."

"We do not turn them over to Congress or the State Department for a diplomatic resolution, do we? If a crime is committed under federal law, even one where international issues are at stake, we try the criminal in our courts. Is that not true?"

She flushed angrily. "Juries are not responsible for setting international policy!"

"No, but they *are* here to determine guilt." Marcus brought the fight straight into that seamed and powerful face. "Courts of law are intended to hold people accountable, are they not? This jury cannot right all the wrongs in this world. But it *can* decide guilt in relation to a specific issue. Is that not true?"

The hostility left a bitter residue. "Not in a case this weak."

"I would say that is for the *court* to decide." He walked back to his table, drained of all fight, all will. It was all he could do to say simply, "No further questions."

Judge Nicols turned to the attorney general and said mildly, "With respect, this court happens to disagree with your assessment of jurisdiction. The defense's motion for dismissal is denied." She banged her gavel. "Court is adjourned until nine tomorrow morning."

★ ★ ★

After the judge departed, Marcus let the seat take his immense encumbrance, and said to Alma and Austin, "We need to talk."

Alma reached for his hand. "You look exhausted."

Charlie shifted his chair closer to the gathering. "Don't you worry about our boy. Any lawyer worth his salt has learned that sleeping easy is something he'll do only after his last case is tried and won." He said to Marcus, "Boomer is dead-worried about you driving around in that Jeep."

"It's fine."

"It's nothing of the sort. Darren showed me. It's got no bumper and the passenger side looks like it's been chewed on by a pit bull with steel teeth."

"It will do for now." He kept his gaze centered upon Alma and Austin. Spoke to the woman, for her gaze was easiest to meet. "My guess is tomorrow the defense is going to rest."

Alma sought reassurance in his features. When she found none, tension raised her voice a notch. "That's good, isn't it?"

Marcus was in no mood for lies. Or, for that matter, too much truth. "With your permission I am going to decline my right of rebuttal. I have no further evidence that will strengthen our case."

Charlie agreed. "Repeating things is dangerous at this stage. It can weaken the power the jury felt when the evidence was first brought forward. And afterward the defense will have another chance to counterattack. We won't catch them with their pants down twice. No sir, not this crowd."

"I don't understand," Alma said, more concerned over Marcus' tone than over his words. "We've won, haven't we? You beat them."

Marcus replied softly, "Alma, their defense is very strong." Punctuating each word with a slight pause.

She turned her plea toward Charlie. "It can't be over. We've got to do more. There must be something —"

"Alma." The one word was enough to turn them all around. Austin Hall sat on the edge of his seat, a hard tight knob of a man. "That's enough."

"But he just said —"

"I heard the man same as you. I've been sitting and listening and thinking for days. If you try you'll hear the only answer that matters, same as me."

The chamber was silent save for the dull sigh of the courtroom's ventilation system. Then, rising in the distance, they heard the faintest clamor. A tide of voices and shouts and loudspeakers and sirens. The courtroom had no windows. Which meant the noise was strong enough to penetrate solid concrete walls.

"Marcus has done all he said he'd do." Austin set up each word as he would the precise formula of a proven theorem. "He gave us more publicity than we ever imagined. The whole world knows our daughter's name. All because of this man."

Austin leaned in close, his voice gentle, but the words rocking his wife nonetheless. "He has done more than we could ask of our closest kin. He's been beaten, burned, battered. He's sat up there and let himself be flayed alive. All for us. And now he's trying to tell us to look and see what we've known all along."

Alma's head began slowly tracking back and forth. Austin took a deep breath, willed himself to hold to his flat, precise control. "Alma, our Gloria is dead."

She gasped in the way of one whose final breath has been torn from her body. Marcus rested a hand on her shoulder, but had no strength for anything else. Nor any comfort to add. Not even for himself.

"If they had her, she'd be free." Austin turned toward Marcus, revealing the struggle to hold himself together. "You do the best you can, Marcus."

"I will."

A single sob escaped from Alma's throat, one wrenching sound cut off as sharp as a broken crystal heart. Austin continued, "You do the best you can. Not for me. Not for Alma. We can't ask a thing more of you. Do it for my Gloria."

He searched about him, as though wanting to be certain his legs were still there and ready to carry him. "Come, Alma. We must go show the world our woes."

"I can't."

"You can. Hold my hand here. Be strong." He lifted his wife with his will. "Gloria is watching."

FORTY-THREE

Marcus watched the news as he breakfasted, taking vague consolation on that wet, gray day from how well Kirsten handled the press. She had been filmed on the court-house steps the day before, with the modern faceless building and lowering clouds for a backdrop. Her hair blew like scattered winter wheat as she fielded question after question, only once losing her calm, when a reporter asked her if Marcus Glenwood was using her as a shield to hide his drinking problem. Her response was quiet, but only because emotion had choked her throat tight. "Marcus Glenwood is the finest man I have ever met," she fired back. "A man who cares so deeply he will sacrifice all he has left to help the Hall family. I wonder who would say the same about you." When the picture switched to the next story, Marcus turned the television off and stood staring out at the dripping rain, reflecting that such moments as this should be savored in si-lence.

The SBI car was there and ready when he and Darren emerged. Marcus waved, but any response was lost to the rain. The drive into town was as silent as ever, a time for watching the highway unfold, slick as a gray-black river. Marcus entered the courthouse at a run, keeping silent as dozens of questions were shouted from beneath a forest of umbrellas. He entered the foyer, brushed rain off his jacket, returned the guards' greetings, then stepped into the elevator alone. Only when the doors closed did he gape like a landed fish, gasping hard and long, releasing his fear.

Within the windowless courtroom, wind and rain and normal light vanished, to be replaced by whatever the judge dictated. Even time was held within her sway.

As expected, after Judge Nicols had given her greeting to the jury, Logan Kendall rose and announced, "Your Honor, the defense rests."

Marcus rose in tandem and said, "The plaintiff waives their right to rebuttal, Your Honor."

Logan's voice betrayed his triumph. "Then we declare our readiness to proceed immediately into closing arguments."

Judge Nicols frowned, a swift notice of concern, there and gone as fast as scuttling clouds. "Counsel may approach the bench."

When they had gathered there before her, she went on, "Does the plaintiff wish further time to prepare?"

"No thank you, Your Honor."

"Very well. I am limiting each side to two hours of closing."

Marcus wished there were some way to thank her for the anxious cast to those stern features. "We would like to take an initial thirty minutes, then hold the right to speak again after the defense."

Logan countered, "Then we request an additional half hour to rebut the plaintiff. It is our right to go last, Your Honor."

"All right. Mr. Glenwood, you may begin."

Marcus rose and walked directly to the podium. He had given scores of closing arguments before all kinds of juries. The words came easily and well. As he spoke, a portion of his mind weighed the jury's reaction. He walked them through the evidence, gave them a careful summary of the early witnesses whom they might otherwise have forgotten. And he studied them. On a majority of faces, he saw concern. This was bad. Even worse was how some now held expressions of pity. Pity was murderous. Charlie Hayes had once said the only time a jury showed pity for a lawyer was when they agreed with him in their guts but had decided to follow their minds. And their minds had chosen for the other side. Marcus had never known Charlie to be wrong on this count.

Marcus began his conclusion. "Through using a pea-in-the-shell game, the defendants have sought to hide their connection to this factory. But the evidence has clearly demonstrated that, in fact, the New Horizons company does not only purchase tens of millions of dollars worth of products from Factory 101, they actually own a significant interest in the factory. One they have sought to hide both from you the jury and from the federal authorities. And we have shown you why.

"Through documentary evidence and the testimony of witnesses, we have revealed that New Horizons Incorporated and Factory 101 were in a conspiracy to profit from the systematic abuse of prisoners of conscience."

"Objection!" Logan bolted from his chair. "Your Honor, the Chinese prison system is not on trial here."

"Overruled. Continue, Mr. Glenwood."

"Thank you, Your Honor." Marcus turned back to the jury and went on, "We have shown how our client was abused because she threatened this profit. She was treated in the same callous manner as their workers. This upstanding American student was made to disappear because she got in the way."

Logan rose another time. "Your Honor, I must protest."

"Overruled."

Marcus fought back the desire to beg the jury to share with him the conviction that Gloria had been right all along. "Gloria Hall was kidnapped and abused by the defendants because she threatened a commercial relationship that was mired in pain and fear and blood. A relationship that cared for nothing save money and power. A relationship that existed purely to exploit those who had no voice to complain. She sought to bring light into the darkness that was endured by many, and for no other reason than because it benefited the company's bottom line. These partners must be punished, ladies and gentlemen of the jury. They must be brought to justice."

Silence followed Marcus back to his seat. He endured the congratulatory pats from Charlie and Alma, though their hands burned like branding irons. He could not face the jury, not until Logan had approached the podium and demanded their attention.

"Ladies and gentlemen of the jury, I am sorry we are here. Sorry we have taken your time and the court's time. Sorry we have dragged us all through this charade for the sake of a lost and forlorn cause. The plaintiff's lawyer has constructed the worst possible kind of case. He has played upon the emotions of two distraught parents and tied us all up with cords of convoluted lies, creating knots of empty half-truths.

"A good case is like a jigsaw puzzle. When things go right, the plaintiff's lawyer should stand up in the beginning and tell us how the puzzle will look at the end. Then we should watch the pieces being set in place, one by one, as the witnesses are presented. Afterward, in what's called the summation or closing argument, the plaintiff should be able to describe the finished scene.

"Unfortunately, ladies and gentlemen of the jury, this has not happened in our case. The puzzle is not complete. The picture is blurred, distorted. The pieces of evidence are mismatched. In fact, I would go so far as to say that we have not arrived at what could be called a real picture at all.

"Let's begin here by listing some of the words we've heard the plaintiff's attorney bandy about." He lifted a printed board and set it on the easel by the lectern. "All right. There was the word *document*. You remember how the lawyer sitting over there used it? He said he would present documentary evidence. That's our second word printed right here, see it? *Evidence.* Then the third word, an accusation of *collusion.* It gets worse, because then comes the word *abuse,* and after that *prisoners of conscience.* And finally there was the word he used to describe the missing woman. Remember that one? *Upstanding.* That's what he said."

Logan left the board and turned his full attention to the jury box. "Now let's take a moment and remember what the experts said about all this so-called evidence. If you're going to look anywhere to decide whether or not there really is any culpability, wouldn't you look to the experts? Of course you would. And what did the experts tell you? That there was no substantive evidence that pointed to New Horizons' being directly involved. None."

He used his silver pen like a wand, punching the air, prodding the jury to pay attention and believe him. Above all, believe him. "Most importantly, we have the woman herself. Someone who has gone out of her way to look for trouble. She has made a profession of standing in harm's way. She protested continuously. She disliked the Chinese government. Why? Who knows? Whatever the reason, we know for certain that Gloria Hall went looking for trouble. Sadly, she probably found it. Is that my clients' fault? No!

"What the plaintiff's lawyer has failed to prove is how New Horizons' *business* relationship with a Chinese factory could be tied in any way to such nasty words as *collusion* and *prisoners of conscience*. Let me remind you, ladies and gentlemen of the jury, that New Horizons Incorporated runs ninety different operations, more than two dozen of them overseas, employing over thirty-seven thousand employees in nineteen different countries." Instantly he held up his hand. "Not that this issue is minor. Not at all. The possibility that Gloria Hall might be missing is terrible. We all hurt for her and for her parents. But ladies and gentlemen of the jury, the opposing counsel has not offered a shred of concrete evidence to tie New Horizons to Gloria's Hall disappearance. Can anyone tell me why these companies would endanger such a lucrative operation by kidnapping a visiting student? Where is the motive?" He paused a moment, then jerked his shoulders in a humorless laugh. "Does this entire supposition seem as ludicrous to you as it does to me?"

Logan left the podium and began a tight little victory parade before the jury box. "Up to this point, our trial has not been about seeking truth at all. Instead, we have watched as the plaintiff has taken an upstanding North Carolina firm, one that employs four thousand people right here in this great state. A company that is in the process of expanding their operations and adding another two thousand employees. A company that supplies more eastern North Carolina families with incomes than almost any other firm. And how do we thank them? By sitting here and watching the plaintiff's lawyer smear their name in the dirt. By tarring and feathering the senior executives. Is this the way we treat our corporate citizens? Threatening them with baseless slurs on their reputation?

"This has been a wet-spaghetti kind of lawsuit, the crudest kind of case. A wet-spaghetti suit is one where you take whatever you can get your hands on and toss it at the ceiling. Whatever sticks makes up the plaintiff's case. What doesn't, well, who loses? Who pays? The answer, I am sorry to say, is a lot of people. In this case, those who are injured are my clients. A fine North Carolina company that has never had any dealings with this Chinese group —"

Marcus was on his feet. "Objection, Your Honor. This is in direct opposition to the defense's prior judicial admission."

"Sustained."

But the silver pen was already out and weaving its spell before the judge had spoken. "Yes. All right. Let me rephrase that. The judicial admission has shown that there was *some* commercial relationship. But what we have also shown is that these relations were nothing like what the plaintiff has claimed. You see how a wet-spaghetti lawsuit works? They claim this. We show that it is something else entirely. They say, But wait, if the one is true, then the other is as well. Do you see? Of course you do. Yes, the judicial admission was that New Horizons had some relation to Factory 101. Yes. But we have not seen any evidence whatsoever that ties the North Carolina firm to responsibility for the acts that have brought us all together. Let us be perfectly clear about that, ladies and gentlemen: New Horizons is on trial here for the disappearance of Gloria Hall in China. And for that there is no evidence. None."

He used both arms to fight the air, since Marcus was too far away to be grappled with personally. "Wrap this up in the personal tragedy of the plaintiff's lawyer, who is desperately trying to jump-start his own life, and what do you have? A mess that should never have entered this courtroom. You remember what I said before introducing my own witnesses, ladies and gentlemen of the jury? I said we would go after the truth. And the truth is that the plaintiff's lawyer has failed on all counts. There are neither credible witnesses nor physical evidence tying New Horizons to any wrongdoing. This is a political matter that belongs in the diplomatic realm. And we have an opportunistic lawyer at the helm of a ship headed toward destruction."

Logan dropped his arms, patted the sides of the podium, gathered himself for the final blow. "The last point I want to leave you with are the words from our very own United States Attorney General. This incredibly powerful and busy woman came here of her own volition to speak with us, simply because she found this trial so vital to our country's interests. She said something very important, and I want to draw your attention to this. She said this trial was a mistake from the beginning." He leaned across the podium, his entire body clenched with the purpose of driving home the point. "I commend this expert intelligence to you. I ask that you consider this very seriously. The Attorney General could not have been any more definite or direct when she told us that this case should never have come to trial." He nodded his conclusion. "Let's wrap this up, ladies and gentlemen of the jury. Let's shut this circus down and allow all of us to return to the real world. Thank you for your time and for your patience with this miserable excuse of a trial."

FORTY-FOUR

When Darren stopped for gas on the way home, Marcus walked across the street to the liquor store. He walked straight over to the inexpensive blends and pulled down a bourbon with a name so cheap it mocked the buyer. He ignored the pricier malts that glittered behind the cashier. He had no interest in anything that spoke of celebration or good times ahead. He wanted something foul and burning and acrid. Something that would smite him hard and hurt him the next day. It was the fate he deserved.

Darren and the man pumping gas both watched his return in silence. He said nothing to either of them, just climbed back into the Jeep and sat there waiting. He did not want any argument. He wanted oblivion.

Darren took his time driving home, meandering through the streets as though seeing them for the first time. Eventually they arrived, however, and pulled in past the SBI car and halted in the drive. Only then did Marcus wish for something to say, some words of thanks for all Darren had done, even an acknowledgment of the comfort Marcus had found in the young man's hulking presence. But there were no words worthy of the man.

Marcus left the brown paper bag on the front hall table as he climbed the stairs and changed his clothes. But when he came back down, it was to the sound of another car pulling into his driveway. He walked out onto the veranda, not feeling much one way or the other, even when he recognized the blond head behind the wheel.

Kirsten climbed the steps in the breathless manner of one pretending not to hurry. She stopped on the third step when his face was clear in the veranda's weak light. Whatever it was she saw there on his features, it stilled her smile of greeting before it had formed.

Marcus said, "I can't even begin to guess how you've come to be here."

"Darren called Deacon."

"Let's see. That must have been on my mobile while I was still in the liquor store."

"Deacon called Alma. Alma started to come herself, but Austin said I should go." She moved one step closer. "Austin said to tell you that sometimes solitude is just another name for death."

Marcus was still trying to frame a reply, one that would keep his way open to temporary amnesia, when the phone rang. He walked back inside, picked up the receiver, and felt as much as heard Kirsten's presence there with him.

Deacon Wilbur's deep, honeyed voice asked, "You all right over there?"

"No." He could almost smell the contents of that unopened bottle. "Not yet."

"The good Lord above tells us He's gonna look after His own."

"You could have fooled me."

"Now you just hold up there. Don't you go looking for fair. Don't you expect a painless life. Don't go hunting for an easy road. Just you settle for wisdom."

The vision of the bag and the first scarring swallow wavered slightly, though Marcus tried hard to hold on. "I've failed. Gloria is lost, the case is lost, it's all over."

"Sometimes the hardest thing a man can do is accept his own humanness," Deacon's tone rumbled soft enough to make the words almost palatable. "Sometimes there ain't no harder road to walk than the one that turns away from the past. Yes, cutting the cords that tie us to what was and never will be again, then turning toward what is yet to come."

Marcus found the pastor's voice rubbing out both the bottle's image and his own desperate hunger. He wanted to hang up, to turn away from this kind man and his painful words, but he merely sighed his defeat and settled into the chair behind his desk.

Deacon waited a moment, and when Marcus remained quiet, he concluded, "Don't know what's harder, saying farewell to the dead-and-gones or hello to what's coming. Sometimes hope is the worst burden of all. One you'll never be able to carry alone. You just think on that, now. Think hard. Try to find some way to take that first small step."

As Marcus hung up the phone, Kirsten walked in and sat in the client's chair. Marcus was angry that they would care so much as to keep him from oblivion. Bitterness over the distance between him and the bottle turned his mood foul. "Gloria knew the whole time she wasn't coming back."

Kirsten nodded slowly. "Yes."

"She went to China planning to place herself in harm's way. She went *expecting* to destroy her parents' lives." He planted his good elbow on the tabletop and aimed a shaky finger at her. "And you knew it all along."

Another slow nod. "Yes."

"She had it planned down to your handing me the documents. She learned that from Dee Gautam, I imagine. Feed the information to the poor dumb slob of an attorney. Do it slowly. Let him hook himself good and hard, then reel him in bit by bit."

"That's right."

Bile rose in his throat. "Shame she didn't mention to Alma and Austin that they needed to find somebody better. Somebody who wouldn't let them crash and burn."

"Nobody could have done a better job," she said, her voice too soft to vanquish even a flickering flame.

Yet it was enough to ignite his fury. He smashed his fist down on the table, but she did not flinch, did not even blink. "Gloria is dead, Kirsten. She's dead. And the case is lost."

Kirsten's gaze seemed made from the same fabric as the night, empty and endless. "She was dead before she left."

He leaned back, searching for a hold on his anger, feeling it seeping away like water through a fist. "What?"

"It's the only thing that has kept me going. Knowing how she was. She was dead inside. She told me that a hundred times. A thousand. She was just looking for a place to lay her body down."

It came to him then, the filtering down from the realm beyond logic. "The boyfriend."

"Gary Loh was finishing medical school when they met. He was brilliant, he loved life, he loved Gloria. They were made for each other. Seeing them together gave you hope for love in a world . . ." She stopped, breathed hard, looked out the window. "Before he started his internship, Gary went to Hong Kong. That was, oh, eighteen months ago now. It was his second trip. There was a missionary group working there, one partnered with our outreach program. They worked in the red-light district down by the docks, mostly with prostitutes and homeless and addicts. They were Hong Kong's only outreach program among the heroin addicts. Gary loved the work. He talked about it all the time. That was just a part of how he was, this mercy he felt for the helpless."

Marcus nodded, not understanding yet, but knowing it was coming. "Britain gave Hong Kong back to China."

"Hong Kong's takeover occurred the year before Gary arrived. The Beijing government treats all addicts as capital offenders, the same as pushers. First they warned the clinic, then they raided it. Gary fought back. We heard about this later, from one of the survivors. He had a number of patients who were too ill to move. He tried to bar the soldiers' entry into the clinic. They beat him with their rifle butts. His skull was crushed. He was flown home in a coma and died three days later."

"And Gloria took it hard."

"She just withered up inside. She was kept so sedated I doubt she even knew there was a funeral at all. For days and days she only said one thing to me that made any sense, one thing you could recognize as real words: Don't tell my parents, I don't want them to know. A week or so after the funeral, she called to tell them she and Gary had broken off the engagement. She had to say something. They knew the instant they heard her voice that she was torn apart." Her gaze revealed a trace of the agony that had emptied her. "I made a terrible mistake then. I should have ignored her and told them everything. They would have stopped her. Had her committed or forced her to get help. I don't know. Something. Then she wouldn't have . . ."

Marcus waited until he was certain she could not go on. "But you didn't."

"She was my friend. As soon as she came off the sedatives, she grew so determined. I mean, the very same *day*. Over and over she said she had to find some way to make them pay. It was like some kind of chant, I heard it that often. Some way to give meaning to Gary's death. She talked about it all the time. I didn't mind so much, at least she was eating again and making sense and getting better. At least she was involved with life. Or so I thought."

"Then she found out about the joint venture."

"Gloria had been working for almost a year on her thesis about New Horizons' labor practices when Gary died. The company was a natural target for her. She had friends from church in almost every corporate department. New Horizons is a foul breed, always had been. Just the kind of group to suck money from kids." She stopped for a breath. "Gloria had pretty much stopped work on her thesis and was spending all her time protesting against the Chinese. Then two things happened at once. An assistant manager at the company heard from somewhere that Gloria was fighting the Chinese on human-rights issues. She handed over documents about the joint venture." Another shaky breath. "And then came the first rumors about New Horizons' wanting to demolish the church."

"You mean the cemetery," Marcus corrected.

She gave a minute shake of her head. "It was never about the cemetery. That was just their opening salvo. Gloria knew because the secretary to the board has a sister in the congregation. Randall Walker appeared before the New Horizons board and said, Complain about the cemetery and ask the city council to condemn it. Do it just before you leave for the conference in Switzerland and let the lawyers take the heat."

"Randall," Marcus said. "I should have smelled his hand in this."

"Once the cemetery was condemned, the plan was to move immediately to include the church as well. They needed the land for further expansion. It was all mapped out. The city council knew and approved."

"Of course they would." The thought of his grandfather's land being handed over to those vultures on the hill sharpened his outrage. "It meant more jobs."

"Jobs and investment and development. The works. Then you showed up, bypassed the council and the local judges, and had a new federal judge overturn all their carefully laid plans."

Marcus rose from his desk and went to inspect the darkness without. "Back up to Gloria and her plan."

"She worked at it night and day. Six months, eight, all the time I was waiting for her to find some reason to live. Something that would keep her here. I thought at times that she'd found it in this battle. But I was wrong. Then she discovered something new, something so urgent and exciting she dropped all her work in my lap and said, I'm going and I'm not coming back."

Marcus said to the night, "General Zhao."

"I should have said something. I should have stopped her. I should have warned her parents and called the police, something."

Marcus shut his eyes to the agony of wrong choices. "The bed in the guest room is made up. You're welcome to stay if you like." When she did not answer, he felt driven from the room by his own lack of answers. "Good night."

FORTY-FIVE

For once it was an idea that woke him, and not the nightmare. Marcus was on his feet and moving before he was even fully awake. He was halfway down the stairs before he registered the change to his home. He sniffed the air, turned, and walked back to the top landing. Marcus walked down the hall, and stood staring at the closed door. The fragrance was stronger there, a taste of softness and light that rested easy on the palate. Marcus knocked on the door. A clear soft voice said come in. Marcus opened the door and stood looking down into eyes that spoke of a heart that was wounded yet still found the strength to care. He found himself thinking of words old Deacon had spoken on the phone the night before, utterances drifting through his mind in time to the faint trace of Kirsten's perfume. Words like *turning* and *hope*.

He said to her, "I'm flying up to Philadelphia. There's something I need to do." When she merely nodded her response, he added, "You need to tell Alma and

647

Austin what you told me."

Clearly this had occupied her thoughts and kept her there the previous night. The pain of resignation was clear in her voice. "They'll never forgive me."

This time Marcus felt certain enough of the people involved to know he was offering more than just words. "Kirsten, they already have."

Marcus had not been to the Rice estate in two years, not since the last time he had come to pick up Carol and the kids. He had never been welcome there. After four years of futile attempts to enter his in-laws' good graces, he had accepted defeat and restricted their meetings to dinners on neutral territory. The manor had not changed in his absence. The same gardener stooped over the same immaculate flower beds; the same butler opened the door they had stripped off some castle in France. The entrance hall was flagstoned and the arched ceiling rose four stories over his head. Sounds mingled with the scents of furniture polish and fresh-cut flowers. It might be autumn outside, but seasons made little difference within this tightly controlled and sterile universe.

Carol's mother appeared in the doorway beside the curved stairway, dressed in silk and gold. Her gaze was as coldly furious as it had been in court. "Get out of my house."

"I'd like to have a word with your daughter."

"She doesn't want to speak with you. Not ever again."

"Nonetheless, I would like to see her." Marcus planted himself, his stance saying what his words would not. "Please, Mrs. Rice. This is important."

"There is nothing you could ever say to any of us that would hold any interest whatsoever." She did not scream. Did not shout. Her breeding permitted no such outburst. But the words cut like daggers. "I await the day your name will be erased from the earth. My greatest regret is that you were ever born at all."

He did not move. "Please, Mrs. Rice."

A voice from the study called out, "It's all right, Mother."

"It's not all right. Nothing about this man is right, and nothing ever will be."

"Let him come in. He'll leave faster if we don't fight him."

"Thank you," Marcus said, taking it as the only invitation he would ever receive. He entered the long side room, with its handmade windows taken from a Kentish palace. He crossed three antique Persian carpets and passed beneath two chandeliers, his way flanked by bookshelves stuffed with leather-bound volumes. He approached the figure seated by a fireplace burning logs thicker than his waist. "Hello, Carol."

"What do you want?"

Marcus halted before his ex-wife. She sat with the regal bearing of a queen. Her chair was drawn up close to the fire, high-backed as a throne. The surgeons had done a wonderful job on her face. With her professional hand at makeup, only a single tiny scar was visible just below her left temple. She held her head precisely as he remembered, the chestnut hair pulled back so tightly it seemed to draw her eyes into a habitual squint, her chin tilted and ready for war.

"Thank you for seeing me."

"I asked you why you were here."

"I've come to apologize." He did not bother to take a seat. Supplicants did not seek chairs or comfort. "You were right about many things. A lot of our arguments happened because I was being too much of a lawyer in our own home, and not enough of a father and husband. You were right about the weekend. I should never have drunk so much the night before. You were right about the accident. If I had been better —"

"You come up here and tell me this

and think I won't tell the newspeople what a snake you really are," she fired back. "I know you. There's got to be some ulterior motive to make you grovel like this."

"No. Not this time."

"You've wasted your time coming here." Her words were etched sharp into the ice of her eyes and face and voice. "Anybody who asks me is going to hear it all."

"That's your privilege." Marcus found gentle relief in the truth that he really did not care. "I didn't come to ask for anything. I just wanted you to know I'm sorry. For everything."

Something flickered deep within her gaze, an instant of indecision. The chin lifted, but there was a slight quiver now threatening her poise. "You never could tell the truth. You never gave anybody anything without exacting your pound of flesh."

"You're probably right." Life had always seemed to cost him more than it gave. He had previously sensed a rightness in using any advantage to win a little back. But not anymore. There was nothing to gain, nothing he sought except an acknowledgment of what truth the moment held. "I used my selfishness to keep from seeing just how hollow I always was."

The quivering rose to touch the words as well. "You're nothing in my life and never will be."

Marcus nodded acceptance of yet another judgment against him. "I don't deserve anything else."

Carol pressed a fist against her face, clenching back the tremors. Only two hoarse words emerged to command, "Get out."

"I'm sorry, Carol. For all I was, and even more for everything I wasn't." He trod the silent carpeted distance.

He reached the doorway when the voice behind him cried, "Marcus!"

He turned back, saw the hand half-raised toward him, saw the tension that marked her face and gaze. He waited, longing for all he had lost, and watched as the hand slowly retreated, and the face lowered to shelter in tearstained palms. Marcus left the house, wishing there were some way to thank her for trying at all.

On the trip home, Marcus watched the flight attendant push the drinks trolley past his row. The tiny bottles clinked their invitation, the light reflecting off the clear and amber liquids as it would the elixir of life. But the momentary feeling of having done the right thing quenched whatever thirst he might have felt. The feeling stayed with him through the night and into the next dawn, which arrived without either sweats or tremors.

Deacon Wilbur was waiting outside to greet him and Darren upon their arrival at church. The press gathered beyond the barriers to watch and film and be held at bay. Deacon asked, "You give thought to what I said?"

"Yes." Marcus spotted Kirsten rising from the car with Alma and Austin, and noted the tension. A note of sorrow pealed with the church bell. He realized that Deacon was waiting for more of a response and added, "I flew up and apologized to my wife."

Deacon Wilbur rewarded him with a single somber nod. "I'd call that a mighty fine first step."

Marcus excused himself and walked over to the trio. Up close the strain was more evident. He greeted them with, "You've discussed it."

Sunlight rested upon Kirsten's head like laurels from another realm. "You were right. It had to be said."

Alma was stiff with sorrow and kept a new distance between herself and the younger woman. Voice tight, she said merely, "We'd figured it was something like this."

The look that Austin gave Alma held

the hoary gaze of shared remorse. "Been thinking it for some time now."

Kirsten quietly announced, "I'm leaving this afternoon. I've caused everybody here enough pain."

Marcus could not protest, except to say, "You've caused me nothing of the sort." But the words were not enough to dispel her sorrow. Nor to prevent her from entering the church alone.

Even so, the service held to its customary gift of space and peace. Marcus sat encircled by noise and friendship. He watched as a trio of youngsters gathered before the choir to add their dancing and high-pitched voices to a modern gospel song. Two of them wore New Horizons shoes; Marcus recognized the glittering rainbow arcs and the metallic glint to the laces.

It was then, as he sat experiencing a bizarre sense of comfort within his own blank world, that the idea formed and took shape. As if it had been waiting for him to reach out and open an unseen door. Marcus rose to his feet, gaping at the youngsters and their dance. He was right. He knew it with utter certainty.

Following the service he reentered the sunlight, marched over to Kirsten, and said, "I need you to come with me back to the house."

She protested weakly. "I'm not sure —"

"I don't have time to argue. I've got to get back and try to raise Charlie. We've got a lot of work to do."

She studied his face. "Something's happened."

"Not yet." He thought of something else that needed to be done and added it to his mental list. "But if we're . . ."

He stopped as Alma approached and demanded, "What is it?"

Marcus could not help responding, "I think I've had an idea. A good one."

Austin's reply almost overlapped his, it was that fast in coming. "We want to help."

He thought of all that needed doing, and could only say, "My place. Fifteen minutes."

FORTY-SIX

The sight of six mortally weary people filing in the next day, all burdened with boxes and books and poster-sized packages, was enough to raise comment from every person in the courtroom, including the defense. Darren dropped his two boxes and retreated with the speed of one fleeing a burning house. Marcus finished stacking his load of books upon the plaintiff's table before glancing toward the defense. There alongside an outraged Logan sat the ever-silent general, his gaze glittering with unspoken wrath. James Southerland, New Horizons' CEO, observed him with the amused contempt no doubt reserved for opponents he was in the process of decimating.

Even Judge Nicols was caught off guard by the sight of the plaintiff's table almost lost under a burden of papers and books. Her gaze lingered longest upon Charlie Hayes, whose face was gray with fatigue. Yet all she said was, "Mr. Glenwood, I believe it is time for your final remarks."

Marcus rose to his feet and announced, "Your Honor, the plaintiff wishes to make an exceptional request for the reopening of evidence."

"Exceptional!" Logan almost shouted the word. "Your Honor, *outrageous* is a better description!"

"Specifically, Your Honor," Marcus continued, "we would like to reexamine a brief thirty-second portion of the video."

"Your Honor, this man is insane!" Logan bounced off the table in his impatience to close the distance between himself and Judge Nicols. "He should be barred from ever entering a courtroom again. Not only do we object, we ask that he and this ludicrous case be thrown out of court! We request the court sanction him, and that you join with us in requesting the state bar revoke his license to practice law!"

Marcus waited until the only sound was Logan's rasping breath, then continued, "There are numerous occasions in the past, Your Honor, where this has been granted." He swept one weary arm over his table. "We have gathered a body of cases to substantiate our claim. I have also prepared a summary sheet of the relevant rulings."

"Let me have it, please."

"Your Honor —"

"One moment, Mr. Kendall." She scanned the three-page summary, set it down, said, "I am familiar with most of these cases. Reexamination has been permitted only where *pivotal* evidence was overlooked."

"Which has happened in this case, Your Honor," Marcus responded.

"Your Honor," Logan was so outraged it took him a moment to gather his thoughts, "we have still not seen any definite proof to connect the video either to the factory or New Horizons! You can't possibly base such an action solely upon the fraudulent testimony of that Chinese girl. She'd say anything and everything to stay in this country. She perjured herself on the stand." Logan had worked himself to the center of the chamber, and stood squared off and ready to battle for his position in the ring. "Your Honor, clearly they wish to reopen this evidence merely to evoke sympathy from the jury just prior to their deliberations. It is the basest sort of maneuver, and must not be permitted!"

Marcus did not argue. He merely stood by his table and waited for the judge's gaze to turn his way. "We had the connection before us the entire time and didn't see it."

"You can support such a claim," Judge Nicols demanded, "without introducing new evidence?"

"That is correct, Your Honor. But it would help if we could recall one witness, the chief executive officer of New Horizons Incorporated."

As Judge Nicols pondered the request, her visage grew steadily sterner. "You may have ten minutes with the witness and one minute of the video. No more."

Logan gaped, could only manage, "Your Honor, I object."

"Your objection is noted."

"We should not even need that much time, Your Honor," Marcus replied, relief robbing him of all but the strength of a murmur.

Judge Nicols leaned over her desk to declare, "Listen up, Mr. Glenwood. If I find that this reexamination of evidence does not indeed merit this highly exceptional move, first I will strike the testimony. Then before the jury I will sanction you to the tune of fifty thousand dollars."

"I understand."

"You just hold on, I'm not finished yet. I will also hold you in contempt and jail you for thirty days. Subsequently, I will add my name to Mr. Logan's request for a review of your license to practice law. And if he so chooses to resubmit his request to have this case dismissed, I will rule in his favor. I will deem your case to be a frivolous claim. And I will accept his request that you be held liable for *all* the legal costs incurred by New Horizons Incorporated." She leaned over, face hard as a hawk's. "Now. Are you absolutely, utterly certain you wish to proceed?"

"I am, Your Honor."

"Very well. Mr. Logan, be seated." She waved her black-robed arm in excommunication. "Call your witness, Mr. Glenwood."

"The plaintiff calls Mr. James Southerland."

The New Horizons CEO approached the witness stand with the stiff dignity of someone unaccustomed to doing anything against his will. James Southerland bore the red beefiness of a very wealthy man who loved to play outdoors. If he hunted, it was with Purdey shotguns, beaters, and chilled champagne. If he skied, it was by chopper. James Southerland seated himself and flashed indignant loathing at Marcus.

The judge leaned over and said to the now-seated witness, "You are still under oath, Mr. Southerland. Proceed, Mr. Glenwood."

Marcus opened one of the boxes and began draping the legal tomes stacked on his desk with brilliantly colored sportswear. "This is what New Horizons refers to as Teen Gear, is it not, Mr. Southerland?"

"Objection, Your Honor, this is new material."

"On the contrary, it was all submitted and accepted in front of the magistrate." Marcus did not even bother to turn around, merely pulled out the final sweatshirt with its world-famous shooting star and rainbow arch, and anchored it into place with a pair of sneakers. He was still smoothing out creases in the sweatshirt when the judge overruled Logan. "Do I need to repeat the question, Mr. Southerland?"

"The answer is yes, everything you have there is New Horizons' Teen Gear."

"Fine. And all this gear comes from one source, is that not true?"

"Objection, Your Honor, this is getting us nowhere."

She wheeled on him then. "My patience has about run dry, Mr. Kendall."

"But Your Honor —"

"I have done everything but put a noose around Mr. Glenwood's neck. If he decides to hang himself, you will be the first to know. Now let us get on with this trial!"

Marcus repeated, "The gear comes from where, Mr. Southerland?"

"Factory 101, China." The chairman wore a checked cashmere jacket, a hundred-dollar hair styling, and a St. Moritz tan. "As I have already explained, the distribution-center chief made a perfectly natural mistake when he did not realize where the goods originated. It is not our intention to —"

The judge broke in with, "Just answer the question, Mr. Southerland."

"Factory 101," Marcus repeated. He hefted the sweatshirt. The light caught the silver threads in the rainbow slash. "This sweatshirt came from there as well, did it not?"

"I just said that."

"Yes, of course you did. And your product lines are all divided by factory, is that not correct?"

The eyes squinted, searching for the purpose behind the question. "I don't follow you."

"There is no overlap at all between factories, is there? What is produced by one factory is produced by no other."

"That is standard company policy. Almost all textile companies —"

"Yes or no, Mr. Southerland."

"Yes."

Marcus gave Kirsten a quick nod. She was instantly on her feet and unwrapping the first group of posters. Along the railing she propped up a series of New Horizons Teen Gear advertisements.

Marcus picked up one of the shoes and approached the witness stand. "These shoes come from your joint venture with Factory 101, do they not?"

"I am not in the habit of being forced to repeat myself!"

Marcus remained unruffled. "Please answer the question, Mr. Southerland."

"I just said so!"

"That is an affirmative answer?"

His face grew red with the effort of restraint. "All right. Yes!"

"Everything about them, right down to the design on the soles of the shoes, is copyrighted by your company, is it not?"

"Yes."

"As a matter of fact, each component of your Teen Gear line is specially designed so that it is exclusive to your company, is that not right?"

"Yes."

"So, for example, you have these distinctive star-and-rainbow designs stitched into the side of the shoe, branded into the rubber stripe around the base, etched into the sole, even woven in special silver thread into the laces. Is that not all correct?"

"You can see it for yourself."

"Answer the question, Mr. Southerland."

He turned his exasperation on the judge. "Your Honor, this is a complete and utter waste of my time."

"If so, Mr. Glenwood is about to pay with his freedom and his career," she responded dryly. "In the meantime, you are hereby ordered to answer counsel's question."

Southerland crossed his arms, clenched his jaw, said, "Yes."

"And all of these components are produced at the Chinese factory and nowhere else?"

Logan jumped to his feet. "Your Honor, please. This has already been stipulated. The lawyer is badgering the witness."

Marcus turned and stared at the judge. Just looked at her. It was enough. Judge Nicols responded, "The information is so stipulated and recorded, Mr. Glenwood. The items originate solely from Factory 101."

"Thank you for the clarification, Your Honor. I now wish to show a brief segment of the digitized video, and present as evidence a still photograph taken from this twenty-second portion of the tape."

"Once again I must protest, Your Honor," Logan continued. "This is being done purely for its inflammatory nature."

"Then Mr. Glenwood will shortly be halted in his tracks." Judge Nicols nodded. "Proceed."

Austin Hall and Charlie Hayes rose at his signal, and left the room. Together with the bailiff they wrestled the television stand back into the courtroom and slid the digitized tape into the VCR. Gloria Hall's image sprang into cruel focus on all four screens. Austin remained crouched over the machine, seemingly untouched by the voice and the image. Only Charlie turned and looked at the New Horizons CEO. And gave him a death's-head grin.

"Send money," Gloria dully intoned, and at Marcus' signal Austin hit the switch, freezing the image.

Marcus accepted the final poster from Kirsten's hands, keeping it turned so that the picture remained facedown as Alma unfolded the easel.

Then one of the jurors cried aloud. She rose in her seat, pointed at the television screen, and shouted, "Look! It's right there! It's been there all along!"

The CEO squinted and leaned forward, searching for what he could not see.

Marcus turned the poster-sized photograph around, revealing a blown-up image of Gloria Hall. Kirsten passed copies to the judge and the defense. This time the entire jury box erupted. Followed by the entire courtroom.

Gloria Hall was bound to her chair so tightly the flesh of her arms and neck ballooned out around the bonds. She was fettered about her chest and neck and arms and hands with long cords. The cords were all made from uncut shoelaces bearing the New Horizons logo.

Marcus caught the movement just in time. He rushed over and steadied Austin with a hand on the man's shoulder and a quiet, "Go sit down."

Austin quivered taut and raging beneath Marcus' hand. He showed the New Horizons chairman a feral snarl. James Southerland cowered in the witness box, recoiling as much from the photograph and the video image as from the man himself.

"Turn that off!" Logan Kendall's cry was almost shrill. "Turn that thing off!"

"You just shut up and *sit down!*" Judge Nicols pounded for order, and turned her growl on Marcus. "Proceed, counselor."

"So, Mr. Southerland," Marcus said, guiding Austin back to the table and into his chair, patting his shoulder one final time. "It appears that we do in fact have a perfect connection between your factory, the video, and the missing young woman. Wouldn't you say that was the case?"

The man looked as haggard as one who had just shaken hands with death itself. "I-I-I don't know what you're talking about."

"By your own admission, the laces that are keeping Gloria Hall captive are made by Factory 101 and nowhere else." Marcus watched as Alma turned slowly, almost creeping about, then pegged the Chinese general where he sat. Marcus waited until he was sure it was a look and nothing more before continuing, "I could have the records read back to you if you wish."

"It was . . . I don't have any understanding . . . I wasn't there . . . I haven't been there in years."

"But this *is* your joint venture, it *is* your product, it *is* your factory, is it not, Mr. Southerland?"

He pointed a finger at General Zhao. "That's the man you have to ask. Not me! I don't know what you're talking about!"

"But I suggest that you did know, Mr. Southerland."

"No! I didn't — you want to blame somebody, go after Randall Walker! It was his plan!"

Marcus moved forward and stood so

that Southerland had to turn toward the jury, or turn away. "I submit that you knew all along. You knew, so you had your people attack me at your Rocky Mount plant."

Logan shouted so hard his voice cracked. "Objection!"

"Sustained."

"You had Randall Walker scare off the first attorney the Halls hired by granting him a partnership. Is that not so?"

"Objection!"

"Sustained."

"You had your people trap me here in the courthouse and beat me and break my arm. You tried to burn down my home."

"Objection!"

"You ordered the murder of Ashley Granger, did you not." He leaned up closer still, hissing, "Just like you ordered the murder of Gloria Hall."

"Your Honor! I object to these unfounded accusations and incendiary theatrics!"

Marcus rapped his knuckles lightly on the witness stand, but even that sound was enough to cause James Southerland to flinch and draw away. "No further questions."

"Mr. Southerland!" Logan bounded forward, seeking to redress the damage by volume alone. "Is it not true that there is a great deal of trademark pirating in China?"

The man slumped toward Logan as he would toward a lifeline. "Yes. Yes. Of course there is."

"Logos and designs are stolen and made by pirate factories all the time." Logan plucked the photograph from the stand and tossed it into the corner. Marcus noticed that several of the jurors and the judge herself flinched at the action. "Is that not true?"

"Absolutely." James Southerland smoothed back his hair, saw the state of his trembling hands, hid them in his lap. "All the time."

"Pirating is a terrible problem in the textile industry." Logan flicked off the televisions, snapped to the bailiff, "Get this out of here." Then turned back to Southerland. "Pirating. A terrible problem in your industry."

"Terrible." The CEO tried but could not keep his eyes from tracking the televisions' progress out of the room.

"Of course it is. It is a well-known and highly documented fact." Logan moved up close enough to block the CEO's view of anything but him. Shot him a warning gaze. "So it is entirely possible, even likely, that one of your illegal competitors stole that design and has been producing

669

these products without your authorization."

"Yes. Of course." Southerland drew himself erect by will alone. "We have strong evidence that this very thing has happened with our shoes."

"And if it happened with your shoes, it would be the laces as well?"

"Of course it would."

"So in truth there is no substantiated evidence whatsoever to suggest that this video was shot in your factory?"

"No. None."

"It could have been any number of places. Done by pirates with morals so low they would be capable of such actions."

"Yes. But not us."

"No further questions."

Judge Nicols watched as James Southerland rose and padded back to the safety of the defense table, a man transformed. She then looked back to Marcus and said quietly, "I believe you have a half hour of closing left."

"Yes, Your Honor."

"Would you care to leave that for tomorrow?"

"I am ready now."

She glanced at the clock. It read only a quarter to ten. Marcus shared her amazement. He felt as if he had been standing in that courtroom through several eons. Judge Nicols banged her gavel. "The court is now recessed for thirty minutes. Counsel is hereby informed that I intend to wrap this up and instruct the jury this very afternoon."

FORTY-SEVEN

They waited until all had departed before braving the courtroom doors. Darren was there in the foyer, ready to offer whatever support they needed. Marcus led them toward the elevators, and was midway down the hall when he caught the first wind of tumult rising in the stairwell and out beyond the windows. A tide of sound pressed in from all directions, enough to raise a look of alarm even from the stoic Austin.

Kirsten turned to him helplessly. "I can't. Not today. Please."

Charlie understood instantly and said, "I'll go down and feed the man-eaters."

Alma and Austin held each other with the numb blindness of emotional exhaustion. Marcus stopped the others with one upraised hand. "Wait here."

He walked to the end of the hall and for the first time passed the point where he had been attacked without cringing. When Jim Bell opened the door to the judge's chambers, Marcus said, "I can't take them out there. We need a place to sit this out."

"Come with me." Bell walked up to the little group, so weary and drained they could only stand around Darren like a woeful flock seeking shelter beneath a storm-tossed tree. The former patrolman approached and said, "How you folks doing? Looks like winter's coming right round the bend, yes sir. Early this year." He pulled a ring of keys from his pocket and jangled them as he walked. "Why don't you join me right on down the hall here. We got us an empty office and a conference room next door."

He opened the door, waved them inside, his voice calming even their internal storms. "That's better now. Darren, why don't you come with me. We'll rustle up some donuts and fresh coffee for these folks."

Marcus offered his hand. "You are a friend."

"That's exactly what I aim to be," the receptionist said, and walked away.

Austin and Alma moved off together into the conference room. Kirsten stood in the doorway, knowing she should not follow, yet uncertain what she should do. Marcus watched the Halls huddle in the far corner for strength, and understood. The morning had stripped away their last vestige of hope. There was no winning here. No triumph, no miracle of reprieve.

At this moment the court's verdict mattered as little as snow falling upon an overwarm earth, a blanketing solution lost before it ever formed. Beyond the windows rose the pandemonium of conquest, a noise that mocked the tragedy within these bare walls.

A deep voice said through the open doorway, "Can I help with anything?"

"Deacon," Marcus cried, feeling that he could finally release his own burden of fatigue. Let it show in his voice and his shoulders. "How long have you been here?"

"Off and on for most of last week and the one before." He offered Marcus no smile, no false words of hope. "You did good in there, brother."

Marcus pointed to the conference room. "They need you."

"Thought they might." He nodded to Kirsten, patted her arm, entered the conference room, and shut the door behind him.

The room was so still that Marcus could sense what he did not hear, which was the burden Kirsten now carried. It was the most natural thing in the world to reach for her shoulder and say, "I've given it a lot of thought."

She turned to him with a look utterly devoid of either hope or a sense of tomorrow.

He studied the violet eyes. "I am certain," he said softly, "that you did exactly the right thing. Every single step of the way."

She balled her fists and held them out to him, clenched around the agony his words had released. He reached up and took hold of those two hands, and said, "Gloria would be so proud of you."

He pulled her toward him and held her as tightly as his weary arms could manage. She clutched him with hands that could not draw him as near as she liked. Her blond head raked back and forth across his chest, the sobs and the words muffled and torn. All Marcus caught for certain was one word: Gary. It was enough.

"Gloria could not let anyone know about Gary's death. Perhaps she just sensed this in the beginning. Or maybe it wasn't that at all. Maybe early on all she wanted was not to have the world try and fit her sorrow into some little box they found comfortable." Marcus could not be certain how much of this Kirsten was catching. It hardly mattered, for her tears and her trembling were lessening, as though the sound of his voice was fortifying enough. He said, as much for himself as for her, "The defense would have crushed us immediately if they knew

Gloria had done this for any reason tied to love and loss. They would have shouted it from the rooftops, and the case would have been dismissed out of hand."

She looked at him then. As Marcus held her and gazed at her tearstained face, he felt as if he were able to see her truly for the very first time. He used two fingers to wipe cheeks soft as the clouds of childhood dreams. She did not move, did not protest, did not draw away. One of her hands clenched the back of his jacket even tighter. So he lay an entire hand along the length of her face, and felt the nerves beneath his skin etch her form into a memory deeper than his mind.

He said, "I don't want you to go back to Washington."

"All right." The words were a whisper, nothing more. But the hand still clutched his jacket, and when she blinked, she pushed out another tear. One Marcus felt might just be for some reason other than mere sorrow.

"Mr. Glenwood, you may now conclude your closing remarks."

"Thank you, Your Honor." Marcus walked over in front of the jury box, picked up the podium, and moved it to one side. He now stood open and defenseless before the gathering of twelve.

Behind and to his right stood two easels, one holding the photograph of Gloria Hall laughing in her evening dress, the other displaying the blowup made from the video, of the same woman tied and beaten and drained of life and hope.

"Ladies and gentlemen of the jury, I will not take long. This is not the time for histrionics. Nor is it the time for mourning. Not yet. The memorial service for Gloria Hall cannot begin until her body is recovered."

"Objection! Those comments are the worst sort of inflammatory —"

"Overruled."

Marcus continued, "The judge in her instructions will charge you with regard to the specific legal issues. You will also have certain factual questions called interrogatories spelled out. These you will answer yes or no. We believe there is substantial evidence justifying a yes vote on each and every one of these questions. After you have answered these questions, you will be asked to assess damages.

"We shouldn't be swayed by glib apologies. The defense's claims of ignorance have come only after their earlier strategy of denial did not work. The judge will instruct you that ignorance is not an acceptable defense, not if they had the means to know. Which New Horizons most certainly did. They could have made a difference. They could have stopped this series of actions long before Gloria Hall ever traveled to China. They chose not to. Instead, they *empowered* their partners."

"Objection!"

"Overruled."

"They empowered General Zhao with their willful ignorance."

"Objection!"

"Overruled."

"We therefore ask that you find *all* these defendants liable. All of them." Marcus looked toward the defense table for the first time since beginning his arguments. "Those present and those not present."

"Your Honor, I protest."

Judge Nicols showed a genuine reluctance to even turn his way. "Mr. Kendall, do not even begin to go down this road."

"What road might that be, Your Honor?"

Her voice grated with irritation. "The road," she replied, "of thinking you can disrupt the plaintiff's arguments with unnecessary objections. Try it and I will find you in contempt." She did not even wait to see if he took his seat again. "Proceed."

Marcus had stood inspecting his shoes

throughout the exchange. When he glanced up, he could see by the look in their eyes that the jury agreed with him on some very deep level. This time he sensed that these were not people who needed further convincing. So he dropped everything he had planned to say except, "We must address the issue of damages. That's really all I feel I should do at this point. Anything more would only detract from what you already know."

To his left stood a third easel, this one holding a white drawing board. As he turned toward it, he caught sight of Judge Nicols glaring down at Logan, holding him in his seat. He picked up the grease pencil and wrote the single word *actual.* "We are just going to assign a number here because we have to. How anyone could set a dollar value on the life of a young woman so full of joy and intelligence and promise is beyond me, so I'm not even going to try." He wrote out the number, and said as he did, "So we'll just say one hundred thousand dollars."

Below that he wrote a second word, *punitive.* "Punitive damages are damages in addition to the actual damages. Here there can be some differences in culpability. You can ask yourselves: Who acted in a malicious manner? Who was more directly responsible for Gloria's kidnapping and imprisonment and torture, and is therefore subject to the more substantial punitive damages?

"You may decide that the U.S. company merely colluded in making this happen. I suggest to you that the evidence has shown otherwise. I propose that their attitude has been very consistent. Whenever anything appeared to threaten their market share or profits, their response was *whatever it takes*. They have never objected in any way to the actions of their partners. They are and always have been concerned with one thing only — their bottom line. No concern was given to the people who suffered at their hands, directly or indirectly."

Beside the first word he wrote *New Horizons*. "Their annual statement shows that the company's turnover last year was just over one billion, eight hundred million dollars. Their profit before taxes was about three hundred and twenty-seven million. They have had a run of several good years, and they currently hold over two hundred million dollars in cash and other liquid assets." He wrote these figures on the board, then stepped back, giving them all a chance to ponder what they meant.

He then stepped up to the easel and wrote *China*. "This morning's *Wall Street*

Journal stated in a front-page article that U.S. financial institutions currently hold frozen Chinese government assets to the tune of eighty-one billion dollars."

"*No!*" The sound tore through the silence like a sword. All eyes turned to where the general stood behind the defense table, his fist held like a gun aimed straight at Marcus. It was the first time Marcus had ever heard the man speak. Only he was not speaking now. He roared the words over the sound of Judge Nicols gavel. "You cannot do this! It is against international law! You must be stopped!" He turned to the judge and shouted, "You have power! Stop this insane man!"

"You sit down!" When the man merely dropped his arm, she pointed the gavel at a uniformed officer. "Bailiff, if he won't be seated, cuff him to the chair."

"Ah, you are crazy." He rammed himself down, muttering furious incantations.

Marcus returned to his board, started to speak, shook his head. He turned back to the jury and merely said, "Thank you."

Judge Nicols allowed the moment to linger, as strong a courtroom accolade as Marcus could ever recall receiving. She then turned to Logan and said, "All right, Mr. Kendall."

He sprang up as though ejected from his seat, and strode to center stage with

Suzie Rikkers in fretful attendance. Together they dismantled the easels and stowed the photographs. Logan did not wait for Suzie to resume her seat before launching into his rebuttal. "Ladies and gentlemen of the jury, the question now is the same question we started out on. That question is: What in the world are we doing here? What in the world have my clients done to justify this circus?"

The silver pen was out and waving like a sparkling baton, but the jury had the look of a band not certain which tune they should be playing. "These guys have drawn up some charges and thrown them against the wall to see what sticks. But you mustn't forget, ladies and gentlemen of the jury, that they have a serious credibility problem here. They have no reliable witness tying anybody to the alleged incident. Remember that. It is crucial."

He paced toward the empty witness box, made a fist and planted it softly upon the railing. He said a final time, "No credible witness. No one to tie the abuses you have seen to my clients."

He then lowered his head a fraction and bulled forward. "I have a story I could tell you, a tragic tale about a factory with conditions so bad it would make you weep to hear about them. Only this factory was not over in China. No. It was here in North Carolina, and the case against this particular factory was tried just twenty-three years ago. Here in our beloved state, ladies and gentlemen of the jury. Less than a quarter of a century ago, we ourselves had factories that were run like prisons."

He raised his gaze to meet theirs. "Yes, China is behind us in some things. But they are working hard to catch up. And what is more important still, ladies and gentlemen of the jury, what is absolutely critical here, what you must never forget, is that these conditions have nothing whatsoever to do with this case. Nothing. We are here because a woman has gone missing. Remember that. This is what has brought us together. The rest is just smoke. Don't let the plaintiff's attorney cloud your vision by blowing smoke at you. Don't you dare let him."

He waved his pen again, and this time they followed. "They say that New Horizons Incorporated and General Zhao should somehow be held liable for the disappearance of a political activist whom they can't find. What they seem to have forgotten is that you do not enter a courtroom without a case that is somehow founded upon *truth*. Law and fact, and nothing else, make up this truth. Law and fact. I submit to you, ladies and gentlemen of the jury, that they remain wide of the mark on both these vital issues. The law is against them. This remains a political issue that should never have entered this courtroom. And the facts are not with them. Remember what I said. No reliable witness." He held them a moment longer, then swept the baton down and away. "They have failed to tie my clients to the alleged misdeed. Do not hold them responsible for what they have not done. I have said it before, I will say it again: Let us wrap this up and go home."

FORTY-EIGHT

The judge's instructions took an hour and a half. The written interrogatories were passed out, the final orders solemnly intoned, and the case handed to the jury.

As soon as the jury retired and the judge departed, Marcus returned his little group to the pair of rooms lent them by Jim Bell. The press had grown impatient and tried to break through the police barrier, but Darren and the guards were ready. Darren and Deacon brought coffee and sandwiches that no one touched. Marcus stared at the food, knowing he was hungry, knowing also he would not keep anything down. He had known such letdowns before, but nothing this complete. He was anxious to learn the verdict, yet he knew it would do little good.

Charlie opened the door and slipped inside. Somehow the man seemed to have drawn both years and energy from the tirade washing against the windows. "Your audience is waiting."

"Not now."

"Come on, son." Charlie walked over

and pulled on his sleeve. "I know how you're feeling, and I'm gonna share with you the barest truth I can. It don't matter."

"Charlie, I don't have a thing to tell those people."

"Sure you do." The second tug was more insistent. "You're a lawyer. You're paid to think on your feet and spout hot air."

Kirsten leaned against the wall, watching them. "He's right, Marcus."

" 'Course I am. Listen to that din out there. They're waiting for you to come out and give them the word from on high."

"They'll eat me alive," Marcus said, but nonetheless allowed himself to be pulled to his feet.

"Naw. Take a little nibble here and there, that's all." Charlie unbuttoned the sleeve covering Marcus' cast. "Roll that up and leave off your coat."

"Charlie, this is absurd."

"I'll tell you what it is, old son. It's a whole ton of solid gold, and they want to just plump it down in your lap." The old man's eyes sparkled like those of someone half his age. "That's the sound of free publicity out there, and a sweeter song they couldn't be singing."

Kirsten walked over, said, "You want to give it all to Logan Kendall?"

"Exactly!" Charlie patted his back, urging him forward. "Listen to the lady, son."

"I don't know what to say," he confessed.

She joined her hand to his, and said, "Tell them what's on your heart."

"You got a smart one here," Charlie agreed, opening the door, then turning back to wink at her. "Believe I'd hold on to the lady if I could."

"All rise." The judge swept in and seated herself. The jury paraded in and took their seats. Marcus felt the tension in the courtroom tighten around his chest like a titanium band.

Judge Nicols observed them solemnly, then asked, "Has the jury reached a verdict?"

"We have, Your Honor."

Marcus glanced at his watch, then the wall clock, saw Charlie do the same. Ninety minutes from the jury's departure to their return. A bad sign. Very bad. Civil-trial juries tended to bring back swift verdicts only when they found against the plaintiff. Discussions about punitive damages alone took hours, sometimes days. Not a good sign at all.

"Very well." Judge Nicols pointed the bailiff toward the slip of paper offered by the jury foreman. She accepted it, unfolded the sheet, read it carefully, shook her head once, handed it back. "The foreman may read the verdict."

The rawboned man held the sheet awkwardly and said, "We find for the plaintiff on all counts."

The court breathed a single sigh, one cut off by the sound of a man's broken sob. The foreman stopped and looked down to where Austin was held by his wife. The foreman's face was clenched up tight as a fist.

Judge Nicols finally said, "Proceed to damages, if you please, sir."

"Yes ma'am." He glanced down at the paper, but did not seem to recognize his own writing. So he looked up and said, "We could never punish them like we'd want, so we decided the two of them ought both to make an atoning tithe."

She shook her head. "Just the damages, please."

"Yes ma'am." He rattled the sheet, cleared his throat, and said, "In the matter of actual damages, we find for the plaintiff in the sum of one hundred thousand dollars, such amount to be shared equally by the defendants."

Austin drew himself up with a shaky breath, wiped his face with an impatient hand. Not wanting to miss any of it, not an instant.

"As to punitive damages," the foreman glanced over at the defense, a spark rising from somewhere down deep, touching the edges of his voice and his features. "We find for the plaintiff and against New Horizons in the sum of one hundred and eighty million dollars."

The courtroom's collective gasp took wings and started to fly, but was hammered down to earth by Judge Nicols. The only sound at the defense table came from Suzie Rikkers, who wheezed a cry as hoarse as a wounded gull.

The foreman's gaze lingered on the general until Judge Nicols said, "Proceed."

"We find against the general and the Chinese government, and hold them to punitive damages of eight billion dollars."

In the stunned silence that followed, two sounds etched themselves deep in Marcus' memory. One was the whoosh of escaped breath as Logan took the news like a fist driven into his sternum.

The other sound was of Suzie Rikkers coming completely and utterly undone. *"No!"* The shriek hurled her from her seat. She tried to ram her way to the left, but James Southerland sat sprawled as if he had taken three bullets to the gut. She shrilled, "You can't *do* this!"

Frantically she clawed her way past

Logan, desperate to escape. When he did not move fast enough, Suzie Rikkers hiked up her skirt and began crawling over the railing. "This is *my* case!"

Judge Nicols clapped one hand over her mouth and leaned back in her chair as Suzie Rikkers fell into the aisle. She came up with clothes and hair awry, her fists swinging at empty air. "I *won* this case! It's *mine!*"

Judge Nicols lowered her hand and revealed her smirk long enough to say simply, "Bailiff, remove this woman."

Suzie Rikkers seemed utterly unaware of the hands that gripped her or the rising tumult that marked her passage. Marcus waited until she had been dragged screaming from the room to turn back to the defense table. Logan Kendall had not moved.

Judge Nicols stood and pointed to the first row of viewers. Marcus turned only because her outstretched arm demanded it. Three gray-suited men rose to their feet and moved to the bar, the wooden gate behind which the public was required to remain. Through the buzzing confusion in his mind Marcus thought that two of the men seemed vaguely familiar.

Judge Nicols did not keep him in suspense. "Two of these men are FBI agents, the other is the district attorney. While the jury was out I met with the DA and the agents, and I have agreed that they should proceed with criminal charges against James Southerland and General Zhao Ren-Fan. A warrant has also been issued for the arrest of Randall Walker. Later this day further warrants will be issued for the entire New Horizons board of directors. They are to be arrested, formally charged, and criminally prosecuted for the kidnapping of Gloria Hall."

The New Horizons chairman remained slumped motionless in his chair. The general tried to make a break for it, leaping over the defense table. The agents and the bailiff moved together and wrestled him to the floor. As they handcuffed him, the general was shouting that they could not do this, and ordering the defense attorney to get him out.

But Logan was still recovering from his body slam, and could only stutter, "General Zhao is covered by diplomatic immunity."

Judge Nicols refused even to look his way. Instead, she remained raptly intent upon watching the general be hauled away. "He is nonetheless charged. These gentlemen will be granted a formal hearing in three days, at which time diplomatic immunity may be invoked for the general." She watched as the agents lifted James Southerland to his feet and cuffed him. She offered the New Horizons CEO the same grim smile she had granted the general, and said, "Until that time, the gentlemen are invited to be guests of our fair state."

FORTY-NINE

Marcus stepped onto the brick portico and rang the doorbell. The night was crisp enough to hold a winter's silence, so quiet he could hear the measured tread of someone walking to the door. Gladys Nicols looked through the narrow side window and showed no surprise at his presence. Instead she opened the door and said merely, "You had me worried for a time there, Marcus."

"Me too. May I come in?"

"Of course." She opened the door and said, "Can I get you something, a coffee?"

"No thanks." He stopped at the sight of two teenagers standing midway down the front hall, a young man of perhaps sixteen and a girl a year or so older.

The young man said, "You did great in there, Mr. Glenwood."

"Yeah," the girl added. "Momma won't let us say anything about a trial, but we were rooting for you all along."

"Thank you."

"Come on in here, Marcus." Gladys Nicols led him into her study and slid the doors shut behind them. "Have a seat there by the fire."

She waited until they had both settled and taken a long look at the fire before asking, "Did you catch the evening news?"

"I missed it on purpose."

"You looked just fine." She gave him the tiniest of smiles. "And my, but you sounded eloquent."

Marcus did not know what to say to that, so he made do with a careful inspection of the flames.

"The press is calling it the 'shoestring defense.' I like that. It holds a certain ring." When he did not respond, she went on, "The Chinese government has recalled its ambassador and declared the verdict to be an act of war. I have declined three invitations so far to travel up to Washington, each one coming from a higher authority. They can't threaten a federal judge for doing her job, but they most certainly can try."

"I'm sorry to have caused you all this trouble."

"Do I look bothered to you?" She snagged a footstool with the toe of her shoe and drew it toward her. Once she had stretched out her legs and settled more deeply into the chair opposite him, she continued, "Let's see, what else did the newscasters say? Three of New Horizons' top sports stars have already declared they are breaking their endorsement contracts. Randall Walker was caught trying to board a plane to London using a false passport. And the State Department is lodging an official complaint against the ruling."

Marcus rubbed his temples against the thought of the battles yet to come. "I'll worry about all that tomorrow."

She shifted in her chair, as though trying for a clearer angle on the issue. "I have been left with the distinct impression that Miss Gloria Hall had this planned from the beginning."

Marcus said to the flames, "If you only knew."

"Not tonight. But soon." She cocked her head to one side. "One question will do for now. She knew the general was coming to America, didn't she?"

"I can't say for certain, but I think so." Marcus felt the fatigue and the release down deep in his bones. "My guess is that she was hoping whoever took over the factory wouldn't be so, well, controlled."

"She wanted to provoke them into doing something that would expose them so that they would wind up in our courts. She wanted it all to happen while the general was over here and in range." Gladys Nicols shook her head. "That poor girl."

"Her poor parents."

"Yes. Them too. How are they?"

"Not good."

The look she gave him was etched with shared sorrow. "And how are you?"

"Surviving." Marcus stretched his back, knew there was no putting it off. "Your Honor —"

"We're done with court for the moment. You may call me Gladys."

His gaze was enough to draw her up tight. "This case will not be finished," he replied, "until we know exactly what happened to Gloria. And maybe not even then." He sat and listened to the fire crackle, then continued, "Next week I'm going to file papers for a new civil action. I felt I owed it to you to see if you wanted me to pass the pressure on to another judge."

She hesitated a long moment. "I am both tired and tempted. But all my life I have heard words about passing cups."

"There is a federal statute framed in the days of the Soviet empire," Marcus explained. "Back then Russia tended to escape responsibility for the misdeeds of state-owned companies by claiming sovereign immunity."

"I imagine we will find the same objection raised when the Chinese government appeals this decision."

Marcus nodded. "I want to head them off at the pass. This particular law says that a foreign government involved in a company for wholly commercial reasons can be held directly liable for the actions of that company. And for all damages."

Judge Nicols sat up straighter still. "My, my."

"Not only that, but there is a legal exception to sovereign immunity. It states that if a single action can be shown to be part of an overall pattern, then the state can be held liable for fomenting this action."

"You want to up the ante, don't you," she demanded softly. "Hit them with more bad publicity. Continue the pressure until they come up with answers."

"As soon as I can get the papers together, I intend to file a civil action against the Chinese government for human rights abuses in its *lao gai* prisons and forced-labor factories," Marcus finished. "Nationwide."

"Then I suppose my questions about Gloria will have to wait a while longer." Judge Nicols rose to her feet, drawing Marcus with her. "I will see you in my office at eight o'clock tomorrow morning."

EPILOGUE

The late November day wore a dress as dark as Alma's. The airport windows overlooking the runway were veiled in a mist so fine and soft it could not be called rain at all. The vast crowd of press and photographers and mourners gathered beside the runway was washed a uniform gray. Marcus stood with one arm around Kirsten's shoulders and looked to a group of television newscasters standing in somber shades and chattering to a horde of electronic eyes. Marcus wished he could somehow grow as impervious to the tumult as he was to winter's approach.

They were all there with him, all the strangers bound to him now, knit into the fabric of his life. All but Gladys Nicols, who had sent Jim Bell in her absence. The retired patrolman and Amos Culpepper had stood sentry at the doors since their arrival two hours earlier.

Together they all had watched the plane land and the passengers disembark. The metal courier stood silent and waiting now, drenched in the same gray sorrow as all the rest of this mournful day.

Jim Bell walked over and said, "You know Judge Nicols would be here if she could."

Marcus nodded, both to the words and his understanding that it was far easier to address him than Austin or Alma Hall. He had two new cases winding their way toward a new jury trial in the judge's courtroom. "It was good of you to come."

Jim Bell offered a paper stiff as folded parchment. "She asked me to give you this."

Marcus unfolded the sheet, read the contents, then called out, "Darren, come over here, please." He handed the tall young man the paper and said, "At the request of Judge Nicols and Charlie Hayes, the governor has agreed to expunge your record. As far as anyone is concerned, you are walking out of here with a clean sheet."

Amos Culpepper joined them. "You still want to join our team at the sheriff's office, Darren?"

The man did not look up from the paper shivering slightly in his hands. "Y-yes sir."

Amos gave a solemn nod. "Nice to know there's some good coming out of this day."

There was a knock at the door. All eyes watched as Amos walked over and exchanged soft words with a uniformed patrolman. He then turned to the couple tucked into the corner shadows and announced, "They're ready to unload the coffin."

Deacon Wilbur rose first, one hand on each of the parents. "Stand tall, now," he said, his voice carrying against the tide trying to press through the open door. "The whole world is gathered out there, ready to watch your Gloria come home."

ACKNOWLEDGMENTS

A number of people proved instrumental to this book's formation. Katie Simon is Staff Attorney and chief aide to U.S. District Court Justice Earl Britt. Her energy and patient explanations were critical to the research's early stages. Kieran Shanahan, an attorney and member of the Raleigh City Council, was instrumental in the shaping of the trial and the defense's strategy. His and Katie's assistance cannot be overstated. It was both an honor and a pleasure to work with them, and come to know a bit more about their world.

Reuben Blackwell, former executive of the Raleigh Chamber of Commerce and now Director of the RMOIC, has been a dear friend for many years. The house where much of this book takes place is modeled after his neighborhood in Rocky Mount. I am indeed grateful to him and his wife, Neva, for seeking to share with me their world. Thanks must also go to the pastor of their church and his wife, Chris and Sherron Jordan, and to all their wonderful congregation. They sang, they danced, they shouted, they put up with my quiet musings, and they made me feel welcome. What a gift.

One of the great delights of this book has been working with my editor at Doubleday, Eric Major, and his assistant Elizabeth Walter. They bring to the table a remarkable level of professionalism and wisdom. I would like to thank two others among the many at Doubleday with whom I have been fortunate to work, Judith Kern and Steve Rubin. My heartfelt appreciation goes as well to the wonderful team at WaterBrook, including Dan Rich, Lisa Bergren, Michelle Tennesen, and Rebecca Price. It is a privilege to call them friends.

My wife, Isabella, is an international attorney who is currently earning degrees in theology and ethics at Oxford University. Her first thesis was on the issue of human rights violations within the Chinese *lao gai* prison network. She has walked with me every step of the way, from dream to realization.

Over a hundred interviews were conducted for this book. Some have requested not to be named, but must be thanked nonetheless. A few of the many others who contributed are: George Ragsdale of Ragsdale, Liggett & Foley; Ashley Thrifte and Lawrence Davis of

Womble Carlyle; State Supreme Court Justice David M. Britt; Federal Justice W. Earl Britt; Alexander B. Denson, United States Magistrate Judge; Ted Borris of Hatch, Little & Bunn; Leslie C. Griffin, Director of Asian Affairs for the U.S. Chamber of Commerce; and the staff at Amnesty International's offices in Washington and London.

And finally I would like to thank my father, a Raleigh-based attorney for more than forty years. Thanks, Dad, both for sharing your wealth of experience, and for opening so many doors.

The employees of Thorndike Press hope you have enjoyed this Large Print book. All our Thorndike and Wheeler Large Print titles are designed for easy reading, and all our books are made to last. Other Thorndike Press Large Print books are available at your library, through selected bookstores, or directly from us.

For information about titles, please call:

(800) 223-1244

or visit our Web site at:

www.gale.com/thorndike
www.gale.com/wheeler

To share your comments, please write:

Publisher
Thorndike Press
295 Kennedy Memorial Drive
Waterville, ME   04901